the absolute

the
absolute

a novel

DANIEL GUEBEL

Translated by Jessica Sequeira

Seven Stories Press
NEW YORK • OAKLAND

Originally published as *El Absoluto* by Literatura Random House, Buenos Aires, 2016.

First Seven Stories Press edition April 2022. Published by arrangement with Casanovas & Lynch Literary Agency, Barcelona, Spain.

Seven Stories Press
140 Watts Street
New York, NY 10013
www.sevenstories.com

College professors and high school and middle school teachers may order free examination copies of Seven Stories Press titles. Visit https://www.sevenstories.com/pg/resources-academics or email academics@sevenstories.com.

Library of Congress Cataloging-in-Publication Data

Names: Guebel, Daniel, 1956- author. | Sequeira, Jessica, translator.
Title: The absolute / Daniel Guebel ; translated by Jessica Sequeira.
Other titles: Absoluto. English
Description: New York : Seven Stories Press, [2022]
Identifiers: LCCN 2021047801 | ISBN 9781644211601 (trade paperback) | ISBN 9781644211618 (ebook)
Subjects: LCGFT: Novels.
Classification: LCC PQ7798.17.U254 A6313 2022 | DDC 863/.64--dc23
LC record available at https://lccn.loc.gov/2021047801

Printed in the USA.

9 8 7 6 5 4 3 2 1

To Pablo Gianera and Luis Mucillo.
For Ana, this novel I dreamed up
while cradling her in my arms.

Who is Scriabin? Who are his ancestors?

—IGOR STRAVINSKY

BOOK 1

FRANTISEK DELIUSKIN

Maybe life is no more than a feverish dream.
So why not take a sleepwalker as a guide?
—MIKA WALTARI, *The Wanderer*

1

A few months before celebrating its hundredth anniversary, the Scriabin-Deliuskin Circle of Buenos Aires commissioned Américo Rabbione (an artist more prolific than talented) to create a sculpture that paid homage to my uncle and father. On the day of the inauguration, the small size of the cloth draped over it surprised me: according to Rabbione's original plans for the project, there should have been at least eight meters separating the black marble base from the bronze heads. The final result would have made my father smile. "Most amateurs think that music ended with Wagner," he once told me. When the Circle's vice president yanked away the mantle covering the statue that would reunite the brothers, my vision was assaulted by a white-winged flutter, the dull gleam of a commemorative plaque and the gloom of a molded concrete block fusing two crude figures into a single embrace.

"If this cubist eyesore represents them," I thought, "then the difference between homage and insult no longer exists."

Within a week, the usual anonymous jokers had improved the monument with a series of slogans and multicolored decorations sprayed in aerosol—filthy remarks, scribbled flowers, jagged stars. And since they pulled off the plaque to sell it for its weight in pesos, there is no longer any sign to exalt the works and lives of Alexander Scriabin and Sebastian Deliuskin.

For the moment, I won't go into the question of the different last names. Of Alexander Scriabin, my uncle, perhaps more than of any other musician, you could say that in the first half of his life he sought the world. He traveled vast distances, living in a way that was at times bold, at times reckless; if in the first half of his existence, his spirit was wide ranging and easily influenced, in the second, preceding his finale, in a move apparently contradictory but actually of equal intensity, having now explored the world, he drew on his resources in a bid to change it; committed to this dramatic and desperate undertaking, he invented the element that heralded total transformation (the mystic chord), and then, with his famous composition *Mysterium*, he poured his energy into an attempt to transform the course of the entire Universe. Of Sebastian Deliuskin, my father, you might say that even when he lived at a distance from (and in the shadow of) this musical explosion, owing to a series of unexpected circumstances, he had to spend the remainder of his days trying to catch hold of what the winds of dispersal had sent spinning, trying to put the pieces back together after catastrophe. But it isn't unusual that this happened to them both, or that the combustion occurred with a particular style.

Alexander Scriabin died too early and was too far away for us to do anything for him; I was just a girl. As for my father, the doctors whom I consulted spoke of a neurophysiological process with degenerative effects on the brain cells; five centuries ago, healers and priests would have made an argument of diabolical possession. The real explanation is simpler: in our family of lunatics, we pay the price of dementia for ascending to the heavens of genius.

If you go back along the genealogical tree of character pathologies, before reaching the original Adam, you'll come across our true predecessor, my great-great-grandfather Frantisek Deliuskin. His father, Vladimir, a typical representative of the adventurousness that a couple of centuries ago distinguished the Russian soul, was a trader in reindeer hides who seized the opportunity to make a fortune, changed sector, and began to work for the different museums of civilized Europe, selling them mammoth skeletons he acquired through the simple means of tossing loads of dynamite into the depths of lakes on the Siberian steppe (from the Baikal to the Kosovskoye). The violence of the explosion detached the blocks of ancient ice from their rocky bed, where these prehistoric beasts are preserved, in such a way that a series of well-timed attempts could as a result send hurling two, three or even five masses with their contents intact; afterward, without fearing the possible revenge that might come from altering the repose of these monsters visible through glinting blue ice (a quivering eye trembling in agony, a fang over five meters long, bristling hairs), Vladimir would "fish" for the huge blocks with harpoons. Thanks to an ingenious system of levers, ropes and pulleys, he would haul them to shore, letting the base of the ice solidify again over the surface of the lake, then proceed to chisel away at these icebergs to get to their core; he had an advantage over any sculptor (or any real artist) in that with his object, the form was given beforehand. Once the frozen mammoth had lost its sheath, Vladimir removed the flesh until he reached bone. This method of obtaining the skeleton destroyed more mammoths than it rescued for science, of course. But these were periods of abundance, and no one cared about such squander . . .

In those days, the father tried to interest the son in the techniques of subaquatic paleontology, but it was useless. For Frantisek, it was as if the time never passed during those excursions; the landscape seemed to him an infinite monotony, an expanse lacking in nuance. His feet grew cold, and a mammoth was a mammoth was a mammoth, even if it emerged suddenly from the waters like an inebriated bubble, a wobbly diadem of frozen beauty. Permanently distracted, idly lashing his whip of braided leather (knout), which for reasons of elegance he wore pressed against his trouser leg, he sneezed, begged for the saving grace of a flu and dreamed of fleeing to warm, distant lands.

When Vladimir arrived at the unhappy conclusion that his heir wasn't cut out for either trade or deepwater fishing, he bought him some versts of territory near Vladivostok, which could be accessed only by sailing up the Vistula River, then advancing deeper inland by means of a snaking branch of a tributary. What could be found there? Muzhiks, forest territory, orange plantations, cattle. The place had been occupied for more than a hundred years by a tribe of gypsies, the blackest in India. The average body temperature of this group—higher by over a degree and a half than the rest of humanity—had produced a microclimate, a kind of subtropical refuge. Frantisek immediately succumbed to the charm of the surroundings. Instead of looking after his interests, he devoted his time to reading, contemplating nature and traveling by boat with the gypsies, who would tell his fortune for free or brazenly steal from him, according to their variations in mood. Sometimes he would spend nights at the shops of these friends, listening to drunken conversations and watching their dances. Occasionally he went upriver, following the salmon. Languid, irresponsible, the new landlord let his harvests of oranges rot in the trees and spill over the earth. The radiance of the fruits could be glimpsed from a distance, like the phosphorescence of ghosts. For a time he scandalized the priests of the Orthodox Church of Irkutsk (the town near his property) by singing in a synagogue choir, excited by the curves of the Ashkenazim insinuated beneath their loose clothing.

At the time, the successive defeats of the Russian armies at the hands of some of the country's historical enemies were destroying the international value of the ruble; since Vladimir charged for the exportation of antediluvian skeletons in European coins of constant value, he grew rich overnight. Frantisek saw his chance;

six months before, he had met Volodia Dutchansky, an organist strapped for cash. In the beginning, less out of interest than out of compassion, he hired him to learn some basic ideas about counterpoint and harmony. Within a month, he'd absorbed everything that Volodia could teach him, and after another month, he could have given classes to the maestro. To put an end to this activity, which now felt superfluous, he granted the organist a salary to work as an oarsman on his boat. He also dictated a letter to him, addressed to his father, in which his maestro added a signature to the phrases exalting his musical virtues ("The Universe has not witnessed a blossoming of such talent since the times of Bach, Pachelbel, Haydn and Albinoni," et cetera), the aim being to gain a stipend generous enough to dedicate himself to music without concerns of an earthly order.

The ruse was a success. Vladimir, surprised by the sudden glorification of the merits of a son who'd always seemed to him useless, with a future that struck him as uncertain, once again felt the pride of blood circulate through his veins, and he took it upon himself to allocate a yearly income.

In honor of my great-great-grandfather, one must say that for a time he did focus on studying the art of composition, even taking up the post of music teacher at the girls' school in Irkutsk. Quickly he transformed into a precious pawn in the complex chess of the town's social relations; the rural property owners in the area competed with one another for him and tried to convince him to give harmonium lessons to their wives. This ambition, laughable in subjects who could barely sing "Volga Volga," can be explained by the mistaken illusion of social climbing that the practice of an art can create. And since these kulaks wanted to refine themselves without effort, it had occurred to them this was a task for their wives; logically, in coming up with the idea—a collective phenomenon—the interested parties themselves oiled the wheels.

"We were all delighted by this modest, well-mannered young man. My husband was so quickly convinced of his virtuosity," one of Frantisek's first and most charming students said, recommending him to her friend. And she added: ". . . especially because of the chromatic quality of his improvisations, which seem to violate every known law of harmony. I remember entering a trance when the maestro played, and couldn't help but think: 'He carries music in his soul.'"

Frantisek's classes were a success; especially in the bedroom. If these women contrasted the dream against the reality (the dream being the "modest, well-mannered young man," a precursor to Chopin with his long delicate fingers trained for delight; and the reality, the brief rough poundings given to them by fat greasy-bearded husbands as they lay on their stomachs or backs), then the second term of comparison couldn't help but vanish away to nothing.

This great triumph, Frantisek's breathtaking sexual apotheosis—which he had expected less than anyone—was not, as so many lush pages in Russian literature have sung of it, a frivolous event that culminated in disaster (lovemaking, challenge, duel, gunshot). The discretion of the Irkutskian ladies played its part, so no one had to lament any tragedy. Frantisek's career as a clandestine lover signified a brief awakening. Foolish is he who seeks in the game of flesh the satisfaction of desire rather than an increase in longing. Although from the very moment of his debut in these duties, my great-great-grandfather had shown talent, versatility, resistance, ardor and a capacity for recuperation that far exceeded the average, the truth is his surrender to the pleasure of these covert adventures was not determined by the frenzy of his discovery, but was secretly regulated by a severe, even ascetic, principle of inquiry, one that would later reveal itself to be a criterion for composition. In effect: the variety of beds, duvets, pillows, floors, smells, breaths, skins and bodies he came to know during these excursions led him to embark on the rigorous task of organizing the priorities of his senses afresh.

An account of his concerns during the period can be given by means of the following conversation (or monologue), which took place with Dutchansky onboard his boat, during an excursion along the Vistula. The setting: Dutchansky rows wearily along a still river as the blades of his oars sink into an algae clump, a miniature sea of kelp. Frantisek tans with his shirt open, lying against big pillows, as he takes bites of a red apple. Bees hum, lichens gleam. Sun above, yellow.

"Am I old?" he says. "Or have I reached the ultimate limit of experience?"

The blade of the left oar strikes the densest mass of water hyacinth, bursting the head of a toad.

"Did you say something, Volodia?" he asks. Dutchansky shakes his head, and Frantisek goes on: "I have no will to transform the memory of my first sexual experiences into a kind of paradise lost, but now that I have some knowledge about my lovers' modulations, I confess the matter has begun to seem a little . . ." Frantişek can't find the exact word, so Dutchansky chimes in:

"What methods did you use to come to your conclusions?" he asks.

"Oh!" Frantisek languidly drops the apple core. Instead of a "plop" when the skeleton of the fruit hits the water, the digestive "gluck" of an opportune salmon can be heard: "Obviously I'm not *that* stupid. By repeating a series of techniques of erotic stimulation over the course of my routine of clandestine encounters, I was able to confirm that by engaging in a series of positions and pelvic rhythms of identical tempo, it is possible to produce a series of equivalent responses in each of my partners."

". . . a little boring?" Dutchansky completes the phrase. "Have you come to the conclusion that sex is essentially monotonous?"

"That would be the necessary conclusion for a mind unlike my own," sighs Frantisek, feeling misunderstood yet again: "In my case, this proof helped me accept the evidence that every feminine instrument possesses particular qualities of timbre, which, if analyzed with the utmost care and sympathy, can be read as a 'theme,' in the musical sense of the word."

To conceal the satisfaction given to him by his ex-student's discovery, Dutchansky takes advantage of the rowing movement to tuck his face under an armpit.

"You look like a fat woman smelling an onion," smiles Frantisek.

"A theme?" says Dutchansky.

"Yes. All of the reactions perceived during a sexual experience and its preliminaries constitute this theme."

"And is there no possibility of variation?"

"Obviously there is," says Frantisek, irritated and already wanting to change the subject. "Under experimental conditions, modifying the antics substantially, it is possible to extract a variation from each one of my companions, but such an effort exceeds the results. The trouble is, working this way, I'd never be able to come up with any musical score at all, much less a composition of great significance!"

Dutchansky, who knows the art of temporarily putting a conversation on hold so a stimulating problem doesn't deteriorate into idle chatter, lifts his head, looks at some exquisite clouds grouped with casual flair and says:

"What a shame. The first drops are falling."

A lie, of course.

"Let's turn back," jokes Frantisek. "The last thing I need now is to get sick."

So they returned home, skirting the shore, gliding through a rain of gold coins shaken down by the canopy of willows.

The interruption led to the creation of a style. After the outing, my great-great-grandfather spent a night of feverish insomnia concentrating on his problem. Early in the morning, he'd arrived at the following conclusions, which he jotted down in his diary:

1) Each woman's body during coitus is the opposite of a blank page. Its sensual manifestations of desire come previously written into it, even its system of combinatorial possibilities.

2) The desired effect of greater melodic and harmonious development, and a richer and more varied orchestral palette, is not to be achieved by means of intense work upon one body in particular. To believe the contrary is the vanity of the novice.

3) A variety of registers can be achieved only in a very primitive and crude way, with the technique employed to this point (an arbitrary and consecutive linkage of one woman after another, in a rapid journey from bed to bed). This is because, engaging with three or four women in a compositionally useful day, the subjacent effects of complementarity or contrast begin to emerge (blondes and brunettes, silent types and screamers, et cetera).

4, and to sum up) How can I create works like the ones burning in my imagination? It is not enough to trace invisible ligatures between these fleeting arpeggios (married women): *I must assemble all the elements of a repertoire, fully prepared to comply with my demands.*

Since his father's economic assistance had reduced difficulties of a material order to the minimum, it was easy for Frantisek to turn his mansion into a kind of phalanstery, where somewhere between twenty and thirty women, generously compensated, submitted to his investigations. Without being aware of it, Frantisek was decidedly an anti-sadist. In advance of his experiments, he prohibited any violence, denigrating act, habit in poor taste or other excess that might distract from his aims of a hedonistic character, celebrating the joys of life. The garments were made of a soft, light material, the kind that clings to the touch; the meals were served on dishes of the best quality and arranged in a way that was pleasing to the eye and sense of smell. Every morning and afternoon, dressed in the costume of the high priest of some fantastic cult, given to him by a designer friend at the Krasnoyarsk Theater, Frantisek presented himself in the secluded premises of the main hall (the windows boarded up, the walls adorned with red velvet tapestries, the sheets woven from linen and silk). Even though during the precise ritual he had organized for his system of compositional coitus, these garments were almost the first thing my great-great-grandfather removed, the outfit stimulated the impulse for profanation in his feminine "instruments," so that a spirit of chance always animated the encounters. In the worst case, it might be a flurry of melancholy, a breeze from another world that enveloped Frantisek in the midst of his coven. But usually it came from something difficult to define, the anticipation of pleasure that transported a woman . . . We won't go into details. In the essentials, Frantisek held to his scheme, which he defined as a "program." Convinced that the simple came before the complex, he began his rituals in the very simplest way, dedicating himself to one at a time.

Knowing by now, from sheer repetition, each woman's ability to become a theme (the personal limits of her amorous capacity), Frantisek decided to investigate whether he could organize these themes into a succession of melodies. His method was so obvious it was even comical. While attending a music hall performance, he'd developed certain fantasies, as aesthetic as they were sensual, around the symmetric revelation of the French dancers' row of panties. And so he decided to line up his partners in a row, hips pressed against hips, waists bent over, backs rigid as planks, hands on knees, breasts dangling. A fragment from his diary: ". . . Sometimes I'd go for the first in a row of twenty, starting from the left, and once I'd drawn the maximum of pleasure from my chosen instrument, I'd move along in order of proximity until reaching the end of the row. Other times, I'd start with the third in line, and pass to the fifth and then the seventh, leaving all those in the middle increasingly excited, before, suddenly and without warning, I'd repeat the procedure with one of those who thought she'd already had her chance, and was beginning to feel the elixirs of her shudders fade away."

My great-great-grandfather referred to his procedure as "the xylophonic performance technique," but didn't linger over it for more than a few days. Interested in the riches that developing two themes in parallel might offer, he applied himself to evaluating them by performing upon two women in the same bed. The results seem to have been promising but inadequate, because very soon he increased the number of women he employed. But now, since it was no longer the concept of succession but simultaneity that dominated, these apparent bacchanals ended up being a work of experimentation as tiring as it was exhaustive.

"The polyphony of voices that sings different things at the same time is what interests me. It's like living in a heaven that flows with scents and skins and moans," he wrote. Soon, however, his enthusiasm began to dull. The multiplicity was overwhelming. Every system of the senses became a chromatic range and long melody of its own, the superpositions of which created new polyphonies. And so, in the long run, his attempt to arrive at the conceptual entirety of the harmonic process had to enter into crisis due to the impossibilities of achieving a totality in perception, and not just in terms of musical production and notation. Not to speak of the limits of his body itself. After this long journey, Frantisek thus came back to the beginning, and he didn't know whether he was turning into a fabulous composer, an undistinguished performer of banal improvisations or a sad degenerate. The system had revealed itself to be a lack of system.

The crisis paralyzes him and Frantisek decides to close the phalanstery. As a good spendthrift who doesn't think about the future, when he says goodbye to his women-instruments, he compensates them with quantities that would be the envy of a king given to lavish splurges. Some use the money to set up their own establishments: restaurants, fashion boutiques, guesthouses, love villas, even musical instrument shops.

His abode now empty, Frantisek mournfully wraps himself in the vestments of solitude. His rhythm of life becomes irregular, no longer respecting the schedules of sleep and food; he spends hours staring with absent gaze at the mounds of cold ash in the fireplace and the advance of damp over the walls. He doesn't answer when people speak to him, or does so with an impossible delay, replying to questions they haven't asked. Human company irritates him, but occasionally a random commentary or gesture can move him to tears, and he ends up hugging the cook or whoever else happens to be near. He suffers from fits of mysticism, although he isn't precise about his devotional object; he surrenders to a confused pantheism that finds divinity in a vase, a glass of water, the broken branch of a larch tree, a couple of dirty socks, tweezers for eyebrow plucking, a Bible, a blazing fire or a pair of jade handcuffs kept in an ebony box.

From this period come the most moving entries in his *Diary*, the ones in which, having lost all reserve, his personality shines through. He writes: "The glances of my fellow men do not escape me, and by their reflection I am given a terrifying idea of my mental state. In the mornings I wake up and hear 'ti-tú, ti-tú' (high, low, high, low). At night the bed gives me no rest, because within my brain's recesses the monsters of dream crouch and mutter inanities."

Frivolous then serious, serious then frivolous, my great-great-grand-father speculates for a time about putting an end to his life. He's convinced of the need to do so, but delays it out of fear of an ugly mutilation. To hide this display of intimate cowardice of an aesthetic kind, and without anything in particular to do, he embraces the cause of dispossession. He survives only with great pains; he sleeps hugging a mangy sheep, shares his food with the poor, turns into an obses-sive Saint Francis of Assisi. But in his attitude, there's a remainder of arrogant anticipation, a lust for contrition. He says: "I want them to forget me," in the vain belief he's done something to be remembered. In the end, he must recognize that his entire peacocking tour through the territories of spiritual humility has done nothing to protect him from the risk of growing resentful—that is, admitting he's failed.

One day he learns of the existence of Afasia Atanasief, a mirac-ulous healer from Murmansk, a small coastal town on the Barents Sea. To visit her, one must cross the entire breadth of Russia, a task for the desperate; therefore, perfect for him. The very idea of sickness is inherently optimistic, because it assumes the idea of its complement, recovery. As soon as he decides to travel the distance, Frantisek's mood improves, which automatically renders the fulfillment of his aim superfluous. But the fantasy of the trip stimulates him, and he writes a long letter to the healer, in which he explains the whole drama of his existence blow by blow; in reply, he receives a telegram with the single word: "Come."

Frantisek makes the appropriate arrangements, leaving Dutchansky in charge of the property, and sets out.

2

The rustic nature of the trip distracted him a little from his obsessive thoughts. The Siberian dogs pulling the sleigh barked in harmony, and transformed their meter into notation by flinging small bubbles into the air of condensed breath, foam and drool. Wrapped in sable skins, Frantisek was lulled to sleep by the shouts of the driver or woken by leaps of the vehicle. It was like a spatial return to his past, when he'd been forced to spend whole days standing next to his father, feigning interest as the latter kept busy extracting his hairy gems from the depths of the lakes, except this time the travel was over the surface; according to his calculations, at one point he'd even have to pass a few kilometers from the place where Vladimir was living out his final days as explorer and tycoon. A beautiful chance to dodge the meeting. But Frantisek was too sensible to the warm radiance of the word "family," which evoked a feeling of belonging in his heart not experienced beyond language, so that when his sleigh was on the verge of making a detour to avoid the town of Lubyanka, he changed his mind and decided to visit his father.

During this period, Lubyanka was barely more than a suburb frayed away from a center that was nowhere. If enemy troops had wanted to stop for food and rest in their transit toward Moscow, they'd never have chosen to stay in the place. The few building structures that went beyond the average level of a shack still had a cow in the kitchen and a dirt floor trampled by pig hooves;

yet from a distance this landscape was an invitation to dreaming, ideally contemplated from the heights of Suiski Hill: the winding glints of the Ubsk River, mute rocks shimmering with mica, surly pine trees tickling the sky, a wicked young thing stealing eggs from the farms, a landowner's bullet setting the henhouse aflutter.

In the midst of this touristic squalor, Vladimir Deliuskin's property on the outskirts of town stood out. Its distinction was rooted less in the lavishness of the house itself than in the difference of size between his place of residence and place of work. When he began to grow hard of hearing after so many years of explosions, Vladimir left the "fieldwork" in the hands of Piotr, his trusty foreman, and built a storehouse comparable in height to some railway stations, with a sheet-metal roof and thick logs from barely planed trees; there, when he had nothing better to do, which was nearly all the time, he dabbled in new methods of "flaying" the mammoths, which faithful Piotr extracted by means of the traditional system and sent along to him. Due to the low temperatures prevailing, even if a month or more had passed since the extraction, at the time of their arrival the mammoths seemed freshly culled. They even let off the vapor of dry ice.

Once the material had been received, Vladimir chiseled the blocks until they took on a zoomorphic shape that vaguely approximated the original; the next step was to pass thick chains over the front and back quarters. Then, through a pneumo-mechanical apparatus of winches, he hoisted the iridescent beast and left it dangling three meters over the ground. When each quarry had been hung up by means of a colossal bellows, connected to a bronze basin, he sent it periodic blasts of hot air that collided with the ice walls, submitting it to a uniform movement of rotation. The result, if we leave out natural asymmetries, was that the ice melted gradually and evenly; of course, this process lasted for weeks, during which the trapped animal began to show inklings of its form, revealing itself in accordance with the differences in surrounding pressure and densities of ice to be a threatening beast or faint ghost; the latter was especially favored on moonlit nights, when the dark blue of the sky bounced off the deep blue of the oldest ice layers; this blue brought out every shadow in silhouette and made the beasts dance to the delicate music of countless water droplets, which skimmed through the cold air and burst against the ground. Mud and specters. The result of all this, once the unfreezing was completed, was those swollen, hairy, foul-smelling masses that Vladimir butchered and sold without wasting a single piece of bone or flesh.

As soon as he reached his father's place, Frantisek headed for the storehouse. Those bulks had always impressed him, and this time the idea of seeing them submitted to such engineering affected him even more. Now that he wasn't forced to accompany his father in his work, and thanks to the distance created by the development of his own activities and the emotional contamination produced by the expectation of meeting again, Frantisek began to discover a link between them going even deeper than the one generated by blood and surname. Beyond the apparent differences in their respective interests, it was enough to observe these beasts hoisted up and submitted to a process that, albeit barbaric, was also wise, an unhurried and painstaking cycle of transformations, to understand that like himself, Vladimir had never accepted things in just the way they were given. "My father, like me, is a slave to form," he told himself, and felt the impulse to run and give him a hug. Obviously, in order to do so, he had to find him first. He shouted his father's name. His voice echoed off the roofs and came back to him muffled, but no one answered. For a few minutes, as he continued to search across the length and breadth of the storehouse, he entertained himself by imagining some explanation for the absence. Just as Vladimir had built a discreet but visible laboratory for his investigations into the revelation of being (the extraction of mammoths from icy masses), it was possible he'd also set up another laboratory, still more secret and difficult to find, where he was giving himself over to new kinds of tests, perhaps to reorganize the parts that he'd obtained in combinations never before imagined (a beast with three legs, five fangs and one eye, with a ridiculously small tail sprouting like a mustache from its face), combinations into which, by means of unknown techniques, he'd later breathe life. What could he do with such things? Give them to the world as foul-smelling golems, perhaps, to see what effect they produced . . .

Frantisek smiled at the excesses of his fantasy. He knew perfectly well that his father possessed too practical a spirit to invest time in playing the demiurge . . . Golems? Only the Jews created those things! But where was Vladimir? Frantisek stopped short. A horrible suspicion, a cold that didn't come only from the hanging mammoths, paralyzed his mind: *His father was dead.* The thought wasn't capricious, even if the associative logic that had brought him to this conclusion seemed a rarefied flourish, a system of legatos akin to those found in a musical caprice. In the beginning was the word "mammoth." In some remote area of Frantisek's brain, this word sent its association tapping along two different channels and from three languages in a single unique direction: "My mother." In effect, "mammoth" can be separated into two syllables, "ma-" and "-mmoth." In French, "ma" is the possessive pronoun "my," while phonetically "-mmoth" becomes "mmouth" sounds the same as the noun "Mutte" ("mother") in German.* And in some sense, mammoths had been and were Frantisek's mother, owing to the fact that, conveniently exploited by Vladimir, they had turned out to be his primary source of nutrition. This is why, when establishing the relationship between "mammoth" and "my mother," he had inevi-

---

* Although one writes "Mutter," in everyday speech the "r" is aspirated.

tably linked the early absence of the latter—a death from typhoid fever when he was just a few months old—with the death of his own father; yet because he had no memory of the first death and his own parallel transformation into an orphan, and given that a wet nurse had substituted immediately for the missing woman, this connection could work only in an indirect form, as the poor mother had never been a real presence for the abandoned child. The mental link that made him suddenly think Vladimir was dead could therefore not be simply the word "mammoth" (my mother). The word that gave the last turn to the pirouette was "Jews." And for this reason, no translation had been needed: when he thought his father could not possibly make golems like the Jews—whom the tsarist authorities during this period had prohibited from all commercial activity—what Frantisek really thought was his father couldn't have behaved like *just another* Jew. If for childish and primitive mentalities—which are identical—every father is a God, that is to say, the one to whom everything is given and whom no negation limits, then in Frantisek's lightning-quick associative system, not being *just another* Jew was equivalent to being the *king* of the Jews: Christ. The Messiah. God, the One and Only, the Anointed One. And how had Christ died? Crucified. Thus Vladimir, who substituted for Frantisek's mother—*ma Mutte*—had, in the process of occupying himself with subsistence—*mammoth*—spent his entire life, despite himself and without knowing it, in adoration of the absent one, rendering her tribute. Every mammoth rescued from the depths of the lakes was a triumph, even if only partial, over the destiny that had prematurely snatched his wife from his side. And in the process of improving the methods of extraction, in their eternal perfecting, what he was doing was building a saga from the perishable yet successive monuments that evoked her. And—here came the conclusion of the thought, of Frantisek's horrible fear—after spending his life in this nostalgic and necrophiliac celebration, immersed in the compulsive repetition of a behavior he couldn't stop, Vladimir had decided to pass to the sentimental act par excellence, becoming one with his lover and fusing with her. In this sense, a destiny that involved "mama"—that is, "mammoth"—which ended with a hanging from hooks, was equivalent to a fulfillment of divine fate and a death crucified like the king of the Jews—in other words, the God of the Christians.

Of course, having arrived at this conclusion, Frantisek wasn't going to pause to notice the logical and theological inconsistencies of his reasoning. Convictions always well up from the soul. Eyes brimming with tears, he lifted his head toward the low ceiling bounded by sheet-metal roofs and looked in every direction for his father, hanged dead. *I go toward you, father, and you abandon me.* The tapping of the water droplets had now lost any festive quality and was the repeated funereal "plop" of endings. Worms garlanded the puddles, bathing in this rain.

"Father!" shouted Frantisek, and let his head fall on his chest, his knees into the mud.

When he looked up again, Vladimir himself was standing before him. If this was a specter, then it was one who seemed to have passed with great realism through the corresponding periods of life: he was fatter, nearly bald, with a black beard sprinkled with white hairs and an alcoholic's nose furrowed by veins. Beyond a doubt, he had aged. From his shoulder there hung a bundle of dead bustards; Vladimir was returning from the hunt.

"Son!" he said, crouching down, picking up Frantisek and submitting him to every display of Russian effusiveness: a hug hard enough to dislocate a joint, a loud wet kiss on the mouth, a rubbing of noses imported from the Eskimos, a friendly fist bump against the chest and a series of cheek pinches and twists, accompanied by the typical phrase:

"*Dorogoy drug*! I cannot believe what this gaze is seeing! My son, light of my eyes, extract of my testicles, adored one never forgotten . . ."

"Yes, your Frantisek," the so-alluded helpfully supplied, knowing that in these moments of emotion, as in so many others, Vladimir suffered from momentary lapses that prevented him from remembering names.

"*Bozhe moi*! Do you think I am a heartless scoundrel, one who does not even know the fruits of his blood?" And stretching out an arm in the attempt to encompass his whole domain, he ended up pointing a finger at the nearest mammoth: "And? What do you think? Gems from the abysses of time! And? Are you coming back to live with your poor father or not?"

To fête his son, Vladimir organized a dinner that from the start threatened to end up a bacchanal. On the pine table from Slavonia all kinds of treats could be found, national and foreign. Among the local delicacies were schmaltz, sweet-and-sour pickles, kimlbroyt, smoked mullet fish, hot and juicy pastrami with sides seasoned with red pepper, tart sauerkraut just drawn from wood barrels, pletzel, little balls of white cheese with miniature green onions or paprika, fresh smetana, duck sausages, debrecener sausages, smoked sprät from the Baltic, fat and slippery úlikes, and hot, just slightly bitter liverwurst, stuffed with black olives and walnuts. From the rest of the world: Greek halva, Polish vodka, Norwegian bacalao, Czech slivovitz, Uruguayan guindado, Portuguese anchovies, Danish sardines . . .

Suffocated by the heat of the logs burning in the fireplace, overwhelmed by the aroma of food and the smell of the bodies of the serving staff who approached to fill his glass or change his plates, Frantisek couldn't help but wonder why the closest person in the world to him, the most intimate and dearest, had always seemed strange. His father went out of the way for him, yet he couldn't help but perceive the involuntary and devastating effect of the chasm that separated them. In fact, he understood, he'd gone to live far away from Vladimir not to build a life tailored to personal necessities, but instead to recuperate, by means of distance and the ennobling effect of time, the sentiment of filial love that proximity had denied him. "I am filth," thought Frantisek, and pitying himself, he once again forgot about his father, who had begun a new monologue by his side:

"What a joy to see you, my son! I didn't expect it. What can we talk about, let's see? Topics. The government. A band of thieves, except for our big boss, the Tsar, who has no clue about anything. The fate of our Holy Russia scares me a lot. Do you go to mass? No? A shame. Anyway. How have you been keeping busy lately? You don't want to talk about it? Even better. Work means problems, and right now we have to enjoy ourselves."

Vladimir gave two claps:

"Music and dance!" he shouted.

From the left side of the gallery came the classic: two bearded old men with fur caps, silk dress coats, wide pants and boots entered jumping and shrieking "Oy, oy, oy!" while they played the accordion and balalaika. From the right side, first came the little foot, then the rosy ankle, then the thick calves and hammy thigh, and finally the rest of the body of the first of five Graces, dressed in transparent tunics that let one see the heavy swaying of their mammary glands to perfection. Vladimir elbowed Frantisek:

"You can sleep with the fat one if you like. Or with two or three of them, even. They sometimes warm my own bed, of course. I won't say they're pure, but I guarantee you they're affectionate. I don't know if you get my drift." Elbow to rib. "If happy coincidence permits, within nine months I might be able to say I'm either the grandfather of a new son or the father of a grandson. No? You're not interested? Do such trifles really worry you? You're not . . . ? Ah, you're taking a purge. What luck, unfortunately. In any case, I don't think any of them are the cleanest. Plague neutralized by plague. Even so, in your place, I wouldn't look down on turning a few over and, with a little ash-tree oil or goat butter, trying out, for example . . ."

While Vladimir babbled away in a kind of alcoholic ode to the charms of his creatures, one of them—laurel crown on her forehead, eyelid drooping over a sclerotic halo of cataracts—recited:

> *Prodigal son, son prodigal*
> *Male son, son most dear*
> *In the steppes I lose myself*
> *To Father's house come I near*

Poem with assonant rhyme. Anonymous Russian author.

Over the course of the night, helped along by libations, Frantisek and his father managed to achieve an imitation of the primordial connection. The son could confide his secret and the reasons for his crisis to his father, and the father pledged to accompany him on the pilgrimage in search of a word from Afasia Atanasief. Comforted by this promise, Frantisek went to sleep as early as he could and left Vladimir, after submitting to all the excesses of his goodnight kiss. But midmorning, when he went to wake him up before departure, he realized his father was totally incapable of any movement. In fact, the vigorous but already senile Vladimir spent twenty-five minutes saying, "Who are you? What do you want? Spiders! Get this filth off me!" and could recognize his son only after half an hour.

The sleigh had been prepared, the dogs were barking. In the distance, on the horizon, black clouds could be seen, increasing in size. The wind was torquing the treetops into right angles. It was time to go. But Frantisek had a question:

"Father, what was Mama like?"

Vladimir made an effort, rubbed his eyes and peered at the deepest spiderweb in the trunk of his memories . . .

"Cintila Alexeievna?" he asked, in a voice tormented by pain or fury. "What was Cintila like?" And instead of having the mercy or decency to say, "She was a fine woman," or "She was the great love of my life," or even "I don't remember her anymore," Vladimir exclaimed: "Your mother was an insufferable beast! What do you want, for me to tell you the truth or a lie? She made my life impossible. With her I wasn't the master of my own house. I had to take off my muddy boots and wear slippers, the drink was rationed . . . She held me in contempt. I had to tolerate that nit, that scrawny pollywog! She thought she was the bee's knees. As if she had a great destiny written out for her beforehand . . . That bloody Polish woman . . ."

"Goodbye, Papa . . ."

"Goodbye? Listen, son . . . When I got sick, your mother, the saint, said to me: 'Flea-ridden dog, when will you have the decency to go ahead and die?' Do you know why you're called Frantisek? Because that was the name of the lover of your mother's mother. I wanted to give you another name, a truly Russian one. But no. She insisted, insisted, and there you have it, see? A *Poilish* name. Humiliation! Why Frantisek and not Volodia or Piotr or Alexei, eh? And what was the problem with naming you after your father? Or isn't it a pretty name, Vladimir? The worst thing about that woman is she never loved me. Frantisek! Listen . . . Where are you going? Never, not for one minute did she love me, your mother! Are you listening? Son . . . !"

Frantisek leaped into his sleigh. Incidental beauty of the tundra. The stormfront pursued him for three days and then dissolved into rain and hail before the very gates of Murmansk. Like the symbol of a good omen, the gentle miracle of an aurora borealis stretched over the town. Frantisek didn't take long to find out the address where Afasia Atanasief attended to patients. It was a modest but spacious house, just overlooking the Barents Sea. On the façade, a worn inscription gave heart to visitors: "Here all suffering ends."

Frantisek went into a kind of waiting room; there were a good number of people there, all miserable, in a typically pious attitude (heads bowed down, hands arranged in prayer). The new arrival leaned over the closest patient and asked whether it would be long. Astonished, the other replied: "Usually it takes a few days." "My God," answered Frantisek, and fell asleep.

When he opened his eyes, he saw that without noticing it, he'd shifted to another space. He was in an empty room, leaving out a couple of chairs, a desk and a middle-aged man observing him in silence. Frantisek felt the intensity and brilliance of this gaze examining his very soul. His life was a skein being unspooled by the man's mind.

"I . . ." he began. "I came here . . ."

"You don't need to explain to me," said the other, and served him a strong brew in a cracked teacup. "*Tey mit limene.*"

"Yes, thank you," said Frantisek, distracted, excited. He took a sip, and it burned him. "You don't need to explain to me." How much wisdom there was in seven words! But he had to express, to justify himself. He set the cup aside and began:

"I'd like to discover the reasons for my crisis," he said. "It requires some kind of introduction." Frantisek waited a few seconds for the other to say, "Go on," or "Continue," or at least "Aha." But his interlocutor remained quiet. Judging that this silence wasn't disapproving (although it wasn't very stimulating either), he decided to proceed at his own risk: "Over time, I've been able to confirm that on every occasion I show up to an activity, a part of me flees. Now then: absence in one place is presence in another. What happens for me, and this is a part of what concerns me, is my presence in this other place is not perceived by me as such, which, in conclusion, leaves me emptied of myself. I want to be cured of this unreality."

"Obviously," said the host, "what you need is to be cured of your ignorance about where your being dwells. Your tea is getting cold."

"I see you've grasped the heart of the matter," said Frantisek, and took a polite sip. The shrewdness of his interlocutor freed him of half his problem; feeling relieved, he was driven to elaborate, to thoroughly analyze his conflict: "How does what's happening to me relate to the music I cannot create? Is it a mystery? At a certain level, it seems very easy to understand . . . Just as I described in my letter of introduction, I don't know whether you remember"—the other nodded—"my fornications were the experimental field, let's call it 'practical,' within an abstract operation of a nature both sensitive and intellectual. It consisted of not the slow development of an idea, limited to, say, the measurement of a plane of melodic thought, but instead was the representation of a figure from different and overlapping visual perspectives . . . What I mean is that as a composer, and I hope you'll take what I say as an element of critical illustration, rather than as a show of presumptuousness, I am characterized by the use of extraordinarily rich, complex polyphonic mechanisms . . ."

Taking advantage of the fact that his interlocutor had deeply inhaled and sighed, Frantisek himself took a breath and drank the rest of his tea. In those seconds of repose, he found that the infusion had an exquisite taste. There were a few small drops of lemon, to be sure, but also something else, something strong and fragrant, which was neither mint nor a camphorated essence of the kind used by old ladies to perfume their bodices and keep their bitches virgin. In the form of steam, the smell of this essence rose from the bottom of the teacup and flooded his nostrils, producing a revitalizing and mentally stimulating effect:

"Clearly the simultaneity of the planes in my creative modus operandi," he went on, "could have been more complete if, at the same time as I spread myself horizontally over the epidermis of my companions, I'd submitted them to the in-depth treatment of relief sculpture—that is, to dissections, trepanations, dismemberments, new assemblages . . ." For a second Frantisek contemplated the landscape of bloody operations that his words spread before them and gave a shiver of pure humanism. "It's obvious that this idea equates absolute aesthetic rigor with universal sacrifice in a dangerous way, and yet . . . I don't know. To sum up, I'm not sure whether my crisis is aesthetic, ethic, vital . . ." Frantisek went silent. All his euphoria had been replaced by a sudden fatigue; it was difficult for him to go on with his explanation: "There's something else too . . . To touch a body, even in the same place where it's been touched on another occasion, is to generate a new moment and at the same time evoke the previous one. It's remarkable: in this repetition, the instrument, the woman, sees emphasis and passion, while the man . . ."

"Please don't explain anything else to me," interrupted the other. And with such authority that Frantisek was sure he'd found a solution to his problem.

"What's wrong with me, maestro?" Frantisek pleaded.

"What's wrong is that you don't even know where you are. And don't call me maestro. Come along."

"Where?"

"To the treatment room. The distinguished Afasia is expecting you."

"Not you . . ."

"*Nyet*. The distinguished is illiterate. I'm the one who reads her letters."

3

Time passed, generations passed, but no one can claim to know in detail what happened during the meeting between my great-great-grandfather and the distinguished Afasia Atanasief; Afasia never made the slightest comment about it, just as she kept silent about all her patients, and Frantisek, after this meeting, which in some way forms the central experience of the first stage of his life, deepened his tendency to reclusion to the point that any knowledge about what happened can be deduced only indirectly, through analysis of the language to which he felt closest.

If in the few surviving musical writings of his first period one can make out a driving will to grasp a sensible and conceptual whole through an intensity and proliferation of experience, then after this encounter with the healer, the compulsion to "tell all" drifts into a far more sweeping and poised form of clear symphonic bent, one that might even sound fatuous and conventional to ears used to the prior saturation. But it's not all arpeggios and glissandos either. In his creation, there is no longer anything that reeks of anguished exhibitionism or a mysterious faith in some deep "inner life." What comes over him is no more and no less than the explosion of maturity, and its effect is that his posterior productions will be marked out by sobriety and an apparent sense of loss, not to do with indifference, but with a feeling of quiet serenity when facing the cosmos.

In accordance with this new attitude, my great-great-grandfather decided to migrate to less traveled landscapes. He left Volodia Dutchansky in charge of his property in Irkutsk and settled on a small farm in Crasneborsk, a region located in the foothills of the Ural Mountains. For those who knew him, this decision revealed that for mysterious reasons he had chosen to flog his consciousness, submerging himself in the idiocy of country living. Yet although it's true that the farm was bursting with chickens, it's also true that in general Frantisek didn't concern himself with domestic tasks. At most, during the winter season he would put on boots and splash around in the mixture of red earth and mud, an inverted twilight, as he went looking for wood. The rest of the time he spent shut away in his cabin, dedicating himself to new works. To compose, he made use of a battered violin he'd procured from a muzhik in the area, swapping it for two very beautiful, just weaned suckling pigs. Despite the difficulty of tuning it and replacing the strings, he fell in love with the instrument: its severe limitations for performance stimulated an unexplored aspect, an extremely austere lyricism. Frantisek was anything but a popular composer, but his innate taste for contrasts had led him to absorb the atmosphere that one breathed in Crasneborsk (sun hitting the eternal white mountain ranges, dawn, mist in the valley) in such a way that sometimes, while practicing his pieces on the violin, the music streaming from those clumsy strings filtered through the treetops and directly entered the souls of those living in the region. As an unexpected effect of this communion between complex beauty and simple spirits, the first caress of his fame arrived. In a progression not worth dwelling upon, the composer of rustic life awoke the curiosity of the big cosmopolitan cities, and precisely because of his absence and reluctance, quickly transformed into the "unmissable" act of the official season. "Ha!" said those in the know, walking along the promenade outside the Saint Petersburg theater where the first concert featuring his music had been offered. "Ha! And to think we'd been about to pass him over . . ."

Of course, the way that my great-great-grandfather presented himself as a rural phenomenon might be seen as an abusive procedure to impose a strong prior belief in the masses about the value of his work, which would create the illusion in most music lovers that they had "instinctively" appreciated his value. At heart, this is how the system of fashion works: as a terrifying model of production for meaning, which dispenses with any reflection about the complex aspects a judgment of quality would entail. Luckily, this wasn't the case with my great-great-grandfather, who was never a social climber and always utterly disregarded the opinions of others about his work. Not only that: so uninterested was he in any expectation of worldly triumph that on the day of his premiere, oblivious to every consideration of an aesthetic order, he walked in his robe and slippers through the city streets, pondering the reasons why he was living through a sentimental revolution.

She: twenty-five years old, daughter of a famous oboist from La Scala in Milan. Sofia Quatrocci. Ugly, a few pounds overweight, with moles, warts and boils scattered all over her dull skin. But intellectually brilliant, with luminous eyes, an imaginative character, an expansive sense of humor and a broad general culture, along with a prodigious memory capable of reproducing to the letter any phrase she found amusing. If any of her admirers presented himself with a worn-out formula, she'd immediately produce a mirror reply:

"*Seye eros rof thgis a tahw*"—or—"*Uoy ees ot eroseye na tahw.*"

Although she occasionally wielded her humor against foreign words, she never did so against the ones who had spoken the phrase. She seemed to consider the rest of human existence a complement to her own happiness, and seemed not to need anyone. She confessed without any sense of shame (or lied like a Cossack) that she remained a virgin at an age when a woman is already considered to be old. She was an accomplished performer. Every one of her shows was guaranteed a full house. Her repertoire was awful, which highlighted her talent. Her voice created gems of enduring beauty, using horse manure as their base. Frantisek, used to treating the female sex as livestock, didn't even dare strike up a conversation with the diva. He waited for her after shows, and sent her bouquets of flowers with no dedication card. Of course, Sofia knew who her anonymous admirer was. It amused her to have such a shy suitor. She was suspicious of him too: there was a risk that all this prowling about was a simulacrum, a charade of seduction carried out by a good-looking but inexperienced composer, its sole purpose to wrangle her commitment to acting in some future monstrosity of his authorship.

At last, the meeting took place. And it was she who took the initiative:

"What should we do with what we feel?" she asked.

"I don't know," replied Frantisek, and fled.

Later there were concerts, social gatherings, friends in common. At a party in the conservatory, they ended up side by side; Frantisek hid behind a glass of champagne.

"Are you a mouse, a man of few words or a half idiot?" she provoked him.

"I can talk about music, travels, mysticism, ice, solitude. I can also talk about orgies and deceptions," replied my great-great-grandfather.

"That is, nothing's ever happened to you," laughed Quatrocci. Then she grew serious: "When singing, I have the impression that my voice occupies more space than I do, which isn't physically true, because my voice comes from my throat, which is itself a small part of my body. This confusion, this error, produces an effect of intensity I call 'art,' and I've always believed that it's enough to fill my life.

But for a while now, I've been feeling something new expanding within me, transforming me into a different woman. I believe it's something that belongs to the order of the emotions. When are we getting married? *Em evol uoy od? Uoy evol i.*"

His composer colleagues decided to pull out all the stops when organizing his bachelor party. After examining and discarding a series of celebratory possibilities (driving a troika along the Nevsky Prospect with Frantisek dressed as a woman, and throwing him naked into a fountain; hiring Tzigane gypsy dancers from a little hut on the outskirts; shutting him away all night in the morgue; et cetera), they opted for the classic formula: a dinner party for the men. There they all were—that is, Constantine Balakov, Nikolai Grigorievich, Kashkin, Broluv, Leonid Katz, Voroszlav Pashulski, Anatol Schneider, Iosef Ostropov, and other greats of the time whose names are today worth less than dust. Vodka, cigar smoke, laughter. Balakov kicked off:

"There's no doubt that by marrying a singer of world renown, poor Frantisek will play a pitiful role." Affectionate fist bump to the back of the one mentioned. "Forced to trail her through Europe playing the contemptible role of the kept husband, he'll lose all passion for work, and before long become incapable of even contemplating a musical stave. *Prosit!*"

"The description is incomplete and even merciful," picked up Kashkin. "As soon as Sofia wearies of her new toy, instead of recognizing that such boredom is in the nature of every human bond, she will unleash a zealous tirade against our friend. Have you ever heard words like 'layabout,' 'idler,' 'wretch'?"

"I think, with complete affection, of 'cuckold.' My wife says it to me every day," joked Balakirev.

The friends gently laughed. Kashkin went on:

"The use of words like these will only mark the beginning of a season in sentimental purgatory. And knowing Frantisek's noble heart, I take it as a given that instead of admitting he's married a shrew, he'll end up blaming himself for what's happened."

"How long do you think it will take her to be unfaithful?" chipped in Broluv.

"Months? Weeks? Days? This very night, during her own bachelorette party? In any case, very soon," added Pashulski.

"Where is Ilya Petrov?" said Deliuskin, uneasy. "He was the one who organized all this, and . . ."

"Petrov can't be relied upon. He arranges meetings and scraps them without any warning. He always leaves you high and dry . . ." said Ostropov. "But let's keep going. All these tragedies could be avoided if she showed an interest in the pathetic living conditions that our friend can offer her."

"I'm not poor," my great-great-grandfather defended himself.

"True. But she's extremely rich," said Ostropov. "Used to luxury and comforts, do you think that Sofia will forgo everything just for your love? Do you imagine that she'll willingly tolerate the charms of the *aurea mediocritas*? There's not a chance that she's going to turn into your maid, so most likely she'll find a way to make you her lackey. You'll have to follow her wherever she goes, you'll have to make do with composing your little works when she leaves you a second free; socially, you'll find yourself exercising at most the role of companion, a decorative figure, the stole on her mink coat that she drags along, picking up the filth of red carpets. Soon Sofia won't even notice your presence. 'Who is that gentleman accompanying you, madame?' 'This one? Ah. Nobody. Only my husband . . .'"

"Is it necessary to continue the joke?" asked Frantisek.

"Joke?" Schneider was scandalized. "Wake up, Deliuskin! Like every prima donna who adores showing her face in sublime realms because what she truly loves is to revel like a swine in the wastelands of abjection, as soon as you're distracted for a second she'll submit herself with absolute pleasure to the aberrant sexual tastes of stagehands, luthiers, hairdressers and singing teachers, marked by their use of all kinds of devices . . ."

"For this class of women, the members of the *lumpenproletariat* playing bit parts in the operatic subworld most completely represent the primal forces of masculinity," added Grigorievich.

"It's already three in the morning and we haven't talked about matrimonial *taedium vitae* . . ." yawned Nikita Ziemkovich. "My experience, which I'll describe for the benefit of our dear Deliuskin, shows that boredom . . ."

While the talks were taking place, Ilya Petrov was conscientiously carrying out the secret task that the group had entrusted to him. Dressed in his best formal wear, an expression of sympathy painted on his face, he had presented himself at the petit hotel where Sofia Quatrocci resided, to confide to her "certain *very* particular particularities in good Frantisek, which make your engagement ceremony inadvisable if you wish to fully realize yourself as a woman, not to mention a mother." Petrov was efficient, persuasive ("Even I, on more than one occasion, have had to brush aside his hand . . ."). While listening to him, the singer went silent, turned pale, denied it and asked for proof, which with the happy ease of the cynic, her visitor invented on the spot, from the names of men to the dates, words, intensities and positions. Sofia broke into sobs, and at dawn, without thinking for even a moment that she had been victim to the cruelest practical joke, she fled Saint Petersburg. A year later, she married a metalworker from Rostow.*

Since he never saw Quatrocci again, my great-great-grandfa-

---

* A note at the margin: God, who doesn't exist—if he did, as my son discovered, it was in the form of a wavelength throbbing at the center of the dense, extremely heavy mass that exploded in a tide of fire at the moment of creation—this God punished Ilya Petrov for his wickedness, envy and resentment. One day, getting out of the bathtub, poor Petrov tripped and broke his spine. A man of solitary habits, he didn't have anyone to come help him. With nothing else to eat, Lila, his Persian cat, had already polished off a sizeable chunk of his body by the time it was found.

ther never found out the reason for this desertion on the verge of the altar, let alone that the cause had been his peers, motivated by envy of his talent.

The abandonment pushed him to take refuge in his work; this loss had opened new seams, new veins from which a superior music bled. In this period, Sofia Quatrocci transformed into a muse, an inspiring saint in a purely imaginary alcove, a figure whose eventual return (in flesh and blood) would have achieved nothing more than duplication and confusion. As is logical, Deliuskin's moral scrupulosity did not bear well with these transitions of his psychic nature, so that in the midst of his compositional vertigo he wept, imagining versions of an impossible reencounter, sublime interpretations of still unwritten works starring the woman who, strictly speaking, he had already begun to forget. Sofia Quatrocci disappeared completely only when my great-great-grandfather finished composing his first opera, *The March of the White Russian Heart*, and had to occupy himself with the directing, staging, dramatization, production . . .

Due to his education and habits (when it came down to it, his father had raised him like a prince), Frantisek was far from imagining what a true descent into the inferno of details involves. The budgetary discussions with the hall's artistic committee, the whims of the singers who always try to tailor each score to their vocal limitations or corrupt aesthetic superstitions, the delays of the makeup artists, the contagious diseases of the instrumentalists . . . The recitals grew exasperating. A week before the premiere, the tenor suffered from an attack of boils and fainted into the arms of the soprano halfway through a love duet; the chorus refused to sing the triplets and the orchestra conductor demanded a change in the arrangement of wind instrumentalists, because the trumpet players were in general too tall and covered up the trombonists.

The day of the general recital . . .

Strident sounds, warm-up of strings, muffled coughs, groans, stifled gases, tuning checks; a double bassist leans over and burps as he smooths the silk stocking over his calf. Deliuskin's peers and colleagues wait in the box seats. "Catastrophe is imminent," predicts Schneider. Nervous whack, the sharp tock tock of the little Grim Reaper's staff, the director's baton on the music stand. A flute solo, the main theme. With the chord of wood instruments, the call of trumpets sounds, then the harp arpeggios. The atmosphere of the Russian steppe, the iridescent splendor of its snows, comes to us in all its trembling beauty. The song of the flute comes back, reflective. Soon another sensual melody is heard; now it's the oboe. A penetrating chord, followed by a wild explosion of orchestral sound . . . "Decadent," opines Ziemkovich. "Morbid, you mean," says Ungarev. "Technically this should be the overture. But what I'm hearing is a prelude!" marvels Balakov. "Yes, to my nap," laughs Grigorievich. "I don't know whether this exemplifies a new concept of nihilism or spinelessness," says Kashkin. Leonid Katz chimes in: "Without a doubt, Deliuskin is the most eccentric composer of our generation . . . and the most mediocre." "Shhh . . . Shhhh. The stage is collapsing," says Anatol Pashulski. "No, they're moving one of the sets. What happens is they're mounted on wheels of different sizes. So that between . . . But is that a boyar, a member of the nobility?!" says Anatol Zinovievk. "I'm afraid it's Merenchokova." "But this woman grows horizontally! From the back I thought she was the incarnation of our longed-for Peter the Great." "Didn't you know that the mother, or perhaps grandmother of Merenchokova, and the dead Tsar . . . ?" "I don't believe you!" "Yes. She was the only one who could swallow his drunken binges." "What a throat!" "Rather. And from that same school, or sequel, we'll now suffer a few indescribable falsettos."

Even though the critics didn't give the work a warm reception, the public made up for it, taking *The March of the White Rus-*

sian Heart as its own and turning it into such a success it became an essential part of the next season's programming. Beyond its intrinsic merits, *The March . . .*, in the history of classical music, was the most serious predecessor to the reclaiming of Russian national sentiment that Glinka would later bring to its peak in his opera *A Life for the Tsar*.

A couple of days after the premiere, Deliuskin decided to consult Avrosim Roittenburg, the fashionable doctor of the moment in the music world: he'd felt slight stabbing pains in his chest.

"Stop smoking," the doctor warned him.

"I've never touched a cigarette," Deliuskin said.

"Ah. Then take off your shirt."

Roittenburg pressed his head against his back and remained silent for a few seconds. Then he said:

"Oy oy oy."

"What's wrong?" Deliuskin nervously asked.

"I wanted to hear how my voice echoed. Get dressed. Nothing's the matter, although the climate of this city isn't good for you."

The doctor's advice fit perfectly with his longings. Frantisek returned to Crasneborsk. There, without knowing it, a special form of tranquility was waiting for him. Not long after his arrival, a knock came at the door of the farm: a Finnish painter. With a sense of vocation, and not lacking in sensibility, Jenka Roszl specialized in the portraits of celebrities. "I have no thought of paying," said Deliuskin. And she said: "I have no thought of charging you." My great-great-grandfather didn't care about the perpetuation of his image, but the idea of sitting quietly for several hours each day tempted him; it seemed like a good chance to concentrate on figuring out certain problems of counterpoint; he also liked this woman's smile, so he accepted. And the moment that Jenka Roszl gave the last brushstrokes to the portrait, he asked her to become his wife.

4

The marriage of my great-great-grandparents was perfect in every way. Both were mature adults, two beautiful examples of the spiritual progress favored by the cultivation of the arts. It's obvious that given his new civil status, Frantisek now found himself prevented from continuing the procedures of compositional research he'd drawn upon in times of bachelorhood. But this didn't entail a loss. On the contrary. These very restrictions on the life of a married man rescued him at last from his anxiety without object, from the challenges of his desperation. Or at least they gave him a new kind of meaning. After a brief honeymoon, my great-great-grandfather surrendered to the charms of domestic life. Everything became repetition: from the morning trickle of honey over butter, spread on dense, crunchy rye bread, to his nocturnal glass of kvass, sitting in his favorite chair. This repetition, which could have worked disastrous influences, weakening his character or ruining his creative impulse, fit Frantisek like the ring on his finger: he started to compose with an unsuspected fluidity and began to transform into a superior musician, approaching ever more closely to his essence.

"Marriage," he wrote to his friend Volodia Dutchansky, "has a religious quality. At some moments (not all, luckily) the rule of abstinence, understood as the fidelity that I owe to my beloved wife, makes me burn and consume myself like a monk in the cloister."

From that moment on, music became his only orgy. Since he was an artist fully conscious of the materials he was using, he saw himself confronted with aesthetic challenges of the first magnitude. Sometimes he chatted about these apprehensions with his wife Jenka:

"What concerns me has nothing to do with pianissimos or fortissimos," he told her, "but with the fate of the series of procedures I've used up to now."

Jenka, who at night swapped out her paintbrushes for knitting needles, threaded another stitch, gave a sigh and smiled lovingly at her husband. Frantisek went on:

"In my case, the most obvious temptation is to squeeze as much as possible from the diversity and combination of sounds I've previously handled, until by means of pure repetition, I obtain the elixir of singularity. To take this temptation to an extreme would mean always writing the same note. The other temptation is its opposite, and thus provokes me even more. It means annihilating myself as an author to become a pure source of absorption, a kind of receptor god: one who does not create worlds, but devours them. Or, to put it less pompously, to become a kind of perfect stenographer."

"..."

"Did you say something? No. I thought you did . . . A third possibility exists, derived from the second, but fuller and more encompassing. This is to do everything and become everyone, turning into a fully inchoate musical being, the most perfect inconsistency, someone or something that comprises what has been done and what hasn't been done, the work of others and anything it occurs to me to write, as well as, in addition, the entire sound of the Universe. What do you think, Jenkele, my love?"

Here, Jenka lifted her head:

"When I paint, I paint."

"Does that mean you don't worry beforehand about even the frame, the canvas, the colors, the palette . . . ? Not to speak of the technique of the brushstrokes, the preceding styles, the objects to portray . . ."

"Let's go to sleep, Frantisek? It's already very late . . ."

"Not yet! There is a problem. If I choose to surrender myself to the third temptation, then soon I will have to admit (as in fact I am already doing now) that the audible totality of what exists is so vast no single being could encompass it (much less perform it) without some kind of formal reduction. Just imagine, the register of only a very tiny portion of the full universal wealth of sound—for instance, what is heard at this precise moment we are exchanging words—would suppose an unlimited quantity of staved paper and copyists, dedicated without rest to automatically and swiftly taking down what they hear . . . ! Which at heart would be no more than to pass a delicate net through fleeting time, and we haven't even begun to talk about the subsequent conversion into an aesthetic product . . ."

Is it possible for two clicking needles to give out sparks? Frantisek saw it, and in their crossing, he too glimpsed the absurdity of his idea, an infinite row of scribes in gray robes losing themselves in the infinity of perspective, their ears straining to capture the static of nothingness; or worse, a constant murmur of quills scoring the paper, each hearing only its own strokes, its own scratchings multiplied to the nth potential.

"Don't fill our house with strangers, Fran . . ." the pleasant voice of reason sprang from Jenka's lips.

My great-great-grandfather understood that his wife's reluctance to debate these questions concealed, in addition to a certain boredom, a message that could be summed up in a single word: "Simplicity!" For her, simplicity was an end in itself, not the prelude to a more rigorous decision. Despite its branching nature and its pleasures, madness in some cases is the easiest option, while simplicity takes work. Jenka was a wonderful woman!

What did Deliuskin do? He cut his losses and seized the best of every possibility (every "temptation"), putting it at the service of his fancy. He hired Lev Isaias Tchachenko, a developmentally disabled man who scrambled around the farms looking for work, instructing him to gather up all the trash, shiny things, loose objects and curiosities that he found in Crasneborsk and its surroundings. Every afternoon, after a meticulous period of collection, Lev would appear with his burlap sack full of treasures: little bells, metal scraps, bolts, fragments of cannonballs, branches polished by water, feathers, worn-out brushes, gnawed bones, teeth, butterfly elytra, scarab beetle carapaces, et cetera, et cetera. With his magic hands, he went about hanging each thing from the ceiling; occasionally, out of pure decorative instinct, Jenka would point out some combination, but in general, Lev worked alone; sometimes, while tying a dried-up wasp or hanging a tuber from a saddle, the idiot would whistle a melody from deep Russia between his teeth, always the same one. (In the third movement of Frantisek's *Slavic Motif* there's a ritornello capriccioso with a carefree air that evokes this whistling.)

Then, and thanks to what Lev had obtained, along with the music that continuously played in his head, which he swiftly transferred to music paper, my great-great-grandfather could hear the system of relationships and allusions produced by this grouping, as objects brushed, collided and rubbed against each other, borne on currents of air. There were even some that spun on their own axes without anything pushing them, out of pure kinetic sympathy, in search of a frequency. These were the privileged objects of pure art, the promise of coming centuries that would run through the whole chromatic scale. One of Frantisek's favorites was a small bent piece of dark-green iron, pure grime and rust hanging from the center of the barn (now transformed into a studio). No doubt it had been the support arch on which the false teeth of a rural noble had been implanted, lost in the midst of a horse ride or the vomiting of a drunken spree. But now it worked as a "basic tuner," because it gathered the vibrations of the objects moving around it and could detect even the slightest differences in tone, correcting, absorbing and launching them once more into the air as a generous collection of harmonious subtleties, a mysterious bouquet.

Of course, no one who wasn't my great-great-grandfather could have extracted music from all this, just as no one but Jenka could find attractive this wilderness where love had brought her to live. Every day, while her husband shut himself away, she put on her rugged boots and wide-brimmed Pre-Raphaelite hat and, with her gaze resting on the distant peaks, entertained herself by painting watercolors of such fine variations they inevitably got lost in the dilution or mist they intended to represent. Those works, which an unsympathetic spectator would catalog as a mere waste of materials, Jenka dubbed "applied replicas of fate." In any case, and except for some news they would find out in a few months, those days were the end of the period when Frantisek and Jenka lived with the feeling that they were on the brink of achieving happiness.

One morning, Frantisek found Lev stretched out a few steps from the door of his house, and not because he'd decided to sleep under the stars. Now he was shapes and colors, nourishment for the retinue of worms. The afternoon that preceded this horrible and fragrant spring morning, the idiot had been going about the fields, carrying his burlap sack brimming with treasures—a wilted petal, a doorknocker, the broken bit of a gentle-sounding flute, a *pileyforus* mushroom of the most poisonous species—when all at once he met with Basia Oprichnick, naked in the weeds, naked and aroused because that scoundrel Anatoli Tarkhov—an adolescent now snoring satisfied under a thicket—had just deflowered her. Basia had been left with the spicy taste of the one she'd just known, and the certainty that this appetizer could be completed with some heartier meal. To catch sight of the idiot—robust, virile, not bad looking—and launch herself upon him was the work of a moment. Everything would have turned out perfectly, and those meetings could have repeated for their mutual diversion, had it not been that as soon as she returned to her hut, Basia realized she could hide *almost* nothing from her mother. Anguish, uncertainty, tears. "Who was it?!" her mother screamed. Basia thought that in the long run Anatoli might be a good candidate for a husband, and so she half confessed: "The idiot."

The pack of avengers from Crasneborsk surrounded Lev in his little fairy-tale cabin, threw him onto the dreamy field of herbs, stripped him, religiously castrated him—one of the enthusiasts belonged to the orthodox Christian sect of the Apokotekai—scorched his nipples with burning irons, pulled out his tongue with pincers, and, after carving the numbers of the Anti-Christ into him with a knife, yanking out his ears by the roots, and destroying his eardrums with kicks so he'd never hear another moan again, dedicated itself to his eyes. "Rapist!" shouted Olega Fyodorovsky Oprichnikova, and unsheathed her claws. In the millionth of a second that distanced the intention from the act, Lev had time to understand that in seeing Basia, he had already experienced all the beauty in the world, and now he had to pay for such abundance. He closed his eyes, not to delay or prevent the inevitable, but to stamp the image on his mind, and as he sobbed with joy, he once again savored, just like the first time, the fresh taste of cherry of his beloved.

A shout and it was done. Two gelatinous little balls to crush in the stone basin where Olega prepared compote. Then came the final moment. Avran Palizin, the strongman of the area, lifted up a big rock and released it over Lev's head. This rock destroyed his cranial cavity; after shattering into thousands of sharp splinters, the bones entered the idiot's cerebral mass (a sponge of exquisite design, reproduced by a drawing of coral reefs in the Kalnuk Sea), perforated and compressed it. And so, in the last moment of his life, amid his final bleat of pain, Lev heard within his head *all* the measures of a music that so many had longed to hear: it was a kind of vastly improved Anton Bruckner, a typical example of the kind of creative influence Frantisek Deliuskin was able to produce on a composer now in the full use of his abilities. But what most called the attention was not that this symphony had been unfurled complete in a moment, or that its supremely elevated level permitted it to aspire to a golden-lettered inscription in the history of music as an unknown masterpiece, the best-kept secret of eternity. No. The strangest thing, the ne plus ultra of absurdity, waste and magnificence, was that in the depths of this enveloping tide of notes, Lev had been able to hear the melodious voice of a lost and distant woman, the voice of a love who moved between tulles and birch trees, singing the folk song "Ochichornia," as Basia's black eyes fused with his fade out.

Given the way events took place, Frantisek would never discover that Lev had been his only disciple, the only heir unrelated to him who had been at his level. All he knew was what lay before him, something he quickly had to hide from Jenka's sight. My great-great-grandfather took off his jacket and covered the destroyed face of the poor fool, already covered by a halo of flies and blood. Why had they thrown him in front of his door? Atavistic mysteries of those barbaric regions. Then he leaned over and, without fully knowing what he was going to do next, picked up the body. As he straightened up, he felt a double stabbing pain that shot through his lungs; it didn't last long, but when it left him, Frantisek was trembling and Lev had once more spilled onto the floor. "It's old age," he thought. "It's the pain of this useless loss." He lifted up the deceased again and carried him deep into the leafy conifers of a nearby forest; there he buried him under a mound of stones. An attentive observer would have detected the similarity between the white color of those rocks, their artistic pink marbling, and the tone that predominated in Frantisek's phlegm in the days that followed. But Frantisek himself was barely attentive to the visual aspects of things—Jenka always made loving jokes about this, because of how terrible he was at matching his clothes—and so the relation in spectrum between the small clots of foam and the tomb of the beloved dead man went unnoticed. In fact, the pink color soon took on almost the opposite meaning, *la vie en rose*, when a few days later he found out that Jenka was pregnant.

Frantisek found himself dreaming of a baby girl, thinking of bibs and nappies and onesies and satin frocks. He also developed a new terror that, with the birth of this creature, his daily existence would see itself annihilated by the entrance into the atmosphere of an unknown dwarf planet, made of diverse materials like nocturnal shrieks, fecal explosions and endless episodes of purple-faced crying. The reign of constant interruption. He also feared that a woman of Jenka's delicate constitution was capable of giving birth only to an angelic being, someone too good for this world and therefore condemned to succumb to the slightest illness. It was necessary to preempt the fulfillment of these dark fantasies, just beginning to blossom in all their richness:

"We urgently need a wet nurse who can serve as governess," he told his wife, and thought the phrase sufficient to leave all matters concerning the decision in her hands.

Jenka, for her part, assumed that the brevity of this spoken comment came as a kind of communication from her husband, and that he planned to take it upon himself to set in motion a process of background checks and selections of local nutrient providers, which she was unable to do given her inadequate command of the language. In her view, the notion of breastfeeding also reinforced the evidence that Frantisek was thinking of getting hold of some fat and cheerful Russian matron, a kind of speckled hen (or *mammoth*), all breasts and no brain. As far as the incomprehensible addition of the final condition went, that the woman also be a governess, well . . . that was definitely a hassle, no doubt one to be dealt with by *him*.

And so, both Frantisek and Jenka waited months for the other to take action. It isn't strange that this happened. Once a plausible idea has been conceived, the whole world moves its head looking for a sacrificial victim to carry it out. And marriage, an institution given to blame and derivative by nature, often generates situations such as the one described. In any case, the matter was far from being explosive. Sometimes, at night, Frantisek would lean his head on the belly of his beloved and comment with a trace of apprehension:

"I don't want to run any risks. We need to get hold of someone . . ."

Jenka, sleepy, preferred not to answer, and Frantisek ended up wondering whether in the end the search wouldn't fall to him. And ultimately, so it did. But not because he'd decided to resolve anything. One day, hearing him cough, Jenka suggested that he visit a doctor. Frantisek decided to listen: he grabbed his cane and set out walking. Of course, Crasneborsk was barely a town at the time: a main avenue, some side streets. A butcher, a carpenter, a blacksmith, a doctor. My great-great-grandfather's knuckle hit the second "o" of Propolski, painted, like the rest of the last name, with an unsteady pulse on the frosted glass divider of the door to the doctor's office.

"*Avanti!*" he heard, in a crescendo not entirely out of tune.

Frantisek was about to flee, having decided not to place himself in the hands of a lover of Italian opera—that is, a dimwit. But a new coughing fit doubled him over; at just that moment, a kind of spreading ectoplasmic projection cast itself over the glass, injecting it with colored phlegm. Once again the *"Avanti!"* sounded, before Propolski himself opened the door, caught him by the handle of his cane, gave a brief but energetic tug, and pulled him inside. Here was his first client of the day, the second of a whole week coming to an end.

Alexei Propolski had spent more than half of his life burning the midnight oil over his books, learning theories and techniques, both ancient and modern, about the art of healing; testing on foreign bodies the efficiency of the concoctions of the pharmacy, the lozenges and poultices of the academy, and the herbs and weeds of popular shamans; and mixing and recombining everything, adding to them some medicinal formulas of his own invention. But his efforts had not served to win him the reputation to which he believed it was his right to aspire. For a couple of decades, this delayed apotheosis had been an incentive; every new discovery, every new understanding, had been for him like the imminence of the moment he was anticipating. Finally, well into middle age, he'd realized that the only experience he would have in this respect was not fulfillment, and never would be, but was rather this wait for an illusory dawn. He had given all of himself, scientifically speaking, and the only thing he'd received in exchange was a perpetual feeling of bitterness, the injustice of knowing himself to be the owner of a talent squandered in solitude. Fed up with everything, he'd decided to bury himself in the most remote corner of the saddest of Russian provinces, and helping along the fickle finger of fate with a map, he ended up choosing Crasneborsk. Of course, in Crasneborsk there is nothing to do, except become a specialist in tedium. Because of this, and because he didn't pursue any policy of constant distraction, however, he now had more free time to go on with his study and research; he dedicated himself to these matters with an impetus even greater than he'd done in his native Moscow. At fifty-four years old, Alexei Propolski was short, broad, extravagant, squat and half-bald, and he suffered from spots and bad breath. He was also professionally brilliant, and without a doubt his work—in the theoretical plane—would have been of enormous use for humankind if it weren't that its author never took the trouble to document his discoveries in accordance with any scientific protocol; his desk was chaos and the best notes fell into the inexpert hands of the various women hired for cleaning, who, owing to the anxious and occasionally successful sieges by the owner of the house, barely stayed on long enough to contain the overflow of that scrap heap. Like so many other doctors, Propolski trusted too much in his own knowledge and very little in the ability of the patient to transmit correct information about his illnesses. Thus, as soon as Frantisek had begun to speak, the doctor raised his hand as if to say "I know, I know." He pensively scratched at the abundant dandruff flakes in his mustache and pronounced: "Excess of greasy humors. Sedentary lifestyle and dyspepsia. We are going to lighten and purify the blood. Take off your clothes and lie down on the table." Over the patient's back he spread a collection of transparent and hungry leeches from the swamps, which immediately swelled and turned red at his expense. Afterward, he pulled them away one by one and threw them in a basket. "It is done. Blessed remedy," he said.

For a week, perhaps thanks to the doctor's claim, Deliuskin believed he was cured. But the cough returned, accompanied by a sensation of growing weakness. He decided to come in for another consultation.

Propolski received him offended, as if the repetition of the inquiry suggested a mute criticism of his healing gifts. Once again he made the patient take off his clothes and lie down on the examination table. He sounded him in an offhand way, slapped him on the back, asked him to yawn, shriek, snore and moan, sniffed his tears and blew into his throat. Then he gave his diagnosis:

"The body isn't so bad, but the mind doesn't help. I'm going to recommend you a treatment for soma and psyche. It's a daily application for at least two months. You must surrender yourself, my friend, you must surrender yourself!" and he gave him the address of a thermal bathhouse in the neighboring village of Taganrog, famous for its gentle climate, which years later Tsarina Elizaveta Alexeievna would enjoy in a brief interlude before her end.

"Is it a brothel?" asked Frantisek.

"If only! If it were, I'd be there myself," Propolski laughed, delighted by his own joke.

5

Pravda, which in Russian means "truth" and also "exact word," was a rather spacious establishment with "Turkish-style private rooms," small and enclosed areas with only a kind of marble bed and a towel for pillow. At eye level for a person of average height, a sign instructed: "Undress."

A curt word is not the same as a complete phrase. Should one undress and remain standing? Or sit? Kneel? Lie down? And if the latter, face up or face down?

"Get into whatever position you like," said a woman's voice, answering a question my great-great-grandfather hadn't asked out loud. Frantisek turned around. The woman was standing just outside the door of the private room, her left hand resting on the jamb. The right was holding a number of slim, flexible, fragrant Asian cane rods. She was dressed in a full-length garment of gray wool, closed at the neck with buttons of austere black coral. "My name is Athenea. Who sent you?"

"Doctor Propolski," said my great-great-grandfather.

"Ah," said Athenea, with a face that seemed to express as much knowledge as contempt. "What's the matter? Aren't you used to being naked in front of a woman?"

Frantisek looked straight at his interlocutor, trying to figure out whether she'd asked him a question or let out a sarcastic comment. Athenea was tall and looked to be over thirty years old. She had dark hair streaked with a little silver, slender yet muscular arms, a severe expression on her even-featured face, and a wild swell at her chest that contrasted with the general austerity of the surroundings. "Impossible to know," he concluded, and preferred to answer:

"Yes, if the woman remains dressed."

"What you see of me now is the most that you'll get from me, apart from the medical treatment," said Athenea. "Do me the favor of lying down here."

"Face up or face down?"

Athenea seemed to consider the question:

"This is supposed to be for your health. But if you don't mind receiving a few lashings to the testicles, you can lie face up."

Frantisek hurried to demonstrate that he was obedient and prudent. As soon as he lay down, he felt the cold marble against his nipples. With his face about fifty centimeters from the floor, he could see the wall was perforated at this height by a series of holes that released a constant steam.

Athenea tested out one of the rods, whipping the air.

"Ready?"

Frantisek, who had retained only the expression "health treatment," suddenly accepted the evidence that Propolski had taken him for a ride. Clearly, all the doctor's chatter about the abnormal thickness of his blood, and the convenience of lightening it, now showed itself to be an elegant withholding of the true—and mistaken—diagnosis: that his ills originated in the lack of an intense and deviant sexual life. That idiot had sent him to a brothel for perverts! Due to his active nature as a creative artist, Frantisek considered himself to be the person furthest from the enjoyment of these erotic prospects, the paradise of public servants and every sort of bureaucrat, which isn't to say that he didn't feel curious about the particular spectrum of humanity that indulged in such pastimes. As it were, now that he found himself, without having wished it, before a priestess of the cult of domination, he could not withhold his purely intellectual interest in the practice. His question was excellently timed. Instead of the first blow, Athenea had to offer her first response. And after some time conversing, Frantisek had rid himself of certain doubts to discover that his interlocutor was a being worthy of the greatest respect. "Mister," she said, "I've never been involved in *that* filth. I congratulate myself on knowing far more aberrations than I practice." Athenea confided her drama: ever since she was a young girl, she'd had a living passion for medical science. But in those times, women had been prohibited from learning it, as the contemplation of naked bodies was considered improper for ladies, even in their condition as corpses. The prohibition hadn't deterred her. At night she studied the discipline from the great texts of Russian medicine, reading, among others, Tcherepnin's *Histopathological Anatomy*, Temirkanov's *Complete Manual of First Aid* and Tibasenko's *General Surgery*. Thanks to her concentration and natural intelligence, she soon turned into a kind of "theoretical doctor." She would have been able to diagnose an illness, prescribe a medicine, even recommend the convenience of a surgery, but she lacked the main thing: she didn't have any firsthand knowledge about the internal organs whose care and attention were her subject. To make up for it, she resorted to a ploy (which later proved to be a joke of fate): pretending she was a prostitute, she followed the trail of the Russian armies that had embarked on a new campaign. In the beginning, everything was a success twice over: the Tsar's troops emerged victorious from their first conflicts, and she had at her disposition all the bodies offered to her by the field of battle. Since war is cruel and doctors are always in short supply, Athenea soon dared to offer her services. A couple of fortunate cures brought her prestige as a miracle worker; some of the ignorant began to murmur that she was the incarnation of the Virgin. In any case, the supernatural blackness of her hair and her paleness from beyond the grave distinguished her from other women. Arkady Troitsky, a lieutenant of hussars, courted her. In wartime, things move quickly. A few days after meeting him, Athenea already knew that she was in love with this man. Arkady was an impeccable soldier and complete gentleman. The evening before the great Battle of Kurland, he found out that he was going to command the left wing of his regiment's cavalry, and that same night, he asked her to marry him. The next morning, due to a series of misunderstandings within the Russian command, the enemy devastated all fronts, resulting in a horrible massacre. By midday, combat had ended and the Russian troops had fled. Arkady preferred not to turn his back on the shame, and he fell in the struggle against superior forces. Athenea found his body only at nightfall. The victors had been merciless with him, as with so many others; or maybe what she saw was the final proof of love by a man who hadn't had time to offer her anything but the essentials, and now offered up his corpse, neatly slashed open with organs exposed, like an anatomy lesson. Athenea fainted; when she opened her eyes, the black night embraced her cold flesh with the strength of a bear, whispering obscenities in the enemy's tongue. That shadow was the first of a long series that possessed her until dawn. Nine months later, the child was born dead: all of its tiny parts were human. From that moment—concluded Athenea—from her swollen breasts, the milk of rage had never stopped flowing.

Frantisek was not insensitive to the suffering of others, nor was he immune to the shock produced in him by this tale, narrated in the hoarse and curiously dispassionate voice of its protagonist. But for the moment, the treatment dealt by fate mattered to him less than the fact this atrocity's consequences were so convenient for his own ends.

This woman was the help his home needed.

Jenka, accustomed to the eccentricities of her husband, wasn't surprised that he'd chosen a person who looked so different. More than a tender governess, Athenea seemed to her a kind of false aristocrat, or worse yet, a lunatic. Secretly she deemed her inept for all service, and certain that being lady of the house had already earned her the new maid's antipathy, she decided to proceed as if the other didn't exist. For her part, Athenea thought Jenka affected the airs of a great lady, something completely inappropriate in a person of true class, and so she immediately cataloged her as a social climber and dilettante. The hatred was reciprocal and instant, but Frantisek didn't notice a thing. At dinnertime, cast into high relief by the venomous candlelight, the women, rather than speaking, exchanged smiles like stabbings.

A few days before the delivery, Jenka confronted her husband:

"I don't want that woman to assist me during birth," she told him.

"Why not?" he asked.

"There's no point explaining to you, because when these sorts of things are explained, they seem to lack justification. Let's just say, I don't like how she looks at me."

My great-great-grandfather saw himself faced with the dilemma of siding with his wife or holding firm in the conviction that Athenea's presence guaranteed a "scientific" and safe birth; in addition, he wasn't insensitive to the effect it might have on Athenea's mood were she suddenly separated from the functions for which she'd been hired. Of course, he also hated to have to broach matters that didn't depend on his own will. How would she take this decision of Jenka's? As an insult, contempt, dismissal? Horrible, horrible . . .

That question, at first glance petty, disturbed him so much that when the moment of the birth arrived, he still hadn't summoned the courage to tell Athenea what Jenka had decided. Truth is, he was less worried about the words to pronounce, or whether Athenea would consider herself dismissed, than about, as just mentioned, the potential effect depriving her of these activities might have on her mind, to which he attributed a critical condition given her dramatic history. To put it concretely, he was overwhelmed by the possibility of having to be present for a fit of dementia. Above all, the dementia of a woman. In his way of thinking, everything necessarily tended toward utopian harmony, such that if something subtracted from or "touched" one of the parts in the order of things, what was lacking had to be compensated by the arrival of a new element. Applied to Athenea's case, this meant that her stillborn son (the son who should have come from Arkady Troitsky, brave lieutenant of hussars, and was instead conceived on the battlefield through the plural member of the enemy) had to be substituted in the imagination with the birth of *his* firstborn.

Naturally, this idea of compensation was the unconscious product of a mind that tended toward disorder and had reached the point of doing away with two planes of reality: the first plane, which points out that children can be lost, stolen, killed, given away, devoured, exchanged or forgotten, but that their loan for therapeutic ends would be no more than risky immaturity; and the second plane, which proves Frantisek's essential naïveté, since at no moment did it occur to him, even to relieve himself from the responsibilities assumed, that the romantic and heartrending story of love and death narrated to him by Athenea in the private room of the Pravda building might be no more than one of many versions of the classic tale of lost illusions and virtues, a useful lie that prostitutes tell often to stimulate those clients who need to dream of a "personal," less mercenary connection.

But Athenea was *not* a prostitute; she didn't go crazy, and she didn't burst violently into the matrimonial bedroom or pull the baby from the hands and breasts of Jenka with the scream: "He's mine!" Hours before the birth, she claimed to suffer from a headache and retired to her bedroom. An old midwife from Crasneborsk replaced her. When the moment arrived, Andrei Evgueni (who, in homage to imprecise Greek ancestors, Jenka would insist on calling Eugenio) was a small silent mask smeared with gray oil and red blood, plus a few lashings of liver yellow. He came out without a gesture, without breathing or even moving. As soon as half of his head appeared, Frantisek was about to beg that they leave him there, that they stop their coercion of the tiny creature. But the little body kept sliding from the canal, a slippery mass that finally emerged with a splash. And the squall of life began.

Frantisek felt that the birth transformed him. "By the mere fact of existing," he wrote to Volodia Dutchansky, "Andrei creates a moral fact: he emphasizes my contingency, reveals my personal nullity, which for years I've tried to alleviate by means of a total surrender to my own problems, my own hesitations and my own desires for experimentation—but for what, for what? All of this has been forgotten. Now Andrei's being hangs from all the branches of the world and reduces me to a dry husk, an insect that has died after giving birth."

It's clear that Frantisek still wasn't dead, either artistically or vitally. It was just that now, without warning, truly and at last, all the illusions he'd put into his achievements and his own being as if they were a precious vessel had ruptured thanks to paternity, so that a new content began to spill out, his love for another creature. This spillage, he soon understood, did not make him disappear. Just the opposite. It was a surprising illumination, the discovery of new perspectives. All at once, he discovered the enormous relief of not paying attention to himself. What is paternity, at the end of the day? A change of focus, the organization of a new system of values, and above all, a question launched toward the future, whose thread, a fishing line with weights, hook and bait included, comes whizzing from the past. Now Frantisek thought he understood his own father, with his useless devotion, his preoccupations, his crude attempts, sometimes emphatic and sometimes outlandish, to carve a path for him. In the long run, he'd shown himself to be a model father. He'd been one as much in his initial hopes as in his dignified acceptance of the evidence that his son wasn't going to continue the legacy of the family business. How his father must have loved him not to hold him in contempt or unmask his tricks, those of a skinny brat who intends to "be an artist"! Or maybe it had been only a matter of pride, of closing his eyes to the evidence that the inheritor of his surname was a fraud, the flesh and blood of his disappointment. Even so, Vladimir had never said anything. He was beyond grateful for that. As part of their late and intimate reconciliation, Frantisek imagined that only now, by having made Vladimir a grandfather, was he beginning to pay for his offenses and become worthy of him. He even thought of writing a letter to express all his admiration. But he didn't do it. Through the simple fact of finding out about the new Deliuskin's birth, Vladimir would know the rest. Or maybe he would realize it when he saw him carrying out the role of a father . . . Something—Frantisek hoped—would happen soon, because surely the old man was burning with desire to meet his grandson.

And in the meantime, what to do? For the first time, Frantisek responsibly faced the evidence of the asymmetry of age in the relationship. Although a rigorous parallel existed between the amount of time he would be Andrei's father and the amount of time Andrei would be his son, if the course of things went the usual way, then he would be a father until the moment of his death, whereas sooner or later, Andrei would lose his status as son and become an *orphan*.

But Frantisek tried not to get lost in these thoughts. He had urgent practical questions to resolve. What did one do with a boy? What did one do at each moment? A child wasn't the same as a compositional problem, something that disappeared from the landscapes of the mind once its formal resolution had been found. To start with, what to say to Andrei, who still didn't talk? Maybe he just had to be at his side, watching him grow, letting love do its work. Beyond this, he didn't know how to change a baby's nappy or make him sleep, he had no clue what to feed him, he hadn't the slightest idea of how his changes in mood were linked to his needs, and he feared for his son's life every time he picked him up in his arms . . . He was immensely useless. In contrast, Jenka had become pure nature applied to child rearing.

Frantisek observed her, studied her gestures and archived in previously unexplored regions his wife's purely instinctive responses to each demand. Despite the novelty of the matter and the interest it woke in him, a region of his mind kept itself free and clear to consider the mystery his wife's new attitude represented. She, who had given him the best gift of his life by ruining her body to grant him the miracle of paternity, seemed after the birth not only ignorant of the dimension of her gift, but openly indifferent or detached from the main object of her sacrifice. "She looks at me like I don't exist anymore," my great-great-grandfather thought. This sudden quality, the abrupt transparency of his person, didn't strengthen his feeling of freedom but made him feel like a kind of scrap metal.

Curiously, at the same time as he was suffering from this phenomenon of "negligence," perhaps less an objective fact than a consequence of his tendency toward melancholy, Frantisek noticed that Athenea seemed to have begun treating him in a different way . . . paying more attention to him. Of course, this could also have been the result of a simple impression of his, with any deference toward his person, minimal as it might be, contrasting with Jenka's hypothetical abandonment; but he thought he was right in noticing this. It wasn't that Athenea granted him the treatment expected from a subordinate who wants to keep her position and goes out of her way to anticipate the necessities and satisfy the whims of her master, but rather that sometimes, especially on days when she presented herself dressed completely in black, her hair gathered into a tight ponytail and her features, as an effect of this fastening, seeming to move forward and grow more rigid, becoming almost a mask of polished marble, Frantisek was surprised to find himself hypnotized by her appearance, which he longed for as some kind of criminal exaggeration of decorum, and that all at once, with the slightest shift in the angle of perspective, threatened him with animal transformation. The pale gleam of Athenea's cheeks, the violence with which the bones of her temples protruded, the warlike blade of her nose and the incredible shine of old black stone in her eyes, transformed her into an enormous bird, a gigantic raven, a primitive entity that observed him from the depths of time with the simultaneously eager and absent attention the bird of prey focuses on a hare. This lasted barely a second; then everything went back to normal, and Athenea reverted to her condition as the help in a marriage that had hired her and now apparently didn't need her. Naturally, if something similar had occurred a few years earlier, a younger Frantisek would have inferred from the fixity of this woman's gaze that she felt desire; but his current reality as a fledgling father and faithful husband led him to dispense with the risk of adventure, and even refuse to admit the possibility that this intensity might constitute a sign of sexual nature. "I'm old, fat, flabby, a physical ruin. I no longer have a body," he thought.

One morning he woke up more tired than ever; in front of the bathroom mirror, he was impressed by his sunken cheeks, the bags of dead skin that spilled out over his dark under-eye circles, the gleam of eczema on the auricles of his ears. At the breakfast table it was impossible for him to swallow a single bite; the smell of coffee nauseated him. Sitting at his desk, he couldn't write a single musical note. Drowsiness, vertigo, headache. He smelled his breath, his armpits. "Corpse," he exaggerated.

When a knock came at the door of his consultancy, Alexei Propolski was sitting in front of his wobbly desk, whose left side he kept balanced with his chubby thigh. He was writing his *Tractatum de Principia Medicamentosum* (Latinization was de rigueur in the period, though he personally didn't know any dead languages), a book that even before starting, he already considered his magnum opus, the one that would justify him to posterity. Since a litterateur in the area had pointed out to him that an unhurried style is suitable for serious writings, Propolski began every paragraph by scanning his sentence, in accordance with the noble classical technique: "Although, the, name, of, a, medicine, can, induce, a, sympathetic, effect, that, contributes, to, a, remission, in, the, illness, experience, indicates, to, me, that, the, opposite, does, not, necessarily, result, in, an, aggravation, of, the, symptoms. Before, writing, out, prescriptions, one, must, never, give, anything . . ." Later, at some point, Propolski forgot the precautions or skipped phrases to directly reach what mattered to him: "Example: if we lay a framed mirror on the ground and allow a rat (big or small, and in whatever color the captor supplies to us) to scurry over the reflective surface, the alteration to the disgusting image these rodents usually offer to our senses cannot permit us to think that we are contemplating a different species of . . ."

The knocks began to sound:

"Just a moment!" shouted the doctor. And he went on:

". . . or that the name is distinct, owing to speculation about the figure."

"No," he thought, "I don't mean 'speculation.'" But the word didn't come to him.

Knocks.

". . . or that the frame contains . . ."

"Doctor Propolski!"

". . . or even that the image formed within our brains . . ."

"Is there anyone there?"

". . . Reflection . . . ?"

End of inspiration.

"Coming!"

Table and papers flew. Propolski didn't even bother to pick up, order and number his pages.

"I'm here!" he said, and opened the door. A clinical, professional glance over his patient: "But how have you let yourself go like this? Do you think I'm a magician who spends the whole day reviving stiffs? What the devil have you been up to all this time, my good man?"

"What's wrong with me?" asked Frantisek.

"I only share my diagnoses with colleagues. It could be a chronic nephritis, an excess of calcium, bronchiectasis, brucellosis, ascites, cancer of the peritoneum, Kruegger-Rand salmonellosis . . . Let's go to the thing and not the name . . ." said Propolski. "Are you prepared?"

"For what?" Frantisek's heart raced as he imagined organ removals, mutilations, agonies . . .

"For a trip to the countryside. Great illnesses require great cures, so I'm going to submit you to some of the methods of modern science . . ."

Although the day was abnormally hot, Propolski swathed the patient's neck in a wool scarf, spun him on his feet and took his arm. As they exited, opening the door of the doctor's office, a draft of air blew through.

"What are those papers flying around?" asked Frantisek.

"Trash," said the doctor, happy.

In the street, as they moved at a brisk pace, Propolski took it upon himself to point out the insignificant details of Crasneborsk's building construction and explain how these trifles affected the habits of people living there ("One day, through a broken window, I could see the very naughty Ecratova bringing her little mouth forward . . ."). From architectural analysis to dissection of neighborhood life: in ten minutes, Frantisek had learned the shameful illnesses, low habits and wretched secrets of half the locals in the census, including their household pets. And the account wasn't interrupted with praise; Propolski had a corrosive remark prepared to dilute the consistency of every virtue, an implacable scalpel at the ready to slice out and bring to light every festering defect. Uncomfortable, Frantisek had the sense his doctor was supplying him with this collection of memorable anecdotes in the same zealous spirit as a wife preparing a suitcase for her husband about to embark on a long journey. "He's offering me the charms and variety of the world as seen through his eyes, as if they were the last images I must preserve before shutting my eyes," he told himself. "But if I were to die at this very moment, the only thing I'd take away is the noise and confusion of his words."

Overcome by the sadness of one who assumes the position of a dying man, my great-great-grandfather was far from grasping the doctor's intention. The gentleness of his end echoed in him like a well-tempered chord, and tinted with the quiet russet of twilight what would otherwise have been a golden morning: sunshine, wheat swayed by gentle wind, the chirping of little birds. Propolski jerked the edge of my great-great-grandfather's bag to make him stop, and with a rather affected gesture of generosity, swept his arm like a fan to offer him the view:

"Someday all this will be yours, musically speaking. Our dear Russian countryside still hasn't yet found the one to express it . . ."

With a low constant buzz, a greenish-blue fly dances in the air. A second later, as it moves away, a hummingbird gobbles it up. The silence lacks semitones. Graphically, a dead fly is worth only an eighth note on the fragile music paper of life, in any case too saturated with circumstantial notes. "But even flies have children," thought Frantisek, and shivered: "That will be devoured by spiders."

". . . if you feel like it, of course."

"Feel like eating flies?" Immediately Frantisek realized that Propolski was still following his own fanciful train of thought. Polite, he tried to make an effort to remember what the other had been saying. "Someday . . ." Ah, yes.

"If I feel like composing," he said. "And have time to do it."

"Time? *Time?*" Propolski's hands fluttered, another proof that in his previous incarnation he'd been a flamenco dancer or master pastry chef. "Time, my dear friend, is composed of a series of unstable units, infinitely reducible or expandable; it's the will that matters. I guarantee you that in possession of a firm will, every temporal unity dilates like a bubble until it creates the shape of eternity itself—a limited eternity, of course. Do you know how old I am?"

"No," admitted Frantisek.

"Nor do I, because I'm not the age I look. And who, at this stage in civilization, believes what the calendar says? To sum up: a balanced diet works miracles. Naturally, mine isn't a religious commentary. Just the opposite. Do you know how to recognize a Jew? You ask, 'Are you a Jew?' and the other answers: 'I reckon so.' Is this a joke? It is! One of the best I know, and I've just invented it. Another version. You ask the same question, and the other answers: 'Are you?' Very good, and it's mine too! But . . . you have a sour face, my friend. *Lajt is lebn*, laughter is life. Joy, joy!"

"If only I could feel it . . ." murmured my great-great-grandfather.

"What's the matter, are you against jokes, or do you happen to belong to the tribe of Abraham, and get a little nervous laughing at yourself? Have you got the traditional *moishe* thin skin? But don't confuse me, eh. In religious terms, my program for the circumcised isn't the pogrom, just indifference. Having said that, I am against Christianity, which turns the simplistic story of resurrection into hope, minimizing the value of every true cure and thus discrediting the achievements of my profession. *That* belief (I refuse to call it religion) is pure psychic blackmail. Who could believe that a sacrifice, the slaughter of a rabbi on the cross, could produce the salvation of all humanity? Eh? What does one thing have to do with another? What is born from the copulation of a donkey and a glass of wormwood? Who could believe that one person can take on the fate of the rest? If you're killed by a hunter's shot . . . how would I be guilty?"

"That's just it, what's the matter with me?" Frantisek thought of asking, but Propolski had already moved on:

". . . naturally, if a miraculous formula were the rule and not the exception the story invents, faith would be called medicine, this world would be taken for Paradise, and our name for God would be the Great Hippocrates . . . Anyway, I don't even know what I'm talking about anymore. My stomach is rumbling. Have you got an appetite? Nearby we have Krasnaya Matryoshka, the inn of Ludmila Orlova, a friend of mine who whips up the typical and atypical plates of this country like a god. You can enjoy lunch and dinner in an agreeable and intimate environment, a gallery with a view of the surrounding landscape, all included in the price of the meal . . . Give me your arm because the path is on a slope and at my age, I'm no longer what I used to be, something true at every moment, unfortunately . . ."

On a peak, after a goat path, a small hut. Propolski's eyes lit up. Frantisek turned his head, looking for some sign of what had been promised, which didn't exist save for some tamped-down land and a slope on which there balanced a few wood tables, straw chairs with and without backs, and wobbly stools made by one-armed carpenters.

"This dive's a little neglected," admitted Propolski, carefully accommodating his bulges. "But simple pleasures are the last refuge of sophisticated men."

Not from the swish of the steps, but from a slight breeze behind him, Frantisek realized that the waiter had appeared.

"Kvass? Beer? Vodka? Water?" said Propolski. "Kvass is going to affect the gallbladder, beer is diuretic but ferments, and you have a delicate stomach; as far as vodka goes, it's not worth going into its harmful effect on the nervous system in general, and the liver in particular. Without a doubt, water is your best bet, to drain the stones and other calcifications lodged in your kidneys. Water for the gentleman and kvass for me, *dorogoy drug*. As for the solids . . . is the herring fresh?"

"Just scooped from the barrel," said the waiter. "Nationality?"

"Norwegian."

"And civil state: hooked." Propolski laughed at his own joke. Then, in a sudden transformation meant to surprise and delight his interlocutor, he wrinkled his forehead, bent over like a hunch-backed old beggar lady, and squinted his eyes so his cheeks rose up like a mantle, a raised curtain of astuteness: "Without bones?"

"I pulled them out myself, one by one," said the waiter, and abstained from adding, "with my teeth."

"Excellent!" Propolski dropped his imitation of a greasy medieval gargoyle and rubbed his cheeks. "Let's begin with a little appetizer of selyodka pod shuboy, with the onion cut fine and a well-whisked mayonnaise, accompanied by a little ovoshnoy salad, so long as the cream is of a suitable acidity . . ."

"Don't worry, doctor. In this heat, milk curdles as soon as it's left the cow's udder. The cream will be like yogurt," said the waiter.

"Good. In that case, add salt. Cut the gherkins thick, and bring the tomato without its peel, which isn't easily digested"—to Frantisek: "He who doesn't peel tomatoes spreads hemorrhoids"—to the waiter: "And so that my distinguished friend here doesn't take me for a xenophobe, let's fill out the previous small selection of entrées with a salad of French origin, the Olivier, provided the meat is fresh . . ."

"If you gentlemen prick up your ears, in a couple of minutes you'll hear the shrieks of the pig beheaded by a saber, an inheritance from my grandfather, once stained in Turkish blood and garlanded by the entrails of janissaries."

"A patriot!" cried out Propolski, and without the slightest caution, he leaned toward my great-great-grandfather and said, in a voice so loud as to make his crude feint of discretion useless: "This one pretends to be a pure white Russian, but with the almond shape of his eyes, the black of those prickly bristles on his head, cheeks and forehead, and his skin's sulfur tone, he looks more Tartar than Genghis Khan." Then he sat up straight and, turning back toward the object of his commentary, he added: "A blade with a good edge prevents the meat from coming apart and the bone from shedding mass, both of which damage the flavor and consistency of the final product. At least this is how it was explained to me by a cannibal whom I had the opportunity to visit in the prison of Smolensk. Now, let's go on with the aperitifs . . . How are the liver and potato pirozhkis?"

"They're finger-licking good, if you'll allow me, doctor."

"Whose fingers?" the joker burst out, and turned back to Frantisek: "How hungry I am, Lord! I'd eat a raw slug, a sick snail. Bring on the pirozhkis, with more garlic than pepper! Or the opposite. And a slew of satiny mushroom soups, the famous solyanka, steaming with fruits of the undergrowth, plus a couple of cold okroshkas. And naturally I expect a complete experience from the classic and irreplaceable little borsch, brimming with grated radish and parsley, good and hot, so the red vapor rises up to our faces like incense. And it wouldn't be unpleasant to evaluate the consistency of a few gribi v smetane . . . As far as main courses go, you know what I'll say: veal stroganoff, kotleti po-kievski and tsyplionok tabaka with a lot of chopped parsley, along with the fragrant green stems, to awaken the passions of women! And some shashlik on the grill, the meat well-cooked but the baby onions juicy, and some pelmenis along with a few varenikis, and of course if there are golubtsis, so much the better. Would you also like some antrikot, *dorogoy* Deliuskin?"

"No. Actually, I doubt . . ."

"You needn't say another word. I'm your doctor. These days I'm sure your stomach only tolerates curd, yes? Yes. In that case, a minor intestinal infection must be irritating those parts. Let's set aside water, by definition innocuous, and drink pure vodka, which either kills or cures."

"Should I get the order started, sir?" asked the waiter.

"Please," Propolski made a sweeping gesture of contempt: "The word belongs partly to the one who pronounces it, and partly to the one who listens, my dear friend. No doubt this *shmutzik* has forgotten half of what I ordered, and to cover the lapse will bring us whatever he feels like." Having said this, he leaned back in his chair; my great-great-grandfather waited with cold satisfaction to witness the scene of the fall. It occurred to him that even at the very moment of collapse, Propolski would find a way to keep spouting poppycock. "Let's see now . . ." said the doctor and leaned back even further, breathing in deeply. The back legs of his chair floated over seventy degrees from the horizontal ground, his nostrils inhaled the fragrance of an intimate evocation, and then, with a knock of spiritual decisiveness, everything fell back into place and Propolski didn't take any tumble, except into the understanding of something: "The question is: Will Ludmila Orlova be here or not? What do you think, Frantisek? Will she have forgiven me, or will I have to forgive her (obviously it will be the latter . . .)? Will we have left behind our mutual offenses? Should I choose to greet her, or is it she who ought to appear? Would it be advisable to make a foray through the service entrance at the side, or through the main door? Will Ludmila be alone or not?"

"Who knows," said my great-great-grandfather.

"True, very true," approved Propolski. "Heaven isn't a petticoat lifted for the benefit of prudes. I'll be back in two minutes, three. Don't wait up."

Propolski stood up, straightened his back, sucked in his belly, puffed out his chest, arranged his hair and launched himself toward the side door. My great-great-grandfather saw him disappear, vanishing into the shadow amid pots of soup stock. He thought of taking advantage of the moment to flee, but didn't. The briefest list of his illnesses kept him anchored to his chair: stabbing pains like blows to his kidneys, dark urine, a confused wild stampede of earthy colors spraying the porcelain of the toilet bowl at his moment of greatest privacy. Not to speak of those moments at night when he was short of breath, his heart seemed to want to burst from his chest and plunge over a cliff, and he felt acidic pinpricks between his ribs . . . "What could Andrei be doing at this moment?" he wondered. "Might he be pinned to his mother's breast? What is the mental world of a baby? Is it words that sound like music, the memory of tastes and smells? Does he know that I exist?" In a shudder of love, he felt the terrible injustice of distance and the violence of time, which would make his son grow up and at some point tear them apart for eternity. This was the clear pain of a belated father, cradling the fierce and anxious dream of tirelessly loving the yield of his seed before he disappeared. And a murmur came to his ears, different from everything else, like a voice speaking to him.

"No," it said.

Could it be—my great-great-grandfather asked himself—that despite the aggregate of sufferings that had led him to tolerate this idiot (Propolski), something objective and superhuman was responding? Was this something providing a response to his unrealized prayers, granting him an extension of his given time?

"No . . ." said the voice, and it was the voice of a woman. "No . . . Not here . . . Take . . . It's not the pla . . . You ungrate . . . No . . . Yes . . . No . . . Yes . . . No . . . Ou . . ."

Sound of pans and other items, something like a bellow from the kitchen—the waiter's grandfather's saber slitting the throat of a cow?—and all at once a voice was heard: "Careful with the hot wat . . ." before seconds later, the classic scalded cat shot out the side door with a meow. "Oy vey, Alexei."

By means of speculation, my great-great-grandfather tried to figure out how he could measure the silence between two moments of time when they formed part of a single unity, desolation. He hadn't reached any conclusion when first the triumphant yet lightly trembling hand, then the rest of the disheveled Propolski's body appeared in the doorframe, resting against it for a few seconds. After these seconds of divine immobility, the doctor put on his best conspiratorial face and approached the table, somewhat unkempt from his efforts and doing up his trouser buttons.

"There's nothing new under the sun, but how many old things there are we don't fully know!" he sighed, plopping into the chair and confidentially leaning his elbow on the table: "The number of tricks Ludmila has learned in the months we haven't seen each other! I can't decide whether I'm happy or getting jealous. How long has it been since I left you?"

"Don't know; I haven't got a watch on me," said my great-great-grandfather.

"Let me be completely honest with you, my dear Frantisek: I have nothing against the idea that pleasure can accumulate and extend with duration, but I swear to you there are intensities directly related to awkwardness, lack and brevity. Do me a favor, check and see there's no sign left on me of those gateways to the little treasure, a spiral whorl of hair or Venusian curlicue adorning my mustache? There isn't? I, if I may put it this way, can still smell the dew, still feel on my lips the sly tingle of those ringlets of happiness . . . What's the matter? You don't see it, or don't want to see? I assume that with you, certain topics . . . how can I put it? Ah, the food! All the better. I'm worn out. Ludmila is a true she-vampire. Lickety-split she drained me of the very last drop of . . . Eh, don't tilt the tray, animal!"

Propolski rushed to help the waiter, busying himself with laying out the plates, dishes, pitchers, glasses, cups, platters and vessels, full of solids and liquids that were charred, crude or chilled, before he then, sweating with pleasure, hurried to mix, taste, separate and recombine the different elements that trickled, stuck together, disintegrated or melted. Frantisek contemplated the pirouettes of his doctor as he tucked into the food, engaging in the seduction of inert worlds (raw and cooked), taking inspiration from the boundless gaze of the hypnotist and the tongue flicks of the lizard, and incorporating a complex series of advances and retreats, satisfied smacks and purrs upon swallowing. The whole series of calibrations, alignments and deflations that took place on Propolski's face made one think of the gesticulations of a robot whose machinery has begun to function poorly, yet it didn't stop him, at the same time as he swallowed each bite, from finding a way to compare it with the others he had sampled over the course of his existence at different restaurants, cafeterias, eateries, taverns, inns and hostelries all over Russia, which seemed to add their pleasures to those of the present, materializing themselves in the imagination as new and ineffable dimensions of quantity, volume, flavor. For my great-great-grandfather, in contrast, the mere sight of this overflow of food made him feel full in advance, while the verbal elaborations induced a kind of moral nausea. Yet again, he asked himself what he was doing there, in the company of this vulgar and contemptible being, a stranger who had dragged him along as a witness and who believed him to be an accomplice in this display of repulsive excess; no doubt a false physician to boot, someone who didn't even have the courage to hurl the fatal diagnosis in his face. But if Propolski was the fleeting and tangible sum of all the misery it was possible to accrete in a day, then what was happening in the larger picture? Why was he consenting in silence to all of this?

"I adore the simple pleasures," repeated Propolski, as he sucked out the white goo at the center of a knobbly, hollow bone, which he'd seized upon with his rubbery tentacles, "the," slurp, "simple, ah, pleasures, are, mmm, the last refuge of complicated men . . . Don't you fancy a little suck? It's exquisite! What? I can't hear you, man, I can't hear you!"

"My incurable weakness, my incurable weakness," whispered Frantisek.

Desserts: snowy blinis with thick cream and a deluge of sugar. Extremely rich khvorost, unpronounceable gurievskaya kasha. There were also khachapuri and pryanikis to throw in the air to a heaven of starving angels. Propolski ate, drummed on his belly and burped in several scales as he recited the names of the most distinguished figures from the current of rural-imaginist poetry that thrived in Odessa from 1660 to 1674 (a bunch of second-rate luminaries), which championed the elimination of rhyme in favor of the groupings of "casual cacophony"; he made noises to dissemble—a trace of modesty, at last—an episode of flatulence, then he stood up, intimating to his table companion that the small detail of the tab would fall to him. My great-great-grandfather paid, and they cleared out.

"To leave is to die a little, to die is to leave a little too much. Ciao, Sofia," Propolski declared as an epitaph. Then, recomposing himself: "What a day, *caro fratello*! We ate, we fornicated (at least I did), we burped, at some point we fucked again . . . and we're just getting started."

"Wasn't her name Ludmila?" said my great-great-grandfather.

"Who?"

"Ludmila. Wasn't your friend named Ludmila Orlova?"

"Yes, and?"

"You said Sofia. 'Ciao, Sofia.'"

"Ah, so I did. Her little ass did seem different, somehow . . . She was so young and so changed that, anyhow, I think there must have been a convenient confusion and I attended to the daughter. At bottom it's the same, and all of it stays in the family! Do you know what we're going to do now, with purely soothing and digestive ends?"

"Go back to Crasneborsk?" ventured my great-great-grandfather.

"*Nein*. We're going to take a splendid little nap in a haystack that's . . ." Propolski raised his hand and pointed forward with his short chubby index. At that very moment, a black bird crossed the ballistic trajectory of his finger: "An oschtropoi. Birds of ill omen. You don't see them often in these parts."

As if to make the word flesh, at that precise moment the oschtropoi gave a couple of spasmodic wingbeats, then plunged to earth, slamming against an invisible barrier and disappearing from the two walkers' views. Seconds later, they heard the shot.

"To shoot down death: is this an unnecessary duplication, a

dire omen or a sign of exceptional luck? Reality, my dear friend, dedicates to us incomprehensible marvels. Sometimes I think that everything—lights, shadows, sounds and colors—alludes in a delicate and infinite way to my distinguished person. I see a blade of grass floating in the air that at a certain moment shapes the first letter of my last name. What cosmic courtesy!" Propolski said.

"Or what an idiotic Universe..." muttered my great-great-grandfather.

Afternoon in the countryside. Every so often, Propolski helped along the process of pollination by leaning over to sniff a flower, in the process covering his nose with talc, the pompom of an inspired clown.

Frantisek was able to leave the doctor only near daybreak. On the road he surrendered to the pure happiness that fills a man when returning home after a long journey of obstacles. To the forgetting of small injuries and daily failures. To the feeling of plenitude. As night frayed at the edges, and he promised himself never to abandon his family again, Frantisek believed that he was going to witness the most beautiful of dawns.

He arrived at his property minutes before the sun came out. The solidity of the heavens had already begun to dissolve into iridescent particles. The first thing that drew his attention was the silence of the roosters. Then Andrei's sobbing. It wasn't the cry of the child who complains to his mother because he's hungry, but the desperation of the one who's called all night long, receiving no answer. Frantisek ran to the bedroom. Sitting on a chair next to the bed where Jenka lay unmoving, there was a black shadow, something that turned toward him. Frantisek recognized the gleam in those eyes.

"I wanted to nurse him, but it's no good. My breasts have dried up," said Athenea.

6

Frantisek understood how important Jenka had been to him only after he'd lost her. Her lightness, that ability of hers to make him happy, began to reveal itself in its totality after the wind scattered her ashes through the larch trees in the valley of Crasneborsk. At that moment he became painfully aware of his love. In his arms, Andrei stared into the embers of the pyre that had consumed his mother. A few steps behind them, Athenea murmured her psalms.

After the cremation, my great-great-grandfather hired Marina Tsvctskaia, a dairy matron, then buried himself in bed. A muffled and persistent pain drilled away at his bones. He chalked up this suffering as the reaction of his organism to Jenka's absence; love was the silent immaterial fire that licked at him before it consumed him. With sheets drawn up to his neck, he noted the most visible signs of life—Marina's laughter as she suckled Andrei, an orange-breasted bird pecking at the green worm of plague that devoured a cedar with blossoming branches on the other side of the window—and slowly he let himself go, surrendering to memories. His mind went back to the first musical experiments, those combinatorial exercises developed on female bodies. Now he could recognize the frivolity of his behavior, the cold deliberation with which he had handled those women, operating with the resentment of someone who knows beforehand he'll never achieve the object of his quest. Frantisek closed his eyes to better evoke the waves of elusive ecstasy that had come over him suddenly in the midst of those covens . . . Such excesses hadn't been useful for anything except perhaps to introduce him to the constant grief that would now forever afflict him, and which had been calmed, for an interval so brief it made the contrast terrible, only by the presence of Jenka. She'd been the great balm of his existence, the true cause and motor that had always driven his actions, and now she'd stayed in the past, leaving him defenseless. All that remained now was to accept the fleeting nature of his existence, which he assumed was reduced to his memory of her.

Slowly, as the days went by, the versions of Jenka that Frantisek remembered came flowing into his mind like an eloquent deluge. In the belief that he survived only to dwell upon her image, he transformed into the sentry who kept watch over the current, awaiting its end. Since this didn't arrive, at least not immediately, my great-great-grandfather decided to accept the rigor of the paradox. Dead, Jenka seemed to become endless, or at least incessant, as if her peaceful appearance, rich with details, formed a prelude to the tribute he needed to make: a lasting goodbye in the form of music.

Clearly, to dedicate himself to the composition of a requiem or solemn mass, Frantisek would have needed a little more health, along with some solitude and concentration. But these last requirements had become tricky, seeing that after Jenka's death, Athenea had decided to take special care of him. First out of courtesy, then out of respect, and finally out of fear, my great-great-grandfather didn't voice any criticism of the new treatment by his housekeeper. Her interventions left his body exhausted and disturbed his spirit, but they were also the perfect excuse to delay the moment of seclusion and creation—that is, the moment of rendering homage to the deceased before he'd have to release her into the slipstream of dissolution.

For her part, even though Athenea's determination was loyal to motives other than preserving fidelity to a life beyond this one, she herself was unaware of the secret impulse behind her actions and, with all her efforts, believed she was doing nothing more than helping a disconsolate widower tend to the garden of his memory. Yet even if she was unaware of her own reasons, she couldn't help but notice the duplicity of her "patient," who on the one hand surrendered to her manipulations, and on the other seemed to take refuge in his despair. This trait of my great-great-grandfather's irritated her. Sometimes she'd gasp in annoyance, "Relax," as she massaged his calves with her strong dry hands, which minutes before she'd sunk into a tub of ice water.

By acting in this way, Athenea was evidently going far beyond the call of duty; in a normal situation, a single word from her employer would have been enough to draw the line. But that word wasn't pronounced, and its omission increased her boldness.

Carried away by a frenzy whose true meaning remained hidden, Athenea overstepped the bounds again and again. These attempts reinforced her perception that Frantisek and his oblique behavior were presenting her with new facets of the masculine universe, but exploring another and more intimate dimension also offered her a mirror of her own emotions, which she hadn't suspected were going to appear. To put it briefly, Athenea didn't know that she'd fallen in love with her master, that sad aloof widower. She was unaware that she loved him with a devotion that was yearning, demanding, anguished, far from tender; she loved him without hopes, without dreams, without feeling herself enveloped by the sweet hypnotic gossamer that casts itself from the gaze of the one in love and projects a ray of light into the beloved, who, in reflecting it, experiences the deceptive illusion of being not the mirror but the source. Instead of all this, she found herself pushed by a brutal and greedy desire, a sordid necessity not happy with anything. In consequence, she began to take on the appearance of a person submitted to a chain of disappointments; her smirk became more serious, her smile turned bitter.

Curiously, Frantisek attributed Athenea's metamorphosis to what he thought was her fear of a decrease in domestic responsibilities: no longer thanks to any cutback by Jenka (she herself cut from life), but because of that sudden dryness that prevented her from feeding Andrei. Even in the midst of his own suffering, he thought of saying a few words to her about this, a comforting phrase or consoling refrain, something that served to cast away her fear. But then, as always, he let the moment slip, and finally forgot about it—or something in him, wiser and more deliberate, opted against it. Was this his small revenge? Maybe not; maybe he was simply dominated by the reign of his own somber meditations and the decisions of an even more somber mind, that of the divinity who presided over his end. To make things worse, his visual capacity was dwindling; instead of that zone of radiance experienced by those affected by a detachment of the retina, which bestows an aura of temporary holiness over objects and people, my great-great-grandfather could perceive only an opaque mist which started to blot out everything.

Frantisek hid this new renunciation by his organism; his situation was complicated enough without divulging a further weakness, which Athenea might use to force him into new extravagances. For this reason he preferred to keep silent, and with the urgency of a condemned man, he tried to memorize the pale remains of the day, leaning over Andrei's cradle to burn those adored features into his retina. Each time seemed like the last, the perfection of the creature already beginning to grow hazy and dissipate (many years later, although for other reasons, my father would live through the same painful situation with me). In the spreading darkness, Andrei stretched out a little hand, clung to one of his fingers, smiled and murmured: "Daddy."

In the spreading darkness. In the spreading darkness of his existence, only in sleep could he still trace the outlines of shapes with precision. That's why he clung to these moments, and even tried to introduce dream to his waking life as a permanent method. He wanted to move in and out, from one state of being to another, as if these were joined by a revolving door. Could Propolski have been right, even though his opinions had seemed a condensation of stupidity in their moment, when he had said that time is made up of infinitely expandable units? Now he wondered whether it would be possible to recuperate the world (what had been lost, what was leaving) by the simple means of injecting into every dream the notion of eternity. To dream the world by parts, with fervor and lucidity, until it could be rebuilt whole. A world shaped to his liking, just as complete and lasting as the real one, and ending only when he wished it.

The way that events turned out, these attempts of Frantisek's never went beyond the initial phase; they never completely transformed into a guided dream. But one night, after falling asleep and waking up several times, he was able to sense the figure of Jenka. She was by his side, in their home library. The novelty of the situation was rooted not so much in the visit by the deceased (who until that moment had been evasive, as the recently dead tend to be), as in the fact that Frantisek had managed to dream himself as an autonomous body within the dream, a being separate from his own consciousness as dreamer, unaware even that his own self was dreaming him. At one point, Jenka, who had been peacefully contemplating the flames in the hearth for some time, came back to her husband and said something like: "Marriage is the performance of just a few notes, but played clearly." Frantisek nodded his head in agreement. With a leap, a fluffy white cat passed through the scene, and went to curl up on the rug less than a meter from the fireplace. "Jan," murmured Jenka. Frantisek was struck by the suspicion that his wife had named a lover. "What?" he said. "Jan, our cat. I gave him that name in homage to Jan Sweelinck," she said. "Who is Sweelinck?" asked Frantisek. Jenka looked at him with pity, moved by his amnesia: "He was an early contrapuntist, who composed music for the organ as if it were meant for a human voice. You always adored his style." "Ah. Right. A precursor of Frescobaldi," said Frantisek, and reclined in his chair. Jenka bent over her husband. "You adore cats," she told him. "I didn't know that," he said. "There are so many things we don't know about ourselves," she commented in a strange tone. Then she added: "Your problem isn't that you don't know, but that you forget you know." Frantisek laughed, uncomfortable, while he asked himself why Jenka had set out so late upon the path of reproaches, and why she was leaning over him in this way, as if collapsing. At such a short distance, he could make out the irregularities of her features and the impurities of her skin. Frantisek noticed that he was sinking into the interior of something that came from his wife's gaze, or maybe from a deeper zone, from her hidden organs. The worst part was that he couldn't escape from this force that took control of him like something inert, without his being able to move even a centimeter, because any backward movement of his body was opposed by the solidity of the chair. "What . . . ?" he trembled. "Shhh," she said. And opening her lips, she stuck out her tongue and started to lick his face with moans of satisfaction. The smell of Jenka's saliva, its density, was different from usual. It wasn't necessarily unpleasant, but it was disconcerting. "You never even imagined what you were missing," said Jenka's new voice. Frantisek closed his eyes . . .

Nobody will be surprised at this point to learn that when he opened his eyes and woke up from his dream, Frantisek discovered he was with Athenea, who was naked and mounted on his member, rocking back and forth.

From then on, for Frantisek, every day was atrocious and every moon bitter. Obviously, with some relief. At the start, and even though it came from a manipulation that took shameless advantage of his sleeping unconsciousness and overall weakness, to the point it almost seemed rape, the sexual act with Athenea affected his entire existence; more than anything because, sure of the power that she held in this respect, Athenea decided to repeat her performance as a way of trapping him, staking all possible love letters against her wisdom in the erotic terrain. She believed that even with her stern yet tremulous look of a constipated noblewoman, her little virgin's tits, man's hips and nun's thin lips, neither Jenka nor her memory could compete with her. But she did not surrender to this belief in the prior certainty of triumph. She didn't trust Frantisek. In bed (or anywhere, beginning that night, where she happened to lead him), she kept an eye on even the tiniest of his gestures, resigning or deferring her own pleasure to acquire evidence of his; sleepless, she pursued him, lying in wait for him in silence or shouting. Frantisek was profoundly shaken by this turn of events. Athenea's frenzy had moved him despite himself and captivated him with its spectacle, and now he had to recognize that he was aroused by a woman he didn't even like. Nevertheless, he thought that his carnal euphoria was a mistaken sign, just like the promise of recovery that appears on the face of a dying person just before the end. And that is why, when all is said and done, despite being immersed in the mechanism of enthusiasms and orgasmic shouts, he gave little importance to these matters; they seemed to him lacking in gravity, save perhaps for the sensation of being unfaithful that sometimes bothered him in the middle of a penetration or that, as he let out the moans and groans usual in such circumstances, made him swallow unpronounced, like an incantation, the name of his deceased beloved.

Of course, his discretion wasn't enough to mislead Athenea. She could see that Frantisek was under the impression he was living out a few nights of light passion. And this terrified her. "What is he really thinking about? Where do I fit into it?" For all that she regretted the little she had gained up to that point, love, with its promise of future bliss, sustained her enough to let her endure the humiliating certainty that Frantisek was taking her like a female animal, one worth as much as an object; at the same time, her love prevented her from recognizing that when he clutched her in his arms, he was dominating all that throbbed within her as a possibility, reducing her to the eternal and palpable terror that dwells within every woman of being unloved—that is, to the condition of nightmare.

With the passing of the days, Athenea gradually adjusted to this situation, and fit herself to his being with the precision of a mask. But before she transformed into this sinister mirror of another's morbidity, she struggled and resisted; she did so with the purity, clumsiness and naïveté (half sentimental delirium, half erroneous calculation) that characterizes everyone in love. To approach my great-great-grandfather's heart, still affected by Jenka's death, maybe it would have suited her to adopt a strategy crafted out of kind actions, understanding, service and patience, which after a period of time, would have received at least some form of response: if not love, at least tenderness and gratitude. But Athenea was too proud, or too anxious, and when she surrendered herself to Frantisek she did so in the hope of achieving with one blow the totality that had been denied her until that moment. Since this didn't happen, finding herself in the trembling emptiness that opened before her dashed expectations, she didn't know how to do anything but double her stakes, trying to give events consistency and make them "real" by the simple means of reminding him of them whenever she could.

Frantisek took this gesture as an imposition or, at least, as a complaint made from a place of strength. He interpreted Athenea's comments to be a request for compensation, the necessary requirement to free him from their exhausting bond of passion, and so, in a shy and ambiguous way, as with people who consider it to be in poor taste to speak of money, he mentioned a figure. He waited for an enthusiastic response and the quick naming of a price. It disconcerted him to meet with an attack of sobbing. Where had he gone wrong? Was the money offered too much or too little? And what if Athenea's reaction didn't have to do with financial matters? But if it wasn't about that, then what was it?

After a few days of doubt, he judged that it was better not to ask for clarifications. Out of prudence, and so long as he couldn't find a way to understand what Athenea intended from him, he decided to cast upon their relationship the shadow of an imaginary shrug: when he crossed paths with her in the hallways, he gave her a vague smile and kept moving. It wouldn't have escaped any objective spectator that this flight had a component of bewilderment to it, and that in his exits from the scene, Frantisek displayed a sort of absorbed haste, like that of a paralytic falling down a staircase. But the worst thing was his vulnerable and shabby appearance: his bowed head, his hunched back, his weak legs, his shirt untucked from trousers and hanging over his belly, his gaze lost in the surrounding darkness.

In the meantime Athenea, although she felt herself ridiculed by an objectively insulting proposition, noticed that her reaction had unexpectedly touched a weak point in Frantisek. This—she deduced—meant she had to keep insisting. And with greater emphasis than ever, she applied herself to talking about the links between them, refreshing for him even the smallest details of every one of their meetings—from her initial appearance up to what had been said and done seconds before—charging even the most minimal conversations with significance. For Frantisek, these emotional deluges were overwhelming, and their flow prevented him from noticing that he could have put a brake on the loquacity by just saying: "My dear, why don't you shut your trap and leave me in peace once and for all?"

But he didn't say that, or anything like it. Such silence seems inexplicable in someone who believed that, save for a few brushes in the night, nothing joined him to this woman. Yet the mixture of regret and spleen that Athenea produced in him, the tortuous way in which she had chosen to impose herself on him, provided a certain density to his existence. Although he wasn't aware of it, although he figuratively continued to light candles at the dead woman's altar, the truth is that his memory of Jenka and her easy ability to make him happy was fading away.

Was it a kind of egoism or inconsistency that my great-great-grandfather, who saw Athenea as an obstacle, ultimately ended up accepting her? She wasn't the woman he loved; she was the one he had by his side. Naturally, these facts don't explain everything. I believe that by keeping her in his home, and progressively submitting to her demands, constant complaints and inconvenient behavior, Frantisek had found a remarkable excuse for not facing his responsibilities to music. The hours of real life and his periods of mental exhaustion consumed him and left him a wreck. Or so he imagined. For him, in some sense Athenea's flow of babble constituted the main obstacle to his musical creation, and she'd become his punishment for what he did not create.

And so, although he couldn't stand her, Frantisek was completely dedicated to her.

Even so, before giving in completely, he made his final attempt, one that was so simplistic it can be thought of only as a spasm of resistance destined to serve as a prelude to surrender. If Athenea—he told himself—had clung to him when he'd revealed he was prepared to compensate her and see her fade away on the horizon, wouldn't the situation be inverted if he now began to woo her, to pretend he couldn't live without her? In practice, his hypothesis fell apart. Since he didn't consider (because he didn't know them) the feelings of the person to whom he was trying to apply his ideas, his effort produced results the opposite of those expected: Athenea interpreted Frantisek's superficial maneuvers in a literal way and, thinking she'd finally pierced the rock-hard soul of the man she loved, surrendered to the sweetness of the new treatment: days of ecstasy, nights of ardor, lyrical formulations of a thicket of shared projects.

Frantisek realized he'd fallen into his own trap the day Athenea said to him:

"I think we should send a letter to your father."

"A letter? Saying what?"

"There's no need to dictate," she said. "I've already written it."

And she recited:

Dear father:

I know it might seem rushed to you that such a short time after becoming a widower, I'm writing to inform you of my next . . .

Et cetera.

The day of the wedding, Athenea flaunted an unusual hairstyle that suited her terribly, the tall headdress of a crazy woman adorned with orange blossoms and a green silk gown embroidered in gold. The anonymous reporter from *Izvestia* who covered the ceremony—clearly Propolski—wrote that "undoubtedly thanks to a scrupulous adherence to the advice of his doctor, a local eminence, our notable composer Frantisek Deliuskin shows himself to have recovered from the series of illnesses that afflicted him in the recent past," while the bride, "slender, very beautiful, with expressive eyes," still couldn't quite seem to believe what was happening. Thanks to a mix-up by the choir director, which only my great-great-grandfather noticed, the voices intoned a Gregorian chant.

Celestial forces rise and fall
And the golden pitchers surrender

As always, Frantisek admired the characteristics of this tradition: its constant circling around a primary note without this creating the sensation of an emerging center, as it would in the posterior tonic, the avoidance of large intervals, and a freely oscillating rhythm that emphasizes not meaning but the suggestive tendencies of language. "An old but solid style," he thought, as he glanced to the right from the corner of his eye. There were his composer friends, making picaresque faces at him. Gregorian. At one time he'd thought of using the severity of this model, wrenching it away from the necessities of the mass for more intimate poetic purposes. A Gregorian chant written for Jenka? In that case . . .

"Fran . . ." Athenea elbowed him.

. . . in that case, taking such a liberty would make it a new form. And if he were to advance outside the framework of the liturgy, and introduce love as an axis . . .

"Frantisek . . ."

"What?" said my great-great-grandfather.

"You may kiss," said the priest.

"Ionic mode," he murmured, leaning toward his bride.

7

Andrei remained in the care of Marina Tsvetskaia, the wet nurse, and the newlyweds set off on vacation; Athenea wanted to get to know *all* of Europe. The first stop was Saint Petersburg. It was summer. In the deserted city there wasn't a single theater open. They didn't go to Pavlovsk either, or to any concerts, or to any of the forty-two islands. Frantisek encouraged his wife to go out alone; he remained shut away in the hotel bedroom with the shutters closed. He tried to get used to the night, or perhaps make out a glimmer of minimal hope, day filtering through darkness. But it was irreparable; he was going blind.

From Saint Petersburg to Narva. From Narva to Tallinn and Tartu. From Tartu to Riga, Klaipeda, Kaliningrad. They arrived in Poland and stayed for several days in Elblag. From there on to Olsztyn, Warsaw, Wroclaw, Krakow . . . In Czechoslovakia, just Prague. Within the Austro-Hungarian empire, Athenea wanted to visit Vienna and Budapest. Berne, in Switzerland. In Italy, Milan (for the fashion), Venice (for the canals), Florence (for the Duomo) and Rome (for the pope). Spain didn't interest her, France did. They crossed the English Channel so she could see London. Taking advantage of the mild climate, they went to the spa town of Brighton. There, on the advice of a hydrotherapist recommended to Athenea by a Polish countess, who had visited the hotel where they were staying by mistake while in search of her lover (an underage olive-colored Tunisian who two hours before had fled to Sfax with all the jewels of the Potocki family via the service entrance of the hotel across the street), Frantisek underwent a series of curative procedures. The first was an inverted crucifixion: replacing the nails with ropes and stretching his arms wide to expand the capacity of his thorax, they hung him upside down, with the theory that the upper part of his lungs would expel the illnesses troubling him. Then a renowned masseuse submitted his body to a series of elongations, twistings of different muscle groups, adjustments of bone structure.

After having endured these cures for some time, Frantisek permitted himself to express certain doubts to Athenea regarding their efficacy. But she paid him no heed: "You must have faith. We're happy. Stop grumbling." At moments like this, my great-great-grandfather became aware of the dimension of his error. His final hope, almost the desire for a miracle, had been that in the way things often happen, the marriage itself would weaken the link by means of routine, mutual boredom and annoyance with the tastes and manias of the other . . . Thus he had imagined that although Athenea's presence would forever remind him of the initial error, the passage of time would soothe the most agonizing areas, leaving behind only a bit of discoloration after the terrible rash. But it hadn't occurred to him to think that against all expectations, his new wife would show greater enthusiasm each day for their life in common. "Happy?" he wondered. "Where, my God, does she find this happiness?" He couldn't tolerate being alone with her. She was a stranger to him, a presence that had imposed itself through the fault of a peculiar weakness in his character. The only thing that brought him relief was to confirm that Athenea didn't notice his anguish. On the contrary, she showed herself to be more passionate than ever. "I'm *so* content to be the wife of the famous Deliuskin," she said. "Famous?" "You are or will be."

"Me?" "Yes. Soon the fellowships, prizes, sales of musical scores and million-dollar concerts will come your way." She had a stunning confidence about all aspects of life. At some point she decided to eliminate the last hints of prudishness, and while he was sitting on the toilet, she'd enter the bathroom for noisy drawn-out gargles, whose contents she'd spit in a gob out the window; she tried to fix their hours of sleep and wakefulness in accordance with the dictates of astrological charts; she was able to spend a whole hour explaining in what way, how much, where and why each vegetable, animal or mineral on the planet ate, digested, defecated. What Frantisek couldn't help but wonder was why she considered this ability to be interesting. A provisional answer was that she was completely fascinated by herself, or at least by the possibility of being heard without interruption. Another was that the marriage (perhaps the fulfillment of an old longing) turned her into a happy chatterbox. This same new condition also rendered impractical the fantasy in which Frantisek had begun to indulge: that of losing her to the brawny embrace of any male specimen in better condition than he was—that is, almost any other male of the human race. He was convinced that he couldn't take any more, yet his list of sufferings had only just begun.

He'd received a card inviting him to *l'obligation* of the summer season, a masquerade ball given by a Chinese tycoon, no doubt an agent of the Peking government. Athenea spent the week going around fashionable shops in search of a suitable outfit and didn't want to delay their arrival by even a minute. In the middle of the winter season, she chose a tilbury carriage without a hood, and forced the coachman to set the horses racing at full gallop. This mad dash, along with the rest of the events that night, would aggravate my great-great-grandfather's state of health.

The Chinese mogul's apartment was located in the residential area. It was a shadowy, clean, spacious place stuffed with little curios.

Velvet tassels hung from the night tables, and there were extra covers on the sofa. The butler explained that Song Li was held up due to an inconvenience but that he'd be there at any moment. In any case, some guests had already arrived. In the living room, with supreme concentration, a Philippine wound a crank to make the images of a magic lantern do turns, projecting phantasmagorias onto the walls. Most of them looked like copulating frogs. "Just lovely," said Athenea. She settled Frantisek on the edge of a sofa, pushed up the glasses that were sliding down his nose, gave him a cup of a sweet yellow drink to hold and dubiously balanced a plate of sandwiches on his lap. "I'll be back in a second," she said and took two steps before her figure vanished. Frantisek had arrived determined not to eat, drink or speak with anyone, but his wife's disappearance made him regret the lack of a companion. Since he didn't know what was around him and didn't want to grope at the emptiness like a blind man, he preferred to avoid the risk of getting his clothes dirty while clutching the food; thus he applied himself to draining the cup and mopping up the plate, before setting them down on a providential table or letting them fall to the floor. The decline in his sense of vision had favored the development of other senses, so as he ate and drank he kept himself entertained listening to fragments of a conversation taking place meters away. One woman was saying there was a colonel in love with her, that her mother was a widow, that she'd inherited a little forest near Stafford-on-Raven and that if everything went to the blazes and the colonel didn't shell out a few pence, they'd see themselves forced to sell every last pine and eucalyptus. Her female interlocutor asked: "But do you love him?" And the first said: "I'm faithful, calm, undemanding and very capable of making any man happy. I don't give a damn about love."

Rustle of feet on the carpet near my great-great-grandfather, puff of air from a nearby couch deflating under the weight of a pair of buttocks:

"We're having a good time, aren't we? I've known you for quite a while now, I think, or at least I've seen you before."

"Impossible," said my great-great-grandfather. "I hardly ever go out."

"Just because you don't see anyone doesn't mean they don't see you. What's your profession?"

Already tired of this conversation, Frantisek preferred to lie: "I'm a machinist . . ."

"Pianist," corrected Athenea, coming back from somewhere.

"Artist? What a coincidence! You're a cellist and I'm an extortionist. Rhyme is proof of affinity," the stranger let out a chuckle. Athenea accompanied it with a sharper smile than usual, which broke into a laughter that evoked the happy clucking of a laying hen at the moment of its annunciation.

"How amusing!" she praised him, when her convulsions had reached an end.

Frantisek felt growing within him the strain of a situation composed of at least two intolerable elements. The first was his anger at this man's ability to cling to him and involve him in a banal conversation, forcing him to continue in the same line or else retreat into silence, an attitude that at a social event could be taken for a display of rudeness. The second was his even greater irritation that without anyone asking it of her, Athenea had decided to reveal to this parasitic plant an item of information he'd prefer to have kept to himself; by doing so, she'd unnecessarily put him in the position of a liar. Why had she opened her mouth? Her mistake of saying "pianist" instead of "composer" didn't matter, and served only to prove once again that she didn't know anything about him. In a gesture of supreme neglect toward the man she claimed to love, Athenea had scattered the decisions about her husband's privacy like so many crumbs, to feed the conversational zeal of this unknown hanger-on . . . And for Frantisek, this was the worst of the worst, because it ushered a third element into an already tremendously complex scene: jealousy. *Athenea*—he thought he understood—*would do anything necessary, even throw him bound by hands and feet to a pack of starving dogs, were it to pique this character's interest.*

Frantisek felt himself struck by the lightning bolt of this unexpected emotion. To feel jealous of a woman he scorned was the deepest humiliation. Jealousy made her indispensable. Desperate, he understood that he had to get her out of there, away from contact with the other. Quickly and in whatever way possible.

"I want more sandwiches," he said with a hoarse voice, stretching his plate toward his wife.

"More?" she protested.

"Yes."

"You're going to turn into a whale," said Athenea, snatching away the plate and getting up from the couch. Before going to the table of cold delicacies, she tossed out her last comment, addressing herself directly to the newcomer: "Would you like anything?"

"And something to drink too," Frantisek voided her offer. "And now that you're standing, why don't you go check when our host is going to arrive?"

"Anything else?" said Athenea with curt irony.

"Nothing. Yes. You should retouch your makeup."

"As if you ever looked at me!" she replied, and left offended.

"A woman who knows how to leave knows far better how to return."

"Are you still here?" asked Frantisek.

"Who, me? Sure."

"I hadn't noticed."

"Don't worry. I know how to go unnoticed," the stranger laughed: "I've spent half my life in the shade and the other half in hiding. Escapades. But now I am midway through a plan of reform! If I were to tell you . . ."

"There's no need."

"It's no trouble. I'll take this opportunity to introduce myself. I'm Alyosha Davidov, my esteemed Deliuskin."

"Do we know each other?"

"Not reciprocally, mister. Ah, here comes your beautiful wife, Deliuskinova, carrying a delicious heap of cold-cut sandwiches and sweet-and-sour pickles! Well, I'll hook into that group dance and leave you in pleasant company . . ." He clapped my great-great-grandfather on the back, greeted Athenea with a wave and disappeared into the crowd.

Athenea occupied the sofa on precisely the sections of velvet that Davidov had warmed.

"Song Li hasn't shown up, but a few minutes ago a young man with striking Nordic features knocked on the door, claiming he was his unrecognized son. *Incroyable!*" said Athenea, who liked to show off her command of languages on special occasions. "Have you noticed the atmosphere? The people are—how to put it?— worked up, in a frenzy . . . I think the sound of wind instruments contributes to it . . . What were you talking about with Alyosha?"

"Do you know that guy?" Another dagger, a new certainty stabbed into Frantisek's heart.

With the same tone of indifference (a topic in itself) that good actresses often affect in bad works, Athenea answered:

"Davidov . . . But if he . . ." and here an abrupt stylistic turn of the period entered reality, or at least the scene between Athenea and my great-great-grandfather: the interruption used to buy time. Turning her head, suppressing her reply, Athenea cried out: "Franti, the door to the dance floor is open! Let's see what's going on inside!"

Frantisek allowed her to drag him along. The hall was blue, and so were the sofas, the plates, the servants' clothes and the fine tablecloth covering the palo santo wood table, painted the color of lapis lazuli. The members of a string quartet were attacking the first measures of a scherzo. "Just because" music, pointless and incidental music, a crackling of sorrowful cicadas attempting pizzicatos of joy, meant to signal that the party was getting started. Timely masks appeared. "Let's dance, let's dance!" shouted falsetto voices. Everyone started to move. Frantisek, sure that this event had been created precisely to add well-defined new episodes to his misfortune, was led, or rather towed, seeing that he was yoked to the neck of his wife. As he rubbed against and was rubbed by her, he also experienced the painful certainty that—even if he was her husband—he was also a convenient substitute for a nearby source, no doubt irradiating waves of stimulating presence.

"Don't lose the rhythm . . ." gasped Athenea.

My great-great-grandfather couldn't help but wonder who his wife's lover might be. Verbose Davidov? The absent master of the house? Someone else? At what point would Athenea disappear with her true love into the crowd? If she was wagering on some base act, her plan was an extraordinary one: to leave him there, practically blind, lost like a scarecrow in a crowd of masked dancers. Such perversity far exceeded Athenea's requirements, since she could have left him immediately, at any moment, in any corner. All she had to do was let go of his hand, and it was over. "No," Frantisek told himself, "this plan's been concocted by her lover." Driven by bitterness, he decided to complicate or directly prevent the operation by his suspected rival, and he suddenly embraced Athenea as if the situation excited him. It didn't surprise him that his wife responded in kind: it was the elation that went with the imminence of flight. Sometimes it's only when we're moving away from a person that they appear to us in all their radiant charm, like the first time we saw them. So it wasn't strange that now, on the verge of leaving him, Athenea felt deeply attracted, fully conscious of the reasons she'd once longed to be his woman. They let themselves be swept along, dancing cheek to cheek, bodies pressed against each other within the increasingly compact mass of people. Frantisek monitored the variations in Athenea's breathing. When he thought that the situation had reached the appropriate temperature, he proceeded to carry out the series of furtive adjustments needed for a fleshly coupling in mobile circumstances. Athenea immediately caught the drift, and as she moved her head, pretending to follow the rhythm of the music, her skillful fingers helped him to liberate his instrument. Frantisek hugged her more tightly, as much to assist the contact of her fingers against his member as to conceal the evidence of exposed goods. In the meantime, she started to wind his crank and whisper to it: "Let me kneel down; I don't care if I'm stepped on or destroyed. I'll go to my death sucking the *potz*." "Bitch!" answered Frantisek. "Yes, yes," said Athenea and let out a couple of hot doggy barks in his ear. At that moment, a couple of powerful hands grabbed Frantisek by the neck and turned him a hundred eighty degrees, as if he were a puppet. The music stopped playing mid-note. Amid the silence of the empty space, Frantisek understood he'd been brought out for everyone's viewing pleasure, a stupid exhibitionist with his piece on full display. Complete humiliation. A foul-smelling rag was clapped over his nose, hiked upward toward his eyes. A blindfold. A shadow to cover his shadow.

"Let's play blindman's bluff!" squealed Athenea.

"No," begged my great-great-grandfather, but the approving shouts of the spectators silenced his protest. Hands spun him around on his feet, again and again, in carousel turns that left him dizzy. He had to stretch out his hands, palms reaching forward, fingers like worms, to keep from falling.

"Cold . . . Cold . . ."

"This is desolation," he thought, and went toward that mocking voice sustained by an immaterial thread of sound. Did he have his cock out? He didn't feel it, nor did he hear any surrounding current of murmurs denouncing his nudity.

"Here . . . No . . . Not there . . . Cold . . . Very cold . . ."

Here or there. Now several called out to him. Carried away by a dull growing fury, Frantisek lunged forward with his head down, aiming at the voices.

"Calm there, toro!"

Laughter, shrieks of women, brushes of skin, rustlings of a crowd as it unfolds like a fan. Frantisek charges. I'm a musician, an artist. Contemplate what I've become: I can't even see anymore. My only remaining pride is to keep my mouth shut, not open my jaws to let out the bellow of a bovine splashing in a swamp, of a mammoth sinking deep into the waters of the Pleistocene.

"Ah . . . Now . . . Warm . . . Yes . . . Hot . . . Very hot! No. No, over here! Here . . . Cold . . . No. Warm. Here! Yes . . . Hot. Hot hot hot . . . On fire!"

Frantisek's hands plunge into something creamy, disgusting. It smears his forehead as he takes off his blindfold.

"What's this?"

There's almost no difference. Shadows and lumps.

"What . . . is . . . this?" he shouts.

"Suck on your finger!"

Athenea approaches. My great-great-grandfather can't see her face, but he knows that she's smiling. She kisses him, lifts up his hand and sucks his finger:

"It's a cream cake . . ." she says.

"Everyone's laughing at me!" sobs my great-great-grandfather.

". . . a birthday cake . . ."

Frantisek escapes, stumbles down the staircase of the mansion, falls on the sidewalk, ripping his trousers, and, without knowing he's doing so, runs toward the jetty. Fiery tears slide down his cheeks, carried away by the wind and dissolving in air, each fragmented part bearing a gleaming shard of a nameless god. As he continues to soak in the diluted salts of his pain, visions of his past attack him in gusts, mucus streams from him like the jeweled sputum of tuberculosis, his lungs start to burn, his legs tremble. Who am I? Fran . . . Frantisek . . . Where are you, Frantisek? It's me, your sweetheart, Jenka. Jenka, light the way for me. I can't, Fran, I'm dead. The dead aren't beings of light? No, Fran, it isn't ash that shines. My glow in this world is already put out. Goodbye, Fran. Old voices. The home where I was born. My family. I'm a child. We're in front of the bathroom mirror, a framed oval with gold adornments, grape leaves and vines. Vladimir, my father, holds me in his arms. Mama is next to us. I look at myself, then at them. I'm so small I think we're not here, on this side of the glass, but on the reflected side, and so I reach out a finger to touch us. Mother is serious, Father too. Against my fingertips I feel the horrible cold of the mirror. My father says: "Frantisek, until today you've been a cretin, a real half-wit. Starting now, you'll begin to understand everything, and be a person like the rest." But I never understood anything, just the opposite, I understood everything in reverse! I'd felt I was pure promise and longing, and now I'm a fraud. A failure, a failure. Human ruin. An idiot, a good-for-nothing. Frantisek. What? Idiot. Me? Yes, you. What is this damp frozen wind? An anticipation of your destiny. You've never understood a thing in your life. So now you must cease living.

The current of the gulf, usually gentle and regular, has given way to a true hurricane: waves beat against the pier of stone and wood. His fall in the water barely raises a few more drops. Drowning by immersion is not a salve, and death in general is no caress. Whirlwinds sink and save him, a courtship with his end. My great-great-grandfather swallows water, hears the roar of the storm as his own cry. He doesn't even faint. All at once, he thinks: Andrei. What am I doing? Son, the sunshine in my music, my complete notation. I abandoned you in the hands of a stranger and launched myself on this frivolous newlyweds' journey, this bitter honeymoon! I am an egoistic monster. I can't let myself sink, I can't die: this self does not belong to me. I owe it to Andrei.

Frantisek's right foot touches the step of an iron staircase; his hands cling to the bars of salvation. With nothing to lose, he goes back to the party as best he can. "I tripped and fell in a puddle," he says, to explain his soaked clothes. Athenea looks prepared to make a scene, but a servant claps his hands together and announces the evening must be interrupted: silken Song Li, in the disguise of Cleopatra, has suffered a heart attack.

When they left the place, Frantisek was shivering from fever. In the tilbury carriage, between one fainting fit and the next, Athenea's explanation came to him confusedly (maybe in just a few words, but he heard them as an interminable string): that the charming young man who'd talked to him at the party, Alyosha Davidov, was in fact Arkady Troitsky, her lieutenant of hussars, dead in the Battle of Kurland. Well, Arkady hadn't really died in combat, but had deserted before the confrontation, owing to quarrels in strategy with the high command. In reality, Arkady had never been her betrothed. That had been his cousin, whom she'd loved like a brother. Frantisek would never believe how closely the two resembled each other, like drops of water. And to tell the truth . . .

Frantisek didn't know how they reached the hotel. The sheets were like a flaming rose garden in which he could only be naked. Something of his ardor had infected Athenea, who lay down beside him and asked him to possess her. "This proves I never had you," he answered, and fainted again. The next morning—in a hallucinatory oasis within the fever that accompanied him for his remaining days—he felt strong enough to decide that the honeymoon was over. They made their way back to Russia.

8

In a display of anger over the interruption of their trip, Athenea remained silent during the return. Back in Crasneborsk, however, she adopted the expansive mode and superior airs of a woman who, after completing her apprenticeship in the school of the world (civilized Europe), can't help but comport herself as a great lady. With little strength now, my great-great-grandfather tried to adapt himself to the consequences of her choice in lifestyle, which showed itself first in the increase of the service staff, then in the appearance of visitors and guests. From the tone of her voice, he knew that Athenea's mother had settled into a room on the first floor, where she directed the operations of the house, and sometimes he heard the contemptible whispers and loud laughter of Alyosha Davidov / Arkady Troitsky, who prowled about the pantry or slipped into the maids' bedrooms.

Deep down, all of this barely mattered to him; even his growing blindness would have seemed only a secondary defect given the circumstances of general collapse in his life, were it not that the progressive annulment of his sense of sight (which had its comings and goings, its shimmerings amid opacity) also went about putting an end to his joy in the contemplation of Andrei's face. Like a tattoo artist who keeps working despite a lack of materials, Frantisek recorded his son's every expression in the pavilions of his memory: every curl of every one of his ringlets, the transparency of his earlobes, the exact pigmentation (splatters of gold on petroleum) of his pupils . . . The loss was infinite, and now he would no longer see him grow up. He solaced himself thinking he would at least enjoy the consolation of his nearby presence. Hear him put together his first words, cry at night, climb into a sleigh, shout in the snow, become a man . . . But not even this would be granted to him.

One morning, yearning for a little solitude, he went to Jenka's studio; the place had remained closed since his wife's death. In the midst of its cold atmosphere of abandonment, as he revised the materials of her work—which also offered him their ceremony of a visual goodbye—he discovered a roll of canvas, hidden behind some stretcher frames and cans of paint. When he unfurled it, he came across a sketch for a portrait of Andrei. More than the detail of technical knowledge, what was impressive about those pale colors was the sentiment of the ineffable, the joy that had suffused Jenka following her maternity. The image of that creature, just a few days old, was pictorial substance infused by light, and now this light infused his memory of the portrait's author. *Andrei. Andrei by Jenka.* Frantisek felt the loving finger of the deceased touching his soul, reminding him he had to protect his son from everything and everyone. Not, obviously, from the small stains of time, which he could make out moderately well with the help of a magnifying glass, but from something less subtle and more macabre, a deliberate work of destruction that had pretended to be time itself, and that had rushed and plunged forward like a Fury, hurrying with treacherous hand to pinch or pluck out Andrei's eyes, and with irregular erosion, attempting to imitate the work of moths. The canvas was already torn across the heart, which simulated the effect of an incorrect rolling technique, but actually came from the slash of a knife blade.

Fearing for his son's life, he secretly sent Andrei to the home of Jenka's parents in Finland.

I won't dwell on the heavy toll the decision took on him, or linger over the desolation that overcame him as he watched his baby boy setting off. Ten dogs, a sleigh, the wet nurse clutching his little one. A cry, immediately soothed. A speck in the midst of the vast expanse. Then nothing.

And that nothing extended to everything. After the departure of Andrei, Frantisek's body reacted like a building of wood attacked by termites. Abscesses formed (every tissue was a niche of pus); he suffered from acetonuria in his urine and acetonemia in his blood; in a preliminary examination, articular lesions, anemia, blepharitis and avitaminosis were also detected; later, he presented cases of bronchopneumonia, tonsillitis, cephalea, cramps and cystitis; he lived from fever to fever, which revealed the effects of an abnormal increase in his bone marrow activity; he suffered from an uncoordinated trembling of the cardiac muscle fibers . . . The day he could no longer get out of bed, Athenea sent for Nikolai Gurevich, a doctor recently settled in the area whom all Crasneborsk (except one of its inhabitants) took for a luminary. Gurevich created such demand that at the moment he presented himself at the home of the sick person, the expectation created by his delay preceded him, forming an important part of his aura as a savior. Frantisek could almost no longer see the movement of a crowd, but no doubt he heard the tumult from the entrance of the doctor's court of followers into his room. Without moving aside the sheet under which my great-great-grandfather was shivering, without lifting an eyelid, sounding him, feeling his stomach, tapping a knuckle against his back . . . without making him cough, spit, exhale, moan, urinate or respire, without even asking him how he felt or the reason for the consultation, Gurevich turned to his students: "Who can correctly tell me what is the matter with this poor fellow?" he said. "Me, doctor." "No, me, me . . ." "I called dibs!" Gurevich pretended to hesitate, poking a cau-

tionary finger over their heads. "Let's see, let's see . . . Orman?"
"Painful swelling!" "*Nyet.* Stulberg?" "General functional impotence, doctor!" "*Nyet, nyet.* Kuperman?" "I don't know, maestro."
"A sincere ignoramus. What are you doing next to me, you dunce?
Let's see . . . Sametskoff?" "Brucellosis, doctor?" "Are you confusing a human being with a cow, simpleton? And you, Sznaider?
Don't let me down . . ." "Hepatic cirrhosis, professor? Look at the
drunkard's face he's got!" Gurevich raised his arms to the sky: "My
God, I'm surrounded by idiots! Do I always have to say it?" And
putting an overfamiliar paternal hand on Frantisek's shoulder, he
said: "Here we have the classic Tetralogy of Fallot, a condition
characterized by four congenital malformations: a) narrowness of
the pulmonary artery; b) hypertrophy of the right ventricle; c)
interventricular communication (the blood flows as if through a
tube, and makes a sound of flatulence); d) displacement of the
aorta toward the right. Treatment: at present, none. I don't know
why they make me waste time on incurables."

And he left.

The second doctor, Vasily Basedow—a true anticipator of
Tolstoy, who crossed part of the steppe barefoot to attend to
him—recommended that he follow a naturist diet, with a soup
made from birch tree bark, juniper roots, insects . . . The third,
the affable Lev Rozenbergstein, an ideal hare to be pursued by the
dogs of any pogrom, would no doubt have been the top choice as
my great-great-grandfather's doctor, were it not that at the end of
the examination he shook his head and confessed: "I don't know
what's wrong with him, and don't know what to do." Finally, by
elimination, Propolski appeared again, filling his mouth with talk
of gastrectomies and ablations, elaborating on his recent liaison
with a foreign beauty and, after encouraging him by saying: "You
look phenomenal, darling," prescribing him laudanum. Frantisek
could work out that he was preparing him for a good death, and

decided to accelerate the process by taking large doses of the medicine, but this opiate served only to intensify his serene detachment toward the things of this world. Dominated by the sensation, he considered all events from the perspective granted by existence in a life beyond; due to a secondary effect of the drug, he even tended to perceive the existence of Athenea and her surroundings in the form of luminous emanations, ordered in thermal chains and lacking a central bone structure, just like worms; he believed that every variation of color transmitted a different thought or emotion in people and had an objective character. Anyone might have said this light show was the system that madness had found to adopt an appearance of truth, but in fact it was precisely the measure my great-great-grandfather needed to embark again down paths of artistic work.

Even that wasn't easy. Frantisek no longer enjoyed tranquility in his studies. Nobody bothered to ask whether he was busy with a new composition. But the papers and books on his desk buried under a pile of gloves, coats, hats and magazines left by visitors, and the manuscripts used in the kitchen to cover jars of curd or line the drawers, didn't seem to bother him. Athenea also began to show signs of delicate health: she suffered from insomnia and walked around the house all night long, tripping over the bodies of guests who dozed in chairs or on the staircase, while in the daytime she tormented him with unnecessary recommendations.

In such conditions, it's a real feat that my great-great-grandfather moved ahead with *Universe*, the symphonic poem that stands out as his musical testament and requiem. Luckily he could count on the help of Volodia Dutchansky, who, prompted by an omen, went to visit him out of the blue and, seeing him reduced to such a state, decided not to leave his side. They often sat together all afternoon in the garden (Volodia carried his friend in his arms and set him down in the lawn chair), where they talked about existing and imaginary music. Frantisek serenely accepted the nearness of his end. Once he confided:

"The blindness doesn't bother me much. I still enjoy the sun on my face. The only thing I regret . . ." and emotion interrupted his secret.

He dedicated at least a couple of hours a day to dictation. It was a difficult task, which demanded great energy from him; he showed an extreme concern for every detail, every note. Sometimes, as soon as he indicated an eighth note and before Volodia had finished jotting it down, my great-great-grandfather, prey to the greatest agitation, would request a change. He gesticulated until he was bathed in sweat and had to stop. Then Volodia would pick him up in his arms once more and lay him down again in bed. Frantisek was so absorbed by the first fruits of his new creation that he didn't realize—despite the efforts against it by his composer friends—that his name had begun to travel beyond the borders of his country. Often musicians of international prestige would introduce themselves to him and kiss his hands. Eager to look after his health, Dutchansky kept him away from these strong emotions; he yielded in his role of a polite guard dog only when the offer was too good to refuse. So it was that my great-great-grandfather left Crasneborsk for the last time and crossed the eighty versts toward Saint Petersburg to attend a great festival dedicated to the performance of his works.

On the night of the premiere, the audience witnessed the entrance of a stretcher bearing a man with white hair covered by an astrakhan cap. His terrible skinniness wasn't hidden by the bearskin coat wrapped around him. Scored by wrinkles, his pale, ascetic face seemed to vanish behind the tortoiseshell glasses that also hid his blind eyes. There were ovations between pieces, and a moving finale ended the concert. Then everyone turned toward the box seat where Deliuskin lay surrounded by flowers. Without rising, in a slow but clear voice, he said: "Thank you."

Despite the triumphal reception, my great-great-grandfather didn't want to attend the rest of the performances, and that same night, he gave the order to go back to Crasneborsk. Throughout the return trip he remained silent. Maybe it irritated him that they'd applauded him for the wrong reasons. Uncomfortable with this silence, Volodia tried to create an environment of conversation, but got off on the wrong foot by mentioning Athenea:

"She looked so moved!"

"Was she there," said Frantisek, his voice lacking coloratura.

After this excursion, my great-great-grandfather showed no further desire for anything but to continue with his final composition. He was anxious to conclude it before his strength deserted him. And so it makes sense that at the dawning of his agony he commenced his greatest artistic effort, rightly considered to have been the first symphonic poem, however much it may weigh on Hector Berlioz, whose *Symphonie fantastique* (1830) dates to over half a century later. Of course, one can't help but point out that to conventional tastes *Universe* lacks those fixed traits that permit one to identify a work and make it possible to mark out details that set it off or bring it into relation with a known model. But no doubt there was a model. Even someone ignorant of music will notice that the work is built on a consecutive series of melodic ideas, in which greater importance is granted to tonal color than to form, to insinuation than to clear exposition, so that a listener has to respond intuitively to its multifaceted portrait in the same way that Deliuskin himself responded intuitively to the beauty and majesty of the Universe he was attempting to portray. The nebulous, harmonious design, the delicate timbres, the iridescent colors . . . everything is definitely new. The initial theme is heard on the woodwinds and repeated by the strings. An English horn adds a brief flourish to a passage of fantasy. Swans drink at the waterfall. Now the music grows lively. The main theme is a sweeping melody played by violas, accompanied by motifs on woodwinds and chords played by strings of a lower register. All of this develops with a pleasurable intensity. The atmosphere then grows calmer, albeit just for a few moments. A feverish new idea seizes the violins and is taken up by the woodwinds. But serenity returns again. The initial material repeats and the symphonic poem ends in an atmosphere of mist, as the music fades out.

9

Frantisek Deliuskin died at the peak of the summer solstice. In accordance with his last will, he was buried alongside Jenka Roszl, his first wife (a small mound of stones at the foot of a larch tree). In the letter he sent to Vladimir Deliuskin (who died the next year in a fishing accident), Volodia Dutchansky narrates my great-great-grandfather's final elegiac moments, the gentle way he expired seconds after dictating the final note. He records how during the funeral ceremony, he almost couldn't hear the priest's oration, because of the heartrending cries of Athenea, the widow.

"Surprise demise," *Izvestia* headlined his obituary. Striking an involuntary comic chord, its anonymous writer—Propolski, needless to say—opened the article with a dubious claim: "Medical science is still unable to explain what happened . . ."

BOOK 2

ANDREI DELIUSKIN

The tragedy, now, is politics.

—NAPOLEON BONAPARTE

1

According to Jean-Philippe Rameau's classic *Treatise on Harmony*, "The world of books doubles the relational system of thought: universal knowledge mirrors the design of a supreme mind." If the latter hadn't been referring to God, it would have served perfectly to describe the tremendous intellectual ability that characterized Andrei Deliuskin, my great-grandfather.

Andrei Deliuskin arrived at his Finnish grandparents' home on the day the fish talked. The aquatic vertebrate was calmly waiting for its turn under the knife, on the counter of the family fish shop, when just as he was about to gut it, as Abraham Roszl was now telling his wife Jamke, the mid-sized carp made a bold move, leaping out of his slippery hands, falling into a bucket of water and popping out its head. Since the Torah doesn't say anything about resurrection, Abraham thought this might be a specimen particularly resistant to changes of habitat. Ah, but it's really something else when a carp—alive or dead—sticks its head out of the bucket, waggles its fins to call your attention, looks you dead in the eye and says: "*Tzaruch shemirah*" and then: "*Hasof bah*"—that is, everyone must take responsibility for their acts, because the end is near! This was a real miracle, not some fake Messiah burdened with good intentions taken down from a cross after passing out!

Then . . . Abraham Roszl had just begun to draw up a comparative list of miracles by the carp and Christ (the first longer by far than the second) when the door to their home opened and a frozen-stiff Marina Tsvetskaia laid an adorable, tiny bundle of life, tucked between layers of wool, in his arms. "Jenka is dead. This is Andrei," she was able to get out. Then she fainted from the cold.

There must be no stronger emotion in the world than simultaneously learning of a daughter's death and grandson's birth. Abraham and Jamke Roszl didn't know whether to thank God or abhor Him. Of course, they had the whole weight of tradition to help them resign themselves to the idea of a trial, not to mention the fact that on this same day full of extraordinary events, a fish had spoken. Late at night, while Andrei and his wet nurse slept, Abraham and Jamke went on with their crying and laughing. When they'd calmed down a bit, Abraham continued his tale:

". . . And then I said: 'You're a dybbuk! Who's ever heard of a talking fish?' 'But Abraham! Abrumi, darling!' the fish said to me, and rolled its eyes just like this. I swear to you, Jamke, if you'd have seen it, it would've broken your heart. 'Don't you know who I am? Doesn't my voice tell you anything? I'm Biniomen Pinkas, your neighbor!' 'You liar! Biniomen died last year!' I told him. 'Of course, I did, do you think if I hadn't died you'd have seen me reincarnated like this?' said the carp. 'And what brings you back? You couldn't stay quiet in your tomb? If you've come back to see your dear Noime, I can assure you you've got the wrong body. Now if you'd taken the form of Motl the milkman, you'd have seen her real up close . . .' I said. 'Abrumi! Always the same joker. No, I didn't come back to life for Noime, though we'll settle our accounts, that loose woman and me. I came for you, pierogi head. I have a message to give you straight from the mouth of G'd,' said the carp. 'What? G'd wants to talk to me, before I've taken my ritual bath?' I said, and took off running . . ."

"But Abraham . . . *Mame Maine*! G'd has a message and my husband makes him wait!" despaired Jamke.

"It was a little lie, woman. I went to look for the rabbi. What else is there to do in a situation like this? Obviously looking for him took some time, since he was on the other side of the city, and when I found him, it was hard for me to convince him I wasn't drunk. 'A talking fish, Abraham! What is this, a Hassidic tale?' 'But seriously, rebbe . . .' 'Abraham, Abraham, do you think that if G'd had wanted to announce the Apocalypse he'd have sent a neighbor of yours turned into a fish that gives big talks at the shop?' 'And what's so strange about that? If the goyim believe the Lord is one and three, why shouldn't we believe the Word of G'd took a little dip in the Baltic?' et cetera, et cetera, and so we took some time getting back to the fish shop . . . And what had happened in the meantime? In the meantime, Kemi, my good employee, had the bright idea to sacrifice the carp and make a tasty gefilte fish of it, which he sold to all the customers in the neighborhood! So the message of G'd is out of my hands now . . ."

"What do you mean? Kemi killed a talking fish?"

"Jamke, woman! Do you think Kemi understands Yiddish?"

"Ah . . . And the message of G'd?"

"Maybe it's better this way . . . Divided up in the stomachs of many good Jews."

"Yes. Maybe you're right. The absolute truth would be indigestible for a single person, no?"

"I think the same. What a day! Better it's over. Good night."

"Good night."

"Jamke . . ."

"What?"

"My heart is destroyed by Jenka's death."

"And what about me?"

"What about your 'me'?"

"What about me, the mother?"

"Yes. I don't even want to imagine."

"Good night. Jenka, Jenka!"

"You have to resign yourself, woman . . ."

"Resign myself, yes. Maybe my belly will burst when I'm sleeping. I'll leave this world in blood."

"Don't tempt the devil."

"The law is that parents walk before their children along the path of shadow. Who runs the Universe? Eh? I think He's dead, and before He died, He left his place to some *schlimazel*."

"Don't talk like that."

"Why not? It would explain everything. Why shouldn't I talk like that?"

"Because it's a sin."

"I'm a woman, and that's enough. Not even G'd can understand what I'm going through."

"I can't take it anymore either!"

"It's not the same thing, how can you compare? A father!"

"All right, enough."

"Whoever says enough is able to put limits on pain."

"I'm going to sleep now."

"All right, sure, leave me alone with my anguish, which is infinite. You can't think of anything else to say? He ruins your life, murders your daughter, our daughter, and here the mister can only say, 'I'm going to sleep now'?! When you die there's not a chance you'll reincarnate as a fish. Even a sturgeon egg would be too big for your soul!"

"Jamke, let's sleep. Tomorrow will be another day."

"Abraham . . ."

"Mmhhh . . ."

"Abrumi . . ."

"Can't I have a little silence? What's the matter now?"

"No, nothing . . . better not to say."

"Let's hear it . . ."

"Our grandson is going to fill us with happiness . . ."

"*Mazel tov*. And now sleep."

"Andrei. What a beautiful name . . ."

Can God—*the* God, a god, any god—distribute the meaning of a message via the infinitesimal portions of material into which a messenger's body has been sliced? Where and in what ways is the content of a truth conserved or destroyed? Does it linger as an aura or is it a purely mental effect, the memory of an existence? Is it possible to transmit it by means of a divided-up body? And if so, through which part? Is the message lodged in the white flesh, the dark bones, the gills, the round strabismic eyes? Or is the Word corrupted if the fleshly bearer is mixed with chopped carrot, grated *jrein*, sautéed onion, flour, pepper and salt? Questions Abraham and Jamke never resolved (or even came to formulate), but that when transfigured into the inquiries of their own experience, both gave and took away justifications for the life of Frantisek and Jenka's only child.

2

Although his existence was full of travel, knowledge and adventure, Andrei Deliuskin's childhood and a good part of his adolescence went by without his leaving the urban radius of Helsinki, submitting to a certain method of concealment that Abraham Roszl had designed for his family as a preventive strategy against all possible representations of the word *joukkovaino* (Finnish translation of the Russian *pogrom*). He believed that abstaining from participation in politics, avoiding intervention in public debates, insisting on holding his head high, keeping off the sunny side of the pavement and steering clear of every opportunity to use pale-colored clothing, expand his property, go for a vacation, take a lover or buy himself a tilbury carriage for outings around town, created a kind of phantasmagoria of nonexistence that helped him merge into the surrounding landscape. As if a chameleon can't be trapped! Sometimes it is, and precisely because of its camouflage. Abraham Roszl's mottos: Don't raise your voice, don't look anyone in the face, don't laugh loudly, don't speak to strangers about religious matters. Every so often, deafening sounds forced him to stay awake, rise in the early morning mist and slip from the house like another shadow to whitewash the phrases painted on the door by terror artists: "Be a patriot, kill a Jew! This is an order of the Finnish Nationalist Civil Guard." The poor old man hurried to wield his anxious brush before any passerby surprised him; he didn't want to make anyone uncomfortable. Naturally, for the perverse hunter, there is no scent more exquisite than the perfume left by a prey seeking to go unnoticed. In this case, the hunter was reality. Due to a shift in the currents and temperatures of the water bodies around Finland, fishing began to grow scarce off the coastlines, which raised the prices of the goods put on counters and reduced demand. The problem grew worse with the arrival of winter. Abraham Roszl spent the few daylight hours wringing his hands over the scene of clean tiles in his deserted fish shop. Sometimes he asked himself whether the phenomenon could have some relationship with the uncommunicated message of the talking fish. What had it wanted to say before its end? Primitive Christians had represented Jesus in the form of a fish. What did that mean? Maybe the Lord had become Catholic and was punishing him for encouraging theophagy . . . !

Doubts. Doubts. All the same, Abraham Roszl didn't give in to the delights of idleness. His task: to put bread in the mouths of his family. He closed the business and with the few savings he'd scraped together after forty years of activity, he bought at a discount price an enormous, fantastic, sophisticated mechanical loom with a movable frame, rusting away in the back shop of Itzak Bialik, a money-changer friend. This loom was a self-sacrificing forerunner of the industrial revolution. In the hands of its inventor, Leibuj Peretz, it would easily have turned out all sorts of knitted, woven and blended fabrics at great speed. Cross-stitched pullovers, puzzle rugs, rhomboidal blankets . . . But Peretz had been forced to part with the machine during his life to pay off debts, and out of resentment he'd barely instructed Bialik about the basic techniques for use of the device. By the time the loom reached Abraham Roszl's hands, there was no longer any instruction manual or oral tradition that could help him decipher his purchase. In short, Andrei's dreamer of a grandfather was forced to come down from the clouds where the golden beak of Bialik had set him and, having shut himself away in his fish shop, confront the evidence of a mystery. Why had he bought this thing? How had he been convinced he could get any value from it? What planet was he living on?

The glinting metal pieces, sprinkled with oil, were scattered over the great black velvet cloth that was like a beautiful spider in the white shop. Even in their asymmetry, their humble disorder, they found a way to suggest a heartbreaking guilt, which to a sensitive observer would have revealed some all-encompassing augury. But for all practical purposes, this luckless Jew was blind to profane signs. And so, lacking even the slightest information about how a given screw might easily tighten a certain bolt, he started to combine and recombine the tubes, pipes and metal frames, working from his fantasies about how basic elemental phrases might be written in a language whose alphabet he didn't know, sure that at some moment, after he'd commended himself to G'd enough times, the correct way to put the loom together would appear traced in the air.

Naturally, until the miracle occurred, he had to make a show of all his devotion, patience and resolve, shrewdly exhibiting his determination not to expect total assistance from the divine (the condition necessary for precisely this to take place). For long hours, he stained his hands with the tools, joining short and long circuits and adjusting them to form squares, rectangles, pentagons, isosceles triangles. But there were always extra or missing parts. Also, who could guarantee that a specific piece—say, a hollow tube with one end dented and the other ending in a point—didn't fulfill a double or even triple function? Not to speak of the rollers, shafts, tommy bars, heddle sticks and other pieces that, out of a love for simplicity, he'd momentarily left aside. By the way, now is the moment to note that if Abraham Roszl had thought of showing the loom to Andrei, either for illustrative ends ("Look what a pretty puzzle, *eyngl!*") or as a pathetic testament to his own stupidity, his grandson would have figured out how to put it together in a few hours. But Andrei was only a child, so this didn't even occur to my grandfather.

The progress of disappointment: a terrible ordeal. Driven by the manic optimism found in all true anxiety, Abraham ended up putting together a shaky construction that held up due less to its structure than to the capricious lattice of threads that crossed it, which got caught on iron, tangled into knots, snarled around bobbins. A metallic grinding bore witness to some kind of functioning. Noise, noise, noise. One can understand why, after a series of attempts, Abraham Roszl preferred to remain alone in silence. After a period of repose and meditation, he disposed of the headache, selling it as scrap metal. Then he opened his business again, turning it into a glass shop.

In the fin-de-siècle Finland that witnessed the upbringing of Andrei Deliuskin, prudent people always walked at the sidewalk's edge, avoiding passing under balconies where flowerpots hung; and they were especially careful about rattling windows, since sudden differences of temperature (radiant days and icy nights) produced a systole and diastole of the material that tended to end with a rain of broken glass. For this reason, Abraham imagined that he had now dedicated himself to a truly surefire line of work. The inauguration was a success at the small-town level. The attendance was made up of traditional clients of the community, who came out of curiosity to find out how at his age old Roszl had managed to change his *gesheft*, and pretended to appreciate the marvels of decoration while they played "now you see me, now you don't" in the elusive plate-glass reflections. Jamke circulated, squeaking affectionate diminutives of recognition as she offered little glasses with *slivovitz*, and snacks of *pletzel* stuffed with pastrami, and pickles in vinegar cut into heart shapes . . . Uncomfortable smiles of acquaintances who always meet face to face and have nothing to say to each other. "How young you look, Iankl!" "Mordecai! I'm so happy to see you!" "The same is true for me, Iankl. How's it going with Leike?" "And how could we be going? On our feet, with her stupid as ever!" Conversations in a low voice: "And that youngster crawling around every corner?" "Shhh. Poor boy. I don't know if he'll last long, just see how skinny he is." "He'll last next to nothing if someone doesn't pick him up off the ground. Who is he?" "What? You haven't met him? He's the orphan Jenka left, after God took her into His glory." "What? Jenka died? When? But she was bursting with health!" "What's this? You don't know anything! What world are you coming from?" "I don't stick my nose into everyone else's life, that's why I'm always the last to know." "Well. It happened like this . . ."

The next morning, Abraham put a couple of flowerpots with newly blossomed geraniums outside the door of his shop. His secret hope was that these flowers would be destroyed in the first downpour, that their stems would be burned by the first frost and then annihilated by a solar flare hotter than the Sahara; through the magical effect of sympathy, any variations in the state of this delicate species would point to variations in the average inner nature of all the picture windows of Helsinki, and would therefore mean a boom and spiking profit arrow for his business in glass manufacturing. But once again he had no luck, except of the bad kind; Finland happened to be visited by a spell of warm gentle winds, a bland summer soup that strained into the country and leaked away after an intense season in Spain. The shop was always empty. And this made him think. Solitude always makes one think, if one lacks the talent for distraction. And it's obvious that this neo-glazier was neither frivolous nor imaginative, which is why in his idle time he could only let himself be carried away by thoughts, jingling with the ominous sound of false coins. For instance: why hadn't the rabbi come to the shop's inauguration? Had he been sick? No. They'd seen him brimming with strength, a real oak, just two days later. Had it been mere chance, an oversight? Or a sign of . . . what?

Abraham tried to concentrate his thoughts, to follow a line of logic, but it was impossible. His brain was an uncultured specimen, devasted by the barbarism of superstitions he confused with adherence to the community's religious traditions. And in addition . . . there were the pieces of glass sitting motionless in his shop, in ordered rows . . . keeping exactly the same distance between themselves . . . like rows of silent assassins.

After spending the day at his workplace, he woke up at night soaked in the sweat of one who's escaped ghosts.

"But what's the matter with you, Abrumi?" his wife asked, mopping his back with a cloth.

"I can't see myself so many times, over and over. I can't take it anymore!" he said.

"And what's the problem? Lucky you! Me, I can rest only when looking in the mirror. I don't know if it's my own self that appears there, but at least it makes me happy to know someone's watching me."

It was a cruel comment, if she'd have understood what he was saying.

"If G'd had wanted to play at repeating himself, he'd have populated the Universe with his images. To open a glass shop is a blasphemous act," muttered Abraham.

"Are you saying that G'd made the world for us to live in darkness and die of cold? What a head case you are! What's got you really feeling bad is the sin of not selling. The more pieces of glass you pack up, the smaller the chance that you'll see yourself reflected. A locale without merchandise. How satisfying would that be? Just imagine the sign: 'Temporarily out of stock.'"

That season, all the city's crystal and glass objects seemed to have achieved a state of supreme physical consolidation, as if they would never need replacement. But even if this weren't the case, even if all of Finland had suddenly experienced an earthquake that left nothing standing, it would have been unlikely for an average person to venture through the door of that dimly lit shop where a trembling Jew sat waiting with a lost gaze. To make his daily situation more bearable, Abraham organized a routine of disappearances and returns, frequently leaving the business and going to a bar to drink and play cards. He'd have preferred the temple, but he considered himself impure. At the bar he studied the game of his future rivals; it relieved him to confirm that every card bore a sign and not a face. One day he summoned up the courage and took a seat at the table. He lost everything left to him, even his business. Not the house, because it was in Jamke's name. He was found sprawled on the outskirts of the city, his face turned toward the sky, in the uncomfortable position of someone who's been waiting for a bush to start burning and instead finds himself—all at once—crucified. His eyes were open.

A few days later it was Jamke's turn.

Andrei was left as the sole and legitimate heir to a disastrous legacy, with Marina Tsvetskaia as his guardian and administrator of assets. The first question that Andrei posed as soon as he could speak, the first that he formulated correctly with both grammar and logic, was: "Who were my parents, and how did they meet and fall in love?" The answer depended on the moment, hour and fickle mood of Marina. In their essence, her stories were versions of the green ogre and blonde princess, the ruler and servant, the magician and frog, the priest and duchess. Andrei didn't object to these variations in the catalog; it was still the moment that things were being named for the first time. At the end of her tales, Marina would insist: "And they lived happily ever after," but when Andrei asked her to tell him where they were alive and happily "ever after," she only pointed upward.

As the worthy grandson of a glazier, Andrei grew up certain that his parents' happiness was a direct result of their invisibility, as opposed to the sadness of his childhood, defined by the material. From his early years, and with the intellectual resources available to him, he applied himself to considering changes in his weight, stature, density, et cetera in relation to abstract concepts like duration, existence, unhappiness, perception, intangibility . . . Concepts that knowledge of his tradition and inheritance would have enabled him to link to the most abstract of arts, music, but that in his case served only to configure a reserved disposition and a strong inclination toward solitude and thought. During school breaks—he was a good student and didn't need to study—he sat quietly in a corner of the patio, contemplating the grain of a stunted, diseased tree trunk that everyone ignored, studying the swarm of locusts that competed to devour every leaf and branch. His classmates took his natural self-absorption for arrogance and decided to punish him, assuming he'd be easy prey. One day Andrei found himself in the midst of a round of hands pushing him. "Wipe your nose, snotface," "faggot," et cetera. This low behavior infuriated him. Closing his eyes, he charged at everyone. A fury he didn't know was inside him surged forward with incredible speed, and even helped him strike the target with a few blows. The circle of aggressors widened for a few seconds, then closed in. He ended up knocked out, but with a reputation for bravery. Starting then, the little thugs of the higher grades would pick on him to test their strength; he was the ideal examiner for the bully in short pants. Provoking him was too easy. It was enough to ask: "Who'd your mom sleep with last night?"

After she saw him come back bruised from a few school fights, Marina Tsvetskaia hired Giacomo Lorenzo Straibani, a Piedmontese immigrant who passed himself off as a gymnastics teacher, to design a routine of exercises that would strengthen her foster son. The *Straibani Method for Physio-Dynamic Development* was no more than a partial and whimsical adaptation of the torture techniques applied during the Visigothic Kingdom, but it helped Andrei to forge his mettle. Truncheons. Weights. Stretches and contractions. Flexes. Imperceptibly, my great-grandfather began to replace the void produced by the absence of Frantisek—a blurry shadow, a faded voice—with the colorful figure of this sympathetic phony showing off swollen biceps. The disciple wanted to look like his maestro and dreamed of flaunting the same handlebar mustache, an identical shiny bald pate, a chest as broad as a tiger cage.

After a few months of exercise, Andrei had developed a solid muscular structure. But neither his momentum nor his devotion for Straibani turned him into one of those languid hedonists who admire themselves in the mirror, tracking the way the tone of their muscular fibers approaches the archetypical perfection of the bulge. He had already experienced the kind of violent emotion the pure ideal of self-contemplation could draw from him (even if it was concealed in the form of body building), and it was this, combined with his primary tendency toward spiritual delight, that later on would result in the synthesis of his adult self. Occasionally he felt *something else* whose nature and characteristics he couldn't precisely describe, and which in the course of his repetitions led him to distraction, a loss of rhythm, forgetfulness of the most basic mechanics . . .

"But what's wrong with you? Inner world or body, pick one!" Straibani griped. "You can't have both at once. What's the matter? Am I talking to a human being or a reindeer?"

Andrei didn't say anything, and so the *professore* went to look for an answer in the private sitting room that Marina had set up with less taste than imagination in dead Jamke's sewing area. Answering his question, Marina, ultimately a solitary soul, tried to express her own bewilderment, in between teas and mint pastilles *au chocolat*:

"What can I say, my dear Giacomo? He's always been a strange boy. In those days of my sad Russia when I suckled him, he'd cling to my breast with such frenzy it rent my soul asunder, but at the same time, he looked at me with those eyes that . . ."

"That what, Marina . . . ?"

"It's not right to say this about a child . . . But his eyes saw into me . . . pierced through me . . ."

Soon the gymnastic activity was pure appearance; the moment he arrived, Straibani would disappear behind the chaste taffeta curtains, trembling in wait for him. After each class, Andrei had to get used to going out by himself, walking through the cold around parks, squares, gardens, frozen lakes and museums, watching each drop of his sweat slowly transform into an ovoid stalactite. Little diamonds of his neglect. What did my great-grandfather think about during those outings? Impossible to know. What did Antonella Scuzzi di Straibani think about when, alone in the small earthen-floored kitchen of her Lombardy shack, she had to decipher those letters crammed with sugary promises and far-fetched excuses, in which her Giacomo excused himself for the paltry funds sent, barely enough for the daily pasta of Antonella Junior, Giacometto, Archimbaldo, Vittorio, Emanuelle and Vicenzo . . . ? Did the *professore*'s wife know that this looping handwriting, crude and full of spelling mistakes, was smudged because of the tears that night after night, in his miserable hovel, under the meager light of an oil lamp, her husband spilled as he named his descendants, as if the magic of evocation could wash away his guilt over having succumbed, repeatedly, to the charms of his fleshy white Russian lover? What did Straibani think about? He could have cut himself on the sharp edges of regret, but the truth is that he never thought about anything. The great tragedy of love is that it rouses even the most lethargic. A generally happy man, for the most part a euphoric idiot, had suddenly been jerked about by the affections . . . One spring contracts, another stretches, and in the end, the metal tires . . .

Harassed by the demands of his desire, agitated by the baby steps of his conscience, Straibani began to abandon his teaching routine. He missed classes without giving warning and took to fainting in front of the stained-glass windows with feminine images at the Pastrognïodk church, episodes of hysterical lust that he interpreted to be experiences of the sublime. Since visions would assault him during these fainting fits, accompanied by music from the solemn mass, Straibani decided to renounce sin, distance himself from every temptation and dedicate what was left of his life to singing the Lord's praises: he signed up for the religious choir. His attractive bass voice (a deep testicular promise) was a hit with the other participants, two *castrati* about to retire and forty-five ladies of different physical, psychological, developmental and civil states. To put it briefly: despite the promises of reform made to his favorite Virgin (an obese and inexpressive Mater Dolorosa who leaned forward from a stained-glass window in the southeast wing of the church, blessing the world), the gymnastics teacher relapsed in error. Now he didn't know whether he was being unfaithful to Marina Tsvetskaia with the irresistible Kymen Lääni, to Antonella with his two lovers, or to the Virgin herself with all three, separately or together.

Of course Marina noted an increase in Straibani's original guilt, as well as a decrease in the stimulus she gave him. Along with this she sensed a certain reticence, that air of a lie that any

woman picks up faster than the flu. Everything sounded unmis-
takably like the prelude to sentimental decline, which in this
case presented itself in the form of a strangely prolonged coda,
a courtship full of odd nuances and transitions, especially of
mood, introspective epiphanies that brought her to a belated
and cruel form of self-knowledge, based on the certainty that
she had always lived a vicarious existence: responsible for a son
who wasn't her own, living in a dead couple's house in a city far
from home, in love with a stranger who was married and, to
make it worse, now leaving her. She firmly adopted this conviction and adhered to its consequences, as if something one's own,
belonging to oneself and no one else . . . in a word, as if such an
essence truly existed. If she was no one and nothing was for her—
she concluded—then she, in contrast, could be everything for
everybody. For a while at least. She started to dress better, to go
out, to charge for her charms. In this activity she obtained neither pleasure nor consolation; to relieve herself from her foster
son's cutting gaze, "which pierces through me with its mute
reproach," she began to advance in the science of combinations:
red kirsch, green absinthe, golden beer, translucent vodka . . .
Mother, mother. Sometimes in the afternoon haze, Andrei was
unable to wake her. Marina would never find out that Straibani, after garnering a certain fame as a "Latin stallion," had
surrendered to another tedious cycle of the dialectic of guilt and
repentance, at the end of which he'd decided that she was his
one true love. She never discovered this because he didn't dare
let her know of his new conviction. He preferred to adore her
from a distance, and limited himself to contemplating her transformation into a great lady of the world. Sometimes, coming or
going from some revelry, Marina caught the fleeting glimpse of
a foreshortened mustache; other times she briefly noticed the
subtle gleam of those memorable eyes, the familiar shine of a

bald head. She attributed these effects not to her lover's relentless pursuit, but to the perpetual shadow of a typically Russian sentiment: nostalgia.

Life went on like this for some time. Then, one summer's evening, one of the mercenary neo-ladies' men who'd wined and dined Marina invited her to go out for a bit of fresh air near Keski Avenue. The street was decorated by a series of arches made from the branches of alcohol-soaked ash trees, stretching from sidewalk to sidewalk. They served as a kind of litmus paper for the town, evoking its atavistic tradition of barbaric and carnivalesque deeds, lustrous rapes in straw huts, triumphs and blazes in the night. Onboard the uncovered vehicle, Marina inhaled the fragrance of the breeze, then waved her shawl as if to say goodbye. The landau passed under the first arch at precisely the moment that Marina lit her cigarette . . . The combustion was immediate and extraordinarily graceful, a ball of fire that engulfed the whole structure of arches with a supreme understanding. Marina herself was the most exquisite part of the scene, perfect in her ordinary dignity, and with the saintly aura of a blue-petaled flower. A bystander reported a curious detail: a tourist disguised as a plush bear had jumped on the landau and tried to extinguish the catastrophe by embracing its victim, but had succeeded only in being consumed by the fire himself, as he let out comical exclamations in Italian.

3

Andrei Deliuskin confronted Marina's death like an adult. He'd loved—and how he'd loved!—his substitute mother, but he'd also been fully aware this love was doomed. For a brief period he surrendered to a calculation of the horrors of the world; when he'd come up with a rough sum, knowledge of the figure left him very near the abyss. He saved himself thanks only to the single reactionary behavior he'd ever allow himself: just as a baby, at the hour of falling asleep, clings to a little pink blanket, a used pacifier or an old green velvet button, he, in the attempt to cobble together from any old thing a certainty that could serve as refuge, went back to the tales that Marina had told him about his true parents. With a handful of vague allusions, the persistent drizzle of memories that had reached him by chance, my great-grandfather invented an ancestry and took possession of a memory, and this helped him to protect himself against the harshness of the elements. He concluded that he didn't need to hurry along his end to reunite with those absent, but should instead make the earth into a heaven where he could recover them. He didn't have the means at the moment, but he did have the determination to see his ideas through. In the meantime, he sold off his grandparents' house at a loss and abandoned Helsinki, leaving nothing behind.

First part of the route, bordering the Baltic Sea: Viipuri, Narva, Tallinn. Detour in Arensburg, just to see how the seagulls descended upon the shoals of herrings. Foam and massacre. In Riga he spent a formative period shut away in the National Library. A stealthy shadow, he hid himself from the eyes of librarians as he made his notes. His wings and wormlike lightning bolts illuminated the written pages at a slant. In the course of a single year he studied texts of ballistics, numismatics, archaeology, physics, metaphysics, chemistry, economics, philosophy . . . And on each one of these works, pressed into the narrow space of the margins, he left unforgettable observations, sketches of systems, new proposals and outlines for treatises whose dimensions will be established by specialists of the future.

One day, a copy of Ignatius of Loyola's *Spiritual Exercises* fell into his hands. It was the first document of a religious character he had examined. At the start, the mixture of hollow emphases and precisions with a coarse administrative tone irritated him; he thought the author was deliberately and frivolously seeking to contrast the ugliness of his prose with the beauties of thought, as if words were a mere means to assure the transmission of a "mental experience" linked to a knowledge of supposed ultimate truths. But soon his perplexity at this stylistic poverty gave way to an intuition. If the scrupulous reckonings and bureaucratic observations of Loyola differed so much from the usual "Church style," this wasn't due to problems of translation or to the author's mistaken decision to write his book in a vulgar language. On the contrary, the choice pointed to a carefully thought-out process in advance of the writing itself. If Latin in those times was the unique language of the Papacy, to use it to write these *Spiritual Exercises* would in principle have signified targeting readers from within the body of Catholicism. But opting for Spanish opened up a breach in this perspective. Had Loyola been plotting schismatic ends? No. Even a distracted reading allowed one to realize that his work had been designed to pass unscathed through the

Inquisitor's fire. Had Loyola been favoring his Spanish compatriots? Was this writing meant to evangelize the semi-illiterate masses of the Kingdom of Castile and Aragon? That wasn't the case either. And here the crucial question of style returned. As part of its evolutionary process (which began with a wretched mob of savage primitive apostles and ended with its current state of petrified perfection), the Church of Rome had elaborated an "allegorical Middle Ages" with apocalyptic tendencies, which, with its terrifying gargoyles and constant appeal to the Mysteries (whether of Eleusinian, Hebrew, Zoroastrian or Mithraic origin), revealed itself to be singularly capable of awing the childish mentality of the masses. In having chosen a humble people for his audience, Loyola ought to have opted for a bombastic prose of *visible* efficiency, since the poor adore exhibitionism and luxuries . . . But what did we have instead? What did my great-grandfather come across in those afternoons of reading?

There wasn't any immediate discovery. Andrei Deliuskin didn't suddenly stumble across all the secrets that the book had kept stored away for him. In fact, any visitor who today gains access to the section "valuable works, rarities and incunabula" on the third floor of the National Library of Latvia and has the necessary authorization to take out and consult the copy of *Spiritual Exercises* resting on a frail, moth-eaten, black plush mitt in the display window, will immediately see that my great-grandfather left an ongoing record of his suspicions and certainties via his annotations. The only reason that the copy enjoys such a privileged exhibition in the first place is, of course, due to the quality and inspiration of this marginal prose questioning it.

Well then. My great-grandfather sweated his share to get to the bottom of it all. But at some point, whether because of his habit of reading or because the key to the book itself lay in undermining the importance of its most visible commands, which served as a distraction mechanism (because at heart, as mystics well know, the sign of God's presence doesn't enter the being through an infinitely progressing chain of syllogisms, but through silence); at some point, and this was the whole of the illumination he was going to receive or produce in his youth, Andrei discovered that Loyola's choice of style required not a religious interpretation but a political one. In truth, for the founder of the Society of Jesus, *God was the mask under which a politics of power was hidden.*

Did this make Loyola a brute atheist, or at the very least an agnostic?

On the face of it, the *Spiritual Exercises* was an intelligent structure or outline that aimed to formalize the teleology of the Middle Ages through a series of practical steps, such as prayer, fasting, supplications, invocations, breathing, exhalations, abstinence, flagellations, et cetera; steps that if carried out with rigor would result in the certainty (or at least strong belief in the possibility) that at some point the one performing them would encounter an undeniable sign of God's presence. God, naturally, not insofar as *He* is, but insofar as He *is*. (Of course, just as in all tales about the arrival of the divine, if He doesn't appear—if the Sign doesn't emerge—then the guilt is our own, and neither hope nor the Ignatian system is invalidated.) But these steps, which are essentially of an overwhelming simplicity, a mere accumulation of time in a relay race, through Loyola's rhetoric, his prose of an exasperating accountant lacking grace, acquire the status of an infinite deferral. His discursive technique, made up of annotations, lists, preliminaries, warnings, repetitions and detours, builds up a formidable defense for the unwary and lightweight reader with quick expectations and petty illusions. Why should this occur if the book were about *religion*? If God is salvation, then the Act is total and there is nothing more to discuss. In contrast, Loyola complicates (or, to be more precise, duplicates), since his aim is human: at least, in the first instance. His arid and underwhelming rhetoric—and *this* is what my great-grandfather discovered—forms a system to reject some readers and choose others.

In conclusion: beneath its innocent appearance as an ascetic manual written to help produce a series of theophanies, the *Spiritual Exercises* is actually a coded treatise that works toward the recruitment, selection and training of a group of enlightened beings that aspires to take power. Understood this way, as my great-grandfather discovered, group prayer becomes a conspiratorial activity, with its rhythms (each utterance of the Pater, each pronounced Name, each intake of breath) turning into a collective meditation about times of political action. Meanwhile, the figure of an expectant or absent God, waiting for the correct invocation to favor an applicant with His presence, becomes a "power vacuum," occupied by a group or council following a series of movements ("political gymnastics") linked not with *what to say* but directly with *what to do*.

Of course, like every text in code, the *Spiritual Exercises* requires an external work or second text, a manual to decipher and activate the first. Andrei looked for it in the Jesuit's *Spiritual Diary*, in his *Commentaries*, in his uncollected articles, in his autobiography, in the allusions of his colleagues, superiors, friends and enemies, in the Papal Encyclicals; never did it occur to him to think of the obvious: that the instruction manual for the formation and training of a militant avant-garde prepared to launch itself into a conquest of the world, a plan invented and cryptically drawn up by Ignatius of Loyola, was—or would be—his own annotations. Evidence of this would be discerned sometime later by the most lucid minds of the Society of Jesus, as well as by, among others, personalities like the Bolshevik revolutionary Vladimir Ilyich Ulyanov, alias Lenin (1870–1924).

But this matter deserves an aside.

4

A little more than a century after my great-grandfather Andrei Deliuskin finished making his notes on Ignatius of Loyola's *Spiritual Exercises*, seemingly neglecting or abandoning them to the consultation or oblivion of humanity, Vladimir Ilyich Ulyanov, Lenin, headed for his first exile in Switzerland, where he planned to found the newspaper *Iskra* (The Spark), envisaged as an instrument to spread his conviction of the need for a revolutionary Marxist party. Its motto was: "A single spark can start a prairie fire," a statement open to both mystical and dialectical materialist interpretations.

From his starting point—Siberia—where he'd been locked up by order of the Tsar, to his place of arrival—Geneva—there is a long stretch, and so the guards (two particularly inept members of the Okhrana) relax their vigilance. Lenin takes advantage of the journey to read. Between Shushenskoye and Omsk he polishes off *The Iliad*; from Omsk to Kurgan he makes short work of *Decline and Fall of the Roman Empire*; from Kurgan to Izhevsk he tucks away *An Inquiry into the Nature and Causes of the Wealth of Nations*; between Izhevsk and Kostroma he pores over the *Principles of Political Economy*; between Kostroma and Novgorod he finally clears an old debt, *The Origin of the Family, Private Property and the State*; and from Novgorod to Pskov he permits himself a literary indulgence: *The Purloined Letter*.

A reader with a good enough map can confirm that by the time the expatriate closes the book of stories by Edgar Allan Poe, the troika is about to reach the Latvian border. Latvia: a small dent in the pockmarked map of post-Bismarckian Europe. A country where all distances are short. From Pskov to Riga there's barely a road. The obvious question: How was Lenin able to make a clandestine escape to Riga, visit the National Library, by chance or intention come across the *Spiritual Exercises* annotated by Andrei Deliuskin, and then use these jottings to further the evolution of Marxist thought . . . ? Did he take advantage of a long nap by Oleg and Magoleg? Did he toss a little sleep-inducing powder into their cups? Is it possible that he poisoned them ("the end sanctifies the means")?

In *My Life with Lenin*, Nadezhda Krupskaya mentions in passing that her husband's journey toward his first exile in Switzerland "was far from being a straight line." What is certain, however, is that Lenin never visited Riga (the closest he got to doing so was in March 1921, when Soviet Russia had to sign the humiliating "Peace of Riga" with Poland, but at the last minute he sent Ioffe in his place, given the latter's experience helping draw up the pragmatic pact of Brest-Litovsk). Since it's also completely obvious that Andrei Deliuskin and Vladimir Ilyich Ulyanov could not have known each other (except if my great-grandfather had been a ghost, immortal being, or vampire), it is clear that the influence of the first on the second, though crucial, was indirect. Or, to put it more clearly, mediated.

So. If Lenin made his journey to Switzerland without passing through Riga, then how did he know about my great-grandfather's annotations in Loyola's book?

To explain this, we have to go back a few years.

Between 1797 (the year Andrei Deliuskin spent a period reading and annotating the *Spiritual Exercises*) and 1850 (when the

Jesuit priest Bernard Stierli enters the scene), a series of minor events took place that suddenly began to draw the attention of religious communities in the area (from Latvia to Switzerland, from Switzerland to Belgium) until they required the intervention of an ecclesiastical authority. The acts in question were no different from those detailed by the tradition of miracles: astonishing conversions, impossible cures, levitations of the deceased, tears of blood spilt by the picture cards of virgins . . . the remarkable thing about these phenomena was that the majority of people attributed them not to the work of saints or the effects of the supernatural, but instead to a volume on a shelf of the National Library of Latvia, deep in the sleep of the rarely visited object: precisely the annotated copy of the *Spiritual Exercises*. Rumor had it that at night, the book radiated a soft golden glow that diffused the mentioned blessings. According to what was said, this wasn't a brilliance without heat but the opposite, a flame without fire, which had scorched to the bone those who'd dared handle it with intentions of theft. But the most astonishing thing was that even though it burned at the temperature of all the blazes of hell every night, the book remained incombustible.

Once news of these events reached his ears, Rigoberto de Nobili, the provincial in charge of the Jesuit monastery in Louvain, decided to order an investigation. It wasn't convenient to give the game away, of course, something that would happen if he were to comply with protocol and request the Latvian government to send him the book for examination; nor could he hire a petty thief to seize it. After thinking it over a bit, Nobili called to his cell Bernard Stierli (his right-hand man and devil's advocate), and after exchanging a few words with him, shared some details about the significance of his mission.

Nobili's decision to appoint him took place at an extremely delicate moment in Bernard Stierli's life. A great admirer of Robert

"Hammer of the Heretics" Bellarmine (he knew his books *Controversiae* and *The Art of Dying Well* like the back of his hand), Father Stierli's only sorrow in this world was never to have been assigned a mission at the level of his abilities. He'd been born too late to meet the founder at the heart of the Company, and had missed out on the missionary feats in Paraguay and the adventures of evangelization in China, Japan and Ethiopia . . . In short, he existed in the perpetual angst of feeling himself consumed by an objectless frenzy, which his rivals in the Company defined as an "eternal succession of small-potatoes crises." As soon as Nobili informed him of his task and destiny, Stierli had to contain himself so as not to cry out with joy. In under two hours, he was on his way.

He reached Riga early in the morning, dressed in civilian clothes. An unnecessary precaution, as no one noticed him. All was turmoil: the police had discovered neatly carved human parts scattered around the city.

Stierli ate a frugal breakfast, chose a pension room that suited the modesty of his funds, picked out an appropriate outfit and made his way toward the National Library. There he was disappointed by the lack of safety measures put in place by the institution to secure its most valuable work; the copy of the *Spiritual Exercises* remained open for public consultation. Out of an elementary impulse for prudence, he filled out the form with a false name, one that had Anglophile echoes and private resonances (to Charles Hope, a dear fellow student of the seminary, now deceased), and—like the Jesuit he was—he practiced a bit of the art of subterfuge by requesting Voltaire's *Candide*.

"Ah. Pornography. The good sir likes it filthy . . ." Gunda Gwrolin, the librarian and non-abstinent widow, licked her lips.

So as not to complicate his character's profile, over the next few days Stierli, disguised as Hope, requested and pretended to read volumes of memoirs by Casanova, by a German singer, by an English erotomaniac and by an unquestionably far more depraved solitary mariner (*Birds and Fish*). In the meantime, he kept an eye on the reading room: the flow of visitors, the bulk or slenderness of the spine in the tomes requested for consultation, the glimpsed contents of a box, the design of a cover. Every two or three hours, with the purported aim of courting Gwrolin, he would approach the counter and compliment the way she ran things, as out of the corner of his eye, he peeked at the form where she transcribed reading requests. Maybe this was a period of obscurity after the book's vulgar explosion of fame, or maybe the residents of Riga were too upset by the succession of murders to worry about the mysterious emanations of this volume or any other; the fact is that since his arrival, no one had requested the annotated copy of the *Spiritual Exercises*.

The days passed in vain. Stierli did all he could to gain the sympathy of Gunda and achieve the position of "trusted reader" (a category that allowed free consultation without prior completion of the form), from bringing her slightly withered bouquets of flowers (the shy plan of attack of the bungling gentleman caller) to inviting her out for an orange liqueur and finding himself being pawed in a dark suburban entryway—the Being, thank God, is not the Thing—as the fat drunk lady sucked on his ear and drew aside the heavy fabric layers of his undergarments. The episode left him perplexed. Technically it was impossible to verify whether he'd broken his vow of chastity or not. In any case, the alleged Hope had little time to verify it. As soon as he'd reached the position at which he'd been aiming, and was already meditating on the risks of stretching out his hand without further formalities toward the Loyolan tome . . . an unnecessary, comforting tragedy occurred. One more episode in the horrifying series of Riga crimes. Stierli felt a warm, Christian, relieved compassion when he found out.

A nice, sharp tip. Plunged straight in the heart. Luckily Gunda hadn't felt a thing.

The next day, there was a new librarian. A man. Everything has its limit and Stierli knew it wasn't time to start again. When he approached the counter and asked for the book, he barely maintained the discretion necessary to keep using his pseudonym. The librarian hesitated—a doubt, a suspicion by a possible police agent?—raised his quill filled with ink and thought for a few seconds. Then he said:

"*Exercises*, requested by Mr. Hope . . . is your surname with or without an 'H' at the start?"

This is the central moment in the life of Bernard Stierli. He's alone, almost alone, in the reading room, and in his hands he's got a treasure to sound out, the possibility of finding a proof for the true existence of the miraculous, a proof that, who knows, might open the closed doors that lead to the abyss: a demonstration of the existence of God. To achieve this leap, this demonstration, would justify his life . . . any life . . . the existence of the Universe itself . . . And to find it in a copy of a book by the founder of the order would be the ne plus ultra. Understandably, the Jesuit returns to his chair racked by emotion (just as fifty years before, Andrei Deliuskin had been *racked by writing*). He taps his fingers against the hard cover, trembling. And what if after the revelation there were no Paradise or truth, but instead . . . ? "Psst. Psst." "Eh?" "Do you feel all right, mister?" "Why?" "Are you shivering?" "Ah, yes, thank you dear, don't worry. It's my excitement, I mean, my age, Saint Vitus's dance." "Do you want me to call a . . . ?" "I don't want you to call anyone, damn it." "Well, pardon me then, what a temper." Chair legs scraping over the floor, the disappearing body of a woman. As always. Desire and regret: woman is a spirit the castles of theology don't know how to accommodate. Now, as he caresses the embossed gold letters with pious dread, Father Stierli remembers that Saint Ignatius was a kind of Don Quixote of the Church; his conversion, his fit of madness, occurred as he was taking a forced rest, following wounds suffered in the Battle of Pamplona, when the only distraction at hand was the New Testament. "What would my fate have been," Stierli wonders as he opens the copy of the *Spiritual Exercises*, "if instead of the Holy Scriptures, Loyola had stumbled upon *Amadís de Gaula*?" Closer than ever to the feeling of personal disappearance, the Jesuit murmurs: "Anima Christi, sanctifica me."

No warm wind sweeps through to rustle the pages of the book, pull it from his hands and send it spinning through the air. And you can forget about the sound of harps (God increases in discretion as he ages). But despite the poverty of effects, the event is of a radical order. Stierli leans over the first page and the reading comes as a shock, a convulsion. At the margin of the author's oracular introductory words (an entire declaration of principles), he finds the first phrases that Andrei Deliuskin, in his small industrious strokes, in his abysmal scribble, wrote over the course of that forgotten Riga summer of 1797. The opening invocation (because some phrases are prayers) already seems to simplify and contain and position in its true dimension the full essence of Loyola's concerns:

How does a spirit move?

Stierli trembles with joy. At night, from his room in the pension, he writes to Rigoberto de Nobili, the brevity of his missive a testament to the happiness that overwhelms him: "Everything is true."

Belief is one thing and proof another. With the perceptiveness that characterizes him, Stierli knows that in addition to being the traditional investigation of a Church expert attempting to disentangle the subtle differences between the mystical trance and the hysterical fit, his work must aim toward a resolution of the following questions: Why is miraculous power attributed to this (and not another) copy of the *Spiritual Exercises*? Is it due to some particularity of design or typography in the printed matter itself? Or is it perhaps due to the annotations made by somebody totally unknown in the margins (as he believes, and wagers on this belief)?

Every morning, Stierli wanders around Riga and the surrounding areas trying to separate the wheat from the chaff, the miracle from the knockoff. And every afternoon, seated at the table of the empty consultation room, supplied with quill and ink, leaning like a cribbing student over the second copy of the *Spiritual Exercises* he's managed to acquire, which every day he brings into the National Library as contraband, he transcribes my great-grandfather's annotations with a reverent and faithful hand, both in the spirit of the letter and in its calligraphic form. The ink is special, acquired at the shop of a known antiquities forger, such that every stroke, as soon as it dries, plausibly imitates the damages of time. But that's important only at the level of visibility. In essence, as his hand goes moving over the pages, the old and devoted Jesuit transforms into the quivering incarnation of a great, already dead young man: my great-grandfather. Stierli reads with him, understands with him, interprets with him, writes with him. And in doing so, slowly, completely, he finds that the extent of Loyola's work begins to open up in its significance. During each of these afternoons of copying, as he advances letter by letter, he feels how the signs of utmost comprehension gradually take possession of his being. "It isn't possible to understand the whole without celestial guidance," he thinks. "What's more, it isn't possible these annotations were written by a single person. They seem to come straight from a divine mind that wants to guide a truth into the world, one hidden until now, an unexpected *reform* in the plan of creation. But why me? Why has it fallen to me to reveal it?"

Stierli suspects and fears, of course. In spite of his role as devil's advocate, it's hard for him to believe in the physical existence of Satan, yet he doesn't reject the possibility that such a being might exist as a complementary figure within the systems of trial and punishment that are part of the economy of salvation. If this is the case, he thinks, then any questioning of his purpose in the Almighty's plan could be the preface to a terrible error, maybe even his own fall. But he consoles himself: "God may not spare His efforts, but neither does He squander them uselessly. He wouldn't do all of this just to condemn me. After all, what am I to Him? Less than nothing." Maybe—he tells himself—he's being overly suspicious about everything. Even so, the figure he's created for himself draws his attention. The greatest nestles within the smallest: a Jesuit copies the texts of an illuminated scribe, God Himself perhaps, who at some moment deigned to silently come down from the throne and sit in a chair at the Riga Library in order to write these marginal notes, corrections, improvements to the work of the founder of the Society of Jesus. Is this a circle? Or might it perhaps be an ascending spiral, an elliptical movement toward a heaven our eyes can't make out?

Astonishment can be a vocation, a sublime aide to faith, but even the most credulous will find his capacity for surprise diminish when such marvel becomes routine. Over the years, Stierli has got used to grinding away at the most arduous texts, a training that allows him to anticipate the moment his intelligence will catch up to or surpass the ideas of the powerful minds whose course he's following, yet now he finds himself before a capacity that exceeds his. He judges the paths taken by my great-grandfather's thought

to be unexpected, his constructions to be fanciful and his deriva-
tions to be abrupt leaps, flares of a truth that doesn't require the
onerous scaling of syllogisms, but whose ultimate logic somehow
knots into a point where it is possible to glimpse infinity. And
the strangest thing is the lack of style, as if this writing didn't
require a man (or any being) to be written. A serene or supreme
impersonality, not urgent or demonstrative, but whose very reticence, when tapped to sound it out, divulges beneath the entire
phrase, as well as within each particular concept, bottomless pits
where dimensions smolder, awaiting discovery. In these moments
of terror or abjection, Stierli believes himself to be in the presence of a machine or monster. He writes to Rigoberto de Nobili
again. His tone is no longer that of a pure, limpid happiness, but
is flecked with anxiety: "Simple in a complicated way. Sublime,
or rather: Ineffable." Nobili doesn't answer: he keeps silent and
waits. Stierli continues his process. The truths, which impose
themselves on him each day as perfections of form, accept a subsequent expansion of meaning that works to either complement
or oppose them, without these scruples invalidating the original
postulations. To sum up: he's stunned by the blast effect that follows the detonation, with its rippling waves of both intellectual
and practical consequences, capable of being measured only at the
moment when these writings—Andrei Deliuskin's annotations—
are distributed to the minds of their intended recipients, whether
these be a universal subject, the entire species or—taking into
account the book where they make their appearance—the members of the Jesuit order.

In any case, and as Loyola himself also said: "Do it yourself."
He has to keep on copying, keep on thinking. And at the same
time, not neglect the world. For some time now, Stierli has begun
to feel he's the object of a number of stares that don't seem incidental. Without effort he notices how an individual wearing

a peculiar jabot, trousers, spats and red trilby follows him over the few blocks of his evening route, then is replaced by another dressed entirely in black. Stierli believes he's been discovered by his fraternal adversaries, the Dominicans, who naturally must also be after the secret in the library copy of the *Spiritual Exercises* (with the likely intention of vilifying it, accusing it of fraudulence or interpreting it in their own way, for the purposes of their own order). But he's wrong. The ones dogging his steps are no more than low-ranking police officers, since his name—that is, his pseudonym, Hope—appears on the list of suspects to be investigated for what Europe has already begun to call the Riga crimes. Ever since the world has been the world, State powers have treated the word "foreigner" as a near synonym for "criminal." In any case, Stierli's inclusion on the list does have a certain degree of relevance, given that as Hope, he enjoyed a fleeting connection with one of the terms in the series, or more precisely one of its victims: Gunda Gwrolin. Both the police and the interested party are unaware of this. Which is a shame, since if Stierli had paid some attention to the matter, following the consecutive links and the sequence, then starting from the third or fourth crime he'd have had no problem deducing the logical criterion and patronymic that guided the hand of the murderer.

Who was it?

Let's leave his identity in suspense for a moment, as we concentrate on his biography: an unhappy childhood with blows of a poker across his knuckles, inflicted by an alcoholic father; incomplete penetrations by an older brother, an unemployed miner. And then, the first acts of revenge: he becomes a specialist in piercing the tiny eyes of larks, and cultivates his aura of doom by pinching useless objects from abandoned houses. In late adolescence, a certainty about the importance of his being fills him, and the consequent need to share this news with the rest of the planet is revealed. Someone tells him that Nero became famous by burning Rome. "Let's see, what can I do to achieve that same end?" he asks himself. In Riga's buildings, there is more stone than wood. That's why he decides to cement his glory without resorting to fire, and instead chooses his victims based on the first letter of their surnames, which, emerging in successive order with the unfolding of events, will announce his own: every small-time criminal harbors the allegorical intent of the lesser intelligence. To kill, to stain his hands with blood, gives him the same amount of pleasure as to imagine the way he'll reveal himself, and the moment an astute detective will proceed to arrest him. And if this doesn't happen at the end of the first struggle, then there will be other, even more spectacularly morbid rounds . . . But just in case (out of fear of being misunderstood), he offers the poor alternative of a coded message, whose text he copies onto sixteen pages of graph paper: "Sixteen people will be annihilated and carved up, their remains scattered through the city, only because I want to proclaim, to the reverence and horror of History, that my surname is composed of the first letters of the surnames of every person dead by my hand." With zero result, Mr. Aglarevopphigius—limping, scrawny, insignificant, bug-eyed, celibate and ugly—pastes up these messages in the bathrooms of the city's bars, after he's accentuated the first letter of his surname with blood.

But it doesn't end here. *There is another sign.* For Aglarevopphigius, the choice of a surname is also the choice of the organ or body part that will be hacked by his dagger, perforated by his bullet, corroded by his poison, squeezed by his rope. Thus the eminent watchmaker **A**cantus receives a gunshot to the **A**bdomen, and **G**immel bleeds to death after his murderer chews his **G**lans . . . The strangest choice by Aglarevopphigius is precisely Gunda **G**wrolin, victim to a dagger that slashes her intestine. Could it be for gassy, gastric, greasy?

How to know? Poor Aglarevopphigius was never arrested, and Stierli, who stayed at the margins of the evolution of this affair (though not at its close) remained convinced that a group of conspirers knew of his mission and was dogging his steps.

Believing the fence of persecution to be closing around him, Stierli hurries. He copies quickly, without stopping or thinking, and runs the risk of committing an error, producing a variation in the handwriting, in the expression, in the meaning of my great-grandfather's annotations.* One afternoon, he marks the dot of a full stop to end his work. It's the most delicate moment of his mission: the one when he must perform the substitution, leaving behind his copy and taking the original to Louvain; it's also, therefore, the moment any enemy would pounce upon to denounce him as a thief and falsifier. This is why, anticipating the trap, Stierli *walks out of the library with the copy*. The operation is typical of his extremely subtle intelligence, and also his propensity for stupendous error. If they trap or capture what's in his hands, the thieves won't have what they're looking for, but its simulacrum. Furthermore, if the transcription is artful in spirit and letter, won't it fundamentally be indistinguishable from the original? For the first time in months, Stierli treads the streets of Riga with the look of a satisfied delinquent. He takes one step, then another. His guilty right hand caresses and reveals the secret pocket in his coat where he stores the book-decoy. To his surprise, no one stops him, no one assaults him, no one asks him to give back or hand over what's been stolen.

At this point in events, some clever reader will question the rationality of the entire operation. Or at least, the grounds for belief in the singular and ambiguously miraculous status conferred on the book annotated by Deliuskin, which wouldn't apply to the

* Some scholars claim that beginning from the "second week" stipulated by Loyola, Father Bernard Stierli's work of transcription moves away from Andrei Deliuskin's text and introduces new clauses.

one that Stierli reproduced in its image and likeness. Doesn't the aura of the first item also extend to its reproductions? If, in this case, the fallacy of the axiom that postulates the uniform value of a series were demonstrated—the axiom that would soon be popularized, among others, by the inventor of the printing press—then wouldn't this constitute a refutation of Catholicism, which grants the same truth-producing ability to the first figure of the faith (be this Christ, the Virgin or the saints) as to supernatural appearances and material copies?

Similar questions hound Stierli himself, but abiding by his subordination to the canon, he suspends his doubt and skepticism. By the time he's at last convinced that no one has mounted guard to catch him red-handed, it's already grown dark.

The oblique Riga night sees him retrace his steps and slip under the banner on the third floor of the library. Agitated (he no longer has the age for such gymnastics), he tiptoes in sandals over the black and white diamonds. In the shadows, every simple line of shelves takes on the density of a gothic thicket. Stierli, who over the past few weeks has memorized the dimensions of the place, walks blindly, arms stretched out, avoiding obstacles by centimeters. It's as if divine providence were guiding him toward the shelf with the book that must be stolen and replaced . . . All at once, just a few steps from the sanctuary, he must stop. He hears a rustle of clothes brush against the walls. Stierli feels a movement of air like a blade, and without thinking he raises an arm. He stops one blow and launches another of his own with the edge of his hand, then hears the music of a stifled whimper, the gurgle of an agony. Everything accelerates. With a confused motion, he pulls the copy from his clothes and substitutes, or thinks he substitutes, the original, which he grabs hold of before he flees. In his flight along the rooftops he doesn't notice the pale crescent moon of the Turkish flag with its two yellow horns, a bite from the heavens soaked in blood, the colors of Islam.

Did our Jesuit think he'd killed someone? A secret and efficient but unlucky pursuer? The night watchman doing his rounds, his furtive lover? It's hard to find a style for presenting events when these take on the inconsistency of the fantastic. In any case, there's no doubt that over the course of the night Stierli *did* commit murder. Obviously it wasn't a voluntary act. An agnostic would claim that the crime can be attributed to the elegance of chance. Yes. *Aglarevopphigius.* Just like every night, he stands leaning dangerously over the parapet of the bridge that crosses the Dvina River, meditating about his scheme for personal advancement. Should he give the world a little help and announce that, scattered throughout the letters of his surname, one can find the first letter of the Hebrew alphabet? Would it suit him to sacrifice a newborn on his birthday (also his own, obviously: Aglarevopphigius gets tangled up with possessives because he has always confused the distinction between himself and others)? And what about turning himself in to the police department (at least it will get him some press coverage)? Or maybe he should put the kibosh on himself in some glorious way?

Meditations. Aglarevopphigius looks without seeing at the dapples of sky-blue color that tint the brown river for a few seconds; then there's a quick gold gleam, and a spermatic furrow traces a little curve with a flick of the tail. A "plic," then nothing. Instead of raising his head to anticipate the burning stripe where the sun will appear, Aglarevopphigius leans over just a bit more, at precisely the moment Stierli runs by his side (his, his). The mere breeze of his movement delivers the fatal push. The waters open up with a murmur of disgust or welcome. Homicide or suicide? In the end, no one can remain indifferent to the dilemma of interpretation this (final) point of encounter suggests between Aglarevopphigius and Stierli, two subjects apparently linked to such disparate forms of the unspeakable.

5

The arrival at the Louvain monastery of Andrei Deliuskin's annotated edition introduced a transformative symbol into the heart
of the Society of Jesus, whose appearance was as radical as the
Spiritual Exercises had been within the landscape of medieval mysticism. Until then, the ideal of perfection had been thought to
be attainable only through union with God, a process that came
about as the effect of a gift, divine grace, not as a consequence
of human merit. This is why the new *inspired contemplation*
established a difference not of degree but of kind with respect to
acquired contemplation, an approach that was praiseworthy and
deserving of every compliment, but possessed only a limited
range, since its origin was found in the will of man to establish
union. By means of the extraordinary gift of *inspired contemplation*, on the other hand, the mystic loses all relationship with
the senses (reason and memory vanish, and images, forms and
comparisons fade away), so that the words later narrating the
experience cannot account for what has occurred; faced with
this impossibility offered as spectacle, the unutterable lashes the
souls of the ones who are not gifted (the mass of practitioners of
acquired contemplation), who feel the uselessness of their efforts to
obtain a contact that in the end will always be of inferior quality.
It isn't strange that the superior capacity of the religious orders to
access an extraordinary state of illumination, supposedly granted

by the transcendental realm to individuals selected at random, finds its analogy in a political state that has no intrinsic justification, but confers every power of authority upon crowned or papal heads. The publication of the *Spiritual Exercises*—as Lenin would clearly understand after reading my great-grandfather Andrei Deliuskin's annotations—produces a breakdown in this theory, as it demolishes the metaphysical foundations of the hypothetical preeminence of the contemplative method for gaining entry to a different arrangement of reality. Although on its face it derives from the religious field, Loyola's book (staying with Lenin) is one of the first ideological productions to wager itself on building a cosmovision suitable to the early bourgeoisie, an emerging social class that invests its egalitarian and proto-democratic force in the desire to possess everything, obtain everything, understand everything, and whose *aspiration* (zealous, though in no way *inspired*) is to *acquire* everything . . . even contact with God.

But let's not anticipate the course of events; we're better off going to the cloisters.

Once back in Louvain, Father Bernard Stierli holds an audience with Rigoberto de Nobili. The contents of this meeting remain secret, like an extraction of confession. But the consequences are sweeping. Briefly: Andrei Deliuskin's annotations transform into an object for reading and discussion within the convent. The atmosphere grows feverish. Different methods are used to approach the text, which produce a variety of readings. Each perspective has its advocates and can boast refined triumphs of interpretation, but none is satisfactory to everybody. The waters divide: from every opinion an internal faction emerges, and within every faction, there bud jealousies, resentments and reproaches. The crisis expands, the dissensions grow serious. Reprimanded by the Head of Rome, Rigoberto de Nobili turns to a model of organized study and debate that reinforces the hierarchical system, limiting the common desire to access a single truth of the text by withdrawing it from consultation: he keeps it in the cupboard of his cell, which always stays locked.

The sudden absence of the annotated copy is felt by the mass of students and priests as a metaphysical void, a whorl that absorbs everything and calms all violence, replacing it with nostalgia. Nobili takes advantage of the dramatic effect and puts himself center stage. He organizes a ceremony to celebrate the end of discord and restores the book to its place, now making it accessible to anyone who wishes to see it, conditional on prior inscription in a "reading circle" of the annotations. As this scheme is an imitation of the concentric model proposed by the *Divine Comedy*, each circle is led by a "guide" (naturally, a member of the group around Nobili) who orients, authorizes or discards the interpretations of the "guided," and regularly informs on possible doctrinal deviations or progress in the correct understanding of the material studied. And it's Nobili, of course, who personally manages the progressions. Occasional rebellions, bouts of free interpretation, are routinely punished with the descent of several circles. Inversely, any promotion suggests prior compliance. Many of those enrolled decide to pay the price of subordination: the rumor spreads that at the last level, called "supreme" or *coelum*, every "ascendant" can leave their "guide" outside the Sancta Sanctorum and enjoy the privilege of direct contact—limited to twenty-four hours—with Andrei Deliuskin's annotations. (In general, out of conviction or hypocrisy, after this complete day of seclusion the "ascendant" leaves the Consultation Room with the expression that ancient tales attribute to mystic union.)

In spite of its thoroughness, this attempt at ordering produces a backlash; some sectors accuse Nobili of being a papist and claim he forms part of a conservative reaction trying to moderate, cover up or eliminate the most piquant meanings that would emerge from a free reading. Believing his condition of "primary witness" puts him above disputes, an already slightly senile Bernard Stierli tries to work as an impartial broker between factions: someone stabs him during a confused nocturnal episode in the refectory. The gesture of terrorized contrition that endures on his face at the wake serves as a balm for spirits wounded by tragedy. After the burial of this illustrious brother, in a grand political gesture, the head monk relaxes some of the strictest policies and eliminates intermediate steps. My great-grandfather's annotations become accessible even to novices. Curiously, this slackening of discipline coincides with a moment when almost no one seeks to consult the copy. It's as if the systole-diastole of prohibition and liberation has made its potentialities less vivid and exhausted its most catalytic truths. Beneath the apparently calm surface of things, my great-grandfather's work turns into a kind of deep-sea fish, a living fossil that continues to move through the murky waters, navigating by its own strange light. Only now it's the book itself, rather than its contents, that makes it a ritual fetish object.

It's lodged in a special air-conditioned room guarded by constantly burning oil lamps, inside a cupboard of palo santo wood, on a mantle of red velvet . . . In parallel with this process, the disillusionment and suspicion keep growing. Some youthful elements, swept up by the agnostic spirit of the period, claim the *Spiritual Exercises* are a mere summary (or plagiarism) of other ascetic-mystical works like the *Book of Exercises* of the Benedictine abbot García de Cisneros, the *Vita Christi* of Ludolph of Saxony and the *Imitatio Christi* of Thomas à Kempis, compendiums in turn of prior books . . . This would of course make my great-grandfather's annotations no more than a tiresome academic exegesis drafted by an anonymous dull-witted scribe, unable to pick up on this disappointing genealogy. The book turns into an irritating vestige of hypothetical fraud. Someone proposes a bonfire to purify everything. One day, an anonymous hand moves forward at last and replaces the copy with a rat's dissected corpse; the scandal of the operation wanes when faced with an absence of repercussions. At some moment, lack of interest and an overwhelming fatigue saturate everything. The annotated edition of the *Spiritual Exercises* returns to its place, the rat's flung in a trash bin and who gives a damn.

The years go by. The new generation of Jesuits is unaware of the peculiar qualities of the book on display and tend to adore it, taking for granted it's an original edition, or the manuscript that Loyola himself wrote. A fresh enthusiasm fills their souls. Prayers, songs, music, trances. Every initiate begins to feel the enormous privilege of being in contact with something whose true dimensions only time will reveal. Slowly, the quiet atmosphere of the room goes about adopting the characteristics of a bazaar. Along with the ritual oil lamps that once illuminated the volume's worn-out edges for nobody, one can now find incense sticks, crosses resting on the glass and portraits of sick family members. One day, a leper sets up at the gates of the monastery and says he won't leave the place until they let him worship the "miracle book." The circuit begins again, but nothing is the same. The subtlety of the debates is now accompanied by a historical investigation that tries to distinguish the relationships and contrasts (if they existed) between Loyola and his commentator; there are even speculations (which there had never been before) about the identity of the author of the annotations. Rigoberto de Nobili, who might have been a special witness to some fragments of what happened, has been impeded from speech and movement for two decades by quadriplegia. Be that as it may, when at the end of the nineteenth century the head monk delivers up his soul to God, the Louvain monastery is renowned as the Church's greatest center of intellectual luminosity.

And here we return to Lenin.

6

Stuttgart, March 1902. Vladimir Ilyich Ulyanov publishes *What Is to Be Done?* In this text, Lenin proposes the creation of a party of professional revolutionaries. His formulations are deliberately simple. In fact, he has read Saint Augustine and recalls his phrase: "When asked the question 'What is to be done?' the ancient world contributed 288 responses." In September of the same year, he writes *A Letter to a Comrade on Our Organizational Tasks*, which gives a new clue about where his concerns are heading. For years he's been embroiled in an unproductive argument with Plekhanov, who accuses him of being excessively "centralist." He, in turn, accuses his comrades of the Russian Social-Democratic Labor Party (RSDLP) of fueling the endless debates, the "verbalism." He is sure he has to impose discipline on the militants, make them conscious they form part of a collective project; his true aim is to build an organism with rigid structures prepared to battle for power. In this sense, Lenin's first impulse is to mimic the operations of the traditional army (whether it be Prussian, Russian or French). But soon he notices that this model, although efficient in many respects, above all in training, discipline and hierarchical subordination, lacks an ethos of finality, and is motivated only by its own preservation as a form. The traditional army—as he understands it—is the crystallization of an idea, an accomplished and intellectually dead machine, not an instrument of possible use. *No recognized army will change the world.* Therefore one must look in another direction. Is there a new kind of army? Does a working model exist?

Yes. Without a doubt. And it's been on earth for several centuries.

Getting his fix of costumes and role play, a vice that marks him out from other revolutionaries, an exiled Lenin leaves his residence in Berne and presents himself at the doors of the Louvain monastery, dressed in the habits of a Benedictine. He claims to be lost and asks permission to spend the night.

"I'll make do with a hard bench in the refectory," he says.

Acknowledging his request, they lead him to a dark silent room. Obedient as a corpse, he lies down in the corner they point out to him. The trip has been exhausting, and he falls asleep immediately. He wakes with the sun. The first thing he sees is the mysterious movement of a painted leather sphere, entranced in circles as by the pull of a magnet and coming to a halt after its final spin: a globe. Then he sees a long, sculpted nail; the index finger that made it turn on its axis. Lenin sits up.

"Am I under arrest?"

Philippe de Groiselliere, the new head of Louvain and owner of the finger, replies:

"To obstruct freedom of movement does not form a part of the training we provide here . . . comrade."

"I see it's no use going on hiding my identity," smiles Lenin.

"Nor do we speculate about the identity of anyone," says Groiselliere. "But we do always enjoy receiving visits from the outside world. Especially if it's someone who doesn't belong to our circle of relations and influences. May I ask to what we owe the honor . . . ? Or will you allow me to go ahead and imagine the reasons?"

"It's the least I can do, as I've already obliged you to play the role of my host."

"Well then. I gather the reason for your arrival at this operational center of the Society of Jesus has nothing to do with the desire to strike up eschatological dialogue. It isn't theory that brings you, but hard practice."

"Is it necessary to so brutally divide the two aspects?" protests Lenin. "The great historical failures have their origin in theoretical deviations that are, in the end, philosophical ones . . . "

Groiselliere interrupts him:

"Far from being philosophy, religion is the field of thought that determines, if not the successes and failures of revolutionary politics, then at least the ability to name and explain them. Indeed, religion builds up a knowledge of universal expedience starting from an administrative criterion: an interpretation of the facts based on how well they fit or diverge from the plan of divine economy."

"That is, religion is the agency responsible for the transcendental nomination of political avatars . . ."

"At least so we Jesuits understand it. And don't play the idiot, because it's precisely thanks to your having understood the results of this insight that you've taken the trouble to briefly escape from your little friends in the Party . . . Martov, Kamenev, Zinoviev, all that lot. Welcome to the game of grand politics . . . Coffee? A glass of water?"

"You don't have vodka? I couldn't find a single bottle in all of Switzerland."

"No."

"Water, then. One question. How do you manage without women? It's not that I . . ."

"Perfectly well, thank you. What, precisely, is the matter that brings you here?"

"I don't know if I should . . ."

"You can call me Philippe, my dear Vladimir Ilyich. You're among people you can trust: the arm of Nicholas II's secret service does not reach here. And, of course, I'll take everything you tell me as a secret of the confessional."

"In that case . . . There's something I want to know!"

"I'm listening . . ."

"If a religion is a State, or at least a State of Matters of the Faith, what I'd like to understand is how Paul the Apostle could invent Catholicism starting from Christ, a subject who lacked being at the moment the Pauline truth was announced. Because, let's not forget, at that moment He was dead, and Paul . . ."

"Saint, please . . ."

". . . and Saint Paul announced as a transcendent truth the only impossible event in the existence of Jesus: the Resurrection. I want to know, basically, how Saint Paul organized his religious party by crossing a subject no longer living with an unprovable event. I want to know how, starting from this convergence of absurdities, he founded the possibility of a doctrine in history that includes the entire human species."

"A Marxist wants to dream up his own Jesus, to generate action in the world through a political law?"

"Yes. Except now it's no longer the Son, but the Party."

"Ah, but how interesting . . . And what is the place of God the Father in your system?"

"With all due respect . . ."

"With all due respect, you want to say that from your point of view God is unnecessary, that theology is a field of study with no object, and that nothing in the Universe is better, greater or truer than what we ourselves are able to create. It means that for you, there are proofs and yet nothing is sacred. And therefore you can absolve yourself of all truth with capital letters, or all illusion of truth, prepared instead to build a conceptual artifact based on efficiency."

"You might say that I want to encourage an ideal, or at least a reflection on the possibility of collective belief . . ."

"If you want it, thy will be done. Do you know the famous phrase 'Cathedrals are made with mud and dung, but are not themselves mud and dung'?"

"No."

"I'll bequeath it to you. Now you can quote it from armored trains, balconies, pulpits and rostrums whenever you want to inflame the proletariat with your speeches. What I can tell you is that Saint Paul's bid for resurrection doesn't require the prior life of Christ; in his opinion the 'realist' biographical story (which the rest of the Apostles take up in detail) even disfigures the story's perfection."

"The resurrection of a being without a previous life to justify it . . . What a splendid idea!"

"Indeed it is . . . the uncaused cause. That is, God, or His most magnificent invention, religion."

"And so . . ."

"And so, brother Vladimir Ilyich Ulyanov, welcome. Brother Francisco will show you to your cell . . ."

"One last question."

"Yes . . . ?"

"There are issues linked to setting up the Party, guiding the masses, and struggling against amateurish enthusiasm and economist tendencies before we seize control of the government. And then, once the stage of triumphant insurrection is complete, there's the question of how to manage the State and build a socialism that . . ."

"Yes . . . ?"

"What I mean is, how did Saint Paul receive . . ."

"Grace?"

"Grace, yes. Or let's say, the miracle of his marvelous invention."

"As the last Christian and founder of Catholicism," said Groiselliere, "he wasn't conditioned or converted by anyone, and so in his case we can dispense with the moralist claptrap about 'mystical illumination' as a prize for effort and suffering. Saint Paul was all bad breath, ferocity, calculation and the will to power. Like Saint Ignatius of Loyola, you might say. Well. Where were we? Ah. As for your stay in this monastery . . . you can leave the door of your cell unlocked."

"But what about my belongings?"

"Don't worry about them; here everything belongs to everyone. We Jesuits consider property to be theft."

To judge by events, Lenin's stay at Louvain monastery bore its fruits. In July 1903, after nine months of seclusion and training, he reappeared in Brussels and London where the Second Congress of the Russian Social-Democratic Labor Party was taking place. By pure strength of determination—"reality is power, everything else is illusion"—he led debates and captured for his faction (the Bolsheviks) a sizable chunk of the leadership and party membership. His firm decision to organize and lead a partisan system that sought to forge an ideology and represent society's transformative forces would in time become a political perspective and modus operandi known as "Leninism." Obviously, those in the know would also have baptized it—the verb isn't accidental—as "practical Loyolism," or better yet, "Deliuskinism." But Philippe de Groiselliere, along with the rest of the Jesuits, preferred to remain silent in this respect. Even after a few decades, works about the Society of Jesus as well as biographies of the Soviet leader neglect to mention the initiation of Vladimir Ilyich Ulyanov (Lenin) into the tactics and strategies that helped him to organize the Party and take power, imparted by the Jesuits and based on my great-grandfather's interpretation of Ignatius of Loyola's *Spir-*

itual Exercises.*

Naturally, having reached this point, many readers will find incomprehensible the blithe way that my great-grandfather washed his hands of all responsibility—or paternity—with respect to his annotations of Loyola, as if he didn't suspect their importance and dimensions, or as if he'd decided to attribute to them a merely provisional character, as a simple draft of future works. Maybe a sudden desire for violent suns and strange moons drove him to cast aside such adventures of thought, or maybe he felt—all at once, as a revelation—that the proper name that emerged from his annotations condensed the meaning of his work. The fact is that one day, in the midst of a phrase that unfolded in a series of variations on the famous "Meditation on Three Binaries," his pen wrote the words: "Napoleon Bonaparte." Andrei stopped, read his writing, gave a quiet sigh, rested his head for a minute on the palm of his hand, then closed the *Spiritual Exercises*, in so doing knocking the inkwell over the table. The ink gave a delicate gurgle before tracing out an anamorphic lake, a chimera, a daguerreotype of Arthur Rimbaud blurred by overexposure to desert fires, and the voluptuous ass of his future wife, appearing in the shadows of the closed room at noon. Then he stood up, walked out of the National Library and left Riga, never to return again.

---

* To establish the causal relationship between Andrei Deliuskin's writings and Leninist praxis, one must keep in mind *the question of procedure.*

As soon as he took control of the government, the Bolshevik leader handed over the exploitation of oil riches drawn from Russian soil to capitalists from the United States and England—something that the deposed Tsar had never dared to do—in exchange for a fabulous injection of money, which he applied to the sustained development of the productive forces. To put it another way, he used imperial powers to invent the working class in his country in order to justify the former Proletarian Revolution. Doesn't this gesture show true understanding of the efficiency of the Pauline achievement, which founds the greatest ideological institution in the West—the Roman Church—on what Lenin calls a "nonexistent event" (the Resurrection of Jesus)? Such a political gesture—which no "leftist" understood at the time—clearly reveals to us that he took maximum advantage of the lessons imparted during his months at the monastery.

7

Andrei Deliuskin leaves the desks behind and reveals himself to be a serious but free young man: available, game for small adventures. He works with the stevedores in Danzig; his back broadens, his muscles swell. Incursion into fishing: tunas. A return to the port: cups and whores. Contrary to all expectations, he doesn't want to rescue them or attempt anything other than to possess them multiple times, with an enthusiasm that recalls his father's early years and notably exceeds his capacity for payment. Andrei fornicates like someone bleeding himself dry. Vlamincka Vilnius, the madame of the establishment (whom the more forward clients call Baby), notes this client's abilities and, taking account of his merits, can't help but admire the length of his carnal baton, the exquisiteness of his lightly schizoid style, the trembling shakes of his head and his general pinkish tone, which makes him look like a sturgeon anxious to swim upstream in search of a corner where he can spawn. The fine braiding of his frenulum, which he occasionally uses as a halter, definitively leaves her in ecstasy. But it's a kind of granule, an oblong formation with sebaceous characteristics, palpitating in an unnerving and independent way, that most takes her breath away: under the smooth, slack skin, which draws back like a virgin's at the slightest graze of her tongue's tip, a society of homunculi seems to doze, the true principle of generation. Lying on the bed, naked, arms behind his head in the form of a pillow, Andrei allows himself to be inspected. His face paints a dandyish smile—unexpected on a young man of his age—as he says: "I'm like a monkey. I can repeat the same act an infinite number of times." Baby offers him a contract with an insanely high figure and the possibility of rejecting clients once he's fulfilled his average daily quota. Andrei rejects the offer and continues on his journey.

Olsztyn. Białystok. Does he go in the direction of Warsaw? No. After a detour, he passes through Lublin and arrives in Radom. Katowice. Krakow. Hungary? The hinterland of Central Europe? His movement forms the sketch of his hesitations. He seems to be guided by a southern tropism, with a slight tendency toward the East. All at once, a turn upward. Budapest, Linz, Munich, Stuttgart, Nuremberg, Erfurt, Leipzig, Dortmund, Hanover. In Amsterdam he gets work at an optician's as a polisher. In his daily activity there's a deceleration of the machine of thought, but since he works with magnifying lenses, he gets used to seeing shapes with an amplified grain. One afternoon, at a café, he meets a young lady. Barely have they exchanged a few words before she reveals her age, confesses she's not a virgin but is single, and tells him that she's in no rush to get married. Immediately Andrei takes these confidences as the flirtatious strategy of a woman presuming to be "modern." While she's speaking, Alicia Varmon's gaze is somewhere else, which doesn't seem to be a consequence of crossed eyes, but a strategy that lets her consider the merits of those present in the abstract. Andrei, in contrast, is perfectly conscious of each one of the details her clothes hide: the full waist, the warm milky thighs, the chestnut-colored pubic hair . . .

"Do you believe that everything that is possible, so long as it's thinkable, exists and is therefore likely to be realized on earth?" he asks.

Varmon smiles for the first time (Andrei sees her uneven, healthy teeth) and looks at him out of the corner of her eye:

"Are you proposing an episode of sexual debauchery, or looking for the perfect definition of utopia?"

Andrei doesn't need to hear anything else to know he's in love.

Despite the promise of immediacy broached by this first dialogue, over the course of the next few meetings my great-grandfather discovers that fleshly access to his beloved is complicated. Although she speaks easily about the habits of different peoples—English pleasures, French tastes, Turkish glandular perversions—the possibilities of concretion go on being delayed. At every meeting, like the act of a malevolent God, Alicia appears escorted by a girlfriend. If this is a plan seeking to exalt her intrinsic merits by means of obstacles and rebuffs . . . then such dubious cleverness doesn't stimulate or excite him. Martha Velin is dark, squat, plump and useless for anything but irritation. Through a strange insistence that Andrei understands to be romantic scruples, Alicia always insists on meeting him at the same time, at the same Viennese café, as their first meeting. And Martha Velin is present at every occasion, silent, impassive, her posture impeccable, her flabby flesh pressing into the iron back of the rococo chair (on the rare occasions she leaves them alone for a moment to go to the ladies' room, Andrei is repulsed to observe the damning mark, the red magnolia-shaped furrow traced into the fat sow's back). With his sensitivity honed by loathing, Andrei, who was never able to draw more than a rude monosyllable from her in the time when he still felt compelled to address her a word, thinks he hears murmurs of decay in that detestable organism. The internal wheezing of emphysema, the overly fluid gurgle of blood overflowing a cerebral artery about to burst, the plops of a chain reaction of explosions in the stomach diverticula.

Occasionally Alicia displays the fickleness of her mood: she prefers to go for a stroll. She takes Andrei's arm, but it's Martha Velin who handles her parasol, who protects her from the sun's rays and whispers in her ear.

One day, however, the unexpected occurs: the chaperone doesn't show up to a meeting. Andrei, who's built up every illusion of happiness (even the ephemeral kind) based on getting rid of her presence, can't help but realize that his budding emotion has a different quality than he'd expected. Being without Martha Velin is like floating in a void—agreeable, yes, but somewhat dull. Joined to Alicia, Martha is a repugnant pustule, a gob of spit in the face of beauty; jerked away all of a sudden, it tears something from the being to which it was attached: it's as if his love were missing a vital element. Free now, Andrei doesn't quite know what to do. And although he can vouch for the continued urgency of his desire, no longer under surveillance—every time he takes Alicia by the elbow to cross the street, every time her breast brushes against his arm—the strength of this emotion remains temporarily displaced by his curiosity about what has happened to his enemy. The rest of the outing is pleasant enough. They visit the Cathedral, where Alicia insists on kneeling before the stone slabs of the high altar that preserve the remains of her most important ancestors. Then they take a stroll around City Park, where they delight in the feats of the giant Belinzone, a Hercules nearly two meters tall, in a muscle shirt and tights glued to his thighs, trained to lift a gypsy caravan with his head as he launches fire from his mouth. She claps like a girl and blushes when Belinzone tosses her a sweet-smelling flower. When they reach Alicia's home again, it's already night. At the moment of the goodbye, believing that Martha's absence permits him to act in a freer way, Andrei makes a move to approach his love and kiss her on the lips, but she anticipates him: she brings up her right hand to Andrei's chest with a gesture to stop his advance, then suddenly lets it drop to his groin, keeping her fist open with its fingers slightly curved as if wanting to take hold of a small caliber cannonball. With remarkable determination she grasps Andrei's testicles, stands on tiptoe and breathes into his ear: "This is all mine, and when the moment for it comes, I'm going to destroy you, I'm going to eat you up piece by piece, I'm not going to leave a single part of you intact. Gorgeous boy." Then, with a little laugh, she goes into her house and slams the door in his face.

Back in the student pension where he's staying, Andrei thinks about what's happened. The combination of incongruous elements disconcerts him. Although in purely intellectual areas he's demonstrated an extraordinary lucidity, in his dealings with women he remains subject to the dominant ideas of the period. The only thing that occurs to him is that Alicia's attitude reveals an intense temperament. He worries over it. Does she consider him to be a prude? "Maybe she hoped for bolder behavior!"

After meditating on it deeply, instead of going to bed he heads back to Varmon's place. When he gets there, he stops for a few seconds to catch his breath. Then, attentive to the hour and respectful of the neighbors' sleep, he knocks gently on the door, murmuring: "Alicia . . ." No one answers. It surprises him. All at once, a horrible suspicion claws its way into his mind: *a delinquent has broken into the house and the worst is already over*. In a vision Andrei sees carved-up limbs, pulled-out eyes, blood-soaked hair. So as not to believe it, he insists with shouts and blows, passing quickly from discretion to anguish. The lamps in the neighborhood begin to turn on. The terror of scandal grinds down all remaining scruples: he finds the half-open window through which the murderer forced entry, and uses it to slip into the home of his beloved.

The first thing that draws his attention is the density of the silence, a rich and saturated silence that's libidinous in its muffled echoes, like the silence of cemeteries; as well as the smell, also dense, with varying levels, delicate lower down and thicker at the heights, every nuance working the deft effects of its peculiarity upon the base of a central tone, a rigorous maceration of tuberoses dissolved in water, plus swirling dust. It's the smell of an imprisoned soul in confinement, he thinks. And for a moment he surrenders to the easy contrast and imagines himself in the role of liberator, entering the room where Alicia moans—in chains but alive, desecrated perhaps, but alive! Then, alert, or maybe influenced by his fantasies, he thinks he hears a murmur, a groan that traces out an arc of agony through the embroidered void of the room, emerging from the upper floor. Andrei runs, leaping up the steps two by two. Right or left? A small radiance, a fleeting twinkle, straight ahead. It's the flame of a candle or its reflection on golden skin, which all at once fades away into a myriad of violet lights, the moon of a mirror attached to the wardrobe door, which as it slowly opens reveals them tangled and naked in bed. Alicia sees him and says only: "Andrei." Martha Velin coldly comments: "This is not real," behind the back of the man who flees the house, sprints down the street, abandons Amsterdam.

8

What path did Andrei Deliuskin take after his great amorous disappointment? When recounting the essential, there's no such thing as an unexpected event. During this period, Napoleon Bonaparte has a group of agents spread out all over continental Europe, tasked with finding scientists, thinkers and adventurers willing to participate in the great Egyptian campaign. The Emperor himself has given instructions: "I want you to get hold of all the unscrupulous poor devils and ruined talents that you can, the ones determined to do anything in order to trim away with the scissors of their ambition some little corner of the shining papier-mâché of glory." The first stop finds my great-grandfather in Bratislava. There he enlists in the ranks of the French expeditionary corps, declaring himself to be a "polygraph and philosopher, optician and orphan."

What leads him to join the French ranks? What does he see in the figure of the Corsican? Does he consider Napoleon to be a contemporary incarnation of the Universal Spirit, as so many thinkers and literati would in decades to come? Or is his selection a product of spite? In any case, while his motives may be varied, the consequences later on will be of indisputable significance for the culture of our time. But this is only a part of the matter. The other question or conundrum is: What leads Bonaparte to organize, assemble and implement a project to invade Egypt? His conflicted dealings with the bungling and jealous members of the French Directorate? The quarrel struck up with the Minister of Foreign Affairs, Charles Maurice de Talleyrand-Périgord, his only rival and countryman with a legitimate claim to be at his level? Maybe France is too small to contain them both, although having said that, it's politically convenient for them to divide the resulting profits from such a campaign (in which the soldier is obviously the one who runs all the risks). Let's also not forget that the plan for conquest derives from a strictly political rationale. Given that it's impossible to defeat England in naval combat, the most logical next step is to generate actions that intend to cut off British commercial routes and put an end to the possession of India, a prerequisite to cutting off, invading and defeating the enemy. Whoever dominates Egypt will hold the key to the Mediterranean and Red Sea. Of course, after his triumphal procession through the country, Napoleon sets his sights on gaining control over Damascus and Aleppo, occupying Constantinople and Turkey, and doing the rounds of the continent through Hadrianopolis or even Vienna, following the annihilation of the Habsburgs. Naturally, beneath the impetus of his attempt to modify the political map, Napoleon harbors the dream of entering into contact with sensual ancient Egyptian wisdom, whose knowledge and use will help him to reconquer his loose Joséphine from the arms of the bloodless Hippolyte Charles, a curly-haired dandy who fascinates her with his amatory techniques. But is this what Napoleon really wants? To be the new Alexander the Great? And what does Andrei Deliuskin want?

In 1798, my great-grandfather travels from Bratislava to Toulon, where he assembles the French fleet. Fifty thousand men—thirty-eight thousand soldiers, ten thousand sailors, two thousand scientists and artists—distribute themselves in fifteen boats, a dozen frigates, a corvette, dozens of avisos, tartanes and bomb vessels, and even a decorative sampan captured from some Malay pirates . . . Names: *Alceste, Aquilon, Franklin, Tonnant* . . . The flagship possesses one hundred twenty cannons and has been baptized *L'Orient*. Andrei travels onboard the *Oiseau*.

The crossing of the Mediterranean is slow and tedious. There are no signals from the English fleet under the command of Admiral Nelson. Life onboard is that of a floating tenement house: songs, card games, charades. Every so often, a drunkard staggers and breaks his neck on deck. The naturalist Geoffroy Saint-Hilaire wins the admiration of the crew members in his launch when he flings himself into the sea and mesmerizes a shark, which is hauled onboard the ship without resistance. On the *Aquilon*, Nouet and Quenot put back and move forward their marine watches, and shift the bisectors of their telescopes' lenses. In his captain's cabin Villiers du Terrage discovers a historical-comparative manual with instructions for sailors' knots, and extrapolating constants, he lays the foundations for infinitesimal analysis. From the forecastle of the prow of *L'Orient*, Vivant Denon loosens his wrist drawing curves and waves, curves and waves. Eventually he makes quick sketches of other boats. It wouldn't be strange if one of the figures depicted was my great-grandfather, although in these drafts it's impossible to make out whether a bulge is a pipe, a heap of clothes or a person. In any case, Andrei Deliuskin spends almost the entire trip in a secluded corner of the vessel, reading.

Twenty-two days after embarking, following a performance of *The Sorrows of Young Werther*, the Corsican decides to offer his troops a morsel: the conquest of the island of Malta. Five hundred elderly gentlemen with musty crosses and rusty armor can do nothing but capitulate. With the aim of publicity, the French liberate a few hundred Muslims from the torments of Maltese prisons. On July 1, 1798, on the coasts of Alexandria, the invasion of Egypt begins. A little disillusioned by the scene that offers itself to his eyes (the vast city Alexander founded is now a dusty village, riddled with mosquitos floating at their ease in cisterns of dark green water), Napoleon barely leaves his residence. While his scientists go about the streets armed, relentlessly pursued by packs of starving dogs, the Corsican throws himself into his first attempts at drawing up a speech for the natives. Attempts:

"Look upon us not as invaders, but as heirs to your civilization . . .";

"We truly delight in your architecture, your past achievements. Any of you who visits Paris will see a number of pyramids and obelisks. To go no further, in the Place de la Bastille there is a fountain that represents the goddess Isis . . .";

"The ancient Egyptian religions gave birth to polytheism and monotheism. Jehovah is no more than an Aten from the mountains, noisy and ill-tempered, and the Kabbalah a confused interpretation of the *Book of the Dead*";

"I am an incarnation of the divine pharaohs. My Italian blood hearkens back to Nubia . . ."

At last, fed up with these preliminaries and faced with the evidence that Talleyrand is conspiring against him, he decides to take a shortcut to Cairo by crossing the desert. A good part of his army dies, melts or goes mad trying to drink the water that is water in a mirage, which Monge will later analyze in a scientific study. There's a skirmish with Mamluks in the village of Chobrakhit, but the final combat, the "Battle of the Pyramids," breaks out in Embabeh. The standard formation of the Napoleonic infantry disconcerts its enemies, who go to combat dressed in their best clothes, believing they'll be confronted with individuals. To shoot against this anonymous and poorly dressed mass seems to be an offense, like aiming at a heap of trash. So the Mamluks fire their guns with indolence, aim just anywhere with their carbines, their blunderbusses, their four pistols per cavalryman. The French receive them with volleys, one after the other, and take the blasé retreat as a sign of victory. This is the first of many misunderstandings that will be produced between the new France and the Egypt of immemorial times, but for Napoleon it is helpful for polishing his first speech addressed to future ages. To his chronicler, he says: "Whereas before combat I addressed soldiers with the following expression: 'Onward, and imagine these monuments have observed us from the heights for forty centuries,' now it would be better to put: 'From the heights of these pyramids, forty centuries contemplate you.'" The chronicler remarks: "But, General . . . it's the same!" Striking him down with one of his classic gazes, Napoleon notes coldly: "The style is not irrelevant."

On August 1, the catastrophe of Aboukir Bay takes place when the fleet of Admiral Nelson surprises the one led by Admiral Brueys, confronting, routing and destroying it in its majority. Now, even if they'd wanted to do so, the French can't return to their country. Informed of the disaster, Napoleon comments: "This leaves us no choice but to advance and found an empire." Looking to find support in the local community, he disseminates a proclamation drawn up with the help of the orientalist Venture de Paradis, which argues for the objectively Muslim nature of the French army that defeated the pope, and presents Napoleon as a representative of Muhammad.

To the members of the Diwan, the document seems to be written by an infidel with only a very crude idea of the true faith, and his anti-Christian fervor demonstrates they are dealing with an atheist dog. As far as the French troops go, the ulema claims there's no real conversion to Islam without appropriate rites of passage, and it proposes a collective day of circumcision and prayer. Napoleon doesn't bother answering. He has himself called "Sultan El-Kebir" and wears a velvet caftan whose hem brushes the floor and gets tangled in his slippers. His view is that it's time to start encouraging a direct connection with the masses, whom he assumes are grateful to him for having defeated the Mamluk caste. To help along this relationship even more, he exempts shop-keepers from the payment of some taxes and dreams up a series of high-quality didactic performances, each of which will culminate in his own unexpected appearance before the Cairenes from the balconies of his new residence, the palace of Elfy Bey, with his arms raised to the sky as if he were a living representation of the Caesars of the Roman Empire (fashions repeat themselves). The generals oppose the idea, accusing it of being a circus spectacle. The scholars, in contrast, turning to various sources of the reli-gious heritage (the resurrection of Osiris, the party following the birth of the Prophet, Christ's bar mitzvah and Buddha's enlight-enment under the sycamore fig tree), advise him to put it into practice during the annual celebration of the Nile's rising waters. This festivity is one of the great events of the season, and the sci-entific cabinet reckons it will be an ideal occasion for the Egyptian people to breakfast on the evidence of its new guests' technical superiority. To this effect, just arrived in Cairo, a team of geolo-gists commanded by the engineer Edme Jomard lays the bases for a dam to regulate the flow of water that passes through the city during the rising.

On the day of the great event, they open the gates of the first sluice. Nervous as a prima donna who peeks out at the audience through a hole in the curtains on her debut night, Napoleon, with the help of a spyglass, admires the rhythm and intensity of the first little jets of water spurting along the canal. For a moment everything seems perfect, exquisite. But—maybe because Jomard's estimate of the levels, rises and drainages was mistaken, or due to some other unknown factor—the next moment all of Cairo floods. Aware of the delicate matter of political implications, the Corsican abstains from greeting the crowd from his balcony, but from his perch he delights in the spectacle: ". . . it was entrancing. People, villages, trees, religious men, minarets, domes of tombs all emerged from the surface of the water, and thickly spread in all directions were thousands of white candles," he recalls in his *Memorial of Saint Helena*.

As a result of this disaster, he postpones his idea of a direct and charismatic contact with the common people, and instead occupies himself with flattering the vanity of powerful locals. He gives instructions to his Garde du Corps that every morning it should carry out a series of pompous and ridiculous movements— weapons displays, genuflections, fanning motions, little jumps, flutterings of lashes and twistings of mustaches—meant to dazzle the doctors of law and the eminences coming to visit him. After this fanfare in the entrance courtyard, the visitors enter a hall built in accordance with the strictest oriental imagery (which to them seems the height of French exoticism), where they drink coffee and sprawl on big pillows stuffed with duck feathers until a very good-natured Napoleon himself appears to consult them about the subtleties of the Qur'an. All of it a dreary but necessary farce.

Then, after some time has passed, comes the second dramatic effect: a fair. In the main square of Ezbekiyé, a wood obelisk imitating pink granite is raised; there are games of chance, and machines to coat apples in caramel or spin sticky sugar clouds. A choir of soldiers sings a cantata about the moral virtues. Under the canopies of a two-hundred-meter-long shop, Arabists give lessons about the difficult art of eating with a fork and knife, and in the souks, the latest marvel of foreign science is revealed: a great flying machine that will rise into the skies, fueled by a source of sacred fire. At the hour planned, an enormous red, blue and white globe takes off in flight, lurching along for twenty or so meters off the ground and then falling onto the spectators, engulfed in flames.

The French are surprised by the indifference of the locals

toward what they don't know. According to the Orientalists (among them the paleontologist Georges Cuvier), this variety of generalized ataraxia has its origin in the successive conquests that razed the old cultures. Egypt, which at its peak was famous for its achievements in science and the arts, the country that astonished the world with its techniques to build pyramids, embalm the dead, multiply the gods and calculate the position of the stars, is now a cesspool. But Napoleon sees a hint of resistance in this apathy, a rudiment of politics. He has to make another effort, and another, and another. He forces his general Jacques Menou to marry a Muslim woman and orders some syphilitic soldiers to be circumcised in accordance with the Law. He fasts. He prays facing the minarets. His favorite verse is: "Glory to God, high above all that is attributed to Him!" His advisers fear that he has truly converted to Islam, but he puts their minds at ease: Egypt is well worth a prayer.

"It is a terrible error to have attempted to persuade the natives of the superior virtues of France," he explains. "We must make the conquered peoples believe that our troops are yielding, even as they continue to forge ahead."

"Naturally," the Corsican goes on, "to be efficient, this 'make them believe' must not be the consequence of verbal communication, since didacticism repels the masses. In contrast, they are attracted by obvious symbols that don't require an explanation. Can anyone think of an essential metaphor, something that reveals our adoration of this old-yet-new world?"

General silence.

"Nothing that touches hearts?"

Idem. But Vivant Denon has an idea:

"I quote an Arab: 'All mortals are afraid of Time, but Time is afraid of the Pyramids,'" he says. "And what if we tried our luck with a French human pyramid?"

"And what might that be?"

Denon takes out his notebook and sketches a diagram: on four slender but solid wood poles arranged in parallel, four acrobats are perched at a short distance from each other. In their turn, another three climb onto their shoulders, who in turn carry another two, over whom the one is raised who "crowns" the ascent. The diagram—notes Denon—is purely tentative. Ideally, a rigorous progression would multiply the number of participants. Five under the four, six under the five, and so on. But it's obvious that an increase in the number of acrobats would also add kilos to hold within each row, directly related to their place in the model, until the weight is impossible to endure for those at the base, and the figure collapses.

"That's why I propose a modest *septimium*," continues Denon. "Seven below, one on top. Twenty-eight poor devils are enough for a human *perpetuum mobile* that evokes the geometric figure par excellence of this region."

"But don't we run the risk of aggravating the tendency we're trying to correct?" asks Napoleon. "Won't every Egyptian who sees the performance think we're trying to show him how everything can be a material to be dominated, a part to be transformed, an object capable of improvement and relocation? Won't these savages end up thinking we want to bring their pyramids to our France, or that anything can become grist to the mill of human effort . . . ? What do you say to these objections?"

"Nothing," says a proud Denon, "except I don't think it will be that way."

"Ah," murmurs Napoleon. "*C'est très intéressant.* Time to set the plan into motion."

The informal fair, precarious in nature, that already exists outside the city now acquires an official character: it becomes the First Inventions Fair organized by the Scientific Institute of

Egypt, and takes place on one of the patios of Hassan Kachef's palace. There, the ingenious acrobatic mechanism is presented. A group of soldiers with very different heights substitutes for the acrobats until they arrive from Paris. You have to work with what you've got. A soldier sneezes and his row trembles, another lets out a fart, everyone laughs and the *septimium* collapses. Vivant Denon comments:

"I suppose this is the end of our experiment."

"On the contrary," answers Napoleon. "We're only getting started."

And so further preparations are made. After the troupe of acrobats disembarks, it's led to an empty plot, where it must practice without rest. The training procedures are in themselves cruel and intolerable, with an inhumanity that grows only more extreme in the heat of that climate. But there's nothing that professionals in any field enjoy more than to sacrifice themselves out of love for their craft. Within a few weeks, the troupe reaches such a high level of professional focus and expertise that it generates its own crowd, an ecstatic and untiring audience that remains silent so as not to disturb it. The acrobats commit themselves to matching the level of their spectators and decide to extend the demonstration for an indefinite length of time. This decision is convenient for the purpose that gathered them, because the Second Inventions Fair—which was going to be its debut—sees itself rescheduled due to a series of administrative circumstances: now the troupe will show up incomparably prepared for the day of their launch. They go on practicing. The concentration that distinguishes them is taken to be a mystical phenomenon, although nothing inspires them but pure adherence to method. Of course, to stay firm, they inject themselves with fortifiers and muscular tonics, and get their calves rubbed by masseuses. When an acrobat can't take any more and begins to wobble (thirst and hunger having turned him into

a sack of bones), the French doctors resort to a solidifying com-
pound, essentially a maceration of ancient mummy, quicklime,
sand and desert dust, enriched with distilled water; the product is
sprinkled over the entire epidermis of the acrobat until he's fixed
in his gesture, unmoving, holding what he bears on his shoulders
without damaging the rest of the structure.

With time, the strict rigidity of the *septimium* ends up affecting
the liveliness of the spectacle, which comes to be replaced by
new attractions. The spot starts to empty out; now the beggars'
chants, Syrian songs and Arabic melodies are no longer heard; the
charmers have taken their snakes elsewhere. In this solitude, the
acrobats remain firm merely to serve as recipients for dog urine
and rat bites. When the Second Fair takes place, no one remembers to inform them, although the empty plot is mere meters away
from the Institute patio, which is bright with lights, sparkling
with fireworks and filled with the cheerful laughter of spectators.
In any case, the acrobats aren't in the mood to rebuke such forgetfulness; strictly speaking, they're dead. Some bodies have been
swapped out for life-sized porcelain reproductions, taken from
the holds of boats bringing new contingents of hussars. One day,
a simoom blows through unexpectedly, and the glorious metaphor of France's love for Egypt is torn to shreds in the warm wind.

9

What does Napoleon Bonaparte want? What is Andrei Deliuskin looking for when he joins the ranks? The answer to the first question is simple and has already been given: the future Emperor hopes to recuperate Joséphine by impressing her with his exploits. Andrei, in contrast, is trying to forget Alicia Varmon. Or is he studying *in situ* the most extreme material form taken by the chessboard of sand—that is, politics? If so, what scenario presents itself to my great-grandfather's vistas of thought as he attempts to interpret his age? Perhaps the matter will be clarified in time. For the moment . . .

Napoleon. *Sentimental Life of the Emperor.* With his head full of rumors about Joséphine's infidelities ("the things Hippolyte Charles says about you, my general," et cetera, et cetera), Bonaparte commits the imprudence of writing a letter to his brother Louis, grumbling about his wife:

> . . . The passion for glory has disappeared. I no longer have any reason to live. I'm fed up with human nature. At twenty-nine years old, *sono finito*. I wanted to lay the world at her feet, and she thinks only of her perfumed idiot. What is this woman doing to me? I don't even know why I married her. She's a far cry from my ideal and she thinks like a seamstress. I don't even like her body odor . . . (et cetera, et cetera).

The letter is intercepted by Nelson's fleet during the crossing of the Mediterranean, when the schooner transporting it is sunk, and the text is reproduced on the front page of all the London newspapers.

For Bonaparte, such indiscretion is exasperating:

"What does private life have to do with war? On this occasion, the British do no honor to their fame as gentlemen," he shouts, kicking the door frames.

But the conduct of the enemy press was foreseeable. What Napoleon truly doesn't anticipate is the reaction of Joséphine, who, in the aftermath of this ridicule before the public opinion of Europe, resolves to make his life impossible. She sends him an average of three letters a week in which she accuses him of the worst crimes, while she claims innocence. These dispatches unsettle the Corsican. What would happen if Nelson were to capture the letters, the ones she wrote . . . ? Also, who should he believe? The general gossip that brands him as a cuckold? Or those tear-soaked pages? (Joséphine strews them with water dispensed from an eye dropper.) At the start, to hide his confusion, Bonaparte responds by affecting a scornful, imperial tone. But the mistreatment doesn't calm Joséphine and, on the contrary, sends her into a state of vengeful fury, full of delirious certainty about the truth of her own assertions; she answers with a torrent of insults. Having never expected to become the object of such a frontal attack, he immediately gives way on all counts and begs her forgiveness. "How could I let myself be led by the winds of defamation to believe that you, precisely you, my only, my adored one, would be capable of . . . ?" "I kiss your feet, I lick your fingers, I submit myself to you as a pitch-black slave, I am your dog . . ." et cetera, et cetera. Anyhow. It's not long before the French fleet comes and goes day and night along the Mediterranean, less to supply the Corsican with fresh troops, provisions and arms than to keep alive the route of a correspondence that torments him. Soon, even this trickle of humiliations is not enough. Having grown used to the role of the lover who repents inflicting on his chaste bride the offense of an imaginary groping, Napoleon racks his brains for an adequate symbol to represent his desire for atonement. Since he knows better than anyone his wife's monetary avarice and childish fascination for trinkets, jewels and antiquities, he dispatches certain shipments of archaeological objects for her amusement, whose natural destination would have been the Egyptology halls of a museum yet to be created—the Louvre—but that through this act of sentimental corruption, end up at his beloved's mansion. Magical, lapis lazuli scarab beetles; miniature, gold-plated pyramids; marble altars; formulas for spells; carvings of the sun god Aten; necklaces with the image of Amun; sapphire seals; carbuncle earrings; perfumed thuribles and mortuary trunks set with precious stones. Objects that leave through the back door almost as quickly as they come in through the front, exchanged for cold hard cash that swells the accounts of the "offended." Despite these brisk dealings, a few knickknacks worthy of Joséphine's garish poor taste remain gleaming on her fingers, fastened to her dresses, tangled in her hair, scattered over the chocolate-colored Chinese silk sheets of the ninny Hippolyte.

Things went on like this for months. But even though the outpouring of gifts didn't let up, Napoleon continued to harbor the exasperating suspicion that Joséphine was taking him for an idiot. Naturally, he had no firsthand testimony that endorsed or refuted his wife's betrayal, beyond rumors; among other reasons because she'd surrounded herself with extremely faithful and well-paid servants who wouldn't open their mouths *this side of the grave*. Consumed as much by his need to know as by his fear of discovering the truth, he whipped up a scheme to introduce the most silent of spies into the heart of this court of the afterlife: a mummy.

Obviously, in this case, it would be a fake mummy. Quiet. Incorruptible. To be placed in the matrimonial bedroom. Pure eyes and memory. Alive. One of his men.

The one concerned with the details is God, not a future Emperor. Once he'd dreamed up the idea, Napoleon delegated the matter of locating a serene or resigned soldier, one who would accept the mission imposed on him, to his assistant Colonel Roger Klab; for his part, Klab thought he had too much on his plate to occupy himself, so he transferred the matter to Lieutenant Vallois, who left it in the hands of Sergeant Mirabeau, who chose one of his more slow-witted men: the hussar Patrice Daudet.

Of course, it wasn't easy to make him understand that he'd been chosen to stay in Joséphine's bedroom with the aim of gathering reliable information about its occupant's activity, and it was even harder to dissuade him of the outlandish idea that his sergeant was asking him to sleep with Bonaparte's wife. Once this had been achieved, Daudet meekly accepted the possibility that the bandages were a kind of uniform and didn't even think to ask how long he would have to remain silent and standing with eyes open, or when he would be relieved of this labor.

Since Napoleon wanted urgent results, the mission was given top priority. The flagship, *L'Orient*, waited in the dock for arrangements to be completed. The bandages set aside for fabrication of the mummy were submitted to a bath of mercury and sulfur salts, and at the moment the spy was wrapped up, the precaution was taken to snip little openings at the level of his eyes and nostrils, a method also followed on the front side of the sarcophagus—this one authentic, from a looting of Thutmose I's tomb. As a preventative measure against defecation, the hussar was submitted to a series of enemas, but in the haste to carry out orders, some elemental matters of logistics were neglected, such that only a short time after having begun the voyage, poor Daudet, squeezed tight by the bandages, stunned by the darkness and lack of air in the sarcophagus, dizzy from the ship's movement, suffocating from the noxious smells in the hold, and already afflicted by the lack of food and drink, started to feel a certain uneasiness regarding his fate; as the days went by, this uneasiness turned to fear, then to anguish, and at last to pure and simple desperation, which manifested itself in the form of shouts, moans, cries, howls and every manner of demand for help, which of course no one heard and which went about diminishing in intensity until death arrived. The fact is that, due to these efforts at survival, or maybe due to the insufficiently developed purgative techniques of the age, as soon as the sarcophagus was unloaded at the port, Noiset, the one responsible for inspecting the consignment and transferring it to its destination, was able to judge by the smell that the contents had decomposed. Working with independence of judgment, instead of bringing it to Joséphine (who would immediately have sent it to be tossed in the dung heap), he lifted the cover, applied an injection of formaldehyde to the dead man, and, after purifying him by spritzing the contents of a bottle of cheap perfume inside, offered the lot to the owner of a circus just arrived in Marseilles . . . none other than Giovanni Battista Belzoni, or Belinzone, a giant over two meters tall with an impressive musculature, known as the Patagonian Samson.

As soon as he got wind of this bargain, Belzoni glimpsed the luminous appearance of a creative possibility: the mummy would add a new number to his spectacle of strength, beauty and ability. But the smell of rotten tinned food that escaped from inside the coffin! Did he have to change its bandages and give it a good immersion bath with scented salts . . . ? Or . . . Or perhaps . . . And if instead . . . Belzoni grasped the air with his fingers in triumph. Castanets. Nutcracker.

First days of January 1799. Night. The Belinzone Circus tent is packed. News has spread through the whole port city that the giant will present something marvelous. The crowd fills all the seats, throngs into the aisles. Ladies sigh with pleasure in anticipated enjoyment from the vision of the New Hercules's bronzed body. All vibrates with excitement. The charm of preambles: a juggler makes five oranges spin on his nose; one cripple pursues another through the crowd, striking his head with a rubber hammer. Voices are heard clamoring for Belzoni. The one named makes his appearance only when he judges that the racket has grown irresistible. Applause. He's half-naked, barely covered by some leather shorts that reach halfway down his thighs. "Studmuffin!" Belzoni winks and strokes the beard that spills like a river of diabolical sperm over his muscularly multifaceted chest. Two assistants carry on their shoulders a metal structure that contains him in a harness. Now another eight men come out who attach the ends to their waists and fall to the ground: Belzoni is the erect corolla, his assistants the fallen petals. The colossus tenses his muscles until they take on exaggerated shapes, then begins to lift up the structure. Slowly, slowly. His assistants now float a few centimeters from the ground, their arms limp as if they've fainted; but Belzoni hasn't yet finished his stunt. On his tiptoes, he begins to spin on an imaginary axis; and if at the start his chained slaves cloak him with their bodies, wrapping themselves around him, seconds later, as they take on speed, they begin to fling away. The ropes that join them to the harnesses grow tense and whip through the air, and the assistants, transformed into spinning tops, splay out their hands, stretch out their legs and give howls of feigned terror. The audience goes wild with enthusiasm. Belzoni stops, and the assistants collapse to the ground, toppling like bowling pins. Trumpets sound. The Patagonian Samson disappears from the ring.

Intermezzo. After a couple of trifles (acrobatics, horsewomen, a human cannonball who shoots through the air without losing his tricorn hat), Mademoiselle Legrini appears. Belzoni has hired her as much for his own consumption (every night he indulges in those beautiful and symmetrical toned thighs, which imprison his neck and bring him to deliriums nearing asphyxia) as to generate in the audience the suspicion that his circus breeds artists able to challenge him for dramatic supremacy. Obviously, the contest is illusory, since what really happens at each performance is a strategic distribution of attractions by gender. While ladies swoon for a primordial macho, men are brought to the point of euphoria and vertigo by the sight of a dancer's legs.

Mademoiselle Legrini's number . . . extraordinary. At the end of it, silence. Coughs. Hurrahs. An empty stage. One minute, two. Then "Firecracker," the dwarf, enters the ring wearing a dress coat and carrying a ladder. The audience whistles, applauds, makes the usual jokes about reversal of size. Making use of the ladder, "Firecracker" sets alight one of the side torches (dangerously close to the red curtains); then he crosses the stage and does the same at the other end. Left and right. The flickering flames are a call to reflection. The moment grows solemn. "Firecracker" leans in the direction of the public, blows out the wick and waves goodbye. The smoke magically spreads through the atmosphere and covers everything; at the same time the moan of a badly played violin is heard. An eastern melody. Over the music floats a hoarse, tremendously masculine voice (Belzoni).

"She's spent more than two thousand years in eternal sleep, guarded from the harassment of profaners. Her dwelling was a tomb of rectangular stone. But today we dare trouble this lady's well-deserved rest for the benefit of knowledge and science. Ladies and gentlemen, just arrived from the Near East and prepared to reveal to us the Enigma of the Other World, with you tonight, Nofretamon, the most beautiful of Egyptian princesses!"

Belzoni enters the ring carrying the sarcophagus that Noiset sold him. He leans it upright against a stand. The light from the torches, unpredictable and partial, carves out areas of shadow. Belzoni's smile is a grimace. He himself looks like Baphomet. Now he whispers:

"This is the moment of your life you have to mint in your minds like a unique coin; this is the moment you will choose to tell your grandchildren about. Today, my friends, for the price of admission, you are about to witness the miracle of miracles: the resurrection of a mummy."

Having said this, and pretending not to notice the exclamations (horror, incredulity, admiration), Belzoni passes a caressing hand over the hieroglyphs that scatter the length and breadth of the sarcophagus:

"According to what can be read in these inscriptions, Nofretamon lived for fifteen years in the city of Thebes, and then died suddenly of an unknown illness; she was the second princess of the dynasty of . . . And today we'll bring her back to life. But I need a collaborator! Does anybody in the audience want to volunteer?"

Before anyone else, a teenager shoots up a delicate white hand: "Me!"

"You? Very well, my boy. Come on up. What's your name?"

"Jean-François Champollion."

"Perfect, Jean-François. How small you look by my side!" (*General laughter.*) "Well then. Now I'm going to pronounce a magic spell that lets me enter the fourth astral state, where I'll make contact with the spirit of this girl. Yes, Jean-François: the soul that two thousand years ago animated this gorgeous bandaged creature will surrender to the influence of my words and leave the heavens to breathe life once again into this body . . . When this happens, my dear boy, I ask you to separate the lid from the sarcophagus, and if it's not too heavy for you" (*to the public*) "—because he looks a little scrawny!—" (*more laughter*) "you can lay it on the sand. All right?"

"All right," says Champollion.

"Good, then let's begin. Ready. Set. Go!"

Belzoni closes his eyes, blinks and lets a mumbo jumbo of pure vocals and consonants flow from his firm lips. Then he rolls his eyes upward, says something like "caramba" and starts to shiver; his entire body trembles, his muscles jump, and he seems to melt and go solid at the same time, like a kind of firm gelatin. Champollion pulls the lid off the sarcophagus and sets it aside. Belzoni, bathed in the sweat of his success, comes out of his self-absorption and proceeds to unwrap the mummy. The first thing that appears to public view is a black wig, cut in Ancient Empire style, which leaves half the forehead free and from its sides reveals some uneven, rebellious locks. The eyelids of the deceased are painted with bitumen or black China ink or antimony (whatever can be got at the druggist); the cheeks are of a spectral paleness; the nose is perfect and lightly aquiline; the lips are full, abundant and quivering with life. Although they've rehearsed the number many times, Mademoiselle Legrini can barely resist the temptation to laugh, and contains herself only out of fear of her master. When Belzoni reaches the level of her breasts, just barely covered by a few shiny-bright tinplate leaves, the dancer shudders with excitement.

"You're coming . . . coming to life," Belzoni says in a false murmur, loud enough to be heard by the last row. "Life is coming to you!"

The bandages fall away. Legrini is revealed like a supernatural apparition, a beauty not of this world.

"Tell me your name, I beg you!"

The woman opens her eyes, summoned by the spell.

"I am Nofretamon, princess of Thebes. Have I returned? Where am I now? Am I alive?"

Mademoiselle Legrini raises her arms. Applause breaks out. Belzoni takes one of the mummy's hands and greets the audience.

Then he leans over to acknowledge Champollion with a condescending hug, as the latter uses the moment to whisper in his ear:

"I won't make any public comment about this crude mystification if you tell me where you got hold of such a magnificent sarcophagus . . . which, in parentheses, as can be read in the inscription, was designed for a male corpse."

The words are lost in the cascade of applause, which doubles in intensity when, as if by mistake, Mademoiselle Legrini lets one of the leaves fall. Her incomparable breast shines like a promise, daubed in oils that frame the perfection of the violet areola.

"How did you realize . . . ?" says Belzoni.

"To start with, the characterization is a pileup of errors in costume design."

"And to continue?"

"Anyone who possesses the slightest knowledge of Egyptian funereal art can't help but recall that the dead, prior to their mummification, were emptied of all their internal organs. In the charming body of this girl, I see no trace of any stitch whatsoever, from which I must infer she is alive and this spectacular 'reincarnation' a mere fraud. Or am I wrong? Not to mention the unlikely circumstance that a two-thousand-year-old mummy would express itself in the accent of a cheap provincial seamstress," sums up Champollion.

"Very good," murmurs the Patagonian Samson, and then adds: "If you keep quiet about what you know, I'll tell you what I know, but if you open your mouth I'll twist your neck like a chicken."

"Deal," says Champollion.

Mademoiselle Legrini bends over again. More applause.

That meeting, and the one the following night, was productive for both of them. Swapping confidences and experiences, they washed down everything with good wine and lavish helpings of food. When speaking of ancient languages and past eras, his young interlocutor's eyes radiated a light in which Belzoni found a cause, something that by far exceeded the pleasures he could obtain from the vain exhibition of his physical strength; this cause would end up changing the path of his life as a circus daredevil, taking him to Egypt, where he'd become an Egyptologist sui generis, one capable both of making the sealed covers of sarcophagi jump with the blows of a battering ram and of chiseling his own name next to those of the pharaohs. For his part, Champollion, beyond the dubious value of the information that Belzoni had supplied him about the "boxes of stiffs," received a powerful stimulus from this companion, which added to the thirst for knowledge that had always obsessed him (at fourteen years old he already knew a dozen languages and was on his way to learning another five). The new impulse was of a different sort, in its way as all-consuming as the first: it was the thirst for adventure.

Champollion's next step was to travel to Egypt. The one after that, to lose himself in its immensity. With the certainty of those who believe the lines of destiny are written beforehand, he abandoned Alexandria, and instead of following the route leading to the pyramids of Giza, strayed away into the Qattara Depression. His clothing was unsuitable, his reserve of water scarce. Drifting like a ghost among the nomadic desert tribes, he begged for shelter in the shadow of the caravans. He rested at Al-Fayyūm. Then he ventured into the sands once again, crossed them and reached Al-Alya, where the fevers of the desert that he had left behind attacked him. He agonized, lying in the concentric interior of a freshly dug mud well. When he wanted to die, he murmured: "I, who have read the *Hieroglyphica* of Horapollo, can say I was put on the balance, and lacked the sufficient weight." Then, surrendering to his taste for dead languages: "*Mene, mene, tekel, upharsin.*" As soon as he'd pronounced these words, he felt the fever give way. Perhaps it was an opportune remission, long enough for his end to take place in the open air. He went out at night, resolved to surrender himself to the moon and the jackals waiting to devour him. He walked until he reached a silt bank full of plants that absorbed all light. In the distance he heard the sound of oars. Champollion fell against the wall that opens, his face sinking into the Nile.

10

While he waited for the reports from his messenger already in the other world, Napoleon continued with his policies to reconquer Joséphine. As soon as he found out about the discovery of an ancient stone covered in notations, mathematical formulas or hieroglyphs in the port city of Rosetta, he decided this would be the final gift, the supreme offering in the series that rendered tribute to his beloved. As a prerequisite, however, the stone in question must be examined. Andrei Deliuskin is chosen by the Egyptian Scientific Institute to look into the matter.

The officer Pierre Bouchard, head of the local detachment, is irritated by my great-grandfather's imminent arrival. He thinks he's an opportunist coming to skim away some of the glory of his discovery. As a precaution, he sends agents to monitor the course of the gondolier transferring him upriver. Every so often, in some bend of the Nile, an arrow flies or a shot is heard. One morning, the bottom of the gondolier appears to have fallen away. Andrei doesn't grow anxious; he moves through the hours and days in a state of drowsiness, as if he's incubating some disease or as if this world's stripped-down forms induce him to the most serene reflection. Few things, but eternal: water, sky, papyrus.

When he arrives in Rosetta and introduces himself, the soldiers lead him with jokes and shoves toward the entrance of a tent, where Bouchard inflicts an hour-long wait on him, then receives him stretched out on a wool rug, reclining on soft velvet pillows; he fondles their tassels, their pompoms, as the chubby imitation of a houri tickles the soles of his feet with an ibis feather. In the background of the scene, on an extra-reinforced campaign desk, the stone is exhibited. Andrei sees its shine and notices that the granite is streaked with mica and feldspar. A quartz rock, about a meter and a half wide, and seventy-five centimeters in height. A discrete black, or rather dark gray, aerolite with fine pink veining. A remnant of dead cultures.

"Oh, Marie! Surprise! We have a visitor! Science has deigned to arrive at our modest home!" warbles Bouchard, his voice choked by resentment. The fat woman applauds half-heartedly as her master leans an elbow on the pillow and turns in the direction of my great-grandfather. He has the wilting petal of a desert flower stuck to the corner of his lips, the absentminded remainder of a libation. No sooner does he pronounce the next word ("before") than the petal comes detached, fluttering away like a butterfly a cat has vomited.

"Before listening to you utter any erudite idiocy, I want you to tell me if you know why we're here. Us. When I say 'us,' I refer to the French expedition," says Bouchard.

Andrei mulls it over for a few seconds. Then he admits:

"I don't know."

"I was afraid of that. Don't irritate me!" says Bouchard, striking Marie's jaw with the heel of his left foot, giving her no option but to draw back. The fat woman goes toward a corner of the tent and crouches down to look for a dagger or prepare an infusion. Bouchard keeps an eye on her movements as he continues: "All the same, I assume you'll have heard thousands of versions about it. Hundreds. I, for one, never believed, not for a moment, that sending this expeditionary advance party to the North of Africa was an innocent event. No. Obviously not. *Prima facie*, I'd say three reasons explain our arrival to this country. A Holy Trinity of converging and complementary motives.

"The first reason, which refers to politics, I'd call *apparent*: Napoleon decided to conquer Egypt as part of his plan to dominate the world. Which didn't start with him, of course. Already back in 1672, Leibniz sent a memorandum to Louis XIV, which argued that to push ahead with a true imperial politics, we must occupy the Gate to the Orient. If you like, we can do a little ancient history, but I think I've said enough.

"The second reason, which implies scientific knowledge, I'd call *allegorical*: At this level, our interest is no longer in taking control of everything, but in knowing everything. We parcel out the world, and our vocation as surveyors of knowledge develops under the premises that any object is worthy of identical interest and equal fascination. Packed up, weighed and measured, everything ends up in the storerooms of the future museum. From the geometric or spatial point of view, it's utter madness. How can the biggest thing end up fitting inside the smallest? Anyway. There you have the natives splitting their sides with laughter when they see Prosper Jollois studying crocodile fangs, Monge sending the tons of bat excrement accumulated in the now empty depths of the pyramids to be weighed . . . ! I myself, I myself was at a session of the Institute when Saint-Hilaire gave a lecture on the puffer fish, which spins like a barrel after absorbing air, floats for a while belly-up, then swells and rises like a balloon. Well then: I remember the commentary of Sheikh Al-Mahdi after our scholar's explanation: 'But what's this? So much yackety-yak about a single fish! The All-Powerful created more than fifty-thousand different species of fish. How many lives does this gentleman think he'll have to waste in order to describe to us this trifling fragment of the whole?' Naturally, the Egyptians are right. But this doesn't prevent *allegorical* reason from lingering as a justification for our presence here. Now, let's get to the:

"Third, or *deep*, reason. This is the level of truth to which I subscribe, and where you find me: alone. At this level, things and entities take on an almost immaterial fluidity; it's the level where research into the past, based on the contemplation of fixed elements, reveals to us events of the future. It's like a form of oneiromancy. Or like the Kabbalah, except that instead of being applied to the name of God, it's used to understand the spheres of sensibility: the world, human relationships. Everything meets at a fixed point. Every element is a piece of a totality in the process of being unveiled. Do you follow me?"

"I'm trying," smiles Andrei.

"Then you have a long way to go," says Bouchard. "*We came to Egypt to find out what the stone will tell us.* That's what I think. Have you seen it? Have you been able to take a look? A mathematical cosmos lies within. Over the length and breadth of the dark surface *all* the algebraic formulas can be found: those that allow pyramids to be built, determine the constant of the rise and descent of the Nile, map out the path of stars and prophesy the course of History. How about it, eh? All we have to do is decipher its meaning, see if it emerges in the course of time (just as the successive reading of sentences allows us to put together their argument), or in the particular spatial relationships between elements, or . . . I assure you that with the solid educational formation given to me at the Military Academy, in two or three more days, a month at most, I'll have understood everything."

My great-grandfather feigns nearsightedness and approaches the stone. At a glance, from the pure algorithm of the shapes, he can see it's carved with writing of three different kinds, in three languages. Not mathematics, but languages. He takes one step back, then another. He says:

"We'll talk tomorrow."

Andrei leaves the tent. He had come in with clarity; mere seconds later, he can no longer see a thing. For a while he entertains himself by listening to the conversations of soldiers around the bonfires of the encampment. But the idea of taking a turn around the desert attracts him more. At night, all sands are black. If it weren't for the hyenas . . . He looks for a campaign official who can find him lodgings, but it's obvious that no one is interested in his comfort. How could they be? They're at war. At any moment there might be another attack by the Mamluks, a disembarkation of Englishmen . . .

In his wanderings he reaches the city walls, recently fortified. If it hadn't been for its color, the stone he was going to study might have ended up as just another one here, heaped up for the defense.

"Are you enjoying the promises of such immensity?"

Andrei doesn't need to turn around to recognize the voice behind him. It's Marie, Bouchard's mistress. They're almost a meter away from each other, but my great-grandfather senses a dense quality in the inexpressible depths this figure radiates.

"Sometimes, when melancholy takes hold of me, I come to feel the freshness that flows from these walls," says Marie. "I lean my cheek against the stones and appreciate their damp. Even in this infernal cauldron, life finds a way to condense into droplets, create moss and decompose. I lean my cheek and feel the freshness and imagine I'm mounted on the hump of a camel spurred into flight by the Bedouin who's kidnapped me. The Bedouin takes me to his oasis, submits me to all the perversions of his libido, introduces me to his culture. I'm shut away in a prison. He comes once a day and feeds me dates, which he pushes one by one into my reluctant mouth with the patience of a saint. Finally, I give way and fall for him. I suck on his fingers while on my knees. This is love. When a patrol rescues me, no one understands my words. Besides, I refuse to speak: my Bedouin has died in combat. I wear black clothes, my eyes grow dark and deep behind the veil . . ."

"It's a pretty fantasy," murmurs Andrei.

"It was. Pierre and I played games like this, until the tragedy of his discovering the stone. Starting from that moment, he's remained awake, walking in circles around those little scratches. How does it make sense to torment himself to the point of losing the happiness that's always been within reach of his fingertips? He acts as if I don't exist. He doesn't listen to me. He doesn't look at me. Now I'm no longer even just a body to him. He caresses the stone. He goes over it like an object under siege, a miniature fortress. Sometimes I catch him passing a feather duster over its grooves, its crevices, its script. He talks to it. I've seen him cry trying to stretch his arms around it. I don't know anything, but I read that the ancient Egyptian gods can metamorphose into any shape if they want to ruin someone's life. If such beastly gods ever did exist, monsieur, what do they want with my man, just a poor devil?"

Marie sighs; she swallows her mucus and dries her tears. Andrei doesn't quite know what to do, so he does nothing. She adds: "If you took away this stone in the middle of the night, I'd know how to thank you. I refer not to my succulent, warm, fragrant sex, but to horses and escape routes. Although there's something I want to ask."

"Yes?" says Andrei.

"Am I beautiful?"

Nile, upriver. Andrei Deliuskin now travels in a decent boat; at least he has his own cabin. Having broken the seal of the envelope ("to open upon return from the city of Rosetta") and read the letter, he's now learned the nature of his mission. He knows that Bonaparte is waiting for him in person, and that he must draft a preliminary report about the hypothetical contents and possible revelations carved into the surface of the Rosetta stone. "Care for this object as if it were your own soul," Napoleon writes to him. "It is of supreme importance that it reach my hands without damage or scratches. I do not want to see any decapitated hieroglyphs, or chisel marks applied in order to censor messages presumed obscene, esoteric or incomprehensible. Legibility goes hand in hand with aesthetics, and I'm not one of those who believe a piece to be more beautiful when amputated." Before throwing the message in the river, Andrei notices that it never mentions the word "stone." The clear and awkward exclusion transmits better than any command his certainty that in some matters one must leave no written evidence.

One night, on the river. A sound of splashing, behind the curtain of water hyacinths and papyri. Is someone eating something, is something eating someone? A black smudge floats at the edge of the bank, a sinking body. European.

Andrei Deliuskin throws himself in the water and rescues the dying man. The crocodiles, glutted with other feasts, don't make a fuss.

Champollion convalesces for two, three days in a fainting spell without dreams. When he opens his eyes, he sees he's on the deck of a vessel, lying on a mat, protected from the sun by a canopy of royal flax. A man with an extremely distinguished appearance leans over him with a smile: it's my great-grandfather. Immediately Champollion feels the impulse to explain, to introduce himself: he tells him about his life, his love for study, his long hours at the Special School for Oriental Languages of the Collège de France (his training in Arabic, Chaldean, Coptic, Ethiopian, Hebrew and Persian, among others), his polemics with high-ranking linguists like Louis-Mathieu Langlès, Prosper Audran and Silvestre de Sacy. Andrei smiles again.

"You've landed in the right place."

He takes him to the tiny ship hold and pulls aside a piece of sackcloth, beneath which a black basalt stone is hidden.

"What do you see?" asks Andrei.

Champollion faints again.

In a hieroglyph, a baboon can mean moon or writing or rage. The head of a donkey can be used to represent the animal or to refer to an animal that's never traveled and doesn't know anything about the world. Leaning on the Rosetta stone, Andrei Deliuskin and Jean-François Champollion (master and disciple) apply logical approaches to meaning in the form of an infinite net. In theory, the Greek and Egyptian writings on the stone are not literal translations but paraphrases of one another—which of which?—communicative signifiers of the general purpose of the text. Does the ancient Egyptian language have a complicated grammar, declinations, a subjunctive? The stone gleams in the darkness. Sometimes, when the course of the Nile grows calm, they hoist it on deck to study better. Andrei elaborates hypotheses—for instance, a principle of acrophonic writing: each image could be a letter. A door could be the letter "p," an ibis the letter "i." Or maybe, proposes Jean-François, everything is gobbledygook, a monstrous polysyllable, an endless and unique word that, if pronounced, replicates chaos. No, says Andrei, pure hieroglyphs represent not the sounds of a language, but the ideas. The problem is that the Egyptian part of the stone uses both hieroglyphs and demotics. Eventually the first name appears: *Ptolemaios*, the Greek form of Ptolemy. A universe of knowledge opens up . . . and Champollion will be the one to make it known. In Al-Minyā, a new outbreak of fever compels him to disembark in search of treatment. Once healed he'll return to France, where he'll reveal what he learned alongside my great-grandfather. A small egoistic detail: for his own greater glory, he'll neglect to mention the name of Andrei Deliuskin. Meanwhile, Andrei must carry on with his journey, since Napoleon is waiting for him at the Valley of the Kings (Biban El-Moluk).

Sky, water.

The sloop runs aground in a narrows of the river. My great-grandfather decides to continue on foot, followed by a couple of bearers transporting the Rosetta stone. Days and nights. Finally, they reach the narrow gorge that forms an entrance to the valley. Andrei sees a cutaway panoramic view, a slash made with a notched knife in the flesh of the world. On the vertical walls of the ravine, worn away by time and about to plummet from the heights, the formless remains of sculptures still survive. They might have been taken for the rugged texture of the stone itself, or the bowel movements of a hippogriff. On both sides, as steep slopes, rocky masses rise up in a sheer vertical, projecting themselves in fantastic perspective against the backdrop of indigo sky. Night is falling. Rays of sun heat one side of the valley to the point of transparency, while the other side floats in the raw blue tint of arid lands.

"Hello," shouts one of the bearers, and explains: "I'm greeting the dead."

The echo of his voice carries into the distance, suffocates in the gorges, dies out and is lost, then comes back a few seconds later, altered:

"Have you arrived safely?"

A dead man? Not yet. It's Napoleon Bonaparte, waiting for them in the middle of a wide plain that opens out after the next bend. Dressed entirely in white. Peeling an orange under a canopy. A pith helmet covering the part of his head where the hair has begun to recede. Andrei approaches. His bearers place the Rosetta stone on the table. For a few moments, Napoleon contemplates the signs as if studying the account of a dream. After looking away, he says:

"Do you know why I asked you to bring it to me? My friends from the Institutes, or to put it more clearly, your colleagues, since in my position I can't presume to have true friends, believe that

my interest in the stone functions at the rhetorical level, as a metaphor for the key that would allow us to establish certain points of
contact between the Egyptians and ourselves. 'Since we're not able
to understand the Egyptians of the present, let's begin from the
origin, searching for the keys of their ancient civilization,' they say.
Starting now, I'd like to make it clear that this hypothesis is ridiculous, and that its practical application would be a complete waste
of time. What are the Egyptians, really? What is this country?
The fetid hole where the Arabs, Greeks and Latins relieved themselves . . . ! Even three hundred years before Christ, the pharaohs
no longer had Egyptian blood . . . Cleopatra herself—of whom
my Joséphine is no more than a pale reflection, a splinter of that
radiance—Jo herself . . . Cleopatra spoke the Egyptian language as
a strategic decision, but her mother tongue was, of course, Greek.
Coptic, with luck, is no more than a simplification of ancient
Egyptian in the shroud of the Greek alphabet, with seven letters
mutilated, an amputated language. In conclusion: Egypt is an act
of the will, a country yet to be born, or else a nostalgic choice. So
what are we going to talk about with them? What could be the
possible basis for an agreement? Nothing. The Egyptians simply
don't exist. And therefore, my friend, no key or code is possible.
What is this about, at heart? Why are we here? What is concealed
by our presence, which I have no qualms about introducing as the
preliminary act that will unleash a series of successive acts, a series
that might be endless? What is it that interests *me*? Very simple:
I'm able to intuit it, but can't yet name it. The mystery of my irres-
olute desire will linger, to be revealed by men who see further and
more clearly than I do. Does this sincerity astonish you? It makes
me happy that someone still finds me unpredictable. I'm dying to
take possession of it. This concept. This thing. Precisely the one
that slips from our grasp. And perhaps this is why I brought my
armies to eat desert sand, using them as a bargaining token. All of

them dead for a yearning. That's how it is. I'm the Moses of my people. Do you know how Moses succumbed? Jehovah says it, not me: 'You'll see the place but never come to dwell in it.' Old Testament. When Moses (or Mashiah) arrived at those boundaries, he claimed that after the horizon line, the Promised Land began. His wife, much younger, said: 'Excuse me, I'll be back soon,' and went ahead on a donkey. Moses watched her fade away in the distance. In a few hours she came back, shouted and threw a handful of sand in his face: 'Promised Land . . . ! You brought us here for this? I'm going back to Egypt right now!' Women always look for security. What one can't understand is why she decided to go with him at all. If in Thebes they had treated her like a queen! Well, in any case, when Moses heard these words of reproach, his heart stopped, his *Ka* rose to the sky to fuse with Aten, and he collapsed heavily to the ground. You get it, don't you? The army is my wife, who asks every day why I brought her to the middle of nowhere. She doesn't notice that I'm the one in agony. Clearly I'm talking about Joséphine now, not my troop of *coglioni*. As you no doubt already know (rumors here travel faster than my infantry), this stone whose protection and deciphering I've entrusted to you is the pearl, the oriental sapphire that I'll hand over to my beloved wife, who will wear it figuratively in her crown of an empress. And, of course, Joséphine will do with the stone what she likes. Break it, sell it, put it on a shelf over the fireplace so the darkest side refracts the heat from the logs, give it to the servants: the material fate of objects doesn't matter to me. By the way, I assume that over the course of the trip you'll have taken precautions to make legible copies of the symbols, so that all of the information contained . . ."

Andrei nodded in confirmation. Napoleon went on.

"Eternity is in love with the productions of time. This explains the descent of Christ from the cross and what I feel for my idiot of a wife. Why so much zeal for Egyptology? Because what we can learn from ancient Egypt no longer means a thing. If you want a Frenchman to be sincere, taking into account that he has Italian blood: Joséphine doesn't mean a thing to me either, and for this very reason she's become precious to the point that I'd do the impossible to recover her. Loot treasures, sacrifice armies, relinquish empires. If hermeneutics is the effort, as bold as it is useless, to make a decayed meaning contemporary, then let me tell you, the entire Egypt campaign is no more than one further attempt to resurrect the meaning of my sacrifice at the altar of love. A room, mine, a bed, mine, and Joséphine and I, naked, playing. She used to wrap me in bandages and tug on them and I'd spin like a top and we'd laugh and she loved me, I swear to you she once loved me. And I promised her we'd go on vacation together, to take salt baths in Lake Mariout—which I now know is empty and dead, just like me. We'd lie there next to each other until the sun roasted us, two mummies preserved by nature in their romantic immersion. Eternal. That's why I no longer have any choice but to be Napoleon Bonaparte, the conqueror, the husband of posterity. A sad consolation. But that's life, no? One flies like an eagle, another slithers like a snake. You just never know which beast you are."

11

On August 23, 1799, Napoleon left Egypt and returned to France. A few days later my great-grandfather also left the country, but instead of returning to Europe, he decided to plunge into the depths of Africa. All trace of him was lost; some say they saw him wrapped in a caftan, leaning on the straw and mud walls of the Berbara citadel as if sinking into their shadow, begging for sustenance as he displayed a mutilated leg; others claim the description is correct, but the setting and oriental attire correspond to the region of Persia. There are those who swear they came across him practicing fasting and prayer mounted on a column, while yet others saw him trafficking opium across the border from China . . . At bottom, these are just versions of the exoticist literature in fashion at the time, which would be picked up again and given a new twist in the works of the devotees of absinthe. What's known for certain is that a few months later my great-great-grandfather reappears in Amsterdam: he's dark as a Moor, burned by multiple suns. His distant air captivates the ladies, including Alicia Varmon, who catches sight of him at a café and approaches, taking him for a stranger.

Alicia Varmon and Andrei Deliuskin married on August 1, 1801. The wife's sizable fortune let the family enjoy a comfortable lifestyle. As was his habit, Andrei spent the days studying and working. He wrote. He was, in short, the only *uomo universale* our species has known since the poisoning of the Renaissance man Pico della Mirandola. His investigations, treatises and essays comprised some hundred manuscripts, venturing into all branches of knowledge. Unhappily, after his premature end—one day, distracted by his affairs, he went out walking without a coat and got caught in the rain, resulting in a cold, followed a few weeks later by pneumonia and death—his widow decided to donate all his papers (with the exception of the *Instrumental Anatomy of Political Praxis*, which the youngest child, Esau Deliuskin, insisted on keeping) to the Amsterdam Public Library, where they succumbed to the flames in the famous fire of 1824.

Alicia Varmon and Andrei Deliuskin had three children, in this order: Athanasius, Elias and Esau.

Athanasius turned out to be a perfectly normal person, someone who never stood out in any field. There's nothing more to say.

The second, Elias, inherited the artistic streak of Frantisek and Jenka, his paternal grandparents. He had a natural gift for music and might have come to be a notable performer of wind instruments . . . Unfortunately, from earliest childhood he had suffered from a deficiency of the acoustic nerve, which had vast repercussions on his mood. As soon as he began to play, the certainty filled him that he could no longer stop. He saw himself forced to avoid any moment of silence between notes, because at that instant a precipice might open up, created exclusively so that he would fall inside. For a steadier or less disturbed spirit, this apparent limitation would have presented itself as a firmament of unexplored possibilities: a vaulted realm of stars in a continuous stream of sound, the accelerated performance ablaze with its unstoppable succession, or—just the opposite—a consummate explosion, the supernova of a single note. Once this perspective had been introduced, the consequences would forever have been happy ones: he'd then face the question of whether to wager on the work that lasted as long as its performer's life in ideal conditions, and focus on writing and playing his own work, or dedicate himself to the invention of new mechanisms to produce independent musical registers, through the fabrication of instruments that served as automatons . . . Two possible ways to have enjoyed a productive life in music . . . But since madness is almost never a source of inspiration, but rather pure and simple human misery, Elias, despite having almost all the cards for triumph in his hands, could inhabit only the narrow fringe of terror made up of those silences he so desperately sought to avoid. In conclusion, and although his performances anticipated by over a hundred years the invention of free jazz (a kind of music prohibited in all asylums), he was respected and admired by nobody, spent his life a lunatic and died an idiot.

The last, my grandfather Esau, is the protagonist of the third book in this chronicle of my family's geniuses.

BOOK 3

ESAU DELIUSKIN

Landscape painting could never have been invented in the Sahara Desert.
—LEON TROTSKY, *My Life*

1

Is the defender of the paternal legacy a figure who courts the abyss?

Andrei Deliuskin's *Instrumental Anatomy of Political Praxis* begins with a series of forceful assertions: "To propose love as a form of behavior, to understand it as a manual of procedures, to claim knowledge of the norms of its intimate grammar, is to condemn a naïve subject to failure; life is an unprecedented wager directed toward a future reality, which by definition is forever postponed." One might even say these phrases describe the limits of the Napoleonic project in its entirety. For Esau Deliuskin, his father's book—the luminous tip of the iceberg of a monumental body of work—formed a fulcrum and lever that, if properly used, would change the world. The life of my family's third genius was arguably a radical and moving way of putting into practice the sentence quoted above. In order to bring Andrei's message into reality, Esau disdained his own singularity and became everyone, nobody and no one at the same time; so intensely did he want to transform what existed (an act of the will that requires a tremendous capacity to love our species), he barely had enough affection left for two individuals he never saw. Esau was made of the same stuff as those who turn away from the lifeboat after a shipwreck and sink into the waters, admiring the shimmer of the Universe. The cold signals of the guiding lights, which for others would be beacons, would for him represent the eyes of his father examining him from the beyond, scrutinizing his soul to see whether he'd been able to position himself at the level of expectations. Of course, this gaze into the void was not the result of Andrei's intentions, but an effect of the rigor his son was determined to apply to the chosen task.

As a boy, and as soon as he learned to read, Esau decided to shut himself away in his room, depriving himself of any contact with family members. They left food in front of his door; when he was hungry, he'd open it, drag the plate inside and shut it again. His mother never knew what to do with him, and considered him to be a kind of monster. There was no way he could be a son of hers, since he lacked her glamour, charm and gift for people. Thinking it over, neither did he possess a single atom from poor Andrei, who'd been a lovable man, albeit terribly boring, always scribbling nonsense and poking about in old papers. Yet even though there didn't exist, nor ever could, the slightest relation between the three of them, by means of a strange transitivity of thought, every time Alicia Varmon, Deliuskin's widow, contemplated Esau with a blend of repulsion and uneasiness, the kind found in mothers who have suffered a profound disappointment, she wondered about her reasons for having "made a family" with the father. Was it perhaps because Andrei had been the sole witness to her only true slipup, the observer of the little secret (her blossoming garden) that had joined her fleetingly to Martha Velin? Alicia didn't know what conclusion to draw in this regard, so as usual, she drew none at all. Waves of ignorance lead people like her to cast works of the quality of her dead husband's into the vast seas of oblivion, and years later placidly succumb to their own fate, forever ignorant about the magnitude of the catastrophe they've unleashed. At any rate. She was what she was, and one April afternoon in bed she kicked the bucket. Her children didn't spend much time crying over her. Alicia Varmon was quickly laid to rest in hallowed ground, and they had to occupy themselves with hiring lawyers to sue for what was left of her inheritance (the third-person plural pronoun should exclude Elias, who could do barely anything but sit in a chair and shiver, his dry lips resting on the mouthpiece of a saxophone in his mother's empty room). It was an unsuccessful struggle, to judge from results. The descendants of Andrei Deliuskin and Alicia Varmon ended up on the streets. For Esau, these circumstances helped him to discover and evaluate the negative virtue of rapaciousness, as well as notice that he had talents for leadership and combat. Man is the wolf of man: he became the leader of a small gang that appropriated the possessions of the rich and distributed them among the needy, in whatever way they liked. As he helped property to circulate and bore witness to the sudden heating of those masses of frozen energy, Esau would experience spikes of wild joy. Such emotions can be linked to a phenomenology of the sacred, except in this case they had nothing to do with the perfect gradations of asceticism. During these convulsions of free will, Esau also discovered the ecstasies of the flesh and, on more than one occasion, experimented with the taste of blood; everything seemed to him underwhelming. The world was an object to be corrected, and according to what was written in his father's book, which he was able to conceal from the inspection of the creditors' flunkies, he was the one destined to take it upon himself to achieve it. He thus came to the obvious conclusion that the actions carried out until that moment had been rudimentary trials for the deed to come. But the future lacks a definite structure. What to do?

As Esau and his gang roam around Europe in a frenzy of exaction and distribution, he considers his next steps. Soon it becomes clear the good times are coming to an end. One of his men is arrested during a robbery. In another heist, his second-in-command dies. The general feeling of carte blanche disappears; they're not invincible or invisible anymore, they're not immortal. Whose fault is it? Esau must parade his bravery to avoid a challenge to his leadership, and even though he's unrivaled at body-to-body combat, he knows that the attempts at rebellion are just the beginning of a series that will inevitably end with his replacement, perhaps death. Less to survive than to triumph, he plots an event whose consequences will uproot his men from their condition as furtive and petty thieves, and elevate them to a heroic dimension. It has to do with eliminating one of the primary figures from the Central European map. Esau calculates that with the assassination, the volatile political stability of the region will go up in flames, just as when someone holds a match to the edge of a spider's web first to eliminate the gossamer, then to scorch the disgusting black body of the spider itself (the Austro-Hungarian Empire crouched at the center). The plan is perfect. Everything has been taken into consideration: the cry of alarm, the guards' reactions, the simulated flight toward the street of the ambush, the bomb, the hidden sharpshooters, the famous man's death. But something goes wrong, the archduke escapes and Esau ends up being the only one arrested.

They tie him down, they beat him until he passes out, they move him in black carriages; every time he wakes, he feels the rattling of the vehicle and the increasing heat. At some point his captors begin to speak an unknown language.

At the end of the trip he's abandoned in a cell. The surroundings distract him. Faraway dunes shifting in the wind, palm trees. If what he sees through the barred window isn't a curtain painted with the deliberate aim to confuse him, then it's possible he finds himself in a penal institution, one of those in the lost provinces of the vast colonies still maintained by empire. Nobody visits him, nobody bothers him; once a day he receives a bowl with a concoction that upsets his stomach as soon as he drinks it. The days are suffocating, the nights freezing. Fleeting stars dart across a transparent sky. Esau looks at them, or doesn't. Most of the time he remains lying on his pallet. He closes his eyes and thinks, or sleeps, or listens to the murmurs outside. His attention is drawn by a dissonant music, a song or lamentation that comes from a nearby cell or fortress. At first it seems to be a mere slur of syllables and vocals, joined by whim; then he discovers it's the sentence that determines the cadence, not vice versa. From there it's just a step to learning the system's rudiments, the syllables' principles; in due course, the low- and high-pitched tones also begin to add fragments of meaning. The music is always identical and repeats over the hours, with the emphasis of grief. By sharpening his hearing, he discovers that what sounds like a lament of love is really the intonation of a political speech, and also understands there isn't one singer but two, the dominating voice and the dominated, like the snake and the branch on which it rests. In this bond, the dominant voice proposes that submission to the regime is the only happiness possible. The second voice, less firm, slipping its tremulous harmony into the silences left by the other, can propose only shy objections, which are rhythmically dismantled by the first. It's obvious there is an agreement between the first and second voice; beneath the appearance of contrast, the second utters only phrases the first can refute, suggesting all opposition derives from a feeble understanding of the reasons presented by the dominant voice.

Esau understands that the music encodes his current position: his captors, whoever they are, want to enlighten him about what's happened. If they've taken the trouble to keep him alive until now, when it would have been so easy to shoot him and toss the corpse in a well, it's because they've decided to use him as a dialectical representative in a cycle where his assassination attempt is read as a negative moment within an overall process aimed at strengthening the regime. (*Instrumental Anatomy of Political Praxis* predicts this and other contingencies.)

Clearly my grandfather doesn't know the language well enough to be sure his interpretation is the correct one. But it's intellectually possible to establish this relation and—even more stimulating for him—think of reversing it. His task would thus become to write lyrics and translate them so they could be sung in that language. His song would reveal the truths hidden by the official model. And with luck, if he finds the appropriate channels of diffusion, it will produce the understanding necessary in listeners so they apply themselves to transforming the world. The only problem is: how to find an acolyte, or better yet a translator, and after that musicians and singers, from a solitary confinement cell?

2

The director of the prison enters, greets Esau and says:

"I imagine you'll have found everything as comfortable as can be under the present circumstances, and that being shut away in isolation has helped you discover that true happiness is to be savored in life's little things. A ray of sun filtering through a tiny window, a cool dawn, the gentle way the hours slip by when one is lucky enough to do nothing. They can say what they want, but you yourself are an example we live in the best of all possible worlds. When have you ever seen a crime punished with a privilege? You should be grateful for the treatment being given to you. Look at those shiny cheeks of yours! You'd see them if you had a mirror. But let me just say that you now have the rested look of someone no longer pestered by everyday problems, the same happy look as a grandmother who's just knitted a blanket for her grandchild. You can't imagine your face when you arrived! An anxious fanatic, warped by the need to understand, consumed by hate. Have you reflected on all this? Is the peace that enlivens your expression a consequence of meditation and repentance? I still don't know, and I've dedicated myself to observing you. I have an infinite number of ways to do so. I've lost sleep following every variation on the map of your face. You could say I've transformed into a specialist in the topography of your soul, if a prisoner's mug can be taken as a faithful mirror, the expression of his sensibility. Let's suppose it can be. Are you cozy here? Is your pillow fluffy? Are you eating well? You may wonder why I take so much trouble over a simple inmate. There are two reasons. The first is of a personal order: I consider myself to be a charitable being. The second, of a professional order, is that I'm responsible for your education. My task is to make you a new man. And to do so I must accompany you in the revision of your past behaviors. In this sense, we must begin with an analysis of your failed attempt on the archduke. You will agree with me that your action resulted from a gross error of perspective, which was to take for granted that individuals are the actors of history. No? You don't think so? What a shame. Well then, patience. Let's go back to the start. The attempt. You thought by assassinating the archduke you could . . . you would achieve . . . But the reality, my dear guest, is that society produces archdukes all the time. If the social order were the equivalent of a game of skittles in which every archduke represents an individual pin, and your bomb had been devastatingly efficient, a ball able to knock down all the pins (archdukes) with a single bowl, then what's certain is that immediately the pinboy—the *system insofar as system*—would have put back the very same pins (archdukes) or, failing this, other identical ones to replace them. Do you think that every individual is unique and inimitable? This is true when applied to the cosmos of the romantic sensibility. I myself, who consider my being exceptional—and don't ask why, as it'd take hours, months, to give you just the barest introduction to the marvels I contain—I myself, at least in theory, am replaceable. Isn't there a horror in that? Yet it's the way of things. Every human being is at once an unexplored universe and a worthless heap of dross. Obviously you could argue that your terrorist activity doesn't operate solely through actions (a shot fired that changes everything) but also takes place in the universe of signs. The message of the archduke's death would thus have been: 'Everything that exists succumbs; even Power collapses.' An instructive demonstration aimed at the masses, one might say. But allow me two observations here, whose relevance won't escape your perceptive nature. First observation: if the attempt on the archduke was an effort to demonstrate the necessarily bloody character of a libertarian alternative—'The flowers of the revolution are watered with the blood of oppressors'—then in principle you'll admit that this attempt was a failure, since no one—except us, the servants of the State who worked to prevent it—found out about the matter. The archduke himself remains unaware he was about to be hit by a bullet. And this is because: a) the archduke has more important things to worry about, and it wouldn't help the performance of his functions in any way should part of his attention be occupied with speculating about delicate questions regarding survival; b) as I've told you before, at an individual scale the archduke is no more than a puppet, a sluggish bass string, a mere pawn in the greater game of politics. So why on earth should we take the trouble to warn him about nothing? Better to let him keep strutting about, here and there. Now let's pass to the second observation: Power. The topic of Power. Let's imagine a successful attempt: one where the archduke and his archducal carriage filled with children, fleas, shields, banners, wife, diplomas, wigs, powder compacts and lap-dogs go flying through the air. What would have happened? What *real* transformation would have followed? Let's even pretend that the pinboy dies and there are no more archdukes. Then what? The State passes into criminal hands, and from a situation of opposition you move into a role of Power . . . Don't you think that at this very moment, or after a few months, a new terrorist would appear trying to eliminate you, to take your place in turn, and so on *per saecula saeculorum . . .*?"

"But . . ." says Esau.

"Don't interrupt. I haven't given you permission to speak! In our respective positions, I'm the one assigned to ease you of the burden of trusting in the importance of the pronounced word. I hope that

224 — Daniel Guebel

one day you thank me for the favor. People think that just because they speak, they utter some truth. And this is false, if you'll allow me the syllogism. What was I saying? Ah. You thought that if the archduke died as a result of your actions, the revolution . . . But why create the revolution, a revolution, any revolution? *What for?* Pascal's argument is perfect, applied to the knowledge of divinity and personal salvation. God as target practice. If he exists and we believe in him, we'll hit the bull's-eye of faith and get it right until kingdom come. Eternity is the best investment on the stock exchange. And if God doesn't exist, well, we made the effort to believe and didn't lose anything that wasn't already lost. But this argument is completely fallacious as applied to earthly subjects. Before I go on with my reasoning: a friend claims the best proof of God's nonexistence is faith. If He existed, then belief wouldn't be necessary: we'd have evidence of His being. In the same way, the best proof a revolution doesn't exist is the hope it will at some point finally happen. Let's go on now. But first . . . is it clear to you that my previous comments have been made in a personal capacity, and that in my role as a public servant of the State, I am a firm defender of Revealed Truths? In this sense, I stand by Spinoza and his *Ethics*: 'We must love God without expecting anything in return.' (How curious a mathematician came up with a formula not based on calculation!) Naturally, in our respective situations, you are in the place of 'we must' and I in that of 'God.' And yet look how things are: I show up to this cell in person to offer you my complete affection, my total protection. And in return I ask for nothing. Yes, nothing. Let's be honest, what could I expect of you? How free you must feel now, enlightened by my words. You, who thought yourself capable of everything, discover your boundless nullity; nothingness opens all paths, although that doesn't mean when I leave I'll forget to shut the cell door. Well. Let's continue. Where were we? The revolution. The revolution, which is the adult

version of the children's tale of earthly paradise, promises an absolute change in the usual parameters. Transformation of the world,
alteration of experience, happiness, vital plenitude. Do you believe
in this stuff? Do you *really* believe in it? And yet it's false, my dear
friend, all of it is false! A hoax stubbornly defended by weak minds
that presume to be educated, to cultivate the ideas in fashion.
(Could someone tell me why the blazes *thought* should be made
contemporary? When and how does thought grow out of date,
such that it must be 'modernized'?) If I may say so . . . You, and
people like you, don't have the slightest idea of the damage that
you do with all this secular preaching about revolution. On this
point, I take off my hat to the clergymen, who strive Sunday after
Sunday to spread the consolations of the otherworldly tale from
their pulpits, no doubt the only happiness within reach for popular consumption. Imagine for a moment the triumphal realization
of this 'revolutionary change'! What would happen with these
domesticated, brainless, undernourished masses if today they all at
once found their every demand satisfied, even beyond their own
expectations? Look at them. Look at the restless flock. Its name is
Legion; now it has nothing to desire, nothing to dream, nothing to
protest. What would happen? Can you tell me? No. Obviously.
You are silent. Paradoxically, your egalitarian spirit has begun to
suspect that in silence you might tap into some principle of superiority. You think so, but it's not true. You're silent, first of all, because
I told you not to speak, and second of all, because you've been
defeated. To speak would imply a recognition of the truth and a
verdict of the facts. What would happen if those in the herd were
submitted to the terrible experience of seeing their longings materialize? Tell me that! I'll say it: as an effect of the sudden increase in
the capacity for discernment, they'd surrender to anguish and
atheism, the requirement for pure intelligence and also the condition for subsequent unhappiness. To be intelligent is to be unhappy,

my dear inmate, and I know what I'm talking about, because I am the most wretched of men. Is this what you want? To transform the world as we see it today into a world of unhappy people? Is that your revolutionary change? Mamma mia! Why such perversity? Don't answer me. Don't say a thing. I'll leave you. I think that's enough. I'll go. For now. I hope you stay here thinking about our little conversation. Goodbye. But what's wrong? Eh? What's wrong? On your face I see an expression of doubt, reserve, even disgust. It makes me think of the look of someone at an evening gala where everything should smell of roses who suddenly gets a whiff of an unexpectedly vulgar sabotage, an inappropriate scent. Let's get to the point. You're silent—you resist. You imagine, aware as you are of our respective positions, that you're not in objective conditions to formulate scruples, intervene in a decisive manner, short-circuit my speech with an objection whose current blazes through what you judge to be the error or falsity of my words. But I'd invert the matter a little. Regardless of the role I perform in this penal institution, a fundamental brace in the scaffolding of the State, do you think what I say is less true because I say it? Do you assume that truths are relative to the power or lack of power seemingly granted to the individuals who pronounce them? Now, yes, I will leave you. I must go to the last turret, into the raw open air, where I'll feed the pigeons. I'll fill my hands with kernels of corn, and let them perch on my shoulders, eat and defecate on me. You should mull this over. But what is it? Say once and for all what you want to say! Speak, or at least make explicit the meaning of your silence! I know already. I talk about 'meaning' and 'explicit,' and you translate: 'truth.' You think that although I'm asking you to spread truth among us, what I'm really proposing is for us to agree on the convenience of spreading lies over the planet. Is that true? Yes, it's true, if we attribute to these words the value of the revelation of a hidden content, as in your case, and not, as in mine, the value of the preservation of already existing values. I, my dear friend—have I already mentioned it?—believe that things are good the way they are, and that a little deceit—a lie, if you like; a cooing, a consolation—harms no one. Think, for instance, of women. I don't mean right now. Soon you'll have hours and hours to think of them. With luck, in a few months you'll be able to think about nothing but what you've been deprived of. Women. You, surely, are one of those gentleman of the view that one must always tell the truth to women, whether they ask for it or not. For someone like you, a man who cheats on a woman is no longer a man, but a scoundrel. Very well. Let me first tell you what distinguishes a gentleman from a scoundrel, then we'll analyze the behavior that best conforms to moral principles. In my opinion, a gentleman is one who, having deceived himself regarding his own conditions, wraps a woman in veils of promise, marries her and accomplishes the mutual ruin of both their lives. A scoundrel, in contrast, has judged his options from the start, coldly and rationally, and foreseeing the results of his behavior, administers his assets like an expert, with the objective that the resulting disappointment—a disappointment inherent in every human doing—will at least bring forth some positive consequence. A scoundrel anticipates with melancholy precision the time of the end of illusions, manipulates the course of events and adapts himself to existing possibilities. The most consummate example of scoundrels I know are the procurers, also known as pimps. The feats of engineering that these martyrs of realism display are to be admired! With the most refined sophistries, they capture the wills of unsuspecting young women who come from the lowest strata of society, and are thus condemned to trudge along the same furrow of matrimonial exploitation, malnourished children and botched abortions already plodded by their mothers. And what do the scoundrels do to 'deceive' them? Instead of a future of relentless misery, they offer them *everything*!

And the best of it is that they fulfill the promises, in their way! Their deceptions complete, they settle these creatures into luxurious brothels, to be educated in the arts of love and seduction; introduced to people of varied customs, cultures and social strata; taught languages; and, in short, made women of the world. And at what cost? In exchange for the surrender of that little thing, that glistening rosy nothing that slashes their inner thighs, and thanks to the generosity of their procurers, these women, after a few years leading a life of entertainment, now in full knowledge of the riches of life and in the prime of their age and learning, can retire to enjoy their income. What can you propose that resembles this in any way? What does the revolution have to offer, compared to the model of cooperative feeling, spiritual progress and administrative wisdom offered by the procurers? I'd even say that for me the brothel represents the ideal of social functioning, and don't hesitate to recommend to all the second-rate political theorists who bandy about outmoded pipe dreams that they study it with great care. You will say, repeating my words: *the girls have been deceived.* Or that even if they take home half the profits, as is often the case, *they remain the victims of an initial deception.* From the factual point of view, this is true. But so what? Isn't it also true that they receive far more than what they imagined as compensation? To put it another way, doesn't it offer them precisely the dose of fantasy and martyrdom to which every female aspires, by legitimate right? Isn't this to give a woman more than she longs for, more than she'd dare request, touching the central point of her desire? What husband could hope to offer such a gift? Leaving out the absolutely secular nature of the matter, and this is the last thing I'll say to you for the moment, in my eyes these procurers are the contemporary version of saints."

3

After the director of the penal institution left, Esau contemplated the reasons for his visit. The way he saw it, the director had come to fulfill the expectations of a ritual, one in which the authority appears before the detained in order to bring about an act of contrition. Since in his case he hadn't shown any hint of accepting the rules of this game, it was to be expected that as a consequence he'd be submitted to reprisals. Esau prepared himself for the torture session by making an exhaustive inventory of the methods to inflict pain. Each individual torment formed a separate chapter: there was no way to compare the rack with the extraction of fingernails, impalement with the bruising of internal organs . . . he had to number each sector of the body and divide it into subsections, take into account the degrees of suffering, differentiate the instruments used in accordance with their specific aims (bleeding, tearing, searing, pressing, flaying, et cetera). Obviously, this anticipation wouldn't help him to alleviate the pain, but he was consoled by the idea there was nothing new about it.

For the time being, however, nothing happened. The days went by with the morbid weariness of expectations unrealized. Was this blow suspended in the air a perfection of his martyrdom? After a while, Esau grew fed up. In some way he'd become indifferent to his future; to be imprisoned was just like being on the outside, save for the absence of the physical detail of weather. Years before, his father Andrei had described to him the impression of extreme solitude and independence that some Bedouins had made on him, lost as they were in the contemplation of bonfires smoldering in the desert night. "Maybe," he'd told him, "they don't need to talk, since they speak endlessly with demons." Something similar happened to him as he now incessantly repeated in his mind the only event that had taken place since his arrival at the prison: the visit from the institution's director. Maybe that—he told himself— had been the chance to implement his plan for rebellion. The director had spoken without drawing a breath, preventing him from answering. And why would he have acted like this, if not from a certain prior knowledge of his defeat? Victory, on the other hand, needs no verbal affirmation: its existence justifies itself.

Esau understood that the director of the institution would not repeat his visit.

One day, while leaving the bowl with his food, the guard let a whip fall on the floor of the cell. It was obvious it wasn't a blunder: Esau was being invited to use the instrument against the guard himself, who had been made a token of sacrifice. Resolved not to obey, Esau began to lash his own body.

As soon as the first drops of blood welled up, the director of the penal institution entered and jerked the whip from his hands.

"What are you doing? Do you call this good behavior?" he asked. "Do you think by putting yourself in my place you make me superfluous? Are you trying to teach me a lesson? If that's your aim, let me say that you still don't grasp a thing. My task isn't to rid myself of your person, but to keep you from harming yourself. Doesn't your attitude shame you? You, who imagined you were carrying out a universal good when you tried to murder an individual, now assume the role of victim with pathological delight. Wretched impostor! If you had a minimum of personal dignity, you'd at least try to grab the whip from me."

And having said this, he offered it to Esau, who didn't make the slightest move except to keep his eyes squeezed shut until he heard the door close.

The next day, the same guard offered to help him escape from the prison. "Flight is an absolute imperative for free spirits," he told him. Esau wanted to know his motive. The guard said he was guided only by the sentiment of humanity. Also, he knew that followers of his were waiting on the outside. Esau asked if this meant his ideology had expanded, but the guard didn't know how to answer: he was only a simple guard, one who didn't follow politics.

They swapped clothes. For a while Esau did turns through the passageways. Architecturally, the prison wasn't overly elaborate, and was very far from complying with any heavy allegorical ideals of oppression or redemption. He went up and down staircases without knowing where he was headed. After all that time locked away, he tended to search out dark corners and closed spaces. Open areas repelled him. Without noticing it, he'd walked around the prison in a direction away from the exit, and all at once, after climbing a steep staircase, he found himself facing a last door. He opened it, convinced that on the other side new jailers would be waiting. Inside he found evidence of a gloomy sanctuary, with the sadness that haunts every demonstration of authority. It was the office of the institution's director. A half-written letter lay on the desk. Or maybe the pages before and after had flown out the open window. My grandfather read:

> . . . the curious thing about modern life, auditor sir, is that every biography can now without loss be reduced to a pattern. As far as the object of your inquisition goes, I am in conditions to reveal to you that all steps are being carried out in accordance with your felicitous planning;

that is, I am slowly turning into the intellectual master of
our prisoner. The unquestionable benefits of doing so . . .

Esau tore up the page and threw the pieces into the air. Then he
retraced his steps. No one stopped him. After a while, the gate
for the exit came into view. He passed the checkpoints and went
out into the street. For a few meters he walked in expectation of
shouts and voices calling halt, then giving the order to shoot. The
outer wall of the prison cast its shadow over a town square. He
lost himself in the crowd. His appearance didn't draw anyone's
attention. In a public bathroom he shaved, washed his body and
exchanged clothes with someone else. He found a little money
in his new trouser pockets. He sat for a while in a café to see a
bit of life. The alcohol went to his head; he wandered without
destination. Battlements, terraces, faces, smells, animals. Confinement had accustomed him to extolling the virtues of scarcity;
now the proliferation of impressions made him feel the loss of
meaning. The world had become a marketplace. And where were
those acolytes, those companions in the cause that the guard had
mentioned? He went into a small restaurant and was served a dish
made with crude ingredients he didn't recognize. Barbarism began
with the palate. Where was he? For a moment he thought he'd got
lost in time, that he was living in a version of Egypt in which the
Mamluks had defeated Napoleon's army, and where he was his
own father, taken prisoner. He fell asleep leaning over his plate.
When he woke up, it was growing dark. A dying red sun baked
the whitewashed walls. Esau climbed uphill for a while. Since he
didn't know where to go, he felt nostalgia for the certainties about
the immediate that the prison had provided him. It was obvious
they had let him escape so he'd grasp the convenience of intern-
ment. At the end of a nearly perpendicular street (weeds growing
between the bricks in the walls; a black dog urinating without

raising its leg, like a lady), he heard a "psst." A veiled woman, resting her elbows on the sill of an oval-shaped window, was gesturing toward him. "So this is the East," he thought, crestfallen. What change could be produced from the most backward part of the globe? The woman called out to him again. "Ara, ara. Mit, mit." Or something like that. Esau came in through the door at street level, which opened onto an inner garden, a tiny pointillist reproduction of the gardens in fairy tales, complete with ridiculous glass chimes and hollow reeds hanging from trees: wind music. "Sut, sut." A soft hand led him to the bedrooms of the house; other hands undressed him; a woman kissed him; he was naked; his body was burning. Esau couldn't recall any experience like this one. Wrapped in the words of an unfamiliar language, he felt racked by tenderness. Before falling asleep, lulled by this voice, he heard himself say that he loved her.

When he woke up, he found himself in the prison again. It didn't surprise him. At every moment throughout his day of apparent freedom, he'd noticed a series of movements being carried out around him, a choreography of secret guardians who took turns to monitor his steps. His flight had thus been a premeditated act devised by the enemy. Perhaps it was a cruel joke meant to destroy his mood, or a test to check the security conditions of the prison, or maybe they'd tried to use him as a lure, to find out whether he'd make contact with the network of his political organization. In any case, what drew his attention was the number of resources used by power to anticipate his actions, as if these were not terribly limited at present. Such disproportion was evidence that his own group had overestimated its revolutionary potential . . . and a further proof that he had to rise to the level of the confrontation. He couldn't be less intelligent than the enemy! In this sense, if—as he took for granted—the prison authorities had made it easy for

234 ➡ Daniel Guebel

him to leave with the intention of using him to detect and capture other political militants, then his task wasn't to "demonstrate his innocence" and offer a "truth" linked to the present, but to produce a mirage of this existence—which might well be genuine in the future—so that a good part of his oppressors' energies would aim to combat him in the wrong time and place. The question was how to create the illusion of a solid political party, a phantom organization—how could he produce a simulacrum? Was it possible to construct a reality that, although lacking a material base, still possessed enough corporeality to make his jailers rush toward it in the attempt to dominate it, and through the very dynamic of political infiltration, which acts through dissimulation and masks, end up providing it an existence of its own? This was the essential problem!* Applying himself to resolving it was his challenge for the moment. He was in an ideal position. In prison he had nothing to lose, and he was no longer dominated by the terror of being pursued, captured and locked up in jail, which had tortured him during periods of freedom.

---

* "The dynamic of political transformation does not respond to the laws of dialectic but to the impulse (ouroboros in shape, atavistic and by nature suicidal) of the scorpion. A spy or agent of the State who embarks on a sting operation in the ranks of a revolutionary party must by necessity make an effort to exhibit—make visible—his 'revolutionary credentials' in order to dissipate any suspicion regarding his true condition. For this reason, in revolutionary activity, it often happens that undercover operatives are the very ones who carry out the tasks necessary for change, and even come to sacrifice themselves for them. An agent provocateur must make himself worthy in the eyes of the 'legitimate members of the party,' going further than anyone else. For example, they might kill a minister in incredible circumstances, demonstrating an extreme courage and an unbending faith in the cause. It is therefore possible that, given the right conditions, the social revolution ends up being the work of a branch of the intelligence forces that carries out its task of infiltrating the revolutionary group with a thoroughly consistent logic" (Andrei Deliuskin, *Instrumental Anatomy of Political Praxis*).

4

No sooner had Esau begun to reflect on these questions than he received a visit from the director of the penal institution, wearing a doctor's coat and sporting a panama hat. He gestured for him to get out of bed:

"I was hard at work drawing up requests for communiqués, replies to solicitudes, petitions of transfer and orders of execution, when a question occurred to me that I judge to be quite timely, one that I thought you might be the suitable person to answer. Naturally, this isn't the appropriate milieu for conversation: the walls are listening."

Once Esau had stood up, the director of the penal institution bent down and fastened a kind of silver anklet ending in a chain to his left ankle, wrapping the end around his own wrist.

"Don't feel like a dog, man, because during a walk it's never clear who leads who."

They left the cell without a word, and set out walking through the desert. My grandfather had lost the habit of exercise, and every so often he tried to stop and catch his breath, but the director yanked on the chain, forcing him to go on. When Esau fell on his face, he dragged him along for a stretch. Instead of mocking his physical inferiority, he encouraged him with tender words, and warned him about the risks of falling asleep in the sun. He even allowed himself an obscene joke:

"Millions of years ago this was a sea, and so every grain of sand is the dust of a clam. But why do you feel the need to sink your nose into it right now? Do you really miss the scent of a woman that much?"

Later he added:

"What happened to your alleged spirit of rebellion? We're completely alone. I don't understand why you haven't tried to take me by surprise. With luck, you could strangle me. Nor would it be a bad idea to try and kick me in the balls. What do you say? If you hit the target, you'd be free. Don't you realize? Free, free as the wind, free as a bird that's escaped its cage. You don't want to fight me hand to hand?"

Gripped by a strange sensation of detachment, Esau understood that all these jests cloaked the intention of ending his life here in the open air.

"I'm going to plant myself right here," he said.

"That's what I call a vision of the future," taunted the director: "To morph into a tree, in this desert of all places! Come on, let's go. On the other side of the dune we'll stop for refreshment." He shook the chain.

A white silk tent. Table, chairs, sofa beds, large pillows. And food and drink in plenty.

"Water, wine, beer, kirsch royal?" said the director. "No? Would you prefer something solid? A finely sliced salami? A sliver of cold blood sausage? Should I make you a little prosciutto-and-cheese sandwich? Not that either? A canapé? Why do you shake your head that way? Fleas? Very well. I wanted to ask you this question: At what point does an idealist turn into a man of ideas—that is, a businessman? That is, how much is what you know, and refuse to confess, worth? Knowledge and organization: these are the pillars that prop up my trade in the administration of captives. A business similar in every way to the one that you manage, which supplies ideological meaning and the production of revolutionary acts. If it weren't the case that mine is thriving and yours is bankrupt, I might say that we're birds of a feather. Have you accounted for that? You should settle for the possibility of being *truly* useful to someone. I tell you with hand over heart, entrepreneur to entrepreneur: you have nothing more to lose, nothing else to give in exchange for what I'm requesting. It's the moment to negotiate."

Esau didn't answer. The director sighed:

"You think you possess something valuable, something that can remain untouched by my knowledge, only because you keep it in reserve. It's one of the best strategies I know, excluding that of pretending to be a mystic or idiot. Naturally, you'll already have noted that given my command over the universe of concentration—in all senses!—I'm in a position to achieve great things. Imagine yourself, for a second, free and associated with me. What we could do! My dear friend: I propose that we use for our own benefit your ability to capture the attention of the masses . . . and charge for it. You have beliefs, I have interests: the perfect team. Have you accounted for that? *Have you accounted for it or not?*"

"But what do you want? You're my jailer . . . !" protested Esau.

"Ah, but I'm no materialist. I'd be happy just taking control of your intelligence. I propose that we enter the world of spectacle together, hand in hand. I can use my influences at the level of the central administration and succeed in getting your file lost. I've achieved more difficult things. Once this is done, and since appointments to State organizations are generally resolved by means of such dubious machinations, I'll be in the perfect conditions to have you named, for instance, Director of the National Opera. What do you think of that, eh? Nor will I reveal to you the benefits that a post of such responsibility would produce on a psyche like yours, molded by the deliriums of the aesthetic of violence! The job would make you a practical

238 — Daniel Guebel

man. Immediately. I'll bet on it. Think it over, the position is at your fingertips."

"Where do I sign?" asked Esau, reaching out his shackled arm.

The director smiled, as if he hadn't noticed the irony:

"I knew you wouldn't be such a fool . . . Now imagine yourself holding the post. I won't describe to you the office, the court of sycophants, the women who will fall at your feet, the suits cut to measure, because I know that you're a high-minded sort. Let's get to the responsibilities. As Director of the National Opera, three matters will personally concern you: artistic programming, institutional funding and individual profits. The first matter depends completely upon your judgment, as applied to the second. What do I mean? The National Opera maintains itself through subsidies, charity evenings, endowments from the Central Administration and revenues from the ticket office itself. To guarantee a high flow of capital from these sources, it's necessary to think on a grand scale and present completely inflated budgets. I want evidence of waste: sumptuous works, foreign casts, orchestras of the highest level, dazzling stage designs, regisseurs of international prestige, expensive whores, dancers, singers, et alia. So let's not delay: think of a program that pulls out all the stops. You're at complete liberty to choose the works performed. You can write them yourself and say what you feel like in them: you can be explicit, whimsical, obscene. Even revolutionary. Not a problem. The sublime work of art or the eyesore that you produce will liquefy the effect of the message within the question of form. People go to the opera to 'see,' not to 'understand.' When it comes right down to it, the content is irrelevant, because the only thing that a message stages is the fact there's someone who acts and another who watches, someone who speaks and another who listens, someone who explains and another who agrees; and both roles, from their respective positions, believe that they run the show. What does this illustrate? That whether or not representation exists, power is a binary structure that *always* remains unalterable. It's not on one side or another, but the result of a relationship between two parts. Obviously, you don't agree with me, and believe the opposite. But that's your challenge, isn't it? To demonstrate that we are the ones mistaken."

"My demonstration, were it truly successful, would have the paradoxical effect of making you rich . . ." said Esau.

"At last we're beginning to understand!" the director enthused.

"I suppose you'll have weighed the risk that this same wealth will lead you before a firing squad . . ."

"Directed by you? How tempting!"

"Doesn't it scare you?"

"On the contrary, it excites me. I adore living dangerously . . ."

"Even so, your proposal is interesting. The other question is not so much who would come see the works, but who would act in them."

"Don't imagine I'm going to enter into the fine details of cast selection . . ." said the director.

"That's not what I mean. I'm seriously considering your offer. What I'm thinking about are the performances for the masses. Those staged not in theaters, but in the great city squares."

"I can't believe my ears!" the director applauded. "The possibility hadn't occurred to me before, but it sounds simply . . . extraordinary. A real revolution! A real theater of the people! Instead of hiring a few highly expensive specialists, we'll multiply costs, not by aristocratic price but by democratic quantity, making actors out of hundreds, thousands . . . the entire mob! We can start practicing here, I mean in prison, staging rehearsals in our microcosm to figure out the best working methods. The prisoners come free, of course, and since they get bored in their cells, we'll have no problem using them. Then we'll transfer the results to a large scale. We must be rigorous. Each one of the actors chosen will earn a salary: the salary that we decide to pay, and that naturally will be much lower than the one we write down in the account submitted to our corresponding minister. Truly marvelous! You can't imagine the profit we're going to wrangle out of this . . ."

5

Back in prison, Esau slept more deeply than he had for a long time. He woke up feeling extremely fresh, renewed. The night had clarified his ideas. The revolution and his own liberation were inevitable. It was a question of mathematics. If the director of the establishment kept his word and transformed some number "x" (almost unlimited) of people in town into actors, then the value of each salary, multiplied by thousands or millions, would require a total exceeding that found in the coffers of the Ministry of Finance, which would produce an immediate liquidity crisis, debt, strikes, inflation, currency devaluation, mass bankruptcy, political chaos and finally the hoped-for revolution. But even if this didn't happen, if the number of actors ended up narrowing down so that the ministry could bear the cost, the final effect would still be favorable, insofar as that with every rehearsal, he'd be training the militants—the political actors—of an avant-garde party *financed by the State itself*. And the work would of course be a performance of the revolutionary act that would later occur in reality, on the day of the premiere, in an extremely didactic staging with perfectly defined movements aimed at the taking of power. It would be a conscientious application of the *Instrumental Anatomy of Political Praxis*, the legacy of his father.

"To think of the revolutionary act as a theatrical performance," he told himself, "to perform acts as if they were true, is ultimately

242 — Daniel Guebel

to construct them as such. At least for as long as the performance lasts. Obviously, if we understand the revolutionary act to be the theatrical act itself, then the events that take place onstage, theater and revolution, become identical. So how can this act be performed? Insofar as it is an act, it cannot be thought of as having a conclusion, because this would transform it into an anti-act—that is, nothingness. Thus, logically, the revolution performed would have to become permanent, an action not conclusive but endless, unstoppable, a series of actions that would inevitably end up radiating throughout the entire world, in such a way that a single moment, in its luminosity and simplicity, in its infinite power of enlightenment, would come to represent the whole and become the emblematic, definitive act—which in turn, and in time, would become material for another theatrical act, a second work or second act that served as a reminder of the first . . . This is what always happens when a revolution triumphs, and the apotheosis of the revolutionary takeover of power comes to be the privileged object of an official art."

Esau came to these conclusions quickly, and after a few seconds was already prepared to receive another visit from the director, to start hammering out the details of the production. But the director never showed up, even though he called out to him for hours . . . It was strange he gave no sign of life. He'd shown such enthusiasm for the project! At the time, zeal had clouded the pure shine of his eyes, and the possibility of an exponential growth in business had lent a touch of dementia to his gaze . . .

After a few days Esau had to admit the director of the penal institution wasn't as much of a fool as he'd thought. In fact, with this sudden disappearance, he'd revealed himself to be more astute than Esau imagined. So all that gastronomical display and persuasion in the desert hadn't been the miscalculation of a dupe blinded by economic considerations who overlooks the implicit consequences of his proposal, but rather an exercise in the cold manipulation of another's enthusiasm—his own. Like a magician who directs the light and shadow of a magic lantern, the director had administered his illusions to make him believe he was being offered the possibility of revolutionary fulfillment, something this functionary had ultimately been appointed to prevent. How had he been able to trick him so easily? The director was the jailer of jailers, his *political enemy*, not an agent of his liberation! And as an enemy, he'd situated him on the battlefield convenient to him. But—and for the first time Esau thought strategically—what if he made the other believe he was still entangled in his deceit? And what if he let the director think he maintained the advantage? Then . . . possessing this advantage himself, he could begin to explore the only possibility within his reach: escape.

In his cell he'd squirreled away metal spoons, blunt-tipped knives, earthenware plates, broom handles, flexible mattress springs, and all kinds of objects that could be used for either fighting or digging. Immediately, and with a ferocity that went against every principle of dissimulation, my grandfather used some of those utensils to begin chipping away at the mortar that joined his legs to the wall. After some time, he managed to free the left leg. He came up against a black base made of earth, sand and gravel, a light enough mixture. This encouraged him. Only at nightfall did he remember his cell was located high up in a projection from the main structure, which roughly imitated a mountain crag jutting over the abyss. If he stuck his hand out the little window, he should be able to feed the birds. Yet now, having at last entirely liberated himself, instead of being able to poke his head outside, he found himself at the start of a kind of cavern. What mystery was this? He ruled out a system that worked as a self-generating prolongation, a mechanism that with every wound to its matrix (every attempt at escape) responded like a microcellular organism, widening in shape and extending its pseudopods. What must really have happened is that at night, as he slept, a regiment of builders and construction workers had been toiling in complete silence to increase the thickness of the cell walls . . .

In any case, the work had to stop at some point, or else the add-on would collapse from its own weight. He would thus achieve freedom due to the efforts by his captors to keep him prisoner. And if it didn't happen this way, if the construction grew until it encompassed all regions, the entire world . . . then the conflict would change meaning, because every member of the struggle would form part of a cycle of transubstantiation, whose ultimate destiny would be included in the figure of the allegory.

But in the meantime, he had to keep digging.

The sensation of embarking on an unpleasant task soon disappeared. A rhythm imposed itself. The tools used for the work started to break. Esau went on with his fingernails. It's true that as a body decomposes, these excrescences are the last thing to stop growing, but while this body is alive and scraping against stone, they are the first to wear out. Esau tried to harden them to create a kind of protective layer, a sheath, using a mixture of clay and filings he attempted to press onto each finger with saliva; soon this mixture was tinged with blood. At least the concoction served as a healing poultice. Along the way he came across worms and maggots. Sometimes, out of fatigue and lack of air, he fell asleep halfway through a movement. His beard grew and stuck to the wall in crusts of grime, to the point that he had to tear it off to continue. Owing to differences in the consistency of materials used to build the penal institution, the tunnel sometimes advanced in a zigzag, other times in a straight line; there were moments the entrance was very wide, over half a meter high, and other moments it became a cylinder through which he could pass only by squeezing his elbows against his chest. To give his hands a rest, Esau used his teeth. His jaw grew stronger with the exercise. At some point he bumped into a lead pipe that channeled the wastewater into the ditch below; he pulled it off with a bite. Weakness and doubt were now bygone passions. He sucked hard on the damp earth and nourished himself on the grubs that sprouted from the walls. The extreme deprivation amplified his capacities. His eyes radiated light . . . Esau began to think of himself as a fireball technologically evolved beyond the merely human, the spiritual weapon of a catastrophe. One day, in the distance, he saw a speck of white dust, a tiny bit of paper that gleamed as if radiant from outside light. Was this an end to his efforts, an escape hatch? He approached, picked up the page with dirty fingers and unfolded it.

Scribbles?

Written in a handwriting he couldn't help but recognize, he read:

Half-wit, moron, filth, excrement, good-for-nothing. You're never going to achieve a thing. Infected pubic louse, nasty vermin, scum from the cesspool, shit in a jar. Death is the only way out for a numbskull in your condition . . .

6

Esau went back to his cell. Reflecting on what had happened, it seemed obvious that the paper had been placed there *so he would find it*. In a clear demonstration of power, he was being warned that his strategies of escape had been predicted and undermined in advance. The situation would have been desperate if these curses inviting him to commit suicide had not also contained a message of salvation. Because read properly—that is, inverting their premises—they conveyed accurate information, the only thing a more prudent writer would have kept to himself: the trace of their processes of reasoning. The use of the word "exit," situated as a possibility only in death, revealed they didn't imagine or expect of him anything other than one form of action: *physical* escape. And in this sense, Esau thought, the advantage could now begin to tilt in his favor, since although his captors believed they'd sized him up to perfection, and by tempting him to do away with himself, had even communicated to him the fact they considered him to be unnecessary, he, now aware of the profile they had on him, could behave *astutely* and allow them to go on expecting that in the future he'd proceed in exactly the same way as he had until that moment. This was his advantage: if he changed his method, then power, a subtle machine applied to registering a past modus operandi, would be unable to detect the variation. Here, in the unperceived difference, lay the key to his success.

And what did this mean in practice?

In the first place, that he had to keep thinking; it was a part of the struggle. To think, to think: to pass through the sieve of his mind all the grains of the message until he had extracted their golden nugget from his own senses. For instance: Why had they urged him to kill himself? Easy: because after a period of shameless flattery and obscene attempts to ingratiate himself, in order to earn his confidence and obtain information, the director of the institution had reached the conclusion that he lacked successors, disciples, followers, groups backing him . . . and hence, that he was *harmless*. Without value. Unproductive. Et cetera. What did he need to do now? Before anything else: shield himself. *Generate doubt in the enemy.* It would be essential for him to work hard at manufacturing smoke signals, signs that might be fantastic but that effectively revived suspicions about his ability to incite crowds, trigger attacks, fabricate martyrs and leaders.

Esau dedicated himself to his own salvation. As a son worthy of his father, he used the talent the latter had applied to reading the secret lines of certain writings (casting the nets of reality to trap what existed, and at the same time anticipate the mesh of what was to come) to instead design appearances of reality that summoned a court of revolutionary ghosts into being, invoked from the nothingness to disturb power. Sometimes he even found it entertaining to arrange the letters of the hieroglyphic alphabet he'd invented to unsettle his captors (twenty-six letters of an oblong shape, some of them halfway between Cyrillic and cuneiform writing, others inspired by the shapes of animals he imagined lived in the desert). Certain that his life depended on it, he made sure the repetition and permutation of these signs took on the appearance of consistency typical of every ideological message. The fact that the result bore a certain resemblance to the Syrian and demotic symbols his father Andrei Deliuskin had known how to read is by this point a mere charming detail. Esau traced out shapes in tiny writing on papers he folded an infinite number of times and hid inside bread crumbs, which he then worked into small sculptures: a house, a rifle, a sickle, a man, a pair of buttocks, a hammer. He set those pieces by the window of his cell, one after another, until the pigeons came to peck at them. His strategy was simple and effective: since the director of the establishment occupied himself personally with the well-being of these infected creatures, he wouldn't take long to notice they'd acquired a new habit. The trail would thus be prepared: as soon as the director cut open the first one to understand its death, he'd find these kneaded bread crumbs, and inside them this handwriting, from which he'd deduce that—contrary to every expectation—his prisoner was still in contact with the forces answering to him.

Yet this was only the beginning of my grandfather's task, aimed at nothing more than concentrating the enemy's surveillance forces in the wrong site. More important, of course, was to keep thinking of a way to escape prison; but above all, and this was the task of tasks, he had to find a practical method to spread a message, as simple as it was effective, that would pave the way for world revolution. Now then, how to do it? In his current state of confinement and forced anonymity, what means could he draw upon to make his ideas known? Of course, he couldn't fall into his own trap and use the pigeons. So what then? No message exists in the abstract, and he was as rich in contents to impart as he was poor in channels to transmit and portray them; he was like a current of water without a pitcher to hold it. In fact, this is exactly what the director told him one day when he entered the cell without warning:

"I must say, you're either a person of superhuman resistance or a complete fraud. You astonish and deceive me in the same instant. All this time you've spent here, and you've invented *nothing*! In prisons like this one, I've been responsible for prisoners of your category before. But were they truly of your category? They wrote. They kept a record of their thoughts. They bequeathed their ideas to humanity. Why not you? Do you consider yourself to be exceptional? Do you possess a prodigious mind able to store chapters and chapters, books and books, written entirely in your brain? Aren't you afraid that when you fall asleep, your ideas will get mixed up? And consider how the progress of science is unstoppable: one day a mechanism will be invented to absorb other people's thoughts. On that day, all of your reserve will be useless. We'll find out everything. Or maybe you aren't as intelligent as we imagined, in which case we'll pass the time analyzing incomplete phrases, stutters, cerebral belches . . . ! And the worst thing is that maybe this is really the case . . . You: an idiot who one day, by chance, decided to kill an archduke because the shine of his medals irritated you . . . while we thought you had conceived of a plan to topple contemporary civilization! Perhaps, and why not? It enters into the calculation of possibilities. Anyhow. Obviously you're an idiot who's useful to us. I'll be completely honest with you: we need the intelligence of the opposition to build a camp of experimentation, where the real is affected by the tensions of the possible. Only then will we be able to evaluate all the alternatives, all the risks. Think, and tell me what you think! But you remain silent. Until now, you haven't earned the crusts that we feed you."

For once, Esau decided to answer:

"I've thought. Your words confirm a few suspicions I've developed. This prison is identical to many others scattered over the face of the earth, and it would be easy to imagine how, if the Universe suffered from a certain limitation of variety in its design, the warden-jail-prisoner schema might repeat across the countless worlds in existence. Innumerable soap bubbles floating in the emptiness of the galaxies, repeating the figure we compose. To apply your example of the dialectic between power and opposition, with the first performing the function of current reality and the second representing the yearning of the new to exist, from my position I can recognize only that a double task awaits me. In the cosmic dimension, I must struggle to annihilate the eternal impoverishing multiplication of possibilities, in order to wager on the natural diversity and richness of the human species, that baroque animal; while in the earthly dimension, it is necessary to continue working for the construction of a world that answers to the most elevated political ideals."

"Ah, now I see where you're headed. You have considered the warden-jail-prisoner schema and asked yourself about the meaning of its tumorous growth. Well, naturally, I have an answer ready," said the director, "although I'm sure you won't share my point of view . . ."

Esau gave a polite nod.

". . . The schema in which we're included," the director went on, "is a simplified and complete representation of the model of production that has imposed itself over the entire planet, and which bears the name 'capitalism.' This model proposes the multiplication of the identical, which was discovered—mark the paradox!—after the invention of the printing press. I wager on this model. In contrast, you . . . you are part of the lyrical reaction that dreams of the survival of the unique in a period unsuited to it. The revolution is a reactionary dream of artisans, displaced by the prevailing industrial logic. Note this detail: under the reigning system of reproduction at a global (and perhaps galactic) scale, we have all become identical, because in the hypothetical situation of possessing an equal value in bills or coins, we would be in a condition to acquire an equal quantity of products. Save for the detail of the amount of capital each individual actually possesses, which makes him rich or poor, isn't capitalism the form of social relations that invokes primitive communism and perfects it? Think about it," said the director, and prepared to leave, but Esau's words kept him for a few more seconds:

"Well, the possibility also exists that in both this world and the cosmos, an infinite number of individuals exist who are just like you and me, but whose systems of relating to each other are different from the ones that join us. If that were the case, even though here it is you submitting me to the reign of your power, in another case (another world, another system), I or someone identical to me would at this very moment be eliminating you and all your alter egos, you and each of your masks and emblems, you and every single one of your horrible figures, and implementing the Revolution on an infinite scale . . ."

"The Universe as a catalog? A museum of endless rooms and objects and beings equal in appearance, but acting in different ways? What an adventure!" said the director of the institution, and left.

After that conversation, the director announced that every day Esau would carry out a series of activities linked to the hygiene and conservation of the penal institution, activities in which he would personally instruct him, as if his function were to supervise the routines of each inmate. Furthermore, he stopped addressing him by his name and number, and with great satisfaction began referring to him as "cretin" or "idiot," perhaps seeking a reaction from his prisoner. Esau responded meekly to the provocations, as if he considered it appropriate to be spoken to like this. He even started to behave in a way that justified them, reacting with bewilderment to the presumed complexities of assigned tasks, even the simplest. In a refinement of irony, the director then began to address him including the customary insult, yet accompanying it with expressions of courtesy:

"By any chance, vermin, do you think you might clean the lavatories?"

Esau replied:

"I take it as a given that such a task would exceed my abilities. At most, I believe I'd be capable of sweeping the floors."

Beyond the insults, the change in regimen was convenient for Esau; it was necessary to achieve a certain degree of visibility and give a proof of his survival, directed toward a network of solidarity that perhaps did truly exist on the outside. In fact, he had no doubt that by making him move about every corner of the institution, forcing him to polish the damp stones of the battlements and contemplate the melancholy twilights of the landscape, the director of the penal institution was using him as bait, exposing him to full view to check whether someone would make a bid for his liberation. Esau's game, in turn, had to consist of putting himself on display without endangering anyone's life. But could he send a danger signal without his captors noticing?

Soon the guards took over the business of monitoring his work and abusing him. Lacking the more refined methods of their superior, they did nothing but kick him, whip him, or smash him headfirst into the liquid and solid dregs he'd just binned. On one of these occasions, while picking the filth from his hair, my grandfather found a crumpled sheet of paper:

I remember every detail of our night together, each time I feel your children move about in my belly, Esau . . .

He was going to be a father.

7

The news changed everything. Thinking about the woman from that night of freedom was like emerging from a dream. Now he remembered the surreptitious ways he'd found to stay in contact; they'd never stopped communicating. The fact these clandestine methods, hidden even from his own awareness, surfaced only now meant the purpose of his confinement was to blur or wipe out his consciousness, a result that his captors had efficiently produced in him. The letter told him that his children would be twins, maybe identical, that an irregular band of paramilitants had entered her house and destroyed everything, and that she'd fled to save her life and the lives growing in her womb; he had to come look for them.

Naturally, given this new incentive, Esau discovered a way to escape the prison. It may seem strange that a man like him, who had meditated on every one of his steps until he was paralyzed by thought, now launched in search of the one who in his heart of hearts he called "my wife," without stopping for a moment to check the direction he'd taken in flight. All at once, my grandfather gambled everything on instinct. Even so, he did have his warnings. One night, at an inn where he'd sought refuge, he was surprised by a messenger who told him that the director of the institution had ordered him to convey his private conviction that this escape was the start of an auspicious career.

"The gentleman, my superior, assures me he's always believed in you, and wishes to express through my person the assurance of his unwavering sympathy. Best of luck!"

Having said this, the messenger withdrew.

Esau redoubled the speed of his search; he at least wanted to meet his children before he was trapped again. In any case, the farther he moved away from the prison, the greater his hopes grew. The landscapes also changed, from desert glare to barren fields. The mutilated limbs of dead warriors floated in the mist, hanging from trees. They might have been remnants of a past century or a testimony of the previous day's battle; frost preserved the remains. Human flesh was a diet like any other; in any case, it was what was available. My grandfather moved forward in the cold, tracing furrows through the snow. It wasn't unusual that in the immensity of the steppe he met with others as absorbed or concentrated as he was; the surprising thing was that others torqued their own paths to start following him. Maybe they took him for a retreating general.

Heat to cold, cold to heat. How much time passed? At some point, and even though his only thought was to unite with his family, Esau understood he had to take responsibility for the subsistence of this horde. They stopped on the banks of a river or canal. There were dozens, thousands; he gave up the count. He ordered a city to be built, since nights were harsh and the spectacle of open-air fornication upset him. As it turned out, there was barely enough material for tents. The inhabitants of neighboring populations, afraid of being looted, contributed food, materials and money. Esau sent missionaries from the settlement in every direction, with the objective of spreading revolutionary proclamations and determining the path the mother of his children might have taken. The missionaries returned in despair. He also had to take over matters of organization. While he and his people had been a sort of nomadic tribe, the illusion of variety provided by changes in scenery had reduced conflicts, but now the sedentary model made them worse. And once it became clear that the world wouldn't yield to his command, he found his capacity for authority threatened. The citadel lacked drains and fountains, and people drank from the same water in which they defecated; constructions grew helter-skelter in total disregard of his instructions to comply with urban statutes. Inaction encouraged rebellion, especially among the strong-bodied youths who hadn't been killed off by typhus or malaria. Sometimes his orders were not just flouted but done so with blatant impertinence. One day, seeing a boy playing in a swamp, he started to explain the dangers of the ooze; at first the boy seemed not to hear, then he lifted an arm as if swatting away a fly and said: "Quit bothering me." Esau couldn't understand this appalling behavior, run rampant. Had they followed him merely to scorn him?

Months passed that could be measured in years. Esau, who had imagined himself in this role—perfectly described and elucidated by his father—as the leader of an avant-garde party, now saw himself reduced to the pitiful figure of a dictator who must lead the rabble with a firm hand. Every so often he escaped for a few days and shut himself away in some caves at a half-day's gallop; there, he meditated on his experiences. He returned with a noticeable improvement in mood. Sometimes he opted for internal espionage and summary executions, other times *laissez-faire*; no one noticed the difference, except the parties involved. Nostalgia for the children he'd never met consumed his soul. Where were they, where was his wife? There was no news. He dedicated himself to growing fatter, turning brutish and forgetting all he'd previously set out to accomplish from the order and clarity of his cell. In his slovenliness he ended up looking like a petty king from some port town, while his own city, which he'd expanded without improving it, transformed into a vast colony of savages . . .

Which had its consequences.

While Esau could attribute this disorder only to the failure of his illusions and the collapse of his mood, the rest of the planet, although it had gently wiped its bottom with his ideological declamations, now attributed an increasingly subversive character to his megalopolis. That hell he renounced, which he wanted to escape, was seen by others as the fulfilled dream of a nefarious political program. Having established this misunderstanding, they made up their minds to destroy him. Just as in the former period of the Holy Alliance, it was the Prussians who sent advance troops to the bloodbath.

Of course, as soon as the enemy troops had gathered, my grandfather knew that combat would be useless; they were doomed. He didn't care too much: the experiment hadn't come off and the citadel was far from being a revolutionary state, so its disappearance would do no harm. What did worry him . . . the idea to which he couldn't bear to resign himself, was that the flames and blood would also annihilate the sign of the revolution that hadn't taken place, but whose sketched outline would be filled in, come better times. With this in mind, in the days or weeks still left to him before the storming of the encampment by the Huns, the only possibility was to stage a goodbye: the aim would no longer be to create a new society, but to produce a new meaning, a demonstration. Something that would permanently engrave itself into the most lucid minds.

What came next can be told in a few lines. Although they were used to victories following just a brief struggle, the Prussians were surprised to meet with *no* resistance. The palisades, ramparts and battlements were deserted. First they thought that all the inhabitants had abandoned the citadel, taking shelter in the night; then they were drawn toward the central plaza by a sad augural sound: the overture to the opera written by Esau Deliuskin.

Against their will, the attackers found themselves enveloped by a dazzling phantasmagoria. The wardrobes were luxurious and the fragile panels illustrated with palaces and palm trees, recalling times unknown to them. The plot of the work spoke of wars and armies, countries and passions, love and death. Taking into account the little time he had and the minimal ability of the participants he supervised, as well as his very restricted literary, imagistic and musical training, it's surprising that my grandfather was able to wield so many elements at once; his leitmotifs captivated the invading army, and under their plumes and helmets, the halberdiers had to hide their tears at this outpouring of beauty. The invading general and his officials (all of them music lovers) immediately recognized that in the entire history of the *bel canto* it was almost impossible to find another composition with as many arias and sung parts, so perfectly justified from the dramatic point of view, and with a mounting of such precision they could give the order to attack only by taking advantage of the impulse given to them by the triumphal march, in which regrettably the inhabitants of the citadel performed the role of the Egyptian army massacred by Nubian hordes.*

Esau was captured alive. At first he wasn't recognized because the smallness of his body and the weakness of his gaze didn't match the archetype of the leader, hero or demigod the winners had formulated of him. He was locked up along with the others in barns or sheds built from the remains of the set design. When his identity was established, they covered his eyes, leaned him against a papier-mâché palm tree and announced they would execute him.

---

* It's obvious that Esau's last invention—his masterpiece and most pronounced stroke of greatness—radiates the spirit of the proposal made by the director of the penal institution. And what does its origin matter? Emptied of its commercial content, the strategy is exceptional. Esau uses the world—the political spirit of the period—and forces it to act within his work: the Prussian army is to be understood precisely in this way, performing as Fate, the inexorable, as it enters the citadel with blood and fire, and emphasizes by means of its bullets and swords the catastrophe of an aborted revolution.

Esau removed the blindfold and shouted at the squad: "I want to see the dogs who are going to kill me!" The sergeant answered: "It was only a joke! We're actors too." Then, pretending he wanted to shake his hand, he grabbed hold of his fingers and broke them, while he said: "Here's something for the letter to your wife."

They beat him until he was almost deaf and blind. He stayed locked up for several days, until his right ear, which festered continuously, began to grow a giant blister, a flower of pus and blood. Then they let a chimpanzee loose on him, believing that in his defenselessness he'd be easy prey for the ape's bite. Yet the beast hung from Esau's neck, hugging and kissing him, and Esau returned the affection as he spoke to it. The guards told him: "This is what happens to your revolutionaries," and tortured the ape in his presence and then killed it. Afterward they offered to let him kill himself, saying that if he didn't have enough strength left, they could help him, but Esau said he wasn't his own executioner. Then came the moment they brought him to the office of the general, who, still moved by the emotions the prisoner had produced in him, begged him to recognize how useless, harmful and stupid it was to dedicate his life to the cause of revolution.

Esau answered:

"You are mistaken. The concept of revolution in this period has the status of an abstract idea: it cannot be carried out under present conditions, and therefore, since it is impossible to gain such knowledge from experience, the imperative takes the form of thought. I am the living proof that the intellectual possibility of a concept does not testify to its prior existence, but can be a condition of its future necessity and realization; I have needed to make use of all kinds of provisional elaborations to compensate for something impossible to know beforehand. Here lies both the highly disturbing character and the fundamental nature of the epistemological leap that my effort implies: it was a first step toward action, which was not an experiment in translating theoretical materials, but a trial without any decisive proof beforehand regarding the truth value of the propositions—without even the certainty that any such theory exists at all. Structurally this riddle calls to mind the distinction between *to know* and *to think*: what cannot be demonstrated in the present still demands to be 'thought' in order to guarantee the work of political praxis. In this way, even if the objects of reason cannot be known—even if they do not enter the framework of information our time offers us—all the same they have directed my political actions, and will allow others to build the theoretical corpus . . ."

The Prussian general answered:

"In a remote cave in the middle of the desert we discovered an old press, its characters faded by time, and next to it a book titled *Instrumental Anatomy of Political Praxis*. Since our task is not to think but to act, we passed the book to our scholars, critics and theologians, who, after studying it, as well as the press, found a kind of relation between these dissimilar objects. The book, in effect, had been printed by that machine, but its typeface had been altered, so that anything printed there would produce a different meaning. Studying it in depth, we realized this press is a barely concealed torture device invented by your father to lead you to your death. Before submitting you to such a design, let me say that if your father planned this education, then his final achievement, which will simultaneously be the most exquisite condemnation for you, is that you will die without ever knowing the true meaning of his words."

8

Was Esau Deliuskin ultimately a footnote to Andrei's colossal endeavor? Or did he fulfill his legacy in a singular way? What can one do but attempt to strike a balance? At least a part of what he sought in life was granted to him posthumously, although obviously not to the letter, if his aspiration was to build on his father's legacy through the construction of a solid political party led by an enlightened avant-garde. What did take place after his death was that his name became a kind of password, and his figure a myth within certain select circles. In these groups, Esau Deliuskin's deeds and writings make him a part of the fertile tradition of utopians who valued the will for practical realization just as much as or more than theoretical effort. My grandfather secured a place in this line alongside names like Condillac, Campanella, Rousseau, Blanqui, Bergerac and Kropotkin, to mention just a few. In certain developments of the contemporary theater of denunciation and the taking of political consciousness, any scholar will also be able to recognize the impulse of a cultural-political tradition that merges art, ideology and life. Although the name of Esau Deliuskin remains—and perhaps will forever remain—hidden from the knowledge of the masses, his achievements are without a doubt crucial to the history of the last few centuries.

To be brief and precise: reflecting on the events of the last century from the perspective of this millennium, it is necessary to admit that the criminal Adolf Hitler knew how to do things with words. And, of course, he was perfectly aware of how to lead others to act the way they did. In this respect, Hitler was a poet of dramatic situations, a theatrical author. Nobody could conclude from this that the Führer knew about my grandfather, or that he took advantage of the lessons imparted by his failure; but nothing prevents us from at least considering the possibility that if in his relevance to his period's scene, Hitler was a sort of demoniacal William Shakespeare, then Esau Deliuskin, attempting to realize through action the work proposed by his father, was a dark rival, precursor and antithesis. If the cause that my grandfather incarnated had triumphed, the phenomenon of Hitler would not have spread and flourished. The rapid end and posterior suppression of my grandfather thus make him a kind of Christopher Marlowe.

BOOK 4

ALEXANDER SCRIABIN

*Mind as the Absolute is outside and beyond
all time, and so is free from all the imperfections of time
experienced by our limited being.*
—DR. MAURICE NICOLL, *Psychological Commentaries
on the Teaching of Gurdjieff and Ouspensky*

1

Every genius faces a different obstacle. Edgard Varèse's father locked the piano, wrapped the instrument in a shroud and hid the key. Pierre Boulez's father bound his son's fingers with wire. Sam Bernstein wrote a letter to his Leonard doling out good measures of self-pity and disapproval: "I fled the Ukraine at sixteen years old to make myself a worthy fate in the United States. In my country I met homeless musicians who performed their songs at bar mitzvahs in exchange for just a few kopeks. I can't believe I had to put up with being shut in the hold of a boat for three weeks, my waist destroyed in New York from hoisting carcasses I had to carve on the icy slabs of a meatpacking depot (arthritis and osteoarthritis), not to mention sweeping up hairs from gentiles' beards at a barber shop in Hartford, Connecticut, and setting up a business to supply items to the Boston beauty salons, all so my firstborn would think the best thing life can offer him is to while away the days playing piano under the artificial waterfall of a cocktail lounge." Stravinsky's mother didn't attend the twenty-fifth anniversary celebrations for the composition of *The Rite of Spring*, because her Igor didn't compose the kind of music she liked: she was a fan of Alexander Scriabin.

As described in the previous book, my grandmother left her home after the far from courteous visit of the henchmen sent by the director of the penal institution. Fleeing through landscape after landscape carrying an enormous belly, her trembling right hand arranged to leave behind couriers and messages addressed to my grandfather Esau. These letters, bottles in the sea, sank to the bottom due to the ambiguity of their recipient's course. And although it's possible that during her journey she passed unaware through the burnt and smoking land where only days before the citadel had risen up, by now it was too late for them to ever find each other.

Out of pity, some peasants let her give birth to the fraternal twins in their stable; the wind lifted the straw in handfuls and my grandmother strained to tear herself open as quickly as possible, as the smell of the blood made the pigs restless. She threw them the placenta, wrapped my father and uncle in some old rags, and named them Sebastian and Alexander. Then she kept going. In her wandering she left the North African coast without realizing it, crossed through Lithuania and Finland, and entered Russia. She fed on rotten tubers, potatoes she found by scraping the hard winter earth; only the memory of Esau's existence allowed her to heat the milk that flowed from her breasts to nourish her little ones. Her extreme destitution separated her from even the benefits of human charity; she saw barbarians holding long sabers, their eyes more or less slanting: she was moving through the land where the Russo-Japanese War (1904–1905) was being waged and approaching the place where the paths of the twins would bifurcate, until their lives entwined again later in a stranger, more intimate way. Alexander, my uncle, and Sebastian, my father, had already turned three years old. They were skeletal pip-squeaks, blue from malnutrition. Terrified of losing them, my grandmother didn't leave their side. They slept together, relieved themselves together. Sometimes, in the dusk, projected against the silvery skies of the tundra, their figures resembled a mystic triad deprived of any power. In her desperation, my grandmother could hear only a continuous bass tone, the laughter of the devil.

The episode that follows is confused. Let's avoid melodrama. Train station. My grandmother and her children stand on the platform. A century, a garrison, is arranged in two columns. Grandmother, father and uncle are swept up into the parade. When the troops finish marching, there's an emptiness. Alexander is gone. The soldiers have boarded a train headed for the front. It's possible to hear the national anthem as it fades into the distance:

God save the Tsar
Grand and powerful
May he reign for our glory
May he reign and our enemies tremble
Oh, orthodox Tsar
God save the Tsar

Faced with the loss, my grandmother thinks she'll go mad. At night Sebastian hugs her and tells her he's still in contact with his brother.

Somehow they manage to climb onboard a boat leaving for another continent. After a calm journey they reach the port of Buenos Aires, capital city of the Argentine Republic. Meanwhile in Russia, my uncle has become a good luck charm. He travels in the soldiers' backpacks, and the regiment becomes a band of adopted fathers seeking relief from nostalgia for their own families. The troop is gradually decimated. Alexander grows up quickly amid gunshots and exploding bombs. The campaign introduces him to the charms of the Trans-Siberian Railway, the only means of arrival for reinforcements to the battlefront. An obligatory stop at the frozen surface of Lake Baikal. Ice skating. Alexander hears the voices in the wind that brings him Sebastian's murmur. It's buzzing with interference, of course, the chatter of lazy soldiers, the swish of the leaves of alder trees. But if he pays attention to the general concert of sounds, he can definitely make out a babble in an unknown quasi-language, its music . . .

The regiment reaches the Far East. The Imperial Japanese Navy, under the command of Admiral Togo Heihachiro, possesses seven battleships (*Asahi, Mikasa, Yashima, Fuji, Shikishima, Hatsuse, Chin-Yen*), eight armored cruisers (*Asama, Tokiwa, Iwate, Izumo, Azuma, Yakumo, Nisshin, Kasuga*), five coastal defense ships (*Fuso, Hei-Yen, Chiyoda, Heien, Kongo*), seventeen protected cruisers, twelve destroyers, one hundred torpedo boats and a series of logistical bases distributed throughout the Yellow Sea. Russia, in contrast, has only outdated naval units, an incompetent high command (Admiral Alekseyev and General Kuropatkin, two of a kind), mediocre training for soldiers and two very distant, strategically useless bases: Port Arthur and Vladivostok.

The night of February 8, the Japanese armada opens fire, torpedoing the boats anchored in Port Arthur without prior notice. A series of indecisive naval actions follow, in which the Japanese show themselves incapable of successfully attacking the enemy fleet protected by ground cannons in the bay, while the Russians refuse to advance into the open sea.

Japan begins its siege of the city. In August, part of the Russian fleet attempts to escape, but is intercepted and defeated in the Battle of the Yellow Sea. The other boats remain anchored and are slowly sunk by artillery. Attempts to assist the city from the continent also fail, and at last, on January 2, 1905, Port Arthur falls.

As part of the defeated army, my uncle, barely four years old, is held prisoner by the Japanese onboard one of their new battleships, the *Bernardino Rivadavia*—which along with the *Mariano Moreno* was acquired from Argentina, the two of them renamed *Nisshin* and *Kasuga*—which due to a secret clause in the sale, also continues to employ some crew members of that nationality, tasked with the functioning and upkeep of the motors. Prisoner is a manner of speaking: my uncle scuttles about as he likes in every corner of the battleship. The Japanese are strange: they are unable to impose limits on children, yet consider every display of affection to be effeminacy. In contrast, whenever the Argentines see this mischievous blond boy, they can't help but pick him up, hug him, burst into tears remembering their own children . . . The head mechanic in the machine room, José Ignacio Vélez, considers adopting him: he's from Santa Rosa, La Pampa, a barren plain in the middle of his country. He has five brown boys and three baby girls, and one more mouth won't even be noticed.

In times of war, bureaucratic paperwork can be a little imprecise. And, of course, Alexander is undocumented, so to do things legally, his original identity has to be restored first, with the aim of quickly swapping it out for the one given to him by his adopter.

What can an Argentine onboard a Japanese ship do to communicate with a Russian? Alexander doesn't understand what the matter is about or what he's being asked. The Argentine gestures and points to his chest with an index finger, which he then lifts to strike his temple; after this, he points behind him with a thumb, crumples a dirty slip of paper on which something is written, and finally, with a knuckle, taps the chest of Alexander, who is knocked down and remains silent. The others, his compatriots, attempt to intervene, only adding to the confusion by repeating the mimes with variations. Each one of them points to himself and repeats something. Of course, these are their names, but they seem to be a mere cacophony. Let's keep in mind Alexander is still a small boy, yet he's lived long enough to understand that language is an articulation of sounds randomly divided into words, which are also organized into particular forms that designate the elements of reality at whim. So at the start, he thinks when they are saying, "Pedro González," "Pablo Fernández," "Atanasio Quilpayen," the foreigners are naming their body parts. "Pedro González," he deduces, is the heart. "Pablo Fernández," the right temple. "Atanasio Quilpayen" is maybe an eye, or two, or first one and then the other. But with the changes in places named and the reiteration of resonant flows, he realizes at last that the unchanging variable defines identity. Then he names himself, producing bewilderment in his listeners. In Russian, vocals have an operatic reverberation: the "a," for instance, stays tucked away until it sounds like an "o," taking on a peculiar stridency, as if the tongue has lost its balance on the edge of the teeth and taken three backward steps, a drunken ballerina, before sinking into the depths of the palate; in contrast, the consonants mellow and clarify, the "ce" and "te" sounds enveloped by the tongue finding decisive points from which to prepare their attack and open fire, out of a love for being pronounced. So when Alexander says "Alexander," the Argentines hear something like Iolexanda . . . Which to them is the name of a woman or Macedonian conqueror. The last name is even more complicated. The first two syllables, De-lius, sound like pure gibberish. The third comes clinging not to meaning but to sound, the "ess": skin. Since the Argentine sailors are practically illiterate and lack the ability to carry out accurate deductive operations, they let themselves be carried away by their own assessments of origin. "Skin sounds like Bin," says Mario Abdallah, "and in Turkish, Bin means 'son of,'" from which they infer the child is telling them he's the son of the so-called Iolexanda. But that doesn't get them very far; besides, for some reason, they start to hear the shouts of the Japs giving orders from deck. An official even sticks his head through the door of the machine room and yells the same thing as ever, incomprehensible. The machinists have to hurry up and get everything going, but they're not going to let some Japanese shithead lead them by the nose either, so they go on with the discussion as soon as his mooncake face disappears from the frame. Someone turns on the motors to make a little noise, in addition to the background provided by the wildly off-target gunshots of the Russian fleet. It's almost impossible to hear anything in the room now. The Bandy-Legged Mulatto tries to wrap up a definition, asking: "So, whose kid is this creature?" Alexander smiles at the words "this creature" and attempts them himself. "Escria," he says, and the false word evokes something he can't define: a precious toy, an imaginary land, words akin to chords, an absolute design. Then he repeats the invented word, an uncanny stagger step of descending foothills, a metaphysical echo. "Escria?" Ramiro Prado says, puzzled. And Alexander says: "Alexander Escria Bin." "Whose son is he then?" asks Vélez. "Who knows," says another. His name is jotted on the temporary paper that serves as a document of fraudulent identity, along with the name of the one writing it. Pardo, as he takes everything down, hesitates: "The other letters I remember," he says, "but how do you write the 'e'?" Vélez gives a huff of annoyance. No son of his has ever given him so much work! He says: "An 'e' is like the drawing of a little fish trying to poke its head out of the water." Pardo wants to be sure: "With little eyes, fins, scales and all that?" Vélez: "Put the letters you remember, and call it a day." Pardo finishes just as a bomb, a bit more inspired than the rest, hits the powder magazine of the *Nisshin* and sinks them in a flash.

If the Russian cannon had fired its shells with less accuracy, in this and other battles, perhaps my uncle would have managed to reach Argentina and—an alternate fate—maybe he'd even have been able to reunite with his mother and brother. The confrontation took place on May 27, 1905, and the history books call it the Battle of Tsushima, in memory of the strait of that name. During the battle, which lasted until May 29, the Japanese fleet—with the exception of the *Nisshin*, burst and sunk—demolished its Russian counterpart, which was, however, able to save a shivering and excited boy from the waters, floating amid corpses. As they lifted him onto the deck of the *Zinovy Petrovich Rozhestvensky*, my uncle sent his brother a telepathic message: "Now my name is Alexander Scriabin."*

---

* Basing himself on somewhat unorthodox chronological grounds, the brilliant musician and prominent Scriabinian Giacinto Scelsi (*Uaxuctum, The Songs of the Capricorn, Aiôn, Four Episodes in One Day of Brahma, Konx-Om-Pax*) concludes that the military incident in which my uncle took part actually corresponds to a previous war, in his judgment, the Crimean (1853–1856).

2

Russia at the start of the twentieth century. The Empire is absorbed in deep industrial change while the reigning couple submerges itself in the dream of autocracy. Alexandra Feodorovna Romanova is an idiot, and better not even to mention her husband, Nicholas II. Thousands of jobs, machines, vehicles and inventions are being created, yet they can only look backward. Whenever a worker appears, folkloric nostalgia (of an aristocratic stamp and reactionary spirit) invents a peasant expelled from paradise. Alexander lives in the district of Khitrovka on the banks of the Yauza River, near the Kremlin in Moscow. The only ones who survive there are alcoholics, thieves, workers and murderers. The police don't enter its alleyways after dusk, not because their horses slip on the muddy slopes reeking of adulterated vodka, but because the mob often rises up, leaving its huts to steal their uniforms and guns and take possession of their cash and even their saddles, leaving only the stirrups and spurs behind. In this filthy rubbish dump, my uncle has lived the experiences of an orphan. At the age he can still be picked up, Alexander offers his services to beggars, who take him for walks as one of their own along the Nevsky Prospect. He learns to make his eyes go blank, let drool fall from the corner of his lips, breathe out hoarse, nasal sounds, and play the polio victim or dead man. You've got to live somehow. Later, a bit older, he learns the basic forms of delinquency: he pickpockets, gets the hang of cutting purse straps, snatches bags as if he were invisible. Rhythmic drumming of feet on asphalt, quick unforeseen sketches, forward movement: the art of flight.

During these years, the contact between Alexander and Sebastian is still in its larval phase. With its delightful simplicity, the literature about paranormal phenomena doesn't address the issue of translation. Is there a universal telepathic language? And where do greater levels of interference take place, in the communication between the dead and the living, or between beings separated by an ocean (the turbulences of the beyond versus the cracklings, aquatic electromagnetisms, whale and dolphin songs, and dolphins in a trance of the here and now)? We should maintain a certain degree of healthy doubt about the likelihood our perceptive organs can faithfully reconstruct the meaning of what is expressed through such contact. Despite all this, and always within certain limits, a transmission did exist between my father and his brother. The information was primitive: resonant masses, undefined voices. Above all they sent each other signals, much as they had during their period in the uterus. Yet the two of them *knew* they were communicating.

Over time, this circuit of dialogue broadened and refined into a special canal. Mediums and seers usually communicate through images or words. My father and uncle did so instead through music. Or, in any case, music transmitted the signals that they addressed to each other. And since music is reluctant to bear meaning, the contact freed them of the problem of interpretation and its consequence, misunderstanding. This could occur only in the situation that—seeing as they were immensely talented in this field—disagreements existed about the *form itself* of the message, in which the problem would be posed as a musical one. Perhaps, to avoid confusions, what went from one to the other was more like a system of notation. I don't know; I can't know *everything* about my family. What I do know is that Alexander and Sebastian fluidly communicated using their own system, and developed their personalities and faculties to such a degree that their abilities came to be noticed by certain people gifted in turn. At least that is how it will be explained to my uncle, a few pages from now.

Within the terribly stratified model found in Russia at the time, Alexander found himself occupying some of the lowest rungs on the scale. Neither the communal settlement where he lived nor the activities in which he spent his time encouraged his growth and personal development. We can imagine how his sensibility of an extraordinary budding artist was affected as he found himself compelled to share his days with a bunch of hoodlums and criminals. In that environment, he didn't even have his short-term survival guaranteed. Making a wise decision, he opted for the path that opens for young people with great ambitions and slender prospects, and taking advantage of his winsome appearance, started work as a bellboy at the Stropanovich, a travelers' hotel near the Bolshoi Theater. Twelve hours of work, accommodation in a room barely larger than an attic, a uniform, changes of clothes and two meals a day. In the salon-bar, there was a fairly decent piano, on which he worked out some ideas when he had free time.

He took care of bureaucratic procedures for the manager; oversaw the cleaning of rooms; helped serve breakfasts, lunches and dinners; filled glasses and lit cigars for gentlemen; closed or opened baggage for ladies; and carried dirty plates to the kitchen. Limited as it was, a milieu like this could encompass the interests of an entire life that aspires to the peaks of modesty: excellence in service, an ascent within hierarchies, secondhand experience (the tales of passengers). Alexander, in contrast, absorbed everything from above for what it was, a structure of relations, a blueprint. This way of seeing distanced him from the facts, and at the same time allowed him to capture them in their true dimension. Obviously the blueprint had movement: sounds and colors and temperatures. Sometimes he felt tempted to transcribe it on music paper, as in fact he ended up doing in his first composition, *Small World* . . . Nor did he abstain from other pleasures that a certain degree of liberalism permitted between staff and clients. But that is of no importance.

One day, the concierge sent him to room 1234, an involuntary homage to the sacred numbers and a display of megalomania by the owner, since the building had no more than forty rooms. There the task awaited him of satisfying the requirements of a difficult guest. The lady in question was accustomed to returning foods because they were dry, raw, overcooked or greasy; she protested because the towels weren't hot enough and the sheets were too cold; she broke mirrors, moved furniture, slammed closet doors, made noises, howled and conversed at the top of her lungs with nonexistent beings until the wee hours of the morning. If she hadn't been a faithful habitué, one of those who punctually settled bills (with inflated costs), the administration would never have tolerated her stay. She wasn't even a distinguished visitor, a Polish princess or English singer. She was merely a fat Russian, a diabetic and lame fifty-something who pushed her snobbery to the limit with her request that she be called *Madame*.

"You'll address me this way. Madame. Madame Helena Petrovna," she said to Alexander as soon as she opened the door. "My last name is Blavatsky, but almost no one calls me that, in theory not even my husband, whom I haven't seen for over ten years now. Speaking of seeing. I saw you. In the hallways. With that sneaky manner. You don't fool me, little mask. You've been called to do great things. There's a portion of being in you . . . an octave, ascendant toward the sun. Do you understand what I'm saying? It doesn't matter now. But don't get confused. To be is not to be perceived, except by chance. In this world, fame is the consequence of an error. The great men, the gurus, the saints, the mahatmas, are often directly intangible. Your mission . . . It's not the moment either. What's your name?"

My uncle said his first and last name, added "ma'am" (the lady blinked) and then asked what she needed. Madame Blavatsky took a seat in a somewhat rickety Louis XVI chair and gestured to the seat beside her. Alexander preferred to remain standing.

"Let's understand each other," Madame Blavatsky said. "The idea of the wheel of life as a cycle, a perpetual return, is the permanent revolution on which a thousand reflections have been spun by the Sumerians, the Buddhists, Plato, Schopenhauer, Nietzsche, the list goes on. In contrast, the channeling of thought based on an oriented turn, in which history develops from a unique start to a definitive and irreversible end, is Zoroastrianism, which has transmitted its dualist perspective and unilateral orientation to Judaism, Christianity and Islam, simultaneously passing it in a different way to Mithraism, Manichaeism and Gnosticism. From which of these waters do I drink? Well . . . Maybe it's time for me to introduce myself, so nothing will lead you into a confusion that doesn't depend on my will. You could say I'm a transmitter of knowledge, and at the same time an inveterate seeker. The mahatmas speak to me of great truths. But why you . . . ? What I saw . . . I know what you need. Let's start from the beginning. Obviously, sometimes I can be wrong. I travel from place to place, spreading . . . And then, as you can imagine, I don't go around carrying giant libraries. My invisible friends 'bring down' to me whatever I need to know, so I can then communicate it to you. I see those words floating in the breeze, pages and pages, books of revelations. There can be errors, of course. Sometimes one reads in the mirror, in darkness. A six becomes a nine, Sanskrit appears as Latin. How is it my fault if I'm not given things already prepared? Anyway, the letters look like each other. That said, even if it's expressed only partially, a truth can never lead to confusion. Except . . . But I shouldn't speak to you of this, yet. Everything in proportion. Melody. Counterpoint. Geometry. Arithmetic. And with harmony."

Madame Blavatsky took out a gigantic Havana cigar from her little raffia handbag and stretched it toward Alexander, who rejected the invitation.

"I want you to light it for me," the woman said. Alexander excused himself. Madame Blavatsky took a couple of drags and watched how the fire burned the tobacco leaf, forming a layer of soft reddish ash. Then she continued:

"Where is the origin of our horror for the infinite? Everything starts with Pythagoras. Or even further back. Fundamentally: Where are we when we listen to music? Where do we go when we listen to it? Where are we guided? Pythagoras. Pythagoras! Of Ionian origin, he was born on the island of Samos in approximately 582 BC. At twenty years of age he was already familiar with Thales and Anaximander, but having heard of the extraordinary knowledge of the Egyptian priests and their mysteries, he decided to go in search of them with the aim of having himself initiated at Memphis. There he could pore more deeply over sacred mathematics, the science of numbers and the universal principles at the center of his philosophical system, which later he would formulate in a new way. His initiation lasted twenty-two years under the pontificate of the high priest Sonchis. Then came the invasion and conquest of Egypt by Cambyses, king of the Persians and the Maedi. Cruel and despotic, after having decapitated thousands of Egyptians, Cambyses took him prisoner. Following a brief and instructive period in prison, similar to the one your father experienced . . . Don't make that face. How do I know? No, no one talked to me about you. I've seen it in the air; I've read it in *your* book. After some time, Cambyses banished Pythagoras to Babylonia. There he made contact with the inheritors of Zoroaster ('The number three reigns the Universe, and the monad—one, unique, unity—is its principle,' says one of his oracles) and with the priests of three different religions: the Chaldean, the Persian and the Jewish, which enabled him to widen his philosophical and scientific horizons. While he was instructed in the sacred rites of the region, he also perfected his knowledge of astrology, geometry and mathematics, and learned that the movements of the stars are regulated by numerical laws. After this, our friend knew more than any of his Greek contemporaries. It was time for him to return to Greece to carry out his mission . . . Pythagoras headed for Delphi, a city located at the foot of Mount Parnassus. There he founded the Temple of Apollo, famous for its oracles. In this temple Pythagoras transmitted the secrets of his doctrine. After a whole year, he left for Crotone, a city in the south of Italy, in Calabria. As soon as he returned to his native land, he founded his own secret society: the Pythagorean sect. The initiates were divided into two categories: the *Mathematicians* ('knowers'), young people especially gifted for abstract thought, and the *Acousmatics* ('auditors'), simpler men who recognized the truth in an intuitive form, through dogmas, beliefs, apologues, indemonstrable oral remarks lacking any grounds, moral principles and aphorisms, the kind of fisherfolk my good friend Maestro Jesus gathered up when he wanted to divulge his more straightforward teachings. The hard nucleus, the firm defense of the Pythagorean doctrine, was clearly made up of the *Mathematicians*—committed to the totality of knowledge—while the *Acousmatics* were entrusted with protecting the gate to the entrance of the temple and with looking after the Sacred Veil. Esoteric and exoteric. Now. Back to Greece. The Pythagorean Arcadia had to do with cultivating mysticism and philosophic thought, whose foundation was a conviction in the possibility of achieving immortality as a series of infinite reincarnations. If you think of this order as not a successive but a combinatory form, you will have summarized the whole of musical possibility . . . But let's go to the numbers. Pythagoras dedicated himself to exploring Everything, the aggregation of all elements, which he named the Cosmos, starting from the assumption (of Eastern root) that this aggregate had certain proportions governed by laws that men can know and understand through the Number, which is the most basic foundation, 'the essence of all things.' Taking it as a given that the cosmos in its totality is subject to progressive and predictable cycles, he decided to measure it with these instruments or first principles. He also claimed that numbers, used to represent mathematical values, are separate from the qualities and characteristics they represent, and have another function: to operate in the spiritual plane. If you don't understand anything, Alexander, just ask me. Your asking something doesn't necessarily imply I can explain it to you. So: for Pythagoras the essence of the number is prior to any tridimensional body and is divine in origin. His premise: 'God geometrizes.' What he learns with the geometers of Egypt and the Babylonian astrologers, added to his own experimentation with musical instruments, helps him establish that the number is the essence of the Universe and the root and source of eternal nature. Therefore, while the Greek thought of the period took for granted that the earth was at the center of its universe, held up by tortoises and elephants, Pythagoras already knew that Earth and other planets turn around the sun. He also thought that celestial bodies move in a harmonious way in accordance with a numerical scheme, separated from each other by intervals corresponding to the length of harmonic chords, whose movement generates a vibration . . . And that vibration is a note. But since every celestial body is in relation with some other at a specific fixed distance, set inside its little glass box like a gear inside a watch . . . What he argued was that the distances between these planets have the same proportions as those existing between the sounds of a musical scale considered 'harmonic,' or consonant. This is starting to interest you a little more now, isn't it? From the Earth to the Moon would be one tone, from the Moon to Mercury a semitone, from Mercury to Venus another semitone, and from Venus to the Sun a tone and a half. Therefore, between the Sun and the Earth there would be a separation corresponding to a fifth interval, and between the Moon and the Sun a distance corresponding to a fourth interval. Give me a glass of water, please. No. The phrase isn't *of* water, it's *with* water, on this planet. On others . . . I can't remember if Pythagoras also said that at the same time the Earth revolves around the Sun, the rest of the planets turn around Earth . . . Who cares? So much time has passed . . . Anyway, all this philosophy had no further object than the purification of the soul, and so . . . Obviously some people will understand anything by purification. Some even drink their own urine. Disgusting. To sum up . . . the tones emitted by spinning planets depend on the arithmetical proportions of their orbits around . . . the Earth? the Sun? The length of the strings of a lyre determines its tones the same way. The spheres closest to . . . the Sun? the Earth? produce deep tones, which grow more high-pitched as the distance increases. In such a way that, have you ever been to a concert? No? Holy mahatma! This boy is a hymn to ignorance! Then just imagine it: you focus your opera glasses into the black velvet depths. It's the firmament. At the start the theater lights seem turned out, and only silence can be heard. Then, slowly—you have all of time ahead of you, eons to get used to it—you start to make out the radiance of stars, dead or not, who knows? Imagine you are eternity itself, to help you settle nice and calm into your seat. Next, tune your hearing. You hear a violin here, a horn there, the bellows of an organ. The instruments breathe. Obviously they aren't *real* instruments. Every planet spins around other planets, and on its own axis, in accordance with its relative position and velocity and angle of spin, to produce a sound or series of sounds that combines with those of the other planets in remarkable synchrony: this is what Pythagoras called 'the music of the spheres.' Of course, all this is a mathematical deduction: no human ear (except the auricle of thought) can hear such blessed music, because it resonates at a frequency impossible to capture. The stars produce ghostly whistlings, tappings, hummings, booming noises. I myself, during one of my astral trips, saw these movements; I heard this concert, conveniently amplified. But I also saw other things. Lots of stellar dross, arias drifting across space, compositions written by those yet unborn. I found myself witnessing the moment a neutron star suffered from a massive earthquake. The poor celestial body vibrated like a bell and let out a note we could define as A major. And that's not all. If you pay attention, you'll realize that everything vibrates at its own frequency. Us, and the cumuli of stars and galaxies. Going no farther, our Milky Way oscillates with music like the head of a drum. So . . . Ah, after so many trips, I'm so tired . . . I need foot massages, an affectionate lover . . . Would it be all right if I put out the cigar I didn't smoke in the water you didn't bring me?"

3

The theosophist made him a very tempting offer, in terms of the amount of payment and work, but also warned him that accepting it might involve him in a few complicated situations. Some understood she was a visionary, but most considered her to be a simple fraud.

They traveled around Russia. There's no need to list the cities. My uncle took advantage of his spare time to fill the gaps in his education. It was obvious that Madame Blavatsky had offered him a summarized version of fundamental topics.

Collating his own readings with what his patroness had told him, he found that she'd been at once succinct and confused. Maybe it was due to strategic motives. In the esoteric tradition, revealed knowledge must possess an appearance that is simultaneously chaotic and incomplete, an overwhelming and obsessive character; the revelation must be the mirror image that the sky casts upon the waters. In this sense, Helena Petrovna had shown herself to be an ideal pedagogue. Alexander threw himself into digging into the ruins of Pythagoreanism to find any fragments of knowledge yet to be drawn out. In Chapter 5 of Book I of the *Metaphysics*, Aristotle recalls the Pythagoreans claimed that the principles of mathematics were the principles of all things, and that things themselves were numbers—meaning not that numbers were a metaphor, but that things and beings were truly *made, composed*, by them. The number is the elemental principle, the essence of what exists, like atoms for

Democritus but with size and extension. And what was impressive was that Pythagoras had reached this conclusion by discovering the numeric base of the musical intervals (1/2, 3/2 and 4/3)! Therefore, since numbers were the key to musical sounds, whoever knew their properties and relations would grasp the laws responsible for the existence of nature and the mechanics of the entire Universe. They were also the foundation of the spirit and the means by which reality presented itself. In a certain way, this derived from mysticism: if numbers possessed reality as a substance that allowed one to discover both the qualities and the physical aspects of things, then this meant they were also hieroglyphs, with which one could perform metaphysical operations of great symbolic significance. Numbers and their sacred character. Numerical mysticism. The cabalistic properties of numbers. Their special attributes. *One*, monad, principle and foundation of all that exists, unique God, Solus, Sun. *Two*, dyad, passive principle, symbol of diversity, expression of nature's contrasts (night and day, light and dark, health and illness, et cetera). Numbers. Numbers. Numbers, and so on until ten, which of course was the most sacred of all, because the first four numbers contained the secret of the musical scale (1 + 2 + 3 + 4 = 10) and its total formed the number of the Universe, the sum of all possible geometric dimensions: one is the point; two is the line; three, the surface; and four, space. The Tetractys.

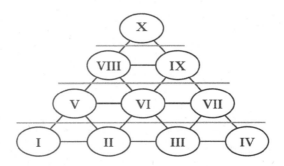

A little patience. Sometimes, while reading, Alexander wondered whether ultimately he wanted to devote himself to geometry, music or cosmology. A matter that wouldn't be resolved immediately, in any case. If veneration for the number ten (the first quadruple) had a transcendental cosmological implication for the Pythagoreans in their doctrine about the arrangement of the Universe (considered for the first time in a non-geocentric way), then it isn't strange their love for proportions and equivalences led them to claim that ten planets were moving through the sky. But since at first glance only nine could be observed (Earth, the Moon, the Sun, Mercury, Venus, Mars, Jupiter, Saturn and the outer Sphere of Fixed Stars, all turning in concentric circular orbits around the *Throne of Zeus*, the central fire), they saw themselves forced to discover or imagine a tenth planet. Invisible but influential, this shimmering black stain closed the account: it was the *Anti-Earth*.

A perfect representation: Alexander understood the schema. His brother and himself, at two extremes. Earth and Anti-Earth. United. The telepathic link and its interferences (minimal dissonance). And the Sun (if it was the father) no longer at the center of the Universe, but spinning like the others around the central fire. The mother also far away. All of them burning, dancing in the cosmos. Earth and Anti-Earth, Sun and Moon. Plump Madame Blavatsky had to be Jupiter.

Let's keep revising. What is the precise relationship between musical harmony and numbers? Pythagoras discovered that certain chords produced by tones, specifically the fourth, fifth and eighth, have proportional lengths of 12, 9, 8 and 6. And given that the ratios between these numbers are equal to those between 1, 3/4, 2/3 and 1/2, which are the simplest that can be formed with the numbers of the Tetractys (1, 2, 3, 4), he deduced that this was the source and root of Eternal Nature. The numbers of the

Tetractys were thus the base for musical harmony as well as the source of knowledge about the harmonic roots of the Cosmos. Numbers were the secret to the musical chord of the whole of nature. Father, one, together with mother, two. A first son comes, three. The second son, four. Added together: a family.

The Deliuskin-Scriabins: a destroyed Tetractys.

What came next was a little easier, and at the same time stranger. The sentiment of beauty that derives from an illusion of perfection ("Numbers are the essence of all things") suddenly saw itself threatened by catastrophe. Poor Pythagoras. Twenty years after the death of the maestro, in 480 BC, it occurred to Hippasus of Metapontum to search for a unit that would allow him to measure in an exact and simultaneous way the diagonal and side of a square, or rather, the diagonal and side of a regular pentagon. What was the use? *It was impossible.* And he thought he'd reveal this to the world: he'd discovered the unfathomable proportion, the irrational (*alogon*) that can't be expressed through reason. If something exists that can't be measured or known, that can't be evaluated or uttered, and this impossible something is multiplied and reproduced as a fire that blazes through all order and predictability, and . . .

The Pythagorean school crucified Hippasus of Metapontum. It expelled him from its community and shared housing, and it raised a tomb for him as if he were dead in life. In Book X of his *Elements*, a severe Euclid gave his opinion that the author of the discovery perished in a shipwreck because *the inexpressible and unimaginable should forever have remained hidden.* A phrase to which maybe Pythagoras would not have subscribed. In any case, the discovery of irrationality and incommensurability, although it destroys the assumptions on which Pythagoreanism rested, putting a momentary limit on knowledge and opening the door to a crisis into which a horror of the infinite wedges, unavoidably also lets slip through the idea of a god (be it single, double or Trinitarian) that manipulates the variables. In any case, the collapse of Pythagoreanism doesn't eliminate the idea of music as an "audible number," which, transmitted by the Hellenist Neoplatonic tradition, passes to the great intellectual figures of late Antiquity (Macrobius, Boethius, Cassiodorus, Aurelian of Réôme, Juan Gil de Zamora, Adelard of Bath, Évrart de Conty, et cetera). Alexander burns the midnight oil reading the *Commentarii in somnium Scipionis, De institutione musica, Institutiones divinarum et saecularium litterarum, Musica disciplina, Ars musicae, De codem et de diverso, Le livre des les échecs amoureux moralisés . . .* He visits libraries, he examines codices. One text sends him to another. When a book is particularly difficult to find, Madame Blavatsky, an understanding patroness, makes contact with her mahatmas and "brings it down" from the heights. Studious, thoughtful, extremely rational, Alexander in this period is the antithesis of the figure a treacherous posterity will define him to be. There is none of the late exaggeration typical of the romantic musician, no such arrogance and ignorance. As far as passion goes, it's enough that it circulates through his veins without it also having to appear as foam in his mouth (as with Nietzsche, Schumann and so many others). He doesn't seem to be a musician at all. It's rare for him to sit at the piano, which doesn't mean he doesn't compose in his mind or practice in his dreams. Besides, in Buenos Aires his brother Sebastian is pursuing a true career as virtuoso, and what one learns is transferred to the other instantaneously, with the exception that Alexander's fingers are slightly shorter and chubbier. In summary, the education he gives himself is classical. This distances him from the trend in fashion, which appears precisely in this industrial age and stakes everything on the reactionary expression of an ineffable "Russian soul" of a clear folkloric type. Taking the sublime as its horizon and the Universe as a program for knowledge, these native concerns seem reductionist and don't tempt him in the slightest. In the present, leaving aside the warm atmosphere of his books and the burning lamp and the silent chords that his hopes play a few meters from his fingers (still not yet converted into music), everything seems horrible. But diagonals and theorems notwithstanding, my uncle continues to believe that beauty will prevail. This enthusiastic wager has the possible appearance of what he vaguely begins to intuit as his mission. Or in reality, a part of it. For him, cosmos and music remain near synonyms. If numbers are the source and rule for the harmony of movement, then aesthetic judgment could eventually be reduced to a mathematical definition, and beauty would be intelligible to everyone, or at least to lucid minds. God as an aesthete. For Saint Augustine, the proportions of music serve as audible metaphors for creation, which lead to revelation and the ecstatic contemplation of divine mystery. Music possesses a highly spiritual character: the movements of acoustic sensation are reflected in the activity of the soul, since this vibrates even after the notes have gone silent.

Next comes Boethius and his triad. My uncle is interested in the belief that the music of the spheres (*Mundane music*), inaudible to our hearing, reverberates through the angels surrounding the celestial throne, and is thrilled by the idea that man is a similar microcosmos ruled by harmony. *Human music* isn't an object of perception but a form of introspection that unifies the life of the body with the life of reason and sensibility, an understanding that evokes the chord between lower and higher-pitched sounds as well as the concert of planetary movements. As for the third branch, the art of sounds and the art of composition in general . . . *Instrumental music* replicates the music of the world, and man, who, like the soul of the world, possesses a musical "chord," becomes its receptacle. External and internal harmony. Microcosmos and macrocosmos. Dialectic of the universal and the particular . . .

These are now associative points in his mental process, which continues to scale the Middle Ages.

In search of themes that interest him, Alexander runs a bit quickly through the distinctions between natural and artificial music. Let's skip over the charming and unsophisticated ideas of Remigius of Auxerre (end of the ninth century AD) about the "perfect song" that incorporates the body's gestures, heights and measurements of performers, and words. Later came William of Conches, unparalleled figure of the School of Chartres. A seductive notion: rhythm is taken to be the point of earthly convergence with the movement of the Universe, which establishes not only a mystical link with all things but also a musical phenomenon equivalent to harmony. And harmony is neither more nor less than the status quo of the Universe, which through art transmits (emanates) true wisdom, the model for every society . . . God, the all-powerful architect, built all that exists and harmonized the variety of created things by way of perfect proportions, of musical consonance. One thousand five hundred years after the birth of Pythagoras, in Conches's rehashing, everything has come back to theocentrism again. The numbers keep telling us the art of music can reach the eternal beauty of the divine. Obviously, although the calculation lets us know or imagine the sounds that celestial bodies produce in their rotation, nobody has ever heard the song of the angels . . .

But what is music, after all? *Mundica*, a contraction of *mundi* and *canto*, the song of the world? According to Juan Gil de Zamora, it really comes from *moys*, which means "water." And doesn't *moys* also allude to *Moyses*—Moses, "saved from the waters"—and wouldn't music thus be what saves man? Questions to which my uncle would have paid no attention had he decided to become a performer rather than composer. Especially the kind of composer he would turn out to be. During those evenings of study, under the permanent effect created by genuine impressions, Alexander Scriabin began to approach the conviction that years later would form the base of his masterpiece: that art is salvation and capable of returning the Universe to its ends.

4

At Madame Blavatsky's place, life runs along the usual tracks. Alexander is her right-hand man: he's in charge of overseeing the staff that does the cleaning, cooking, washing and ironing. He also devotes some attention to the visits piling up in the waiting room. His patroness is careless with details and because of this sometimes finds herself at the center of minor scandals, subject to a variety of accusations. Russia is a provincial society and in the emptiness of its cities surrounded by tundras and taigas and steppes, any sound echoes as after a boom.

"They're slandering me! I want a lawyer!" shouts Helena Petrovna.

Everything kicked off after a whirlwind tour the Madame undertook in Bombay for reasons of health and instruction. She stopped in London on the return, visiting the local branch of the Theosophical Society, with the aim of resolving certain philosophical, dogmatic and financial conflicts with its members. The start of the meeting had taken place with all the appearances of great friendliness. The eccentric Lady Anna Kingsford, responsible for the English branch of the Masonic lodge, greeted her with a warm reception *comme il faut*, a platter of tree-shaped delicacies, fiorituras, cherries jubilee. Naturally, with the wicked intention of catching her sweetened up, with her guard down. At the third meeting, Alexander's patroness was surprised by the presence of new arrivals. They were introduced to her as recently joined members, but Lady Kingsford finally confessed they were examiners from the city's Society for Psychical Research, founded two or three years before with the stated intention of "providing a framework of objective security for the development and knowledge of paranormal events." According to the hostess, the two gentlemen, F. W. H. Myers and J. H. Stack, merely intended to observe the display of the guest's remarkable abilities with their own eyes. Naïve as she was, or claimed to be before the world, Blavatsky accepted this examination, and over the course of several nights, she demonstrated her talent for summoning the ghosts of beings still living, projecting and materializing human doubles, encouraging the appearance of objects, bringing forth the sound of astral bells, using ink and solution to reproduce the handwriting in sealed letters with postage stamps from different countries, making flowers, brooches and cowbells turn up with the help of doubles of the Initiates . . . According to what Blavatsky confided to my uncle in the midst of a fit of weeping and convulsions, she'd also revealed a whole series of experiences of the most deeply sacred character—"I even spoke to them of the golden city, Shambhala!"—with the aim of helping the cause of spiritist science. But it was no good. The others stripped away their masks, and Madame realized she was in the presence of a committee that nobody had invited. The accusations still hadn't been formulated, but already she felt the malevolence emitted by these people's heads as an oppressive yellow light.

The interrogation began. A stenographer registered the questions and answers: while Mr. Stack zeroed in on her hygienic habits, sexual preferences and gastronomic tastes, Mr. Myers knuckled down to his attempt at deciphering the sources of the Society's financing. Sometimes the two spoke at the same time. The façade of affability having long since dissipated, Madame wasn't even able to get them to serve her a refreshment. The interrogators raised the tone of their voices to criticize her statements, made it clear they intended to expose her contradictions, revealed themselves to be cruel and skeptical, and showed no consideration whatsoever for her feelings. Finally they were able to anger her, and she accused them of being incompetent and completely lacking experience in the study of psychic laws. This reply immediately seemed to calm the pair, and they withdrew from the meeting uttering every kind of excuse.

The next day, an article signed by the two of them appeared in the *Christian College Magazine* of London, accusing Blavatsky of being "one of the most astute and dangerous impostors we have ever known."

Madame boarded a ship that took her to the continent, and from there headed for Russia. By the time she arrived in Moscow, the media was already informed of the scandal. Furthermore, some newspapers linked to the Society for Psychical Research had published a series of letters whose authorship they traced to her, in which Helena Petrovna had allegedly written to two ex-employees ordering them to build false walls with sliding doors and all kinds of other contraptions to dupe the gullible. They repeated old complaints too: that she manipulated the game with the cup, that objects vibrated at the contact of her hand because she put subtle motors inside them . . . They even tried to explain the miracle of teletransportation as a magic trick in which a passage connects one cabin to another, or failing that, attributed its success to the use of twins . . .

"I'm not afraid of these blackmailers' claims, Alexander," Blavatsky told my uncle. "While we're being honest, though, I must confess a few gimcrack miracles are necessary to bolster the faith of the inferior majority of our acolytes. The higher truths that live within me or manifest themselves through my presence are more arduous to demonstrate. And that's why I need a lawyer."

Alexander made his inquiries and finally tracked down a professional whom he thought was an excellent fit. Short, bald, with a thin beard that narrowed to a sharp tip and eyes that flashed with resentment and the imperious will to triumph at something, whatever it might be. He wore a shabby and badly mended suit. It was obvious he lacked a woman. His hole-in-the-wall office, two rooms whose windows faced the Red Plaza and the back part of the Kremlin (servants' courtyards and abandoned towers) were full of books written in German. To Helena Petrovna, this ostentatious flourish seemed a display of ignorance. All the same, not knowing where else to turn, she told him the situation.

While the theosophist dawdled over the fine points of the case, the lawyer paced around his office, poked his head out the windows (as if preparing to give instructions to the government building's personnel), smoothed his eyebrows, clasped his hands behind his back in an unconscious imitation of the dead French emperor's preferred gesture and buried his thumbs in the pockets of his waistcoat like a shopkeeper. At last he took out a gold watch, checked the time and spoke:

"In my opinion, your problem is totally insignificant and therefore highly risky. A single spark can start a prairie fire. My brother is dissolved in the ether of the Universe because a thug from the Okhrana discovered pamphlets from a terrorist organization in his home. They hanged him, and I had to flee to Switzerland because the tsarist persecution extended to the rest of the family. As if politics were borne in the blood! The trip had its advantages: I played chess and met unconventional people, avant-gardes . . . What I mean to say is we live in a closed society, most obviously symbolized by a low fluidity in the circulation of news. That's why anything fresh tends to solidify, and every person and practice are immediately made visible. In your case, the fact that they first attributed to you the gift of speaking with the dead, then accused you of having helped this rumor along with tricks, puts you square in the eye of authority. And in Russia, that means danger. Just imagine: tomorrow or the next day, any of these days, in some remote part of our country, a pack of wolves devours some number of sheep. In his own defense, the muzhik, who can never repay the owner for the value of the lost livestock, alleges he saw a horde of the dead rise up from the mud and drag the animals into the abyss . . . And who does he accuse of such an act? You, ma'am, naturally."

"What are my options?" Madame Blavatsky wanted to know.

"I'd say you have two options left: either acknowledge you can speak with the dead and produce a satisfactory demonstration of this talent, or declare you're unable to do so and accuse your accusers of imputing to you a gift you never claimed to possess."

"But what about the letters? I never . . ."

". . . in any case, my advice is: patience, money and terror. I can put you in contact with a bank and train robber in Siberia, who occasionally undertakes certain tasks for me. For a few rubles my friend can travel to London, visit these adversaries of yours, take out his knout and lash their incredulous backs, or directly tattoo his last name into them with the tip of his knife. Nor is it inadvisable to fire a few shots. Result: the next day, Yosip is on his journey back and your prudent enemies are issuing a denial that leaves you free of all suspicion. What do you think?"

"I think you show contempt for me without knowing me and don't even grasp what's at stake in this case," said Madame.

"I occupy myself not with the truth, but with the state of the claim," replied the lawyer.

This reply exasperated Helena Petrovna even more:

"My dear pen pusher: I can read in your mind that you consider me to be an old hen and think the wisdom I transmit is nothing but neighborhood ladies' gossip. Vulgar empiricist, you confuse the real with the visible. Your insensitivity toward the drama I'm suffering exposes that you believe yourself to be fated for great things, which may be true, if we take into account that the great isn't always synonymous with the good. Up to a certain point, you can be forgiven for not caring about who I'm talking to, but just who do you think *you're* talking to?"

Madame Blavatsky left the interview furious, and calmed down that night only when one of her obliging mahatmas materialized the copy of a notification for her, which ninety-nine years later would appear in the Official Bulletin of the Society for Psychical Research. In it the institution, admitting that it had worked with excessive haste, judged her free of guilt and responsibility. The next morning, Alexander sent this notice from posterity to be framed and hung on one of the walls of her study. But the document didn't seem to fully calm the exonerated one. Returning to the *petit hotel* one afternoon, following his usual shopping run, my uncle entered the theosophist's private room and found it to be strangely free of presences, beginning with that of its owner. On the table was a letter:

> Auguries, curses and premonitions. I must attend to . . .
> But tell me something, my dear Alexander. Do you think
> that if I'd done what they say I did, I'd have left written
> evidence of the fraud? The purpose of this accusation is to
> discredit me before the world by painting me as a kind of
> idiot, along the way ridiculing the mission to which I've
> dedicated my life. In all of this I see the black hand of the
> Roman Church . . . For the moment my only refuge lies
> in making a hidden pilgrimage toward the fate my spiri-
> tual guides indicate to me.

Next to the letter was a little silk bag with a not overly modest quantity of bills and coins, enough to see my uncle through the winter.

5

With the money that Madame Helena Petrovna Blavatsky had left
to him, my uncle didn't need to worry about material concerns for
a while, a period he used to broaden his education. He took composition classes with Nikolai Zverev and later enrolled at the Music
Conservatory in Moscow. He learned a few things from Arensky,
Taneyev and Safonov. From this period we still have some pianistic
miniatures, brief morceaux that more superficial readings attribute
to the influence of Tchaikovsky. But it's obvious the contemplative
aspects of these short pieces go beyond the abilities of that sappy
melody maker, to instead become a totalizing reflection (the first of
them) summing up the best legacies of Romanticism: the pleasant
sound and small-scale forms of Chopin, the constructive mentality
of Liszt and the base of the Russian pianistic tradition. And this,
paradoxically, would be seen most clearly in preludes like his opus
11 and 33, which he'd write a few years later. Meanwhile, a time for
learning. His teachers were astonished by the speed of his progress;
in just a few months he had transformed into an impressive pianist, although his small hands could barely stretch more than an
octave; in his efforts to achieve greater spread, he sometimes hurt
his fingers until they were bleeding. And although in the contest at
the end of the year (category: performance) Rachmaninov won the
gold metal and my uncle had to resign himself to second prize, it
was obvious to those who attended the event that in the future, the

winner would have to settle for developing a virtuoso career that peaked with the ephemeral glories of a circus pageant, while Alexander Scriabin, even with his physical limitations, had shown the material of a true artist: he had played in a trance. From this period we have some of his first annotations of a philosophical character, very elemental but not at all incorrect, in which he vindicates the redemptive Promethean character of Luciferianism. Luci-fer: *he who brings fire*. And, no doubt, he who sacrifices everything to its light.

But one must also live: my uncle starts to give concerts. In Saint Petersburg he meets the patron and editor Belyayev, who will pay him generously for his compositions and lend him money. Tours: Germany, Switzerland, Italy, France. It's the period of his preludes, along with his Second Sonata and Symphonic Poem. On his return to Moscow he meets Vera Ivanovna Isakovich, a pianist also graduated from the Conservatory and a great admirer of his music. They get married. A period of success begins. Russia itself seems young and thriving. Summer. By invitation of one of those flamboyant ministerial programs that take entertainment for culture, they board a steamboat, the *Ivotknik*, which lazily rotates the blades of its turbine down the Volga. Every evening the boat drops anchor near some riverside town, the grand piano is hoisted on deck, and Alexander and his wife offer concerts for four hands to ecstatic provincials. It isn't strange that in a sudden impulse of pride, my uncle declares: "I am God." In a sense, he is. He's become the most famous musician in the whole of Russia. Vera, who adores him, occupies herself with making sure he doesn't have to worry about any practical concerns. She picks out clothes for him, cuts his hair and styles his mustache, looks over contracts. For the first time, his foundling's heart experiences the warm current of affection. Love makes him sensitive to the fragility of things; through the influence of love, his music leaves behind its purely cerebral aspect, its trace of the "thinking reed," and opens in a more spontaneous direction, taking feeling to be the reflection, echo or chord that pairs with the throbbing of the Universe. This form of vibratory pantheism—a reaffirmation of knowledge through the senses—will have long-term consequences for his work, but let's not get ahead of ourselves. In the immediate present, a maturation of the romantic gesture can be noted in a more complete unfolding of the mass of sound—that is, its "rapture." Despite his obvious progress, Alexander knows he's far from having been able to express the abstract in the concrete; during performances, he even sees the public celebrate specific moments of prowess he privately takes for occasions of despair, flare-ups of resentment at the evanescence of those voluptuous dream figures he aspires, without success, to bring into being.

Of course, this state of anguish—which he calls insatiability—isn't constant, but it does upset his life enough to leave a mark. Alexander suffers from allergies, his hair comes out in clumps, even in summer he can't go out without a hat. In the mirror he sees eczemas, blackheads, bags under his eyes. He becomes peevish; sometimes he's absent and bad-tempered. Young admirers continuously visit him at his home in Saint Petersburg, bringing their compositions to submit to the maestro's judgment; but my uncle passes weeks without receiving anyone or, instead of the hoped-for gesture of approval, offers only curt and far from stimulating replies—"Try again," "Doesn't work," "Nothing in this"—or quotes the bitter pearls of the Russian phrase book: "What can a donkey know of sweets?" "Don't make a tower of excrement to reach the sun," "The jolting of the cart settles the melons," et cetera. Vera, who knows the private reasons for the pain behind her husband's edginess, tries to calm him by making his surroundings more comfortable. Medicine helps too: Alexander always has constipation or excess blood flow or circulatory problems or a dilated heart. Trifles. I don't know what happens all those years between my father and uncle, telepathically speaking. I do know that Alexander continues playing and composing in a room draped in sumptuous fabrics, which muffle the too bright, too pale light, along with his children's voices. One night . . .

One night he dreams of a family. It's a complete family, with servants. Half-covered by clothes of the most refined taste, they wait in a basement, posing for a daguerreotype camera. The paterfamilias, standing and dressed as a soldier, rests his hand on the shoulder of his wife, sitting on a rustic wood chair. The children are arranged by height, in *dégradé*. What draws the attention is the atmosphere of serenity without hope. A little one hugs a pillow. Another begins to cry, and the father takes off a medal hanging from his chest and gives it to her to play with. In the dream, Scriabin thinks he recognizes the medal: it's the first of many he's won over the course of his career. It means this must be *his* family. All of a sudden, steps are heard. A row of soldiers positions itself in front of them, blocking the exit, and opens fire. Alexander knows it's a dream, and he could interrupt it if he knew how to wake up. But the shots continue, and when there are only corpses left, the killers drag them toward a cart . . .

In light of historical facts, one might venture this was a dream anticipating the tragic end of the Romanov dynasty, probably induced from afar by Madame Blavatsky. But for Alexander, the clarity of what he's envisioned prevents him from even considering the possibility this is the royal family, which in any case has nothing to do with him. It's his own. My uncle wakes up convinced he must save Vera and the children from this fate. The decision is terrible: he must take himself far away from his current life, as it's the only protection for his loved ones against these bullets of the future.

At no point in the years that followed, up to the instant of his death, did my uncle have the slightest clue about the nature of this threat. Who were the ones firing in the dream? And why? His sacrifice had to be fulfilled in silence, since any comment on his part might provoke what at all costs must be avoided. Put simply, he believed in the reality of the terror, and acted accordingly. He left his wife and four children and never saw them again.

6

A dream produces events, and events generate works. The sudden abandonment of his home, whether considered as the first element in a series of hallucinations that would end up plunging him into abysses of genius and madness, or as the obedient response to a warning from the Fates, led to powerful shifts in Alexander Scriabin's cosmovision and work as a musician and composer. Starting from this moment, he occasionally compared himself with Christ, who needed to leave his loved ones on behalf of a supernatural mission. Some speculated his growing penchant for religious figures was the channel his mood had found to rescue him from a ray of depression. Luckily, his renunciation of domestic happiness didn't leave him feeling empty. On the contrary, he discovered new areas to cultivate; the suggestion of imaginative freedom in his beginnings gave way to a kind of technique or procedure of insistent repetition that heralded what would soon follow: his discovery of the mystic chord. Solemnity unfurled its wings above him. Now his works flowed at a marvelously intense emotional register, without being pathetic or strident. His way of expressing pain turned out to be a supreme elegance. This didn't prevent his concerts, which kindled both sensibility and understanding, from sometimes eliciting paroxysmal tensions or unstoppable fits of tears in the audience. My uncle's devastated soul transmitted its desolation, which ironically assumed the form of a public tri-

umph. In homage to Vera Ivanova, he composed some pieces of
the most exquisite lyricism, his *Feuilletes d'album*.

In this time of renunciations and gifts, my aunt's reaction was
even more extreme and poignant. She, without knowing the reasons for it, "understood" Alexander's flight and devoted the rest of
her life to teaching and praising the music of the man who had
left her. Certain that they inhabited a dimension of love beyond
the flesh, convinced that Scriabin's decision (which consumed her
like a cancer of the pancreas) had to have been the best thing
for both of them, to make their link more transcendent and thus
deeper, she did not let a single day go by without playing her husband's works. For Russian theosophical circles, this "afterimage"
of a relationship mirrored the kind of arrangement that Madame
Blavatsky, in her own sphere, had created with her mahatmas. A
supra-reality. Which was confirmed in the growing mysticism of
Alexander's music, now packed with metaphysical descriptions
in which he tested out, sometimes groping his way, the explosion of the cosmological thought that would occupy him in his
period of maturity until the end. It isn't surprising that at the start
of his great achievements, we also find the first false note in his
reception by the public and specialized critics, objections to the
complexity of his ideas and the "pretentious ambitions of this
crackpot" (Rimsky-Korsakov *dixit*); some who had previously cel-
ebrated his works' surrender and delirium now mentioned formal
imprecision. Despite this, the wave of Scriabin fever was still on
the rise: my uncle incarnated the essence of the creative spirit. And
its afflictions: hypochondria tormented him, so he found himself
obliged to consume medicine in alarming proportions; out of fear
of germs, he never took off his gloves in public; in the presence of
strangers, he increased the intensity of his gaze to generate a "visual
barrier" that blocked intrusions into his psychology. The Russian
critic Sabaneyev observed the effect attending the performance

of his own compositions produced on Scriabin: "Sometimes he bent his head down in a strange way, with eyes closed. His face expressed an almost physical pleasure. Then he opened his eyes and looked up, as if he wanted to fly; but at tense moments of the music he breathed violently and nervously, sometimes grabbing hold of his chair with both hands. Rarely have I seen the face and figure of an artist change so much while listening to his own music. He seemed unable to conceal the deep experiences he took from it." Solitude had made him hypersensitive, given to excess demonstration. He kissed his piano as if it were a living thing, and grew anguished when it had to be tuned; he slept with scores under his pillow so at night the intensity of the contact didn't fade away. It isn't strange that in this period of surplus vibration of his primordial elements, he became involved with another woman.

Tatiana Schloezer was a somewhat inexperienced pianist who at eighteen years old had listened to one of Alexander's compositions and decided it had been the most powerful impression of her life, to the point she gave up her own ambitions out of a desire to understand the work and personality of her new god. Tatiana: tall, blonde, rosy-cheeked, with extremely pure blue eyes (though a bit nearsighted) and pale skin soft to the touch. A dream come true, for those who like to dream of women as flesh bibelots. In the beginning Alexander paid no attention to the commentaries that people let slip around him. But my uncle's great weakness, or if you like, his distinctive mark, was that just like the prophets and evangelizers, he needed a favorable environment that approved and helped spread his thought, a need that increased after he tore himself away from Vera. In these circumstances, he couldn't remain indifferent for too long to Tatiana, who showed herself prepared to give him everything, and content herself with whatever little he might offer her in return, even were it no more than the opportunity to forever continue in her role as silent witness to the existence of her beloved. Without anyone asking it of her, she began to assume the different functions that ease the life of a solitary man. She served tea to guests, prepared snacks, arranged pillowcases, aired out rooms, and took responsibility for regulating the entrance and exit times of visits . . .

Although he didn't show it, Alexander felt grateful for the domestic assistance. Of course, the intensity, the fire that burned in Tatiana's eyes, hadn't escaped him, but since this was an effect he was used to provoking, and not only in people of the opposite sex, he took it to be natural. He saw Tatiana as a young girl, and this is how he treated her. As a show of his regard, however, from time to time he made her the object of something vaguely akin to gallantry; Tatiana took her nourishment from these sentimental alms. Of course, she never mentioned her expectations, because she'd taken careful note of the limits that Alexander himself had imposed. Wasn't it true that among the many tasks she was assigned, one was to keep the bedroom free of dust where like an altar, illuminated by candles, the portraits of Vera Ivanovna and her children were displayed? Certainly, in this period Tatiana respected the emotional privacy of my uncle like no other, but sometimes, daring to lean her ear against the closed door, she heard the spasmodic moans, the babyish sobbing of the man she loved, for the woman he'd abandoned.

Were they an unusual case? Two artists curbing the satisfaction of their basic impulses out of a sense of decorum? At some point my uncle realized Tatiana's presence was essential to him, and inevitably he'd have to resign himself to losing her, if he didn't add something beyond these crusts to the relationship. Somehow he had to bring her up to his level, even if this equality was only a pretense. At the same time, keeping in mind Tatiana's active and sensitive intelligence, he couldn't just butter her up with flattery but had to respect the delicacy of their respective positions.

Finally, my uncle decided Tatiana had grown accomplished enough to *participate* in some aspect of his creative process, even if she didn't *compose* with him.

Alexander transformed his disciple into his first listener by submitting all works in process to her opinion. There's no need to draw any mistaken conclusions from this attitude. Although Tatiana was still a hesitant pianist, she had a solid theoretical formation. Given permission, she was even capable of educating Scriabin about certain aspects of his own work, concealed to himself.* At such moments, Alexander felt delighted gratitude at the presence of this self-effacing treasure. And it wasn't about greed or egocentrism, at least my uncle didn't see it that way, but about asymmetrical reciprocity. Tatiana was like a wishing well: he'd thrown in a ruble, and the fountain had returned so much more. But he couldn't rule out that it was a temporary phenomenon, since there's no woman who at her peak doesn't produce a radiant effect on some man. Maybe—thought my uncle—the balance would change over time. When that happened, he might find out what he'd offered her, thinking it meager, had represented an immeasurable vastness for Tatiana. As a music teacher, at least, he'd confirmed it was almost always this way with his students.

For a while, everything seemed to be going smoothly. Everything worked to the point that my uncle decided to entrust his disciple with some tasks that, while of vital importance to

---

* Decades later, Glenn Gould would discover recordings in which Tatiana Schloezer performs Alexander Scriabin. Even with her untrained playing, accentuated by the jerkiness of the needle sinking into the plastic record's groove, the organization of the work comes through clearly. Tatiana rarely used the pedal, which in his own performances my uncle emphasized heavily to forefront the aspects that most interested him (echoing and inchoate sound, Eastern fantasies and hypnotic, mist-filled atmospheres). With this omission, Schloezer emphasized what, following the impulses of his romantic character, Alexander had hoped to disguise in his compositions: the evident presence of a powerful contrapuntal structure, learned under Taneyev, who had studied it in J. S. Bach. Needless to say, in his own versions, Gould drew out this tendency.

his career, were secondary to his more permanent interests; for example, the drafting of texts for concert programs. The result was ideal. Tatiana had penetrated so deeply into Alexander's thought that her writings seemed to flow from the composer's own hand. In them, Scriabin's conception of music at that moment found its most complete expression. Through Tatiana's words, the compositions of Alexander Scriabin challenged the dominant trends of the period . . .

The appearance of these texts reinforced the musical influence my uncle now had over the cultured youth, eager for more sophisticated and rebellious forms than traditional composers could give them. Somehow, with Tatiana's help, Alexander's music found a reading in keeping with the thought of advanced sectors of society.

Initially, my uncle agreed to sign off on even the paragraphs in which Tatiana presented an explicit reading of his work as somewhere between lyrical yearning and the desire to oust Nicholas II's autocratic government. But an artist, a true artist, must always remain a bit ubiquitous and fluctuating, else he turn into a mere bourgeois.

"Tatiana's impulsiveness," he confessed to friends, "helps me understand it makes no sense to write one work after another, if the effort is preserved only by the superstitious will to profess a 'stylistic identity.' In its reiteration, this identity makes all new creation superfluous. When I recognize the work of some colleague as soon as the first chords have sounded, I know it's time to leave the room. The small yet great secret true artists cultivate is to distort the automatic program of their tastes and tendencies, making each composition into something new over the course of its development, in order to radically differentiate each work from the previous ones. Simply put: We have to invent ourselves every morning, make ourselves magicians and keep surprising until the end!"*

With the slowness of those affected by an excess of discretion, Alexander at last decided to thank Tatiana for the lesson she'd given him without his having looked for it. When he did so—in a way he considered explicit, hoping his gesture of recognition didn't escape her—he found it curious that Tatiana's reception was colder than expected. Used to her displays of veneration every day, the disciple's aloofness irritated my uncle, and he was about to react negatively but preferred to curb his anger. It was the first time she'd ever behaved this way.

But what was happening to Tatiana?

Nothing is more disturbing than the fear of suddenly losing what we've always taken to be ours. By virtue of a simple and unexpected gesture, Tatiana, who for months had barely stood out from the decor, was now the element that disturbed his life. It isn't strange that as a consequence of this discovery, Alexander forced things along, bringing them to a point only he considered unexpected and surprising.

---

* Typical of the "middle period" of his creative evolution, this statement by my uncle anticipates the central problem of modern art. Alexander Scriabin notes the paradoxical character of an aesthetic creation that stakes itself on a constant cycle of transformations, which—at its logical extreme—will necessarily produce the result that an artist doesn't recognize himself in his own works (not to mention the other kind of recognition from the public, permanently lost to him in advance). At this indeterminate moment in an aesthetic career, some come up against the horror, the very substance of emptiness, while others discover in it the ultimate gamble, the supreme achievement. Naturally, since art is made by limited subjects, imperfect and finite, once the artist is dead, the cycle of mutations in their work concludes. And what remains? A gallery of mutilated statues at the mercy of the elements.

As we know, in his glorious "final stage," Alexander Scriabin clearly understood the bounds of his aesthetic project of constant change and resolved to surpass them, proposing to go beyond the frontiers of art and transform the course of the Universe in its entirety.

7

Beyond the refreshing impression it gave my uncle to find himself with a young, flexible and available body, which gave way to his vigor after months of abstinence, the fact Tatiana went from the living room to the bedroom didn't seem to produce a substantial change in their relationship; at least, it wasn't a complete change. The difference could be perceived in the greater pleasantness (the relief) that Alexander showed, and his willingness to reduce the distance between them. Yet Tatiana continued to wear a surly expression, the imperturbable look one expects from governesses and servants.

For a while, he preferred to understand this attitude as the obedience to appearances a single woman must display if she lives in a man's house. But truth is, their environment didn't pay the slightest attention to convention, so at some point my uncle had to ask himself about the reasons that made Tatiana wear a scowl. The most obvious thing, to ask the woman herself, would have been at once tricky and useless. With sensitive women like her, every question is a torment, every interrogation an accusation. To force on her the dilemma of either babbling inanities (if she herself didn't know) or lying deliberately (if she wanted to hide the reasons for the behavior) would mean to act under false premises to obtain a single result: moral violence. It was better—he thought—to diminish the risks of conflict by turning to indirect methods.

Thus Alexander decided to accept the degree of hypocrisy implicit in the act of proceeding with a delicate inquiry. Taking Tatiana's hands and guiding her to sit beside him, he told her he wanted to speak to her as one speaks to a dear friend with whom there are no more secrets. Tatiana, who in general was used to answering even his most trivial comments, didn't let out a word. If the evening light that came in through the window had been slightly more intense, if my uncle had been a little less concerned with picking out the phrases he was about to utter, he'd have noticed Tatiana's slowness in taking a seat and the paleness that spread over her whole face, and would have anticipated the situation was taking on an aspect rather different from what he'd imagined for developing events. Whatever the case, he tackled the matter. He declared he had no complaints or resentments, only gratitude, and claimed it was solely concern about Tatiana and her state that encouraged him to beg that she freely express any uneasiness or disturbance she might feel. Was she comfortable in the house? Sometimes he saw her looking absorbed, overwhelmed, listless. Did she find herself with too many responsibilities? Did she perhaps need to take a vacation, continue her studies? Or did she need some free time to work on her own compositions . . . ?

Tatiana listened to these suggestions in silence, then bowed her head a little, slowly rubbed her eyes—was that a tear or the shine of makeup on her cheeks?—and fixing her gaze on some indefinable point in the room, murmured:

"Idiot."

Alexander didn't know whether she was referring to herself, him, the whole world or the situation. But he noticed she was now crying without covering her face. The tears kept sliding down, perfect ovoid drops that barely grazed the perfect skin, now redly haloed by rays of sun going to hide beyond the golden domes of Saint Peter's fortress. Before he was forced to turn on a lamp, my uncle had the opportunity to discover the beauty that flooded through Tatiana, the terrible beauty that streamed from this woman. Racked by terror, enveloped in the aura of a new kind of inspiration, he wanted to say something she would understand as a request for forgiveness or proposal to begin again, but he didn't have the chance to open his mouth, since she spoke first. She said that he rejected her, he'd always rejected her; that when he hugged her in his arms, when he kissed or caressed her, every one of his gestures demonstrated he was only offering her a miserly and short-lived scrap of his attention. From the start, she said, Alexander had presented her with a coldness able to freeze the center of the earth, yet she'd kept silent and remained by his side, hoping that at some point things would change, and dreaming of a moment that would never arrive, because from the very start it had been clear that he'd never take responsibility for anything, never really look at her in the way she hoped he would, that his mission in this world was not to make her happy.

Taken aback by the violence of this claim, Alexander left the room and went to his bedroom to think. When he came out, it was night. Dinner hadn't been served and Tatiana had shut herself away in the guest room.

By the next morning, my uncle had thought over the matter enough to recognize that, notwithstanding the way they'd been presented, to a certain degree the woman's arguments expressed the truth. From the moment they'd met, she'd left behind everything for him, even pretense. Tatiana had been the ideal student, and he hadn't known how to see her in that light because her natural modesty had emphasized her virtues and concealed her gifts. To put it bluntly, he used her without noticing her, without contributing to the development of her talents. Tatiana had made every effort, but now he had to devote part of his time to *her*, to getting her to return to composing and playing.

8

Tatiana showed herself to be a hardworking student. Her progress was so quick that after a few months Alexander pushed her to sit for the annual pianists' competition at the Moscow Conservatory. If she achieved one of the first positions in the selection, her career as a professional of the instrument would be assured. Although she didn't display great enthusiasm about the proposal, my uncle was confident in advance of a favorable result. His laughter could be heard, clear and high-pitched, through the hallways of the building as they waited to enter the concert hall.

"Joy, joy!" he said as he rubbed his pupil's hands wrapped in ermine gloves. "Everything will go splendidly. The jury isn't used to performances like the ones you're capable of offering. And if out of stage fright you aren't at your usual level of quality, don't worry. They're friends of mine and will be understanding. Beruloff even owes me a few favors."

"The only thing I want is for this to be over soon," she whispered.

It was a somewhat gloomy comment, but Alexander attributed it to her great sensibility. After all, they'd seen several candidates leave the exam hall in a state of total devastation.

When her turn came, Tatiana moved stiffly into the hall. She'd adopted an updo for the occasion, hair pulled back into a tight ballerina bun, which gave her a severe, disciplined, angular look.

Without greeting anyone, she took a seat on the stool and waited. Taneyev—by now an old alcoholic—leaned over the table and gave her a friendly once-over:

"Your maestro, my most esteemed Alexander Nikolayevich Scriabin, present here today, let slip to us you greatly esteem our dear Ludwig van . . ." he said. "It would be most appreciated if you could offer us a movement or, if you like, just a few measures of one of his sonatas. What would you prefer?"

"She knows them all to perfection," my uncle answered for her.

"Ah, good, good, very nice. It's terribly cold out today. Would you like to loosen up your hands by starting with something simple, like *Clair de Lune* . . . ?"

"She'll play whatever you ask," said my uncle.

"But my cherished Alexander Nikolayevich . . . Beethoven composed thirty-two sonatas! Only a pianist with substantial experience could know them all . . ."

"You'll be astonished by the speed and clarity of her performance, her talent for double thirds, octaves, sixths and chromatic sequences, her unparalleled ability for sight reading . . ."

"In that case, my admired . . ." sighed Taneyev. "She can begin wherever she feels like."

"First movement of Sonata no. 8 in C Minor, op. 13," announced Tatiana.

"The *Pathétique!*" rejoiced Taneyev. "*Grave; allegro di molto e con brio.* Light and pain. A concentrated movement, detailed and intricate. Go ahead, please."

Alexander held the view that before launching into the first strokes, a pianist must feel the secret vibration of energy that flows from the instrument and communicate one's own to it. When Tatiana gently placed her fingers on the keys and seemed to be resting, or perhaps listening to something, he realized (yet again, as he had so many times in the last months) she'd fully embraced his approach, and wagered everything on the magic of this initial contact. He also observed, content, the way his pupil's white skin stood out from the ash yellow and black ivories. A triple checkerboard. The reflection of her fingers on the polished wood. Tatiana crouched over, her shoulders curved as if to concentrate the fury of her body as pale as it was strong, and with a sharp jerk of the head, she began. For a few seconds, in which he kept his eyes closed, my uncle let himself be carried away by the excellence of the performance. There, in the mountains and valleys of time, was what he'd taught her, enhanced by the sensitive gentleness of her touch, which sought to transmit to each note her yearning to draw out its intimate resonance, its duration exceeding the possibilities of acoustics and amplitude. Going beyond the spectrum, even . . .

Suddenly, a false note. And silence.

Tatiana remained unmoving, sitting up straight. She stared into the angular abyss of the piano's open lid.

"It's nothing. You can start over, most valued one," proposed Taneyev. "This often happens when one has learned a piece well: one trusts too much in mechanics, in corporal mnemotechnics, and wham! The error of memory is followed by a physical stumble. All you need is to recover your automatism."

"Absurd," my uncle said. "Tatiana isn't the victim of a breakdown in the performance sequence. She isn't a little drummer girl. She knows what she's playing very well."

"Memory is trivial, writing is permanent. I think the problem would be solved if someone brought her the score . . ." proposed Beruloff.

"Sonata for Piano no. 29 in B-flat Major, op. 106," announced Tatiana.

Her left hand rose up.

"Just a second, most precious one," said Taneyev. "This sonata poses colossal technical difficulties. For years no one dared perform it publicly. Liszt was the first. As you know, it was Liszt who promoted the idea of the performer as a specialized object of astonishment for a public of middle-class ignoramuses, who, knowing nothing about music, pay their entrance fee to see a kind of illusionist of high-speed percussion, a monkey dressed in a tailcoat. And so . . . Those are not the only difficulties to overcome either. You also have to shift between many different registers . . ."

". . . Like a fish in water, our Tatiana," said my uncle.

"Third movement. *Adagio sostenuto. Appassionato e con molto sentimento*," added Tatiana.

The same bend, the same gesture. She was made for the instrument. Who wouldn't have written for her? She began. The A and C-sharp. A whole temple enters through the narrow door of the first two notes. Scriabin looked at the jury; the jury smiled. Everyone remembered, everything flowed. After the scherzo *assai vivace*, which closes in an enigmatic way with what seems to be a question mark, the crystal clear tinkling of these two notes forms the start to one of the most beautiful sonata movements ever written. Here, in the theme with variations, Beethoven is an Olympian maestro. What a risk! The main theme, written in an almost polyphonic form, transforms with the first variation into a melody that prefigures Chopin and accentuates the tormented character of the movement . . .

Feeling that Tatiana was playing it safe, my uncle's consciousness went ahead in its necessity to grasp the piece, to enjoy not only the moment but also the unfurling of the form in its wider structures: after a few measures in which the deaf author pretends to feel disoriented, he begins the second variation, superbly constructed as a melody with wide intervals, and after this modulation appears the third variation, in truth a modified form of the first . . . Here it seems Beethoven wanted to shout, to do away with all the preceding anguish, and in the end the main theme returns like a memory, the twilight glow of a Russian or German sun falling over the fields . . .

Another false note, and silence.

Taneyev had a hard time opening his lips.

"And now what, *carissima*?"

"Maybe you're a little nervous, and . . ." said Nikolai Tcherepnin.

"First movement of the Sonata for Piano no. 27 in E Minor, op. 90," announced Tatiana.

"*Mit Lebhaftigkeit und durchaus mit Empfindung und Ausdruck*," whispered Tebalski, as correct as he was disheartened.

After a couple of chords that dissolved into arpeggios, the same thing happened.

Why, during this setback, did the figure of the woman dressed in black take on the appearance of a mechanical bird?

Alexander left his seat, climbed up to the platform and, taking Tatiana by the arm, gently said: "Let's go."

When she'd stood up, my uncle acknowledged the jury with a slight bow of the head.

Back at home, Tatiana showed signs of a strong headache and went to her room. She spent the whole afternoon sleeping, and in the evening began to cry out in her dreams; all her bedclothes were soaked and she burned with fever, but she refused to receive the visit of a doctor and swore she'd be cured only if my uncle promised he'd never submit her to a test like that again.

Alexander promised what she wanted, and by the next morning Tatiana had recovered.

Distressed by the evidence that Tatiana had shown herself to be incapable of facing challenges others consider to be a powerful stimulus, my uncle asked himself what it was this woman expected or wanted. Was it something he could offer, allow or obtain for her? Something within reach of his fingertips? Or was it something abstract, ineffable, lacking substance?

On this point, it's impossible not to wonder how my uncle could have been such a genius of Romanticism, and such a hopeless case when it came to sentimental matters.

In his position, even an individual gifted with a minimum of perceptiveness, someone barely above the level of the subnormal, would have noticed that Tatiana's fury (her irritation, her spite, her bad mood) was the natural consequence of a hope forever disappointed, of a heart tired of never receiving the consolation of which it dreamed. Of course, love was the dark area in my uncle's life, both what he felt for Tatiana—which beat away inside him, a dull unnamed throbbing—and the agony he'd felt for Vera, from whom he'd ripped himself away in the belief it would save his family. Maybe the hard time he had bringing love into his life again can be understood as the tremendously paralyzing but understandable manifestation of the terror the body feels during dark hours of the soul, the nightmarish possibility it will experience the effects of another amputation. For him, Tatiana could be anything—student, concubine, grantee or benefactress—except the region of flesh and blood where a wound could reopen, one that still hadn't stopped bleeding.

It's because his whole being refused to suffer again after the loss of Vera that Alexander couldn't know or accept, much less say to Tatiana, that every one of his words and thoughts and acts in the last months had been dedicated to her. This recognition would have been equivalent to admitting he was losing Vera again. Pain thus opposed itself to the confession of the truth, and exerted its tyrannical hold; instead of embracing the truth that saw itself prevented from coming to light, and unaware of the true reasons for his difficulty behaving the right way, my uncle went over events, trying to analyze their respective positions, seeking alternatives, justifying himself or, what comes to the same thing, beginning to ask whether error could exist if he hadn't encouraged it. At heart—he thought—Tatiana was also responsible . . . Sometimes she was a little unfair. Not just a little. She exaggerated. All women did. It was imprinted on their character to mark the force of a conviction with an abuse of brio. The problem came from an absence of regulation of this excess, a riot of this intemperance. In Tatiana, a lack of control made her *too* unjust. After all, he'd tried, he'd done things for her! Hadn't he?

Convinced he wouldn't be able to discover what Tatiana wanted from him through logic (if she did want something), my uncle opted to trust instinct. Working from intuition, he chose to respond to the request that, strictly speaking, Tatiana had never formulated and to go deeper in the direction he'd already chosen, which had given such poor results. Like a physician who calculates the success or failure of a cure by adjusting the proportions of a tincture, the subtle oscillation between poison and medicine, he judged that the error had its origin in an insufficient dose of his music: Tatiana had come to know it, she'd been sufficiently steeped within it, but she hadn't sunk deeply into it enough times for this act of spiritual communion to transport her to a higher dimension. Additional and heavy measures of his gift were needed to produce a transformative experience, something that raised her to his heights and made her just like him, a part of his own being.

"I want the torrents of my music to pass through her metaphysical body and flood her with an orgy of sensations," he wrote to his friend and agent Koussevitzky.

9

Unable to know exactly what was going through Alexander's head, Tatiana saw in his didactic insistence only the violent gesture of a man who lacked consideration for anyone's feelings but his own. In fact, one of the most irritating elements in the matter was that my uncle was publicly taken to be a champion of the new aesthetic sensibility, along with Blok, Diaghilev, Nijinsky, Stanislavski, Artsybashev and Kschessinska, among others. What could one think but that this conduct put him at the border of moral duplicity, or straightforward hypocrisy? For Tatiana, these characteristics affected his music, or at least began to affect the perception she had of it. Gradually, the exasperations, romantic outbursts and passages of misty emotion (the famous "atmospheres") in his compositions began to grow intolerable to her. And this wasn't only because Alexander's demands on her functioned as an imposition, but also, and above all, because in their unfolding, every one of the features of his style worked as a layer that enveloped and lulled to sleep her own tastes, the manifestation of her own artistic possibilities. Alexander—Tatiana believed—was the vampire who drank from her blood to make her his mirror, the sole reflection in which one of his species can contemplate himself. But this swapping of youth for immortality demanded two things of her she was no longer prepared to give: admiration for the usurper of her identity (tenuous as this was) and agreement to the operation. So, at the same time as she remained by his side despite everything—because love exercises a reign superior to the reasons used by intelligence to disparage it—Tatiana offered a growing resistance, and used the flame of her hate as the key element of her individuation. She became cynical and, in public, allowed herself cutting comments and belittling remarks such as: "I know his true self all too well."

Faced with this state of things, and with the greatest delicacy, Alexander's circle of friends suggested to him the convenience of distancing himself a bit from a woman who seemed to have applied the better part of her energies to making his life miserable. The curious thing—the curious thing for these friends—was that my uncle stubbornly rejected these ideas. In his pupil's harshness he seemed to find the material for a shameful satisfaction. So his friends went silent or themselves avoided being present for further scenes of the uncomfortable performance. Especially because after a while, these displays of feminine irritation, which these friends tolerated only because they seemed to have become a requirement for approaching or staying close to Scriabin, took on the form of unwanted confidences. Tatiana had modified her form of behavior, and rather than confront him directly, she availed herself of Alexander's friends as the repositories of her disappointment, the witnesses to her everlasting suffering. As if it hadn't been enough to openly harass and belittle him, she now used them to complain. Some of these friends, equipped with a reasonable share of subtlety, saw a certain degree of progress in this change. If rage had begun to give way to grievance, then once its litany had been exhausted, it could yield to some form of reconciliation. But this didn't seem to happen, or at least not immediately. The grievance extended over time, and in Tatiana's voice it sounded like a high-pitched noise, not projected but natural, a perpetual piercing sound that drilled into their eardrums and their patience. During this period, many friends moved away from my uncle, alleging he'd been hypnotized by a Medea capable of ruining everything. Others denounced the effect of my uncle's vanity, in negative: Tatiana spun around him at the rhythm of her accusations, and in the dark waters churned up by her insolence, my uncle found the dregs of an unequaled devotion.

One night, however . . .

As they did every night at the same time, the circle of intimates had gathered in the big living room, hoping Alexander would perform something new from what he was working on. Instead, as was usual now, they received only his silence, a silence that looked thoughtful but was oppressive, and was accompanied by the sharp contrast of Tatiana's commentaries. The moment was despicable; Tatiana revealed the wounds of unsuccessful love as she'd never dared before with such rawness; her usual biting criticisms were accompanied by dredged-up intimacies: she said the ardor my uncle offered the world, the torrent of the music that sent dupes and music lovers into ecstasy, motivating hope or overwhelming them with the promise of an infinite deluge, was actually a leftover trickle of energy limited to expansion in a single direction, because—and here Tatiana raised her tone of voice, went pale, and hitting sternum with right thumb, presented herself as testament and proof—*she* knew well the price to pay for the composition of these fatuous enchantments, a mere *mélange* of hysterical chords and capricious arabesques (the hysterical arabesque of his capricious chord), was the withdrawal of the author from every human contact. Tired of putting up with his fussy behavior and prudishness, she could no longer conceal the fact that Alexander spent days, weeks, even months showing signs of terminal exhaustion: he lay beside her as if he were a dead man. His supposed absorbing passion, which led him to fill one sheet of music paper after another, after another, with his scribbles, thus represented a gift that cloaked a shameful farce, the overblown lyrical imitation of an impotent Casanova. Obviously, *sometimes*—here Tatiana rushed to dismiss an objection no one had formulated—Alexander attempted to lurch himself out of inaction; abandoning his position as a living mummy, he'd sometimes lean toward her, make a move in search of her love, but at those moments she'd reject him with anger and disgust. Why did she do that? Why not accept these tokens of effort? Not because it was far too late: she'd already offered enough demonstrations of her patience, her personal sacrifice for him, a sacrifice by now part of her deepest past, tucked away in a pouch of the most gorgeous and expensive velvet, kept in a glass jewelry box in the most isolated corner of the museum of her naïveté. Of course, it would never have been too late if Alexander were operating *sincerely*. But alas, she knew him: in his every dying bishop's gesture to appeal to her as a companion and woman, there was nothing but fear and calculation; calculation of the advantages and disadvantages of keeping or losing her, and fear his rejection of a normal and regular contact would at some point force her to declare, precisely as she was doing now, the impossibility of maintaining a link of convenience in which she'd given everything to the point of exhaustion, until she was a wreck, whereas he hadn't given anything in the slightest. Nothing. Not a thing, not the slightest damn thing. Have I explained myself, do I need to say any more, or do you understand me now?

After saying all of this, Tatiana went quiet, exhausted and also a little frightened. What she'd said had broken something; her excess had courted the specter of the irreparable. Alexander, who throughout the whole of the woman's monologue had kept silent, jaw resting gravely on his chest, now lifted his head and remarked in a casual tone:

"For some time now, I've felt the need to travel."

After these words, his friends made their excuses and left. This time it was Tatiana who visited my uncle's bedroom. She stayed all night long.

Branded by many as an "aspiring aristocrat," my uncle set off on a journey identical to those so beloved by the nomadic mysticism of the Russian peasantry. These aren't about clothes worn or deities worshipped but the idea of abandoning everything, of cutting ties from a previous existence and symbolically "dying" for one's fellow man. The outer path, the pilgrimage, becomes the inner path, and the pilgrim, the restless dead man, is a *stranniki* . . .

This period of wandering is one of the most fascinating and least known periods of his life. The lack of precise information and contradictory versions locate it on the narrow fringe between myth and legend.* His trip was drawn out in time and spread out in space. He contracted malaria in Bukhara, dysentery in Balochistan, scurvy in Kurdistan, *bedinka* in Aschkabadian and dropsy in Tibet. He met priests, engineers, doctors and princes,

---

* Imprecise and vague as it was, this journey was powerfully inspiring for a good part of the Russian intelligentsia, especially the "exoticists" of various kinds. His influence grew to fever pitch in the case of George Ivanovich Gurdjieff, who in his invented autobiography *Meetings with Remarkable Men* attributes to himself each and every one of my uncle's vital experiences.

Mimetically following this journey, the self-proclaimed "maestro of the Fourth Way" also claims to possess abilities as a composer, inspired by his disciple and companion, the pianist Thomas de Hartmann, who studied with Arensky and Taneyev and had my uncle's work strongly recommended to him. Strictly speaking, all the Gurdjieffian hot air about a supposed "System" of his invention, his convoluted Law of Seven and Law of Three, and his "Ray of Creation" that transforms the Universe into a cosmological musical scale ("do" as God, "si" as Universe, "la" as Milky Way, "sol" as Sun, "fa" as planets of the Sun, "mi" as Earth and "re" as Moon) can be understood as a gaudy vulgarization of Alexander Scriabin's work.

people who stood out due to not only their appearances but also their vigor, self-control and compassion. He traveled for part of his journey with some of them. Rocky wildernesses, inaccessible locations. Some of this, especially in places where the nature had a desolate splendor, transmitted itself to him as a vibration of the material, as sound. Here was the truth of Madame Blavatsky's words, now as firsthand evidence. This vibration, which went from the world to the Universe, or maybe from the Universe to the world, ricocheted against his own body, or reverberated through it, in accordance with his height and tonality. The intense yet delicate experience, of an extremely refined subtlety, united him with physical things even as it detached him from his being, separated him into an infinite number of slender psychic layers and recomposed him, folding him into a totality while preserving his difference from it.

In Tabriz, he learned the secrets of hypnosis, a skill he promised never to use. He traveled through Turkistan, Orenburg, Sverdlovsk, Merv, Kafiristan, the Gobi Desert. He followed the golden path to Samarkand. At some point, he visited the monastery of Sarmoung, and walked around the three main patios (which represent the exoteric, mesoteric and esoteric circles of humanity). Although it's probable that this visit occurred only on the allegorical plane, or that he gained admission to its patios and cloisters by the privileged route granted to some eminent men through the door of dream, what's certain is that he was present for the demonstrations of sacred dances. At the monastery, Sufis introduced him to the knowledge of the *mehkeness*, and Talmudists enlightened him about the mysteries of the Merkabah. One night, under a full moon, an old priest supplied him with a concoction that produced mydriasis: with his pupil dilated to the level of absurdity, and his visual and auditory sensations increased, he experienced colors, tones, reflections, iridescences he'd never dreamed possible. The real world and its miseries and torments disappeared from his mind as a truly divine atmosphere surrounded him. Scriabin understands what his compositions have been missing until now; his task as an artist is only getting started. Projected against a background of black sky, the lustrous stars tremble and begin to move as matter loses reality to become essence.

Then he loses himself in Asia. Some travelers see him circulating amid the gymnosophists of Gedrosia, the koinobis of Egypt and the rishis of Kashmir. It's said that he makes a pilgrimage with the monks of India called Hossein, and that he seeks the worshippers of the fire of Zoroaster and the Persian and Chaldean magicians, who want to impose primeval truth by reading the uncorrupted original version of Zend Avesta. In the mountain chain that borders the Tibetan Plateau, he discovers that under the scrubland of dry grass and slopes of sand, ancient civilizations are buried that competed in pomp with Babylon. At the edge of the oasis of Tchertchen he stumbles across the ruins of immense cities, destroyed in the tenth century by Mongols. The wind, which blows endlessly, sweeps through to conceal and reveal copper coins, shards of broken glass, coffins that hold the perfectly conserved mummified remains of tall men with thick heads of hair, their skin ravaged by psoriasis. Alexander finds the real Nofretamon, a smiling young man with eyes closed by gold discs.

There are some who calculate that in earthly terms, this entire period of spiritual initiation should be measured in years. The near exact authentic figure, however, can be deduced from the fact that Julian Scriabin was born a few days after my uncle returned to Saint Petersburg.

The arrival of a son seemed to ease the couple's tensions. With Tatiana busy breastfeeding, Alexander could at last go back to composing and giving concerts without greater disturbances. Of course, this claim is relative, given the serenity of the environment found itself somewhat altered: the use of the trill, which in my uncle's works abandons all decorative function to repeat with dramatic insistence, should be read in direct relation with the protests of the baby, who was born with certain digestive disorders. The use he makes of this circumstance shows him to be a mature artist capable of incorporating any element, even the most unlikely, into the development of his work. And it's precisely during this period that Alexander notes the possibility his work might have a "use" different from the expressive and aesthetic intentions that produced it.

This discovery was a consequence of his link to a couple of infamous personalities.

11

P. Badmayev, a famous doctor or unscrupulous fraud who claimed to have a solid grasp of Tibetan medicine, was the one who supplied Grigori Yefimovich Rasputin with the herbs, perfumes and poultices he used to treat the hysteria of the Tsarina and the hemophilia of the heir Prince Alexei. The crooked *staretz* and his dealer had become an influential pair in the private life of the imperial family. Of the two, Rasputin functioned as the prima donna, the public figure, while Badmayev served as the power behind the throne. Through their actions, both of them had earned the hate of the most undeviating Slavophile sectors of the Russian army, which accused them of being spies in the service of foreign powers, ironic because if the foolish Nicholas II had paid attention to the lewd monk's warnings when the time came, Russia wouldn't have got involved in the war against Germany that resulted in the October Revolution or the massacre that liquidated the Romanov dynasty, broke up its imperial army and installed the Bolshevik leadership in the Kremlin, which was manipulated by William of Prussia's intelligence services and ended up signing away a good part of its territory to German barbarians at Brest-Litovsk. It's true that, being the sort they were, only the idiot of the Tsar and the cretin of his imported wife could believe in the sincerity and purity of intention of the miracle-working duo, which demonstrates that stupidity hits the mark more often than good judgment. In effect, although they got together "with the political dregs of Saint Petersburg" (the phrase belongs to the delicate Prince Yusupov), formed by characters like the journalist Manasevich-Manuylov and the prince M. M. Andron-ikov, in political terms Rasputin and Badmayev looked out only for the superior interests of the nation and its monarch. Of course, this doesn't conceal the flagrant fact that they took advantage of the autocrat's gifts to grow rich with impunity. In addition, the royal affection made them arrogant and vulgar. Rasputin didn't hush up his opinion that the aristocracy lacked Russian blood, calling its members dogs and accusing them of being parasites implanted in a generous soil that at any point might brutally cull them, while he defined himself as "the truth of the future and the lion of two worlds that will save them from revolutionary catastrophe." In fact, in the court's strained atmosphere, there weren't lacking those who argued that his unbearable conduct, baffling fragmentary statements and incorrect speech had to be understood as a sign of the new times, to which nobles had to adapt for the sake of their own survival. And for this reason, they adored him even as they loathed him, and gave him their daughters, mothers, wives and lovers.

Badmayev, who had less intense sexual appetites or more diversified interests, observed that Rasputin's brutal conduct did nothing but fuel the conditions for their near disgrace, and so he applied himself to looking for a solution that favored them. Especially since the latest political and military setbacks had struck a severe blow to the general belief in monarchy by divine right. To sum up: it was a situation that guaranteed life to nobody, much less this couple of outsiders. It isn't strange that in his desperate search for protection, after running around several government offices requesting endorsements from functionaries who days later were riddled with bullets or blown to pieces, Badmayev thought of Alexander Scriabin.

The Tibetan doctor presented himself before my uncle with the justification that he wanted to commission a piece celebrating the court gardener's birthday. My uncle, despite having heard a few things about his visitor, didn't show much interest in the offer. Alarmed by the curt reception, Badmayev scrapped his excuses and revealed his true aim:

"My dear Alexander Nikolayevich, I come like a pilgrim begging you to hear his supplications. I have detailed information about your recent trip and have been able to make an accurate evaluation of the planes on which your current preoccupations unfold, and so I know well—better even than you do!—the dimensions and reach of your future concerns."

"What are you talking about?" said my uncle.

"My dear Alexander Nikolayevich! Of all the current composers, you are the only one who understands music to be a superior revelation transfused with invisible energy that could influence the world of phenomena; you are the only inheritor of ancient knowledge. This is why I have dared bother you with a request that might seem an absurdity, nearly an infamy, but that at heart is directly linked to the development of your labors. It involves protecting the earthly sheath of a soul that is holy, though in appearance wayward, along with, of course, my own . . . I need . . . it's a small thing to ask of you, but it would be a miracle to obtain it . . . I need a harmony, a specific vibration appropriate for that soul, something like a chord of the pleroma, a kind of plenitude able to modify the rules of the physical universe and grant invulnerability to the person to whom the harmony corresponds. Is it possible to achieve this?"

"Are you asking me for a personal aura made out of music?" asked Scriabin.

Noticing a mocking lilt in the tone of my uncle's voice, Badmayev stood up and coldly responded:

"Honor among mystics . . . If some reincarnation of your

Greek maestro were present, I'd ask him for this favor. Since that is impossible, I'm asking it of you. And of course, your efforts will be splendidly compensated. In this and other worlds."

And with a gesture more elegant than might be expected from someone of his physique and appearance, he let go of his visiting card, which gave three turns in the air (Alexander heard its journey as a succession of fourth intervals in different variations), before it dropped with a clean flutter onto a pewter tray gathering the ashes of a fragrant incense stick from India.

12

No more than a week had passed since the visit before my uncle decided to study the contents of Badmayev's offer. Perhaps, as the doctor claimed, the proposal was in line with his interests and pointed toward the development of the traditional knowledge he'd renewed contact with during his trip. In addition, something about Badmayev was very familiar to him . . . Could he think of him as a pale Asian version of Madame Blavatsky, come back as one of her multifaceted mirrors to give him another shove toward some form of truth?

The period of collaboration between Alexander Scriabin, P. Badmayev and Grigori Rasputin is a little-known chapter in the history of music and Russian mysticism. Generally, my uncle tends to be thought about as yet another victim to the forceful magnetism of the Tsarina's protégé. Truth is, Rasputin was little more to him than a freakish laboratory specimen and object of curiosity, whom he had the good judgment to keep away from his home. But he was intrigued by the monk's unkempt and slovenly appearance, by his fascination with the tedious ceremonies of dissolute life, by his apathy toward the joys of the intelligence.

"My thoughts are like birds in the sky, they flit this way and that, and I can't do anything to stop it," said Rasputin.

He was a man who read badly, wrote lopsidedly and was ignorant of the rules of orthography, not to mention one who never memorized his acquaintances' last names—after submitting women to his instincts, he'd refer to them by nicknames like Beauty, Little Star, Baby Bee, Curls or Gorgeous, just to avoid mix-ups. He was a theatrical show-off, the kind of feminine male who needed to reaffirm his personality by making himself the permanent center of attention.

"Everybody wants to be on top, but only one manages it," he told my uncle the day Badmayev introduced them. Then he showed him around his rooms and gave him a tour of his properties: "I had a filthy shack and now just look at the big house I've laid my hands on. This pillow costs six hundred rubles and this gold crucifix is priceless, because the Tsar gave it to me as a mark of distinction. See? It has N, N for Nicholas, engraved into it with a blowtorch. And this portrait of *me*, what do you think? What burning eyes! Don't think I'm picking bits of food from my beard while the artist paints me. I'm thinking. I have so much to think about. You'd be astonished if I told you just one of my thoughts. Do you see these Easter icons, these miniature golden eggs? If you turn a crank, you can split the ruby down the middle so a diamond-studded carriage pops out. Inside are the Tsar and Tsarina and the children, and I am that little doll doing turns as it waves, blessing the world. Look, look at this letter from Alexandra Feodorovna! She gave it to me herself, from her own hand. What do you say? Can you read? I don't know where I left my glasses . . ."

"I am incapable of making any decision, Grigori, without having consulted you first; I will always ask you everything . . . Even if they all rise up against you, I shall not abandon you," read my uncle.

"Mama loves me a lot," Rasputin shed a false tear. Then he put away the letter and showed him to his favorite tavern, where they spent most of the night. While Alexander looked on, the monk drank, shrieked as he danced, clicked his heels, yelled, hugged the balalaika players, threw glasses into the air, stomped on them with his reindeer-fur boots and opened his shirt to bare his hairy chest. Then, exhausted, he sat down next to my uncle and confided in him:

"Although some think I'm acting, I'm not a clown. Ever since I was a boy, I've understood there's an enormous force inside me and I have no power over it. The only thing I know is all that one needs to know in life: how to impress others. If you want to create a strong effect, you have to speak little, restricting yourself to pronouncing brief, clipped, even incomprehensible phrases. No need to worry about meaning; the rest will take it upon themselves to find it. The less people understand something, the more value they give to it. Idiots are everywhere and the Spirit blows where it pleases. I'm aware what you're thinking, my dear . . . ! Where's Badmayev? Sometimes, I suspect that instead of giving me Tibetan medicines he stocks me with chemical products. At least, the smell . . . What's doing turns through that little head of yours? I'd like you to hug me! You're my friend, aren't you? The people suffer greatly and no day or hour goes by that their Little Father doesn't think of them. War would be insanity. I behold red seas. Our army isn't prepared for confrontation. Much less against a precise, machine-like Germany. In battle we'll know only how to generously spill our Slavic blood. War is brutal slaughter, and there's no truth or beauty in it. While drinking, I talk about our country, but I never let slip anything a foreign power might use. Of course, I accept any contribution to the cause of peace. Etch this on your brain: soon, very soon, there will be a tremendous fire. It will engulf everything. If before you finish your work, I am the victim of a criminal attempt, I want you to make it known that the intellectual author of the event was not our poor Tsar but those nasty red bugs. Do politics interest you? To conquer a walled fort and conquer a woman requires the same strategy. One must treat ladies like whores and whores like ladies: that's the key to success in love. What differentiates a lady from a whore? Money and position. Everyone is equal and nobody's a nobody. And who am I? Father Grigori, he who lets Russia speak from his mouth. You must protect me, because if I were to die, the catastrophe would be to our land. Embrace me! Are you my friend or not?"

After that long night that ended with the *staretz* baptizing the sawdust on the floor with his vomit, my uncle accepted Badmayev's request. Even though the Tibetan doctor had offered him an astronomical figure for the creation of an effective musical carapace, my uncle was moved not by an interest in the money, but by the fact that in the request he'd glimpsed an element, as old as it was new, that would turn out to be of central importance when plotting the coordinates of the *Mysterium*.

Of course, there will be those who point out a certain contradiction in the fact that a work like this one, whose purpose and results have no comparison in the entire history of humanity, found a point of origin in Rasputin. Why him instead of any other? Why surround that beast with a protective aura?

Beyond the fact that the blend of the crude and the sublime forms a part of the aesthetic panorama in this period, it remains understandable that because of the life he lived, the dissolute monk embodied an interesting figure for my uncle; in a sense, he could be compared with a Judas of the tavern, a representative of our degraded species. As such, to rescue him from the darkness with the fiery magic of his art would be a Promethean task or, to continue the comparison and extend the use of hyperbole, would mean his transformation into a new Jesus.*

Now Alexander faced the problem of making good on the

---

* Of course, just a short time later, driven by unhappiness, my uncle would notice that the balance necessary to preserve the microcosmos of every individual from catastrophe is correlated with the one indispensable for sustaining the macrocosmos. In this respect, we can now reveal that the most well-known aspect of his work, the "mystic chord," expresses at a human level what the *Mysterium* does at a universal one. And it's because of this difference in magnitude that the chord produces a practically instantaneous effect, while the *Mysterium* is a work that must develop over time, so its benefit spreads through all of Creation.

request. Badmayev's assignment hadn't been a mere allegory but a desperate plea. Badmayev was convinced of the possibility that music could "materialize." And after all . . . if Pythagoras had said that the Universe vibrated in C, why wouldn't it be possible to create a musical field around a body . . . ? A specific vibration at a specific frequency could produce physical results. The chords on Piano A that reverberate on Piano B in another room ("sympathetic resonance"). The contralto breaking a crystal glass with her high pitch, a B note. Obviously those were easy exercises. But Badmayev had turned to him precisely for that reason: to go beyond this, to make the difficult possible until the unlikely became real. Now then, what notes or sounds might work to protect Rasputin from a murder, turning him into someone invulnerable or perhaps invisible?

Determined not to let himself be consumed by uncertainty, my uncle chose to advance in his hypothesis that the "carapace" had to respond somehow to the essence of Rasputin, to express, through musical notation, the very being of the monk, which should begin to vibrate when the melodies, harmonies and chords specially chosen for him were performed. His idea, although it evoked the new discoveries about electrical current, possesses more affinities with certain experiments carried out by entomologists of the period, who had come to the conclusion that chitinous surface coverings typically found on cockroaches, dung beetles, snails and ladybugs were not the product of the chance phenomena that evolutionary fates incorporate into the development of a species, but the result of a programmed internal secretion: as if these brainless critters were an integral part of a plan that included the perfection of their natural defenses, for the benefit of their survival and preservation. Obviously the process could be measured in millennia, in millions of years, and he didn't have that much time to help the Tsarina's favorite: he had to quickly find the few carapace-notes equivalent to the monk's crude individual substance. If my uncle was wrong about the appropriate notation, and when the chord was performed, Rasputin's being vibrated at an erroneous frequency, then the monk (among others) would run the risk of dissolving into a puddle of water.

The question was, at what frequency did the chords of this individual's soul vibrate? Scrupulous historians might ask whether the tragic end of the *staretz* put Rasputin's assassin, Prince Felix Yusupov, in a role as unexpected as it was fearsome: if he became the musical critic of Alexander Scriabin's attempts. But this would be a myopic perspective for reflecting on the course of events.

For some time, my uncle tried to complete the assignment. He followed Rasputin everywhere, studying his gestures, behavior, relationships. Yet he sensed a dark energy in him, something untamable, a kind of internal shield or low emanation that blocked any scrutiny of his interior. In fact, there are still some who believe the mystic chord

(C/F#/Bb/E/A/D) was a failed and provisional attempt to express the monk's diabolical character. The only thing certain is that my uncle made a series of attempts, and these didn't give the best results. When he communicated to Badmayev that the soul or essence of Rasputin had the opacity of a latrine and it was time to abandon him to his fate, the Tibetan doctor didn't formulate any objection. With a sad and somewhat enigmatic smile, he answered that although Alexander could not appreciate it at the moment, his efforts would bear fruit in the course of time.*

---

* Did Badmayev have premonitions? Was the Tibetan doctor a master of the anticipatory arts? The fact he turned to my uncle demonstrates he possessed at least enough knowledge of physics and acoustics to know that objects vibrate at specific frequencies, and that given two sensitive objects of the same frequency, near each other or connected in space, a vibration of one will produce a vibration in the other as echo or response. Strictly speaking, knowledge about these matters does not imply any particular hermetic knowledge: the newspapers in those days, for instance, reported that a scientist from the United States had built a "phonautographic ear" using a stalk of hay, at the end of which he'd placed the ear of a dead man. When the scientist spoke into the ear, the hay traced sound waves over the surface of a piece of tinted glass. The result seemed to imitate fog waves over water.

Were Badmayev and Alexander Scriabin aware of further details about this experiment? What we do know is that the unusual combination throws a certain light on the purpose of the *Mysterium*: a composition, a vibration (or rather, an organized combination of vibrations) whose ultimate aim was to contrive a rippling series of modifications over the whole profane epidermis of the Universe.

13

Saint Petersburg is at the height of its glory. The sound of bells cleanses the air. Gold domes of orthodox churches, the sparkle of snow, ice skaters tracing arabesques over the frozen surface of the Neva River, which will soon hide the crazy monk's dead body under its white cape. After a day spent on composition, Alexander celebrates the evening's beauties by playing piano with his son Julian. Life spills like liquid honey over a crunchy slice of black bread, spread thick with butter. They entertain each other performing some very difficult pieces for four hands. Julian is a young genius, a musical phenomenon at his age, and, of course, my uncle is convinced that with the years his fame will eclipse that of Mozart. Although this isn't his first born, only with him has he discovered the joys of paternity, owing to no fault in the children from his marriage with Vera, whose absence continues to cut him to the quick. But he was too busy with his own concerns at the start of his artistic vocation and heard the shouts and sobs and complaints as a disturbance to his work, while now, he no longer minds giving up the use of his hours. There's an incomparable pleasure in witnessing the growth of offspring from our own blood, as we learn to cultivate the virtues of our own disappearance. Julian: his sallow skin, his gray steel eyes, his clear gaze, his dark ringlets like those of an Arab . . . His clear laugh. Arpeggios.

The seasons pass. We will speak only a few more words about this boy, my cousin, although the rest of this chronicle dedicated to Alexander Scriabin is marked by his breath. Summer. Tatiana (a Tatiana incredibly reconciled to her fate; a loving mother, a tender and faithful wife) prepares him for an outing with his classmates (lunch and afternoon snack on the banks of the Dnieper). Little sailor suit, short pants, blue and white jacket over dark blue shirt (linen and pearl buttons), black leather shoes, white socks pulled up to his knees. Tie? No. A straw hat circled by a black velvet ribbon, to protect him from the glare. Tremolo of leaves. Birches. Julian sets out onboard a steaming modern machine called an *auto mobile*. He arrives to medallions of light and shadow, snaking waterways. There's a small boat anchored in the cove, unexpected in the landscape. The boys are naughty. Julian has just composed his four preludes for piano (even today they can be acquired in a rather sedate version played by Evgeny Zarafiants). He and a couple of friends climb into the boat, pushed by the gentle governess. There's no wind; it's a floration toy. Slow, then presto. A ripple. Pointillism in the landscape. Bubbles.

Suggestion is not enough; the production of an effect invoking what's vanished through a description of what alludes to it. But it's impossible to repeat everything again, to say it over and over until the word and the thing become one. To speak into being that finger that came from nowhere, that warm pink flesh once curled in trust around the finger of my uncle. Goodbye, Julian. Life. Life. Life.

I can't say much about my uncle's pain, about its endless succession. He had a father he didn't know, searching for whom he'd lost his mother and misplaced his brother; he'd pushed away his first wife and children to avoid tragedy; and now Julian . . .

When she got the news, Tatiana succumbed to her suffering. We won't have anything more to say about her. Alexander went gray overnight; his hands trembled and his gaze became a blank stare, even though his pupils shone more fiercely than ever. He didn't stop working for a moment.

From this period comes his opus 60, *Prometheus: The Poem of Fire*, which begins the cycle of the most remarkable accomplishments of this exceptional genius. Maybe it's a risk to say my uncle composed this work to literally and symbolically rescue his son from the clutches of death. But it's true. The influence of theosophy, his spiritist practices . . . the somber and sentimental worlds of necrophilia are capable of encouraging beliefs even more fantastic than this one. Just as the experience with Rasputin's "protective shield" had been his first technical attempt to produce a physical effect through acoustic vibration, the tragedy of Julian would push him to multiply his efforts, because for him this death would be the clearest evidence that—cosmically speaking—instability is the prevailing order.

Prometheus: the Titan opposed to Zeus that bears a flaming torch to illuminate a humanity in darkness. Then, via Christian syncretism, he becomes Lucifer, *Luce ferre*, the giver of light. How can one avoid thinking that Alexander Scriabin wanted to seek amid the waters for the lifeless body of my cousin Julian? To search for him, to rescue him. The whole of humanity in a son. Of course, the lesson of Christianity is that an Occult God closes His eyes to tragedy, something my uncle was unable to do.

Prometheus is thus written in opposition to a divine plan that tends toward annihilation, both out of indifference toward the created and as punishment for human actions, or perhaps out of the desire for reconciliation and reformation of the divine with his work—that is, an impulse to return to the Initial Void. Alexander Scriabin rebels against this gesture that he believes immoral, because it doesn't take human opinion or will into consideration. "If God exists and has created all beings, whether it's a fragment of plenitude He chooses to inhabit, His pleroma, or a little private hell, a region He descends toward concealed in different forms . . . what's certain is that men also live in their own universe, even if they haven't created it, and have the right to live in it and opine about the conditions of their being and duration, since within this general Universe they've created their own particular universes and own worlds, and reign over them as gods of their own creations," he wrote for the program of the work, on the occasion of its premiere—which took place in Moscow on March 15, 1911, with conducting by Serge Koussevitzky.

Musically . . . *Prometheus* is a composition for piano, orchestra, and a light keyboard called a "chromola" or *tastiera per luce*, a kind of "color organ" my uncle ordered custom-made from one Preston Millar (I have no further references). The result is in general highly dissonant; the mystic chord takes precedence, above all at the start, as an expression of the dominant chaos, then the work rises up with gradually increasing discipline until apotheosis comes in the promise of resurrection—whose intensity leaves far behind the efforts of Gustav Mahler in his *Kindertotenlieder*, which concludes with a more traditional sharp chord in the key of F.

While he was working on the manuscript, my uncle had visions of radiant axes, leaves in flames and fiery tongues, images surging up in his thought he attempted to translate into the staging. In addition to the strictly compositional aspects, the messianic character of the work is marked by the choristers' white vestments and the "chromola," which projected colors associated with the harmonic plane onto a screen over the aisles of the hall as well as the audience, so as to induce its spiritual evolution.

Beyond a doubt, in this relationship between music, light and message, elements of both theosophical and Kabbalistic inspiration can be found; in fact, the concept of the ascension seems a direct allusion to the tree of Sephirot. Above all, however, *Prometheus* is the mature and luminous blueprint of an approaching comprehension. Fury as a response to the indifference or will to destruction that animates the divine element will yield to a full consciousness of the impending catastrophe, and the subsequent understanding that the emptiness through which apocalypse infiltrates must be fended off at all costs: and so, from denunciation of the present horror, Alexander Scriabin will progress after only a brief period to his concept of the *Mysterium*, the total work of art aimed at the salvation of the Universe.

14

Frightened of the novelty implicit in the *Prometheus* project, or maybe of his own transfiguration, Koussevitzky, during the premiere, omitted use of the light machine, claiming the images in color would distract the audience, which led to a personal confrontation with my uncle. All the same, beyond the painful betrayal of his patron and representative, what most affected Alexander was knowing that apart from the reception obtained, his music hadn't been effective in the dimension where he'd proposed to triumph. *His opus 60 hadn't changed anything.* Neither transformed the audience nor returned to Alexander the beloved and now dissolved body of Julian and his pure little soul, which kept on calling out to him . . . The evidence shook him. Was it a technical error to insist on the chord of his invention, to the point it became central to his aesthetic? Or . . . ?

It's curious to note that while critics considered him the most prominent champion of a current of subjective art, the boldest example of the renovation of formal structures in pursuit of the extreme imperative of personal emotion, Alexander Scriabin thought of himself—and worked in consequence—as the inheritor of a tradition of objective art, one that over the course of time had been reduced to a kind of psychic realism arguing the particular configuration of sounds evokes some response in the human mind, translated into the form of "inner experience." Of course, this *reductio ad hominem* had its importance: it pointed to a specific mathematical relation between the properties of sound and some aspect in our system of receptors, which for instance determines the ability of a certain music, within the framework of a certain defined culture, to generate a certain sort of instinctive reaction (Gregorian chant / kneeling / prayer, military marches / parades / belligerent feeling); its highest aspiration thus limited itself to inducing the repetition of predetermined, codified behaviors. For my uncle, it was necessary to go further (even if this journey pushed him very far back in time), to amplify the possibilities. If mankind was conceived within the mark of difference of heterogeneous creation, then it should do something more than reproduce what has already been given, using the elements within reach. The weakness of every reflection theory is that it postulates a total identification between the Being and the Copy, when, as we know, no body circulates without some loss of energy over the course of its journey. So—my uncle believed—in order to be truly powerful, music had to abandon its character of an echo and turn into action.

In this sense, Alexander now recognized his error with Rasputin had been to believe that by the simple act of providing him with a series of particular chords, the *staretz* would ultimately have been able to generate a field of his own, an inner emanation, a reflection of the vibration of his atoms in the form of a "shield" . . . as if music were a vaccine that generates an immunological reaction in the affected organism. But that was like producing something to expand the limits of a prior condition, like teaching a boy in front of the piano to perceive the subtle vibration of the energetic field between E and F and between B and C. The truth was that he had to produce a difference of degree that could tear people and things from their beings to hurl them directly toward the new, toward a Universal Prometheus!

But what was the new, and how to find it? And what was the direction to go?

Driven by these questions, my uncle went backward. Yet again he went over Pythagoras, via Aristotle. Everything is mathematical. The movement of the celestial bodies must produce a sound, given that on Earth the movement of bodies of much smaller size produces this effect. Given the sun, moon and stars move so quickly, why don't they produce a louder sound? The measurements of their speeds and distances retain the same proportions as in the consonances of music, so the sound coming from the circular movement of stars must produce a harmony . . . If we don't hear the sound, the music of this circular movement, it's because it's accompanied us ever since we were born, and therefore we do not distinguish it from silence . . .

Then, following the logical drift of his reading, he consulted the work of Johannes Kepler, one of the great geniuses of the High Middle Ages, perhaps the first tormented mind of modernity.

How did my uncle develop the truths of this scientist within his conceptual scheme? No doubt, there were elements with which he felt allied: Kepler again took up the idea of the totality and unity of existence, typical of the ancient cosmogonies. For Kepler, the individual soul contains the potential of the entire heavens, and reacts to the light of planets in the same way as the ear reacts to mathematical harmonies in music and the eye to harmonies in color. Thus the myriad stars of the galaxies farthest away and the defecations of a Cossack are related, not because they're made of the same material or because of any identity of form (the diversity of what exists refutes this assumption), but because of their arrangement. If the planets affect us according to the angles that form between them and their resulting geometric harmonies or dissonances, then the affinity of our individual souls with the *anima mundi*, subject to strict laws, is a fact. Kepler picked up the ideas of Pythagoras and his theory of the harmony of the spheres, and used them to look toward the future.

Essentially, in his first book, *Mysterium cosmographicum,* Kepler affirms that the spheres of the planets (the five he knew) are separated from each other by five perfect solids, which were symmetrical, located in a tridimensional space and placed between the six planetary orbits, where "they fit to perfection." These "perfect solids" (the tetrahedron, cube, octahedron, dodecahedron and icosahedron) have equal sizes and can be inscribed within a sphere, so all their vertices touch the sphere's surface. Kepler's idea: "geometry has existed since before the Creation, it is coeternal with the mind of God, it is God Himself." And if God created what exists according to a geometrical model, and equipped man with an understanding of geometry, then it must be possible—he thought—to deduce the whole system of the Universe through pure reasoning, thus reading the mind of the Creator. The astronomers are priests of God, called upon to interpret the Book of Nature.

Clearly Kepler was in search of a mathematical law to explain universal harmony . . .

But later, with time, he understood things don't work like this. The way the planets moved . . . They shifted in such a way that if perfect solids really existed, they'd have ended up exploding in space, blasted apart by the displacement . . . This also annihilated the possibility that universal movement worked in accordance with the musical harmonies of the Pythagorean scale. A planet doesn't move at a uniform velocity, but it moves more quickly as it approaches the sun; it doesn't "sound" at a stable tone but oscillates between notes that are lower and higher, and the interval between the two notes depends on the asymmetry or eccentricity of their orbit. Then . . . "Then," said my uncle, on the night of his readings, "if the harmony of the spheres existed as the ancient Greeks thought it did, perfection would be a fact and Julian would not have died."

Incapable of accepting that God hadn't arranged things so the planets traced out simple geometric figures (perfect polyhedrons), Kepler tried out all sorts of combinations until he at last discovered the planets turned around the sun not in circular orbits, but in elliptical ones (as Tycho Brahe already knew) . . . What did that say about the Universe? What did it say about God? Or about his mind? Where one wanted to find divine symmetry . . . there appears . . . an ellipse!

For a Christian spirit like his, the effort to accept the truth of his own conclusions must have been gargantuan. And strictly speaking, only when he admitted his error was to be found in having attributed a specific hierarchy of values to a specific choice of form (no doubt a remnant of the Pythagorean influence, or perhaps an effect of his incursions into occult science, astrology and numerology) could the scientist hit upon his Three Laws,* which earned him fame and resulted in a new world. In *Astronomia nova*, but especially in *Harmonices mundi*, Kepler, at the end of his journey, went back to his origins in a different way. Along with insisting on the old and beloved concept of "the great music of the world," which at this stage of his understanding seems as much knowledge as metaphor, he showed that the sounds of the planets are related to the varying degrees of speed at which they turn, and demonstrated that the faster the movement of a star, the more high-pitched its sound (if we know the mass and velocity of a spinning object, we'll be able to calculate its sound at every one of the points of its trajectory), such that there are well-defined musical intervals in the Universe.

Wasn't it extraordinary—thought my uncle—that a man who was born and died more than two centuries ago was showing him

---

* First Law: The planets move around the sun in elliptical orbits, with the sun located at one of the foci of the ellipse. Second Law: The planets, in their paths around the ellipse, sweep out equal areas in equal lengths of time. Third Law: The square of the orbital period of each planet is proportional to the cube of its mean distance from the sun.

the way? Poor Johannes—scrofulous, syphilitic, a witch's son—had been able to compose six melodies, based on the six planets of the solar system known in that period. When laid over one another, these melodies could produce four different chords . . . And Kepler believed that one of these was the music at the beginning of the Universe, and another would accompany its end . . .

The totality . . . the totality of all that existed. The same one he'd already tepidly approached—getting warm?—with his *Prometheus*.

15

"Spring day. A flock of seagulls crosses the clear sky and vanishes from sight in the firmament, a shoal of salmon swims upstream to spawn. When moving at great speed, fish and birds trace complicated figures. The question is, why don't they crash? What is the enigmatic factor that eases the way for them or, which comes to the same thing, that prevents them from straying and generating confusion and chaos with their activity? Is it instinctive, is there some kind of agreement . . . ? Put another way: Can we conceive of a hypothetical field of study that would explain the simultaneous evolution of the same function in biological populations not in contact? Since I'm sure that no one will come up with a reply, let me state for the record my question is purely rhetorical . . ."

The voice of Vladimir Ivanovich Vernadsky vibrates like a bass singer's through the Assembly Hall of the Russian Academy of Sciences. Arms crossed, rear leaning on the edge of the table, the professor of mineralogy and crystallography makes good use of his position on the platform to contemplate with evident scorn and unconcealed disappointment (melancholy, melancholy) the confused sea of heads that sways, following his movements. Except one, which answers:

"Perhaps we could think of that flock and that shoal as not a sum of singularities but a unity composed of some number of elements that reverberate in unison, or share a consciousness, even an intelligence. That resonance would be identical to the one expressed in music as harmonic sounds. But the relevant question here is whether this unity of action can be understood as a manifestation of the particular nature of certain species or as a constant of the universal plan."

Vernadsky opens and shuts his mouth, and studies his interlocutor for a moment: pleasant appearance, restless gaze, clear skin, handlebar mustache, prematurely graying hair. Could he have seen his photograph in a newspaper, his portrait in some oil painting, his features copied in a program? Or has he crossed paths with him at some academic meeting, clandestine political gathering, cabaret?

"You," he says at last, "represent a ray of light amid so much darkness."

Alexander Nikolayevich Scriabin and Vladimir Ivanovich Vernadsky became friends. When they had a free moment, they went out walking around the outskirts of the city. Even though the surroundings of Saint Petersburg were little more than a quagmire, a testimony to its boggy past, in those surroundings Vernadsky found geological remains of great interest. With his walking stick he poked through the opaque rocks and dirty sand looking for stellar dust and Precambrian ash. Sometimes he leaned on my uncle's shoulder. There's no point in reproducing every chance snatch of dialogue, but it does make sense to transcribe the moment of their most important conversation:

"Can organic life alter the course of inert being? That is the question," says Vernadsky.

"What do you mean, my esteemed Vladimir Ivanovich?"

"A rock is a rock, always. In the Cryptozoic Eon, the same minerals and rocks were formed as now. Over the course of geological time, in contrast, living material has changed. And its history is the story of the modification of the organisms that compose it: a slow and extraordinary history. My thesis is that the evolution of matter moves in a particular direction. Is it toward God? Harmony? Before attempting a response, let's consider a series of factors"—Vernadsky smiles—"In a series of investigations undertaken in the Pacific ocean by Johann von Krusenstern, trawl nets cast into deep-sea pits gathered crustacean specimens at the start of the process of cephalization. The development of the central nervous system is irregular, but once it reaches a certain evolutionary level, the brain isn't subject to retrogression: it's only able to progress. This implies that we can imagine the biosphere as a dazzling choir of extremely powerful intelligences . . . twenty thousand million years from now. In the meantime . . . we have man as the advance party of this progression. His achievements are remarkable. Over some thirty centuries he has colonized every one of the territories, even coming to transfigure what is lifeless, producing artificial minerals. And this is only the beginning of a radical modification. Can our ideals establish relations in accordance with the laws of nature? It's necessary to find out. Meanwhile . . . Let's agree that man has become a geological force at a huge scale, able to change life beyond his own environment. That's why I wager everything on the struggle of our species. To avoid catastrophe."

"Are you talking about . . . ?"

"Isn't it an astonishing paradox that although we're an almost infinitesimal fraction of this planet's total mass, our fate is to worry about the cosmos? If man has been able to alter the biosphere, with an expansion of his talents one might also expect transformation at a universal scale. In any case, I'm somewhat pessimistic about our possibilities. Maybe we should have been born a few million years ago: we would have had time to truly develop our brains . . ."

"When you say catastrophe, is that a kind of allegory?"

"No. I'm sure about the existence of a direction, not a destiny. And I've observed that something like the end of times . . . is approaching. In *Alaska at the Edge of the Pole*, my colleague Jacob Tujacevich wrote about how we're experiencing the slide of Earth's mantle and crust over the liquid nucleus of the planet. The movement is growing progressively faster. As this displacement makes the equator move over new regions of the Earth's surface, these will begin to suffer changes in their centrifugal force and sea level, which will produce new distributions of sea and earth, meltings of glaciers that keep the crust's tectonic plates in position, seismic and volcanic calamities. In addition, it won't be long before the sun begins a cycle of unusual activity, generating more spots, launching enormous gas clouds into space, basically acting as it hasn't since the start of the last Ice Age. This is probably due, although it's not the only reason, to a modification of the Earth's magnetic field, and therefore to its gravitational field. Of course, the Earth-Sun attraction works both ways. Luckily, until now we've been saved from burning to a crisp since the effect of both masses dissolves over distance. Is the increase in effect, the proliferation of sun spots, due perhaps to a change in our planet's alignment? Could we be leaving our orbit? Getting too close to the sun? It's not absurd to think that . . . Ultimately, even with its size, our sun is no more than an immense flaming globule to which we remain joined through the effect of gravity, one that is susceptible to the tugs and pushes of the harder, denser, colder planets that orbit it. Like Earth."

"Do you think this double attraction will end up throwing our planet off its axis . . . ?"

"Yes. The sun will come up against it, just as an elephant's backside comes up against the mosquito that stings it. Before this kind of coupling takes place, of course, the Earth will have first burned to a cinder. Usually what happens is that the sun doesn't lean or fall but wobbles and expands in the direction of the center of the solar system mass. The stronger the gravitational effect, the greater the probability that there will be fissures or tearing in its surface. If this happens, it will release an incredible amount of the radiation trapped inside the fireball. Imagine that explosion in interstellar space! A spectacle worth contemplating, though obviously we won't manage to enjoy it for more than a millionth of a second. Naturally, I don't think of the Apocalypse in religious terms, although the Sumerian astronomers thought that the orbital anomalies of the sun were due less to Earth than to an external gravitational influence, to a binary companion we've never yet been able to observe: they called it Nibiru and said our planet will end when it appears in the sky as a red sun. Of course, the feeble-minded courtesans that swarmed around Nicholas I tried to link this prophecy to the ritual appearance of red flags in anti-government protests, but they were too inept even to put together a convincing metaphorical system to explain it. In any case, this isn't the only danger. Remember the explosion of Irkutsk, a few years ago? Thousands of hectares devastated in a remote part of Siberia, and a single victim, a dead shepherd, testimony to the faulty population scheme of our empire. Well then: this absolutely was not the 'Death Ray' Nikola Tesla is supposed to have invented, but the result of a meteorite's fall. The truth is that every sixty-two million years, the orbit of our solar system passes through a region of the Milky Way that possesses an extraordinary gravitational density. Some sixty-two million years ago, one of these meteorites fell on our planet and extinguished the majority of life, including the dinosaurs, what I supposedly study. And one hundred twenty-four million years ago, there was another similar impact, as the previous fossil layer proves . . . In reality, I am a biogeochemist and eschaton-paleontologist, one who seeks amid the ashes of the past and the deceptive greenery of the present for the traces that herald the end. Here I must repeat a truth that never ceases to be relevant: despite what ordinary perception indicates, the stars are not fixed in space. They move on a colossal journey through the galaxies. The Universe is a romantic date in which like seeks like. Women will talk of the soul, but we men are right when we say that the only motor of love is attraction: the laws of physics themselves indicate it. In this sense, our Milky Way is being attracted toward a massive grouping of stars called the Virgo Cluster. There . . ."

"I'm unable to appreciate the technical details," says my uncle.

"Briefly, when we're a few million kilometers away, the process of this approach will undergo a qualitative leap, and the combination of light and gases and color . . ."

"We'll crash?"

"Yes."

"That is the end, and you're satisfied just formulating it?"

"Do you want me to blink to make my uneasiness clear?" says Vernadsky. "I don't have a wife or kids; I don't have to worry about descendants."

"If you study a planet or, going even further, the cosmos to the point of understanding everything, what sense does it make to scorn humanity to the point of washing your hands of its fate?" says my uncle.

"But are you crying, my friend? Why? Before the irreparable, stoicism . . ."

"You seem to possess equal doses of fascination for the achievements of knowledge and the vistas of annihilation, my dear Vladimir Ivanovich. In any case, the announcement of evil does not justify complacence, based on the miserable argument that one has nothing to lose. What we've seen . . . what we've known . . . I don't know what might be at the limits of the Universe, I don't know what will happen to us. But no worthier task occurs to me now than to wager everything on the preservation of our species."

"Do you really think there's something worthy of being rescued? Your own work, *Prometheus: Poem of Fire*, encapsulates the dilemma between salvation and condemnation! The flame that Titan raises up to illuminate humanity is the same one lit during the fall . . ."

"True," says Alexander. "But the question that opened our little chat isn't simply rhetorical, is it? I think you formulated it as a provocation."

Vernadsky smiles:

"In the solitude of my laboratory, I hear the notes the stars produce through their vibrations. The sun sings. The stars sing. Ghostly whistlings, drummings, buzzings. In the case of the sun and other radiant bodies, they express the passage of energy from the inferno of the nucleus toward the surface, and its escape into space. The entire Milky Way oscillates and vibrates like a drum. But this sound has become . . . out of tune, and therein lies the danger."

"So," says Scriabin, "the harmony of the spheres exists . . ."

"Existed. The relationship has been destroyed. The question, my dear savior of humanity, is whether we can succeed in restoring that lost order."

16

Why does a musician, just a musician, no more or less than a musician, decide to set in motion the impossible? How can someone transform into a savior of the cosmos, a crusader of humanity? There's no question that with *Prometheus* my uncle had made his first great effort to transform the consciousness of our species (even if it was limited only to those who happened to listen to it). But ultimately, that had been no more than a game for children, compared with the task Vernadsky had entrusted to him: to modify the structure of reality, thus restoring the Universe to its harmonious order to prevent the final Apocalypse.

Now then, how could he do so? Was it about augmenting the previous techniques, intensifying them to an unthinkable level until the extraordinary occurred? If Vernadsky was right, it was a matter of pure logic: life is a cosmic process, a progressive colonization in which the self-conscious elements work radical reforms upon the ones that lack knowledge. The Universe, in contrast, works in ways that may be amusing or terrible, but are always involuntary: it may be a Great Thing, but it's not a Being. It was from this point, and from his own actions, that my uncle had to start, assuming his mission (like Prometheus). Of course, he had to consider the extent of it: one man, One against the faulty tropism of the Universe. But what means did he have? His mystic chord, perhaps? It hadn't even given results with Rasputin's harmonic shield!

The challenge couldn't be compared with any other; the probability of success was tiny, but the result wasn't determined beforehand. Perhaps this is why my uncle decided to give his project of transformative mega-composition, which would be projected into the infinite abyss, the name *Mysterium*. The title alludes, of course, to Johannes Kepler's *Mysterium cosmographicum*.

Posterity has collaborated to cast this activity into the shadow through the deceptive light of myth and legend. The disciples of Madame Blavatsky, both the orthodox and the unconventional, share a great deal of the responsibility for this. The following narrative has an air of undeniable theosophical exoticism.

According to this version, my uncle planned the performance of the *Mysterium* in the Himalayas. For seven days, an orchestra made up of two thousand musicians, situated near the peak of Mount Everest, would play the composition, while a multitude of chromolas or *tastieras per luce* spread out at different heights across the neighboring mountains (Annapurna, Shishapangma, Makalu, Cho Oyu, et cetera) cast their colors into the sky. Flames of blue-gold-red-blue fire would shoot up over them, as machines like modern sprinklers released perfumes for the rapture and elevation of a crowd of participants dressed in white togas, who would follow the concert and let themselves be mystically enveloped by its effects, or braid themselves into ecstatic-orgiastic forms with Indian dancers. Every dawn would be a prelude, every nightfall a coda. But this wasn't all: hanging from the skies (no doubt held by the invisible mahatmas), bells of alchemical gold shining like mirrors would make the celestial spaces vibrate. And at the end of the seven days, like a sudden rainfall, the entire Totality would change.

Of course, since this event did not take place, the Blavatsky-ites argue that a few months before the culmination of his work, fully engaged in the task of editing the draft of his *Mysterium*— titled *Final Sketch, Preparation for the Final Mystery* or *Preparatory*

Action—Alexander Scriabin had an illumination: the work he planned to carry out was contradictory in its aim, and so he had to abandon it.

It seems madness to think that my uncle imagined for even a moment that his coherency as an artist depended on relinquishing his work, but on this matter, the lapse by Madame Blavatsky's disciples isn't without a certain sound judgment, at least going by the assumptions of theosophy. According to them, what happened is that a radiance spilled over him, instantly flooding everything, such that he suddenly grasped the Truth, once and for all. And this Truth revealed to him that the material attributes of the phenomenal world are only apparent. In this sense—he'd have thought—music, his music, *all* music, was a concept, but first and foremost it was also material, the acoustic expression of an idea transmitted through physical objects that vibrate at their own spectrum of frequencies. Hence both the initial outline, the *Preparatory Action*, and its next step, the great work of the *Mysterium*, would be just as illusory, weavings of the veil of Maya they themselves were attempting to tear apart. The idea (or Idea) would thus be: if the phenomenological world is a deception, the only way for the *Mysterium* to find success as a means of universal transformation would be for it to remain in the sphere of the absolute concept, because once translated into sound, its power would fade.

Having understood this, my uncle would thus have taken the only coherent next step: his artistic transfiguration and physical death, resigning the corporeal nature of his being and the material of his work to a dissolution in prolonged Nirvana, a delightful insubstantiality.

The only problem with this theory (as idealistic as it is moving) is that it's false. We could even say that Alexander Scriabin's great wager was for an extreme materialism: the construction of a great musical-physical-acoustic system to alter the course of reality. Whether death took him before or after he achieved the results he sought . . . is the question we'll take up next. But there isn't the slightest doubt that his purpose was neither mystical nor ineffable but aesthetic, political, cosmic and cosmological. What importance does it have if material is a form of energy, or the opposite? What he proposed was to generate a steady musical ray transmitted in the form of a constant luminous vibration, which, projecting itself toward the farthest reaches of the Universe, would generate a shock wave able to realign all the planets with its impact.

Energy? Matter? Music? Wave? Vibration?

Now, at last, the moment has come to take up the *Mysterium*.

17

In the Middle Ages, Rudolf de St. Trond (*Quaestiones in musica*) attributed a color to each musical mode. In the sixteenth century, Franchinus Gaffurius touched the soul of more than one damsel by comparing the effect of a *glissando* with the image of a rainbow, because in both, sounds and colors follow each other in an interrupted metamorphosis. In the eighteenth century, Marin Cureau de la Chambre and Marin Mersenne designed new acoustic-chromatic scales, and Isaac Newton laid the scientific foundation for the existence of a musical division of the luminous spectrum according to seven natural sounds, on whose chromatic base Louis Bertrand Castel invented his "ocular harpsichord," the instrument for which Jean-Philippe Rameau wrote some of his compositions. Alexander Scriabin picked up the tradition of joining colors to sounds and gave it an extraordinary turn when he decided to appeal to the first and primordial symbol of all colors, their source of origin, the step prior to the decomposition of the prism, light itself, with the aim this would transmit every one of the notes composing it to all the corners of the Universe.

In that sense, the metaphor of the Himalayas might be useful as a testament to the dimension of its ambitions, but nothing more. What's true is that to reach his objective, my uncle had to turn to the science and technology of the period for help. Because, as we all know, unlike light, sound cannot travel through a vacuum.

"Luminous music." Maybe the explanation should be brief. Light waves are electromagnetic energy and sound waves are mechanical energy, and due to their nature, the latter are able to change their range. A telephone: the transmitter contains a coil of wire and a magnetic field, which turn the sound wave—the speaker's voice—into an electric signal that can be transmitted through the telephone cable. The receptor coil receives the electric signal and generates a second field, which makes a slender membrane—an ordinary and effective simile for the marvelous human ear, with its fossa and lobule and delicate pinkness and golden layers of wax—vibrate in response to the electric signal, changing it back to sound.

Now then, the planets lack a similar system. The Universe exists but doesn't speak. Maybe the time has come to reveal that the bells that would hang from the Himalayas, "shiny as mirrors," *were*, in fact, mirrors. The ones my uncle would use to transpose the key of his music. And that the machine used to launch the *Mysterium* into the depths of heaven . . . that machine was built.

To do so Vernadsky had to draw on his resources, among them deceit and flattery. The funds a useless minister collected for the restoration of the Pulkovo Observatory building and the improvement of its telescope were diverted toward assembling a cannon that could shoot the most powerful luminous beams history had ever known, something unique of its kind, although technically it was no more than a practical application, colossal in size but theoretically identical in aim, of the design of the photophone invented in 1880 by Alexander Graham Bell.*

Of course, Vernadsky couldn't deceive his colleagues for long

---

* Invented as a logical byproduct of the telephone, and of greater importance, the photophone was supposed to have transmitted the voice (or any other sound) through a mirrored layer called a parabolic-vibratory mirror (or transmitter), which reflected sunlight and focused it through a lens toward a receptor, placed about seven hundred feet away, at whose center a selenium detector was connected to a battery and a receiver with built-in telephone.

about the true character of the machine he was building, and he had to use a good part of his prestige and the weight of his authority to silence grumblers and avoid the spread of rumors. Even so, buried though they'd been, voices were heard whispering, almost always reaching ears not properly trained to interpret the contents of the message, so that over the years the version that ended up prevailing—the most ludicrous, but also the one most in keeping with the spirit of the period—alleged that my uncle had managed to convince Vernadsky of the need to build a device able to establish communication with ghosts and apparitions. It isn't strange this occurred. Spiritism is no more than a dark appropriation of the clear technical solution genuinely found—or perhaps it's the opposite, and science makes the absurd dreams of our species a reality: Thomas Alva Edison tried to profit from his venture by claiming that thanks to the telephone, it was possible to speak with the dead, such that Mary Baker Eddy, founder of the Church of Christ, Scientist, ordered loyal followers to bury one of these devices with her, in case she wanted to transmit new revelations from the afterlife. Following this logic, Alexander Scriabin would have used Vernadsky in order to speak with Julian again.

The photophone—which was consumed by flames during the October Revolution of 1917, and whose small-scale replica is now on display in the Green Room of the Observatory—measured twenty-five meters in height and ten meters in diameter, and thanks to its double tubes, it looked remarkably similar to a Triceratops.

In his time, Bell had problems making his machine work on cloudy days and managed only to transmit sound within a maximum radius of a couple dozen meters. Essentially, the sound came from a human speaker who had to articulate with extreme slowness and precision, in words that were generally of one syllable, at most two. Maybe because with the telephone he'd resolved the matter by applying another technique, or maybe because he didn't see immediate possibilities for development and financial gain, Bell forgot about the photophone, so that when Vernadsky and my uncle applied themselves to the matter, it had been over three decades since the last update of the machine, which was now little more than a piece of junk destined for a technological museum. For Vernadsky, improving the optical part was almost a game; selenium arranged in the form of a diaphragm over the listening tube allowed for a clear and instantaneous emission of sounds when illuminated by the modulated light sent through a perforated spinning disc. By adding a "spectrophone," he was even able to achieve a different intensity in the sound emitted, depending on the wavelength (or color) of the light entering the device through the telescope. The sound waves that were generated rippled through the listening tube and produced the desired photoacoustic sound.

At the technical level, then, the matter was resolved. Of course, for skeptics of every kind, the fact that a great musician and a single scientist could have believed it was possible to cross through space, realign the planets, and avoid apocalypse simply by adapting an obsolete machine might seem to express a moving and pathetic naïveté, bordering on stupidity. Can a Triceratops defeat a Tyrannosaurus, the king of creation? Scriabin and Vernadsky thought so. The principle of time that governed the conception of the *Mysterium* seems to point in this direction. It's obvious that the two men had decided mass had to be opposed with mass, length with length, and musical time with the time of the end. It's also obvious that they knew it wouldn't be enough to play a single note at regular intervals to change the direction of the Universe. A minimum constant ringing wouldn't suffice to alter the transit of the Milky Way, on its path toward destruction. Thinking of the cosmos as a billiards table, the *Mysterium* had to become a sort of acoustic mechanism with a practically unlimited number of shining balls of white light ("solids"), which would spin over the black felt of space and by means of the effect of their proportions, relations and intensities, collide with and knock from their orbits an innumerable series of planets in motion ("stripes").

Now then, for the limited purposes of this history of music, the fact the *Mysterium* was left incomplete due to my uncle's unexpected death . . . in no way diminishes what he'd done up to then. The *Preparatory Action* is an advanced blueprint of what would come, and is in itself a work as magnificent as it is strange. Anyone who decides to listen to it will clearly understand, after just a few measures, that neither Scriabin nor Vernadsky believed in the existence of pure chaos. Neither the *Preparatory Action* nor the *Mysterium* would be a haphazard succession of notes thrown out without rhyme or reason, in the extravagant hope that once released into space they'd somehow arrange themselves to avoid the disastrous collision of our galaxy with the Virgo Cluster and subsequent combustion. The *Mysterium* wasn't designed to be only an acoustic mass transfigured into light, an accumulative buildup of noise. Just the opposite. It would be a carefully thought-out globe of music, a system rigorously composed to generate a predictable and formulaic effect in accordance with the rules of science. In that sense, its forced incompletion leaves everything, if not adrift, then at a point of suspension, which allows for more hypotheses than certainties.

Alexander Scriabin woke up one morning feeling a sharp pain in his upper lip; over the course of the day a boil formed. Accustomed to disdain for his body and respect for alternative forms of medicine, he consulted his old acquaintance Badmayev, who supplied him with a few homeopathic globules or clots or Tibetan herbs, which he had to boil, then drink as an infusion. As a result of this treatment, the illness seemed to let up at first, but then the boil grew even more inflamed, and his face swelled and deformed; it was like the warty, multilayered epidermis of a prehistoric beast, some cold-blooded monster, except it itched and spread with an inflammatory appetite over his whole body. It's striking that someone pursuing the highest good suffered from such an infernal appearance. Several incisions were made but the swelling didn't go down, and foul-smelling pus streamed from the wounds, a kind of lava whose constant flow weakened him. He was convinced this mortification of the flesh was necessary. Or maybe he believed, as the Babylonians, the Assyrians, the Mayans, the Egyptians, the Sumerians and the Jews had believed before him, that a body submitted to bleeding can through its sacrifice preserve the lives of loved ones, and in the process open itself to ritual contact with the spirits of the beyond. They say at the final moment he kissed a cross, though we don't know whether it was Coptic, Russian Orthodox or Apostolic Catholic. In any case, his last thoughts were of his absent family and of Julian, his dead son. On April 27, 1915, Easter Sunday, Alexander Scriabin died of sepsis. Which brings us to wonder what it is that yields, and why, how, in what form something may resurrect.

18

Leibniz said the relations between things are organized according to specific and complex laws that depend on the environments in which the elements move. In the case concerning us, which includes the totality of all that exists, we must agree this system of laws is particularly intricate.

A brutal way to address the matter would be to state that we don't know whether in the end the *Mysterium* was "projected" or not; if conscious of the nearness of his death, my uncle persuaded Vernadsky to send the *Preparatory Action* into space through some form of transcription, not even as a primitive yet reliable recording of this early version, but merely as its notation. Nor do we know whether, even if this were carried out, the transmission managed to prevent the Armageddon of the Milky Way, or owing to the shortcomings of this approach, and emphasizing the uselessness of all human efforts, our galaxy will someday end up slamming into clusters, pocket universes or stellar clouds, lighting up the night of the cosmos with Vernadsky's predicted radiance. Even in the case the geologist and musician did manage to launch the music into the heart of the firmament, and it survived, we wouldn't be able to conclude from this event that the "acoustic light" would necessarily spread endlessly through the depths of space. But we can't write off the opposite possibility either. Maybe my uncle sent the notes into the stratosphere as he thought them up, maybe the *Preparatory Action* was in itself a complete, self-sufficient work (while the *Mysterium* would perhaps have been too strong for our galaxy); maybe, to preserve the universal order, it was enough to send a single note.

And that's not all. Other enigmas linger, which no doubt science will someday resolve. What was the force of the music projected as light, and what was its fulcrum? Or did its state as vibrational energy render the existence of a material base for projection unnecessary, whether this be the photophone, the Pulkovo Observatory or our entire planet? Another question: how to alter the trajectory of the Milky Way with a ray of light emitted from one of its corners and sent *beyond this*? Or, to put it another way, where should Scriabin and his device have located themselves to readjust the course of our solar system? The famous cosmist Nikolai Aleksandrovich Kozyrev contributed a new purpose to the photophone, besides its anti-apocalyptic use, which was to help experimentally confirm one of Vernadsky's last theories, according to which having overcome some distance "x," *light does not continue advancing but folds back on itself*, so at some point my uncle's acoustic or musical light would return to its source of emission. I suspect this hypothesis attempts to demonstrate that the Universe is not infinite, or in any case that time, not space, is infinite. If this were so, Vernadsky must have imagined that having traveled the complete ellipse of his journey, the light emitted by the photophone would be captured by the receiver tube, reprocessed inside the machine and launched once again into the cosmos, giving way to a perpetual circulation without interruption.

Of course, Kozyrev's theory is based on an ideal calculation, and doesn't take into account the fallibility of objects and erosion of materials. But it also displays a flaw that results in an unsuspected aesthetic richness: during its journey, in its contact with the things it brushed against or passed through, amid the galactic tides it experienced, submitted to the shockwaves of space and density of the planets, and reaching its final limit, Scriabin's music (that light), for all it folded, wouldn't have been able to return to its point of origin in conditions identical to those of its launch. By necessity, it must have returned transformed. Better or worse? We don't know. But yes, different. Maybe, in the end, that process of endless change is the solution to an impossibility, the music of the spheres of which Pythagoras dreamed and which Alexander Scriabin set into motion with his *Mysterium*.

19

Did the photophone ultimately launch its musical cargo? Did the Universe receive its impact, and did it continue to receive it in an imperceptible yet constant form? I think it did. And it also occurs to me that the *Preparatory Action* is the decoy my uncle left, so the world would believe the only thing he'd been able to achieve and produce was the evidence of his failure. Maybe he did so out of modesty, because he believed that the appearance of the unrealized was a worthier representation of human possibility than a clear and obvious demonstration of having crossed every limit and entered the peaks of absolute glory. It occurs to me that in his dealings with Vernadsky, Alexander Scriabin arrived at greater truths than those I am capable of knowing, and that after carrying out his task, he decided to pass on to a fuller dimension. Did he project his music onto himself, and thus materially and spiritually move himself to another plane? Perhaps Madame Blavatsky was right, perhaps the Universe contains a myriad of infinitely faceted universes (the noosphere of Vernadsky being one of them). In that case, maybe it's true that like a new god, another one of many, my uncle decided to keep spinning through some of these universes, and that from there, from wherever he was, he began to call out to my father. And that he went on calling out to him, went on dragging him along and taking him with him, telling him they needed to be One again, just as they had been in the belly of their mother.

BOOK 5

SEBASTIAN DELIUSKIN

*The true musician is not the one
who composes or performs music,
but the one who uses reason
to understand the laws of music,
and through them,
the order of the world.*

—BERNARD FOCCROULLE,
La naissance de l'individu dans l'art

1

Giovanni and Giacomo Tocci shared two heads and two necks, four arms, two hearts, four lungs, two diaphragms, a digestive system, an anus and a reproductive system; for their parents it was difficult to punish one's offense because the other had to suffer the consequences in solidarity. In adulthood they married two sisters, although the Church refused to bless the links, as anatomical fusion prevented sexual consummation (of either one) from taking place with due modesty. In the inventory of circus monsters, one can find individuals with two heads or linked by two or four arms, alongside those conjoined by the head, thorax, backs, coccyx, sacrum or sacred omphalos that joins waist to chest . . . The lists that the science of anomalies provides will always be behind the whims of a nature that celebrates piecemeal a sudden impulse for the baroque, but such blossomings are nothing when compared with the bond that existed for years between Alexander Scriabin and Sebastian Deliuskin, which made two extraordinary artists into a single unit.

Of my uncle's work, how much came from Alexander? What did Sebastian dictate from the other side of the ocean? Did Alexander compose and Sebastian correct, or vice versa? Did they do so in unison, as a duo, and was Alexander the one who transcribed the notes on music paper? Did what echoed in one brain find its form in the other? Sometimes I have the suspicion that the writing of the *Mysterium* didn't end with my uncle's death or with the "progressive cerebral hemorrhage" (as the neurologists branded it) that afflicted my father. In any case, I'm sure that Sebastian Deliuskin continued the work to the extent his strength permitted. I imagine the deterioration of his faculties as a *diminuendo* written by his body in the same way a composition approaches its end, a cultivation of the arts of silence after he'd developed an entire system of procedures, even as in the will to endure, he attempted to write new pages that rose up in glory over his progressive ruin. It might not sound as if I'm talking about music anymore, but that's not true.

In my first memory I'm three years old. It's a winter morning; I'm going into the open patio of the kindergarten. A leaky faucet. It's so cold it seems the drop sliding from my nose will freeze in the air. Like the girls of the time, I'm wearing lace-up shoes over cream-colored tights and a blue skirt made of coarse fabric. I feel the wind hugging my legs. My waterproof raincoat keeps me dry, but I shiver.

Who took me to school each day? Who waited for me at the exit? Of course, at that age I couldn't dress or travel without company, so . . . The only thing I know is that a couple of hours later, while I was in my favorite corner stacking up colored blocks, the director on shift appeared in the Little Blue Room, putting on a face of exaggerated pity when she saw me, the compassion appropriate for a poor little darling. She came, she pressed me against her, she crushed my hood any which way, she picked me up in her arms and took me away from there, cramming me against her armpit, suffocating me with the reek that permeated the damp wool of her sweater. Some distance away, framed by the lozenges of red and yellow glass in the door at the entrance, my grandmother was waiting. From that day, I also remember the paleness of my knuckle after it was crushed by my grandmother's hand as we walked toward a train station. My grandmother spoke to me in a low, gentle voice, but I couldn't understand what she was saying, since she mixed Spanish words with others of stronger accents. Then we reached a rectangular park, bordered by rows of poplars. At the end of it was an old building, painted with whitewash. There were men in smocks, rooms with beds and people in the beds. A long, melancholy figure was lying down, eyes closed, head wrapped in a sort of turban. A paper card written in black ink on the headboard said: "Sebastian Delivsky." My grandmother took out her fountain pen, tried to correct it. All at once she stopped:

"Your father's dressed like he's from India because he's going to perform at a costume party," she said, bursting into tears.

"Is he dead?"

"No, honeybunch. They put a spell on him, but he'll wake up soon."

"Why did they operate on him, grandma?"

"Don't talk. He's resting now."

For years, I thought my father's brain seizure was the result of my mother's having left us, or having disappeared, and not the effect of my uncle's sudden death. For someone who hasn't experienced the symbiotic communion of those two brothers—and my child's mind still didn't know anything about it—it's hard to imagine any phenomenon like it. Alexander's death was an abrupt red ray that split Sebastian down the middle.

My father's recovery. My father's recovery. On sunny days a nurse pushed him around the plate-glass corridors in a wheelchair. He had a lost expression, he was absent from conversations, he seemed not to be listening when people spoke to him. It was as if the burst blood vessel had produced a radical suppression of his senses. Everyone—the doctors, the physiotherapists, the blackbirds that operated the electroshock machines and their

vulturelike court of psychiatric institutions, straitjacket manufac-
turers, hawkers of cemetery niches—assumed his hand motions
corresponded to the impulses of an unhinged nervous system. But
I already knew then, even if I couldn't explain it with the right
words, that this trembling of the index finger (which rose and fell
just slightly on the chair's armrest, and rose again, and fell again)
mirrored the impulse to follow the musical movements that kept
on playing in his brain.

2

It's not unusual for the world to admire the blossoming of one genius while ignoring the appearance of another of equal relevance, but what's truly astonishing is for both prodigies to have occurred in perfect symmetry, and for the two geniuses to have ultimately been the same. The continued posthumous fame of Alexander Scriabin and the apparent progressive collapse of Sebastian Deliuskin were plotted onto this map of inequalities. As my father's finger wore out the plush cover of the armrest with its *ostinato,* performatively demonstrating—nobody noticed (except me)—his resistance to making me an orphan, after my uncle's death, high European culture lived through a period of Scriabinian fanaticism, even if this apotheosis, not interrupted even under Stalinism, tended to limit itself to the strictly musical and washed its hands of the cosmogonic dimension of his work; prevailing judgment held this dimension was a purely metaphorical one, an effect of mixing theosophical pastiche with the ferment of anarcho-socialist ideals. So the idea that the *Mysterium* had been composed and performed to save our Milky Way—perhaps the entire Universe—was understood to result from the megalomania of Alexander Scriabin, who turned to exaggerations to promote his own legend. Be that as it may, my uncle's name was still far from having disappeared into the cone of oblivion, or into a footnote to the motley history of the past century, when my father achieved what doctors called his "partial recuperation." Blessed is God, who doesn't exist, for having worked this miracle that allowed him to leave the hospital and hold my hand when we climbed onboard our first train.

I remember, as if it were today, the feeling of watching the open countryside pass with its contrasts and delights—pastures, dopey cows, wheat fields—visible through the fogged-up windows. At the time, every wagon had a small firewood brazier, the only thing needed to heat the compartment. My father remained in silence, though he smiled at me now and then. We got down from the train at nightfall. Someone had come to pick us up at the end of our journey, the representative of a local cultural committee, cap removed, exposing his baldness to the air, a bouquet of flowers in hand to receive the distinguished pianist and his little daughter. Except for the local details of chickens pecking by the side of the road and dogs sprawled out licking each other, the place seemed deserted. We prepared ourselves while walking toward the venue, the salon at the club. I can't say anything specific about the concert that night, referred to by the presenter as a "musical potpourri": neither what my father played, nor the size of the audience, nor the quality of the piano, nor its temperature and tuning. But I do vividly recall the sadness of the hotel we were given for the night: the fake alpine exterior with broken tiles and a dry branch poking out of the drainage pipe, the faded red carpet in the reception hall where a ghost who's seen better days glances at the cuckoo clock just as the little wood bird sings, then scratches an ear with a pencil before filling in the form with our names and guiding us up the spiral staircase, pointing out the black hole of a bathroom (with broken lavatory, without toilet paper or mirror) at the end of the corridor, and the door of room 313, where squeaky spring mattresses, a vase with dirty plastic roses, damp sheets, and a fly-spattered hunting scene knit from wool await us. My father and I, alone. Our suitcase leans against one of the two beds. As he changes clothes for dinner, I glance toward the street. A tube of violet light snakes around a metal cross: "Vivoratá Drugstore."

For a time I kept believing our tours around the country were an excuse to look for my mother. Wrapped with a golden aura I polished in my mind, Mama came back again and again, a serious, elevated, noble figure and the deity of my repeated dream, although at the center of that radiance was a face whose features I couldn't summon. Details I'd have been able to retain were I to have had a photograph, even one tiny enough to press under the hair snippet of a locket. But I didn't have one, and it seems my father's were lost with the rest of his belongings. As with so many other things, he couldn't remember where and with whom we'd been living before he suffered the accident. Of course, I trusted that if doctors had given him the all clear, it was because they were sure at some point the lacunae of his memory would fill in, and we'd get hold of the missing information. What I didn't know was that they'd allowed him to go only because they thought they'd done everything possible.

And in the meantime, we traveled. We presented ourselves at hotel dining rooms, trade union assembly halls, social clubs, concert venues shut down from lack of use and reopened for the occasion, and homes of retired lady piano teachers, encouraged by the renown of the performer and the news his marvelous abilities could be hired at a discount. I've seen more than one variety show huckster bargain down to a cut-rate offer with my father, drawing on arguments about his reduction of musicality (*pianissimo*) and his imbalance and fluctuation of intensity, demonstrating it with a wavering left pinky.

What made my father at first accept these shameful fees, then later complain they'd swindled him? The throbbing red vein in his temple, the threats . . . It's true that more than once his protests led to an improvement in payment, but they also left the link with his employers in a jittery state of nervous tension and, in the long run, put our sources of income at risk.

Somehow my father considered such scenes to be a part of the concert. But these gestures, frequent in star performers and contemporary musicians, met with an inappropriate public in his case, unable to appreciate his kind of aesthetic wager. How much is a concert *worth*? How much is the uniqueness of a performance worth? Maybe he no longer noticed the difference, or maybe he knew too much, and what everyone—including me—thought of as the effects of his stroke were no more than the mark of that devastating singularity, that sign of genius now transformed into stigma. Only he knew the enormous distance that existed between his current reality as a pianist touring the provinces, and what he truly represented. With his brother dead, Sebastian Deliuskin was the world's only standard bearer of something that had changed everything but gone unnoticed, or that hadn't yet revealed itself.

3

On free days between concerts, if the weather was good, my father would dress me as a princess and take me for ice cream. We'd sit on the wood benches in some plaza and look at the fancy people walking their dogs. We never talked about my mother, but for me those outings were like meetings glued together with hope. At the end of the afternoon, the chill forced us to go back to our hotel room.

I remember a few outings in particular. Something like the anticipation of a realization—or maybe the simple wish to forestall deception—made him alter the route. We would change plans and go to the cinema. In one of those warehouses turned into projection halls, sliding roofs had been installed. On summer nights, between films, the electric humming of the motor could be heard as it started to operate cables and pulleys, then the structure of iron and sheet metal slid aside to display a piece of gleaming and rectangular architecture: the landscape of the sky with its constellations. I don't really know what he was thinking about then, maybe the music he'd composed with Alexander Scriabin that continued ricocheting through the faraway galaxies, but in those moments he almost seemed happy. Even his feverish finger grew calm on the armrest of his theater seat. He didn't care about the films. He closed his eyes, and instead of following the moving images of the story, he listened to the actors' voices as formless noise, or random uncomposed music.

4

Even in the first months after he was authorized to leave the hospital, my father knew his cerebral processes remained irregular. If memory is like a tapestry woven with different colored threads, which intertwine to create a general shape and complete design for the past, what happened to him is that the most fragile connections, which he'd supposed would be restored over time, saw themselves instead damaged by erosion. The threads were *cut*, consumed by the termites of that process of deterioration. Even though he still recognized the "general shape" in broad strokes, a moment would come when the image could no longer be made out. In some of his notes (which I won't transcribe), he mentioned that instant as the one when his consciousness would cease to recognize its own being. He was worried not so much about losing himself, as about at some point not remembering I was his daughter. His deepest fear was that he'd even forget he loved me, and this terror drove him to love me with desperation. I was his precious thing, fragile and fleeting. Above all he dreaded losing his mind for good before I was ready to live without him. That's why he hunted for ways to delay this point in time and space, in which he'd no longer know what the world was, or who I was, or what he himself would be. His notes were a method of safekeeping: there he wrote descriptions, included pictures and registered the way his mind organized and cataloged memories, which he tried to mark off clearly from dreams and nightmares, anticipating the final period. A few months ago, going through these papers, I found an old photograph stuck to one of the pages. We are at the zoo in La Plata, and I'm wearing a heavy dark wool jacket and cap with earflaps. He, in contrast, has on a short-sleeved shirt and is crouched down so our heads are the same height. My little arm hangs from his shoulder as I look at the camera and Dad looks at me. His emotions are difficult to read, the hieroglyphs of an absent mind, but in his look I now think I see an infinite gentleness, an infinite sadness. Next to the photo, in shaky handwriting: "This is me. This is my daughter. Alejandra Deliuskin-Scriabin."

Obviously . . . obviously in this process of decomposition that swept away everything in its tides of blood and neurons, its eddies of knowledge and memories, one might assume that someday he wouldn't be able to read what he'd written either. That's why, in his struggle against the inevitable, my father drew up a series of unusual procedures for each one of his concerts. How can you play something without remembering the music? How can you sit in front of the audience knowing that someday you won't even recall the words that name what you're doing? Of course my father was an extraordinary pianist, perfectly conscious of the significance of instrumental technique, which is why he knew that after the worst happened, the imprint of his learning would let him keep playing for a time, even if only like a sleepwalking pianist or a machine gone haywire, unaware of what it spits out. That extra time would have its duration and end too, but my father trusted he could stretch out the period. So his concerts began to give way to a deeply considered strategy: improvisation as second memory. Instead of what the programs announced, what he performed was a subtle web of deviations that in their melodies and harmonies progressed a very long way from acoustic and conceptual repetitions, those limits that allow one to recognize a composer's "personal style": while leading others to believe he was strictly adhering to his repertoire, he was performing in austere solitude the music of the future.

5

I don't know exactly when I realized that what affected my father wasn't characteristic of every adult, but a trait particular to him. Darkly I intuited that the tours were no longer aimed at reuniting with my mother and rebuilding the family, but formed part of his desperate attempt to get hold of some protection for me before illness claimed him forever. At night, when he thought I was asleep, he wrote letters: to acquaintances, to child welfare services. In the morning we tossed them in mailboxes, waiting for answers that never came, because he gave no return address. Maybe he assumed that anyone interested could trace us through the reviews in local newspapers, the posters stuck on the doors of little theaters, the voices in the air broadcasting his name over radio stations in the provinces.

I understand his pain at the certainty he'd never know where his daughter would end up. Even then, I was sometimes able to sink deep into the orbit of his thoughts, advancing in a connection made possible by our flesh and blood, the community of our being. Those thoughts might be described as impressions and tonalities, letters and sounds, moving shapes. My vital risk, the scenario I'd have to face when he was no longer with me, could be heard as something throbbing in the silence, forever about to be performed. That devastated him: to read my thoughts (as I was doing with his) and know I was starting to realize everything.

That's why he turned to irrational methods in the attempt to preserve my innocence. As if he could veil himself from the excess light that displayed his mind for my scrutiny, he surrendered to music, in order to stun himself, and to drink, in order to avoid suffering. It's clear he maintained enough control that no one noticed (except me). Inebriated, with his neurons bloated and moving in all directions thanks to the alcohol, he forgot about time and was able to climb onstage: there he felt every note achieved its own weight and duration, vibrating in the ether, radiant, while the transitions between them took on a lively and exultant spirit, as in a Christmas carol. Of course, for this effect to maintain its intensity, he had to drink more each time, and once the moment of initial splendor had passed, the effect of the alcohol faded and everything sounded hollow. No one understood better than he did how awful the situation was. Canceled performances, migraines, shaking hands. Without seeking it, that brief period gave him an artificial preview of what everything would be like when I'd have to look after him. Of course, there were things I couldn't do, like pick him up in my arms and lay him in bed, although I was able to take off his shoes, serve him a glass of water, tuck him in and stay up at night to watch over his sleep. When he caught on to this, my father stopped drinking. His attempt at recovery went beyond the limits of mere abstinence; he tried to climb back up the hill.

He started to take notes on everything. As if each letter could inscribe a new order in his mind, he became an obsessive of the systems that govern the connections between things: limits, signs, ratios. He wrote the distances between one town and another, the slight variations in landscape, the names of hospitals, the number of trees on each street, what he put in his suitcase for each trip, the items of clothing we wore, the color of each anti-seizure pill, the description of a golden patch in the pupil of my left eye, the letters of my name. At night he went over these jottings: with a fine-tipped pen, he even traced a few faint lines that joined an address to an object, an object to a number, a number to an unfinished word; the design of those geometries may not seem to have pointed toward any specific meaning, but such mechanics of habit no doubt led him to engage in certain forms of thinking. That visual grammar was his last effort to conserve the world, his final truly organic and conscious attempt at healing.

6

I think this account of his life—of our joined lives—should come to an end like a coda interrupted by the unexpected end of its composer. But like him, I resist the end. With his deteriorated abilities, my father occasionally sat in front of the blank music paper and tried to write something, I don't know what, though I suspect he was trying to complete the *Mysterium*, a task whose fulfillment had been postponed or interrupted after Alexander Scriabin's death. Of course, as we know, the first draft, the *Preparatory Action*, might have worked to prevent the Apocalypse—or at least defer it. But the fact that in his condition Sebastian Deliuskin attempted to take on a venture like this one, that with disturbed faculties he tried to continue and conclude the project of transforming the Universe . . . that speaks to a particularly human attempt to cross through the barriers of the possible to reach the dimensions of holiness.

The ancient mystics, musicians and mathematicians would never have thought of their words, formulas and compositions as being linked with objects in the physical world, and much less with totality; instinctively they believed that their practices were parallel worlds that didn't align with the workings of the material spheres. Only the Gnostics, before Alexander Scriabin and Sebastian Deliuskin, showed themselves capable of discovering in each word of their religious books a sign or the name of one of the "spiritual places" whose relations determine the law of the cosmos. My uncle and my father were the ones who found a way to read the Absolute as a sheet of music with notes in the wrong places, and set their minds to ordering them by means of a work and an action destined to endure. In that sense, both are the highest point of the family evolution, the geniuses of geniuses, the ones who reached the furthest by traveling along the path of their predecessors. In their case, it was no longer just about composing a symphony that gave voice to a powerful intuition, a tide of exceptional music that interpreted the meaning of life and situation of man in the world (Frantisek), or about reading religion in a political key and drawing up a plan of action (Andrei), or about trying to carry it out in the world (Esau), but rather about directly taking the intimate structure of the Universe by storm and submitting it to a colossal transfiguration.

But what if that is what the *Mysterium* does? And what if I myself, driven by the same ambition that inspired my family, have also tried to change reality and the perception of it, even if just in the minds of readers? This chronicle: a series of ascending and descending scales, glimmers of information made possible by old family archives, a few books, Stravinsky's bold and timely question—"*Who is Scriabin? Who are his ancestors?*"—and my will that everything change once and for all, or if not, explode into eternity.

Maybe that's how it is, how this is. Maybe my father's dying life was plotted like an encrypted composition, a work capable of being read only when the world was prepared to understand it. Sometimes I imagine that if I could manage to sink deeply enough into the damaged abysses of his consciousness, if I could reconstruct the meaning of his experience, I'd be able to deduce the complete *Mysterium*, its purpose and significance. Then I concentrate on the final moment; I close my eyes and see it. One afternoon, just before giving another concert, my father lies down to rest on the bed of the last hotel room. The putrid blues of twilight can be seen through the window. With his clothes on, Sebastian Deliuskin looks as if he's sleeping, as a trickle of blood slides from his ear and marks a red circle on the sheet. My father. The years pass and I think of him and feel so alone, but it consoles me to know I wasn't so while writing. Until the very end, I have lived with my ancestors.

BOOK 6

ME

*I write this bitterly . . . because I do not believe
this leap into limitation will ever happen to me.
The cosmos will continue to devour me.*
—WITOLD GOMBROWICZ, *Diary: Volume 2 (1957–1961)*

*All time machines are likely to self-destruct
the moment they are activated.*

—KIP THORNE

Once, as part of a classroom demonstration, my teacher lined up ten crystal glasses on her desk and filled them with water based on an increasing progression, an approximate mathematical calculation. Then she began to strike them with a teaspoon, one at a time. Since we'd never seen an experiment like this before, we were astonished to notice that after each tap, instead of a sharp, complete sound, there was a kind of flowing acoustic vibration, which remained trembling for a few seconds without fading. Over the first vibration the teacher introduced another, and another, and this first glass turned into a rainbow of vibrations, identical in pattern yet discrete in time; this difference of identity was a miracle the teacher multiplied over all the glasses, moving the teaspoon to the side of the next one and striking it in such a way that a second sound (I can't remember now whether lower- or higher-pitched) superimposed itself on the first, thus beginning to unfurl with its own identity. She struck one glass after another, faster and faster, until the jingling echo drowned out the vibration of the entire row and each one of the individual glasses, made to perform again before its original tremor had ended. That angelic music was played to illustrate some law of physics I've forgotten.

"Everything sings," the teacher said.

Years later, I'd see each planet slide through space like a drop of vibrating water, sounding according to the blow given to it by an external stimulus and the anti-gravitational force of its own mass, determined by the angle of its elliptical movement, but back then, in those days of my childhood, I could understand this trembling elemental music only as the triumph of a supreme harmony. The humiliations of life at school, the tedious succession of lessons that didn't matter in the slightest, had given way to a lesson about beauty and truth. And this mystery that opened up like a flower (thanks only to the graze of a teaspoon against a glass) would soon yield to another, for which I hadn't yet found an explanation, which I would resolve only when traveling through time: the mystery of my mother's absence.

1

In those days I'd sometimes catch my mother absorbed, staring into the imaginary horizon that stretched beyond the mirror. When I found her like this, seated unmoving before the reflection of her own image, I couldn't help but think she'd been arrested by a fascination with her own beauty, to the point she didn't notice me. Later on I'd understand that this gleam in her eyes was an indication she was trying to save herself from her own thoughts, adrift in some region of the past—for instance, the hour she lost her father, Sebastian Deliuskin. The intensity of these ideas or memories took such hold of her that everything else, including me, seemed to become a pale shade. During these episodes of immersion, which would grow more marked with the passing of time, one can no doubt find the nucleus of her decision to write the biography of each one of our family's geniuses.

A good part of my childhood went by in the scrutiny of a closed door. The one that hid my mother behind it. I know every mark in that rough wood rectangle, every grain of its material, by heart. Since I was just a boy, unable to decipher the secrets of her behavior, I understood that concealment as a rejection. Her dedication to a cause did not include my upbringing. At school I was bad-tempered, irritable, too sensitive to be accepted by my classmates. Solitude, solitude. She never came into my bedroom to give me a goodnight kiss. How to win a mother's love? Maybe the drama of my life is knotted into this question, whose disentangling would lead me to behaviors unlike those accepted by most mortals. I'd find that love in an infinite wager, in the particular form our encounter would take.

Besides, the rest of my family looked after me. In our suburban area of the provinces, my grandparents and father headed a small business whose earnings allowed us to live with dignity, even if they had to keep an eye on every coin spent. I was raised on chicken stews prepared at a low boil in huge pots, so during the cooking the flesh material would slowly release its nutrients, which disintegrated into the thick broth. The chicken was chopped up and flung into the pot without first disposing of the red and black viscera, and these parts bubbled away with the legumes and vegetables. The resulting stew was a constellation of yellow grease spots and lumps gleaming on the surface, sometimes pierced by a claw of the boiled chicken as it rose up from the depths.

I'd be lying if I said this disgusted me. On the contrary, the remains of beastly origin linked me with the remote past, in a chain of generations. Just as the chicken was once a dinosaur, and the dinosaur emerged as an amphibian from the water, we, who were once apes and, before that, fishes, all found ourselves together in the primal broth. To grab hold of that claw as prey, to bite with relish into the part of the muscle where the leg begins, was in some way to turn, coil around and give myself a painful, happy bite, to seize hold of a part of my own self. That's also why I liked to go with my grandmother, my father's mother, to the local neighborhood market. At a supermarket I'd sit in the shopping cart, but here she carried me inside her bag like a kangaroo. It was an open-air fair that condensed the modern life of the time in its variety—blenders, nutritional mixes in yellow packets, wire flyswatters, multicolored plastic curtains (the poor man's rainbow)—but also remained just the way it had in medieval times: dead and living beasts were displayed on the wood counters. Anticipating that moment, I wanted to get there right away, without pausing at the stands where bazaar trinkets were sold. All that junk was irritating: the porcelain cups and teapots painted with fake Chinese words, on mountain landscapes that smudged at first wash; the metallic smell of the aluminum pressure cookers; the tastelessness of the pewter cutlery and gaping mouths of the glazed porcelain jars like those of sleeping monsters. In contrast, my interest grew as we approached the area where, under a thick canopy that filtered out sunlight, the fishmongers handled their merchandise in front of the public. They wore black rubber boots and very thick white cotton trousers and shirts, which at the start of their work, at least for a couple of hours, retained an immaculate appearance, but over the course of the day ended up getting stained by the material of the inner organs from the species they carved with their short, incredibly sharp knives, by the small amount of liquid that could spurt from any one of those bodies, but above all with their own blood, since they sometimes hurt themselves opening the stomach of a fish, or pricked their flesh against some spine or fin. Occupational hazards. It was interesting to note the contrast, depending on the time my grandmother and I arrived at the fair. If it was early, they seemed to be barely a rung under doctors and surgeons in the hierarchy, resembling them in the use of their caps to hold back hair. Later on, they were surrounded by chopped-off heads, their clothes were daubed with grease spots, their stalls reeked of fish and buzzing flies circled them. The eyes of the fish drew my fascinated attention. Those little spheres had the fixedness of death, yet maintained a certain vital intensity in their yellow point that glowed inside the expressionless black circle when the fish was fresh, and grew increasingly opaque as the hours went on, until their shine dimmed forever and the sclera and its orb sank into the hollow. What had those eyes seen, what had they wanted to see? It seemed as if in their final moments, those nearly brainless creatures had discovered something, a remainder of will, a determination to bear witness to their existence.

But for me the center of that universe was the stall where live chickens were sold. Out of principles of economy or conveniences of transportation, the vendors brought them there squeezed together in cages, so the ones that were pushed in first ended up with wings battered by the pressure of the ones pushed in afterward, clucking with ignored desperation. They could protest to exhaustion, and no one would stop to analyze whether that noise held longings of the soul or messages about a strange new world: their fuss soon grew weaker in volume, a decrease inversely proportional to the number of their peers taken from the cage for sale and extermination. The vendor sacrificed the chicken by abruptly twisting its neck; he did so with such precision and speed that the animal collapsed, never aware of the finality of the event. After its neck had been broken, its thickest feathers were plucked and its belly was sliced open to remove the viscera, both edible organs like heart and lungs, and disposable ones like the black straps of intestines. At home the job was carried out by plunging the chicken into boiling water. The heat loosened the skin and dilated the pores, making it easier to pluck out the remaining feathers . . .

The fate of those beasts never mattered to me much, nor was I concerned with the greater or lesser measure of suffering with which they met their end. As adult animals, they'd reached their full stage of development, and no further illusions could be entertained about an unfurling of their possibilities for being (save for if the miracle of a total mutation took place) . . . The same could be said of their young, the chicks that tugged at your heartstrings with the warmth of their little bodies and the softness of their golden down. As soon as they were born, they began taking on their final form and were thus condemned. On the other hand, I was very interested in the prior phenomenon: the egg. It was there, in that zone of transparencies, that small patches or gleams or substances went about growing thicker and denser, negating over the lapse of a few hours the solidification of any possible alternative future, even as those colloidal substances were also a verification of being. For a mind abstracted from the spectacle of time, this was a tragedy; the absolute present was indeterminacy, pure potential. What also caught my attention was the incompatibility between this developing alchemy inside the fragile structure nature had molded as its vessel (the spherical shell that enclosed a helix, an object of supreme craftsmanship), and the crude and singularly vulgar method by which the egg, after the series of mitosis had concluded, made its appearance: through the chicken's asshole.

For years I refused to eat eggs. I was disgusted by the blatant signs that before turning into food it had passed through a bird's rectum. Whether they be white, greenish or grayish, the chicken's shit stains produced a repulsion in me I couldn't manage to overcome, even if my grandma washed the shell in a blast of water under the faucet, soaping and scrubbing it hard with a brush. For me, this changed nothing. To eat the contents of an egg assumed some form of contact with the filth that surrounded it en route to the exit. It also implied the annihilation of the possibilities of a life to be born. In some way, this egg paralleled my own existence as someone who'd just begun to glimpse the incredible potentialities of his development and encountered a hostile universe resolved to devour him, endlessly.

2

Every day, at five o'clock in the afternoon, my grandmother took me to the San Martín pastry shop. It was a building from the start of the last century, the size of five barns, with a dining area and a private room for families. As soon as spring arrived, the owners dragged the tables to the street, and my grandma and I would sit at one near the sidewalk's edge. My grandma was an immigrant who in all the years she'd lived in exile could never correctly pronounce a word with a diphthong (when she offered me a boiled egg, she'd always say "bodeg"), but all her nightmares, embarrassments and humiliations vanished when she raised her hand to call for Héctor, the waiter who served us. Then she became truly imperial, an effect of her joy: she was going to feed her grandson. She raised her hand again and ordered a soda and "teeny sambich," a ham-and-tomato triple-decker.

"The usual," said Héctor, and after a while came back with a round tray holding a gleaming porcelain plate laden with crustless, rectangle-shaped white-bread sandwiches, and next to it a thick glass bottle modeled on a woman's ideal curves, inside of which one could see the thick red syrup that started to bubble as soon as Héctor set it down on the table, and, with a single, sharp, precise movement of the hand, uncapped it. That movement and the resulting sound—an amalgam of suction and liberation—distracted me, and for a fraction of a second, my gaze moved from his hand to the bottle's mouth, hoping to witness a bubbling overflow of its contents. Then, since this explosion didn't happen, my eyes flicked back toward Héctor's hand, but he'd already taken advantage of the second to operate his true magic, which he began by hiding the star of the performance: the little metal soda cap. Some waiters tucked them away in their white uniform pockets as soon as they moved off. But the disappearance that Héctor produced was merely temporary, a few moments of slight suspense to accentuate what happened next. In some unknown way, without my grandmother and I able to figure out how, the cap, which we'd assumed was hidden in the hollow of his palm, all at once flew through the air as if it had dematerialized for a moment, freeing itself from any grasp, and having done so, had materialized again, which supposed not just an alteration of the laws of gravity but also a new scientific principle, the sudden animation or self-propulsion of the inert—although it's obvious it was just a trick meant to impress me. Anyway, this cap made its journey through the air. Circular in shape, as with beverages of this kind, it also had a sort of jagged edge used to hermetically seal the glass mouth of the bottle, so that in flight the spinning teeth let one imagine the journey of a star toward the outer limits of the known. In this case, the street's black asphalt was equivalent to the night sky of the Universe, with its background radiation temporarily absent, and if the cap fell next to so many others tossed previously, over the course of days and months and years, it was because it had gone to occupy its destined location after traveling for ages, in the wake of the original explosion: there it would remain until the passage of some vehicle ended up flattening it like its sisters, a constellation of discs that gleamed on the pavement in summertime. Fanta, Coke, Crush, Bidu, Miranda, 7 Up, Indian Tonic, Aldebaran.

After uncapping the bottle and serving our glasses to the halfway mark, Héctor left the plate with the sandwiches on the table, turned around and exited the scene, tray under arm.

My grandma looked at me with a question in her eyes. Let's? I smiled. Then she took hold of one edge of a sandwich and raised it up—moving her fingers twisted by osteoarthritis with indescribable delicacy—to peer inside. Here was the privileged object of her very closest study: a tasty morsel for her grandson. The two slices of tomato had to be fresh, impeccably so, just sliced and thick enough for the redness of the fruit not to be threatened by any transparency that would reveal an ungenerous knife, yet slender enough for their flavor to be clearly distinguishable from the ham. The bread had to be fluffy, yet within limits, because if not, when spread with butter, the solid dairy product might tear its surface. That's why the San Martín pastry shop, which knew the tastes of its clientele and was prepared to satisfy them, took out the portion of butter from the refrigerator an hour before our visit, which gave it time to acquire the necessary softness to be spread without difficulties, while avoiding excess exposure to room temperature, which would turn it rancid. But what made me consider a ham-and-tomato sandwich to be the ne plus ultra of exquisiteness was the thickness of the slice of ham, which at the moment of tasting allowed one to appreciate the texture and flavor of the flesh; this precise cut, which combined a density of material with the greatest lightness, rendered the work of the teeth unnecessary. Its suppleness brushed pleasantly against the tip of the tongue. There, in such tenderness, I found the secret to the deepest appreciation of the savory tidbit, which turned again and again within the cavity of my mouth, ended up dissolving after a sequence of ecstasy, thus harmonizing with my grandma's belief that this was precisely the way that—to state it plainly—the food's nutrients were most effectively absorbed into the body without loss.

That belief, which derived from her personal history full of ethnic crimes, sudden orphanhoods, confinements, deprivations and miseries, had made scarcity into a condition from which a system of values could be drawn. Not only that. It had become an exercise in nutritious regulation that offered a lesson: saving was an aspect of morality. Those heaps of triple-decker sandwiches accompanied my childhood because, out of love for my grandmother, I transformed what was no more than a series of slices into the highest instance of the desirable. My first personal investigations into the science of duration advanced in more than one sense through the territory she had marked out.

This research began in the days her illness took a turn for the worse.

Before then, I'd never been present for anyone's last days; still less had I formulated to myself the idea that a sick person's pain, when one harbors no reasonable illusion of a cure, produces an ambiguous feeling in relatives, which includes both kindhearted longing for the cease of the loved one's pain and brutal and blind desire for the torment to end once and for all. In the wilderness, a dying person is a wounded beast whose elimination doesn't make one wait. But in our so-called civilized world, thanks to the palliatives of medicine, the end of a condemned being can linger on for months or years. When the final horizon is no longer recovery, such prolongation seems futile, but deep down it expresses a desire more human than any other, the preservation of an individuality at all costs. It's true that in my grandmother's case, as soon as things grew complicated, she firmly expressed her decision to die in peace. But none of the adults in our family accepted this command without resistance, one that would have entailed the suspension of treatments and operations that had already been programmed, from which nothing more could be expected but progressive deteriorations and higher doses of pain. Somehow her will to depart once and for all clashed with the general will, which preferred to dole out gratuitous suffering rather than admit something hadn't been tried. On this matter, of course, my elders' attitude was like a sign launched toward the future, a warning inscribed in my memory and that of my cousins: when it was their turn to occupy the place of the dying, we'd have to look after them and fight for their lives even if the effort was hopeless. The position was a legitimate one. Back then, I myself would have given the impossible for my grandma to be cured. I was prepared to accept her in conditions of extreme decrepitude and old age, so long as I didn't lose her. There was always something more to do, by the looks of it. Doctors opened my grandma, sewed her shut, swapped the positions of her organs, stitched her up, cut out meters and meters of her intestine . . . It was a long journey during which I contemplated the meaning and conditions of existence. I reached my conclusion during the wake. As the only species gifted with reason, language and understanding, we are also the only ones who unfairly possess the ability to comprehend the dimensions of our tragedy.

In that sense, and although I still wasn't aware of it, I was turning into a worthy representative of my family. If—something I still didn't know—one of my ancestors had composed his music to save the Universe, I was resolved to do everything possible for my grandma's love to forever remain by my side. I wanted to find a way for the human race to become immortal.

3

After my grandmother's death, a heavy, black cloth fell over me: the ugliness of the world. The ugliness of the world hiding the beauty of all that existed, stretching out its dark fabric. The cold of the mornings on the way to school, with the acidic remains of breakfast rising up my throat and exploding as vomit through my mouth. The dirty blocks of mud and frost, the low windows with grillwork, the withered flowers around the garden gnome lifting a cement wheelbarrow. The sound of the church bells on Sundays calling everyone to mass and the coldness of that salvation being delivered in Latin through the loudspeakers. The prayer echoes off the bleeding windows, frightening the birds and their lice. *Sancta Maria, Mater Dei, ora pro nobis peccatoribus, nunc et in hora mortis* . . . Yet at the same time, and having discovered the nature of my mission, everything became more luminous. The capacity of my brain expanded. The force of a nervous impulse started to circle through my neurons. I could identify the secret connections between things. This wasn't a mystical process, as far as I knew. To bring to light, within our nature, the conditions of an immortality which until then had denied itself to everything in existence (save the dead, which is thing, not being), in order to enter the perspective of a boundless temporality, involved a foray less into the promises of theology than into the material forms assumed by duration.

Since my aim was to resolve the central problem of humanity,

I knew from the start that I must not distract myself carrying out tasks of an academic caliber, the sort that research the techniques for mummifying Egyptians, the supernatural preferences of the Babylonians or the magical potions of Druids; nor was it necessary to apply myself to the knowledge of the historical evolution of medicine and its usual applications. My field of operations was situated between the coordinates established by mathematics, physics and geometry. The mental perception of this objective reality would provide me with other friendships: Euler, Gauss, Hippasus, Minkowski, Heisenberg, Einstein, Park-Button, Maxwell . . .

As I've said, thanks to my grandma's influence, I had established that a certain relationship between the density of material and the empty space allowed one to establish some kind of conservation of energy. Although in its origin this applied only to gastronomy, the principle could be extended to wider spheres, since essentially organic life assumes the existence of a healthy (rational) administration of energy sources while its cessation or extreme imbalance tends toward a mutation of life, or directly its end. So it wasn't strange that in the disordered and eager universe of my readings, I ended up getting interested in the contributions of the Russian astrophysicist Nikolai Kardashev and the contributions of another scientist, from the United States, Freeman John Dyson.

In 1964, Kardashev drew up a scale with three categories that could measure the level of a civilization's technological evolution, based on its amount of energy. Those situated in the first degree, or Type I, were able to use all the energy available on a single planet. Those in Type II could use the energy of a single star, external to the planet taking advantage of it, while those in Type III were capable of using the energy of an entire galaxy.*

---

* Kardashev calculated the energy available on Earth at approximately 10 (to 16) W. That of an average star would be around 10 to 26 W, compared to that of the sun, 3.86×10^{26} W. Of course, the present-day existence of civilizations like the ones described is hypothetical.

Considered from the perspective of Earth, it was obvious that our planet hadn't managed to arrive even by a long shot at the first stage. Difficulties with conversion of the oceanic thermal gradient, an insufficient number of wind turbines and chemical plants to process volcanic gas . . . Impatient with this scenario of a delay that would take centuries or millennia to overcome, and swept up by the demands of the present, Freeman Dyson conceived of a mechanism able to move us from the nearly absolute zero, to which we seemed condemned, straight into Type II. His invention was a delicate synthetic warp, an artificial and opaque megastructure that in his own honor he named the "Dyson sphere." This structure or space mantle orbiting at some antigravitational distance from Earth would be composed of billions of solar collector panels, which would derive part of their igneous energy from nearby living areas, spatial cities that would constitute the platform for the launch of humanity into other galaxies. Meanwhile, the majority of the energy captured would be sent back to Earth in an exogenous-endogenous procedure.

The conceptual simplicity of Kardashev's theories and the geometric character of Dyson's invention led to the rapid dissemination of his proposals: the searches for life on other planets were motivated by both these factors. The astronomers aimed their telescopes toward the sky looking for stars with an unusual infrared glow, which could be explained only by the addition of an artificial sphere. The movie theaters in the neighborhood began to alternate their usual programming of cowboy and spy films with science fiction ones, featuring astronauts who visited planets with modules forged from Styrofoam mock-ups of Dyson spheres. Dyson himself contributed to this development of popular culture by serving as a consultant for the screenwriters of stories. In its turn, the contact with or transfusion of the preferences of the masses had its effects on the scientist, who dedicated his final years to making an inventory of the characteristics a genetically designed bush must possess in order to grow and develop from the solid material of the comets. By scattering its seeds, he argued, it might produce a mass of oxygen large enough to generate the existential conditions for an atmosphere in which the human species could breathe.

After Dyson's death, his heirs quietly donated his sketches to Yale University, taking for granted that his fantasies were impracticable. But neither the tact of this gesture nor its character of a posthumous judgment muted his detractors, who by slandering him kept the cult of his memory alive and made the theoretical possibilities of his inventions known. "How does one sow a vegetal species in a comet? Where does its nourishment come from? Who waters it? If it doesn't burn up during the friction of the journey, how does it process the elements of the atmosphere it encounters, converting them into something like oxygen?" (Albert Geobb). "The new composition of the atmospheres might ironically signify the annihilation of Dyson's neo-civilizations distributed in hyperspace, since in the case that they do exist, we know nothing about what they breathe" (Friedrich Mittelhaus).

Jumping off from these speculations, the Dyson sphere—its delightful combination of original materials, avant-garde design, classic geometry and contemporary hallucination, aimed at a total use of the sources of energy—was a perfect orb that took up my thoughts over long nights. But even in my obsession with this form, I knew that if one morning I woke up to a horizon concealed behind a series of reflecting and absorbing panels, even though these worked to protect humanity from meteor showers and provided an inexhaustible energy source, they wouldn't help me achieve my ambition to become immortal.

Reflecting on possible methods, the first ones that occurred to me were related to the medical techniques of the period: surgeries, transplants, et cetera. Material ways to supplant organs worn out from use, prostheses for a body able to survive as long as each part could be substituted, and endure even if the outer structure continued to age, with skin becoming flaps that were trimmed and sewn up, bones swapped out for alloys of plastic and titanium . . . but this preservation had its limits and some day it would grow intolerable for its bearer. Not to speak of the decline of faculties inherent in the parts without replacement (the brain, for instance, the nucleus of memory and linchpin of identity). Having ruled out this option, I also passed over the religious tales, which can't explain the reason why an omnipresent figure to whom paternal qualities are attributed, whether in the form of soul, spirit or sigh, might have any interest whatsoever in our ongoing existence. From the treatises on reincarnation, I concluded that the story about bodies occupied by migrating identities served as a way to portray to weak minds the greater mystery: that of time. The journey in time was the great collective dream, another floating bubble that carried the spirit of the age. I still didn't know enough to actively participate in a project of that magnitude—in fact, I hadn't even finished primary school—but I did have the basic information necessary to understand that space and time make up four continuous dimensions, so that if the gravitational path of a star can give a twist to that dimensional kaleidoscope—that is, if a mass can curve space-time through the effect of a gravitational interaction—then it is also possible that time can curve with the help of space, time's arrow coiling to form the blessed loop that lets us travel into the past.

Of course, to make this trip it would be necessary to build a time machine, with the basic conditions that allow passengers to travel. The only inconvenience, which could not be overcome for the moment, was that in practice the machine would be a tunnel, with the entrance subject to the evolution of time, synchronized with it in a perpetual present (i.e., the perpetual succession of the present of each moment), whereas the exit would remain unmoving in the moment and place of its creation, so that only those alive *after* the machine created the loop could travel into the past, and only so long as this machine continued to exist. To sum up: no Neanderthal carrying his stone axe could climb onboard and fiddle with the commands, which was an advantage, but also a serious inconvenience, since the machine did not exist yet and I had no certainty it would be produced during the course of my lifetime. In addition, there were not insignificant theoretical problems linked to the matter of the return, which might well exit onto a parallel door in a parallel and different space-time . . . Not to mention the paradoxes that intellectually stimulated families across the world, gathered every evening in front of their home television screens to witness the broadcast of a new episode of the series *The Time Tunnel*.

Hidden inside a mountain in Arizona, a base harbors the biggest secret project of the United States government: a time tunnel. The machine is a kind of gigantic spiral inductor that hypnotically turns, carrying two scientists, Tony and Douglas, through time. Due to a flaw, after the inaugural trip Tony and Douglas can't return to the present of the series, and so they go bouncing around different periods of history. One would have to be very coldhearted not to be moved by the black-and-white spectacle of the two adventurers, flying as they wave their hands against a white background, a fan ruffling their hair and pressing their clothes against their bodies . . .

Beyond the predictability of the narrative device and the repetition in each episode—a risky situation for the scientists, a rescue planned from the laboratory in Arizona, a transfer to a new period—what the series questioned was the possibility of altering the course of history on the basis of an intervention by a protagonist from our present in an event of the past. For example: if Tony and Douglas crossed paths with the greatest of criminals, Adolf Hitler, should they kill him, or would doing so unleash a catastrophe even worse than the one they sought to prevent through their action? The interesting thing about the series was that it contrasted the will of the protagonists to make the good triumph at all costs with the iron determinism of the script, whose ups and downs were plotted to demonstrate that the past cannot be modified. Of course, part of its charm was rooted in the ease with which the tale convinced us our heroes hadn't achieved their objectives due to chance or pure bad luck. But at the same time, what else would have been feasible? If the duo had managed, for instance, to abolish a historically dated milestone—the French Revolution, the fall of Constantinople, the annotations of Andrei Deliuskin in Loyola's *Spiritual Exercises*, et cetera—then this abolition would no doubt have modified the sequence of virtual futures that hung from the eternal tree of unrealized alternatives, resulting in a chain reaction of effects that would perhaps have ended up annihilating our time as we know it. Let's imagine for a moment that having just arrived in the Paleolithic, Tony tenderly picks up a baby Velociraptor in his arms, in doing so preventing the antediluvian beast from stepping on a slug, so that the slug survives, climbs up a plant, devours its leaves. Because the slug ingests these leaves, the caterpillar that would have fed on them perishes, so the bird that would have trapped it changes its flight path and doesn't become the prey of a reptile, which in turn . . . and so on successively until the explosion or entropic dissolution of the televised time tunnel, television, civilization and ourselves. At the same time, the fact that the series continued to exist and we were still watching it demonstrated that the dinosaur-cause and its string of effects had not been altered.*

Unfortunately, in April 1967, a brutal cut to the studio budget forced the sudden interruption of *The Time Tunnel* and liquidated these guarantees. No further recordings were made, and Tony and Douglas were left floating adrift in the darkness of the incomplete. In any case, the message had already been sown, and the seed of speculative thought germinated across school playgrounds and at family dinner tables. In my class at least, intellectually worked up by the first stirrings of prepuberty, there was no young man who didn't consider the alternative that during a trip one of the two scientists would sleep with his own great-great-grandmother, becoming his own great-great-grandchild. Or to complicate the matter a little more: What would happen if Tony met his grandfather and killed him in a drunken bar fight? In doing so, of course, he'd also eliminate his future self. But if this crime suppressed his birth, then how was it possible he had existed and killed his father's father? And in turn, if he could travel to the past, stay there a while and come back, wasn't it also possible that our present was the past of hundreds or thousands of travelers from the future? Wasn't it possible and beautiful that the world and time were just as we knew them *precisely because* there were legions and legions of time travelers who from every future age were descending in parachutes or landing in spaceships or floating in on iridescent petals

---

* In his self-consistency principle, Igor Novikov states that if an event takes place and results in a paradox—for example, if a traveler goes to the near past to prevent a fire in which his mother dies and, upon arriving, "accidentally" knocks over the lamp that starts the fire—then the probability of occurrence of this event is zero, not a matricide. Hugh Everett rejects this principle and claims that the universe divides every time a new possibility of physics is explored. Given a number of alternative possible results, each one of them takes place within its own universe. Thus the condition of the pluri- or multiverse is that the blaze the firefighter of the time must combat will multiply across all existing universes. Furthermore, the initial firefighter will act within the original universe where the involuntary blaze started, but *not* the one created by the lamp spill, which generates its own series. Therefore, no effect can nullify its cause, but effects can create new causes in infinite loops.

from all corners of space-time, entering and modifying things so that we (and our ancestors and descendants) continued to perceive what existed just as we did?

In that case, time travel would be like the luminous art of fairies, who, with the rhythm of their magic wands, uphold the threads of reality to ward off the advent of nothingness.

4

My mother got pregnant shortly after my grandmother died. The news didn't change her routine of seclusion, whose true meaning I didn't yet know. But it did bring a series of builders, plumbers and carpenters to our home, hired to build a room for the new member of the family and, along the way, add a garage, extending it into the front yard. The remodel of the house, with its alteration of space, changed it for me not so much into a territory for games as into a field of experimentation: each beam of wood stacked on a heap of bricks in the patio and covered by a galvanized metal sheet became a hideout where I could spend hours until it was dismantled to form part of the siding or new wall, which implied another modification. The curious thing was that just as these temporary environments changed locations every so often, it was also obvious these workers spent hours without doing anything but collecting those metal sheets, sawing apart those beams of wood and heaping up a small pile of bricks for the preparation of the afternoon barbecue, which made my father despair, since the house was still under construction with the date of my sister's birth approaching. But the workers listened to him as if to the rain. They lacked any sensitivity about the needs of others, or simply lived at their own rhythm (on their own time), so that first came the grill setup, then the preparation of the fire and the heating of the wood to make charcoal, then the slicing and salting of the meat, its careful distribution over the wire rack, the attention to cooking times . . . followed by the chopping of vegetables for salads, the setting of the table, the purchase of bread and drinks. After their lunch, washed down with bottles and bottles of wine spritzed briefly with jets of soda that added a purple foam to the tops of the glasses, a nap was necessary. It was summer. They flopped in the shadow of the vine arbor, taking care to lay down, between the mosaics and their tired bodies, a few pages of the newspapers previously read during long breakfasts of mortadella-and-cheese sandwiches, accompanied by *maté*. Perhaps because coolness was prized over the slight softness those pages could give, however, many of the newspapers were tossed away during sleep, and left piled or scattered around the yard. They were popular newspapers glutted with information about film and theater stars' romances, soccer victories, criminal deeds and television programs. A few of these newspapers also included supplementary magazines, a hard nucleus. Due to their vulgar wording and scandalous intention, my father had forbidden me from touching, let alone reading them, so I had no choice but to squirrel them away with the greatest discretion and devour them in my hideouts. The magazine that most attracted my attention was called *How It Is*. The tabloid format featured enormous photos with brief captions; on the even pages, known and unknown beauties appeared, dressed or undressed to the limit of the age's standards—bloomers that offered just a glimpse of buttock, hands covering swollen breasts, the smile of an actress, model, contestant or prostitute looking at the camera—while the odd pages ran photographs of criminals riddled with bullets by the police, children mutilated and tossed in trash cans, remains of human torsos, unwary or suicidal victims of speeding trains, women raped and murdered. With the opened pages alternating like this, from those with a flash of pubis to those with a segment of eviscerated intestine, one could imagine that when the magazine was folded shut, the parts would mix together, and the bloody slash would become a penetration. The editorial judgment of *How It Is* favored such associations, and it wasn't strange when one day I saw the subliminal intentions had reached their apotheosis.

A photograph on the cover showed the dead wife of the deposed president, Juan Domingo Perón, referred to as a "tyrant on the run." Eva Duarte, "Evita." The mummy was in her coffin. Her braided hair looked like straw, and her white face was a mortuary mask. On her shoulders and neck one could see the evidence of hammer blows and slashes, dealt to her by the same rebels who had previously toppled her husband, blows and slashes that had torn gashes into her skin and that permitted, or so it seemed to me, the burlap of her stuffing to appear. In addition . . . In addition, there were her small hard breasts, the fragility of her thorax bones, her elegant waist, the algebra of her navel over the mystery of her belly's curve, her mount of Venus where the stiff hairs of her pubis sprouted.

There isn't much point in describing the nature of the emotions that flooded through a boy experiencing, for the first time, the complex blend of stimuli produced by a naked body surrendered to the unmoving pleasure of life in the beyond. The source of eroticism itself gushed toward me. Never before had I been struck by an image with such intensity. I gazed at this translucent skin, the taut remains of this flesh that revealed to me its particular way of embodying the secrets of death, and at the same time I tried to find out the material explanation for its charm, focusing on the journalistic account that told of the secret pilgrimages of the corpse and the ancestral techniques used to conserve it. But these words were pure typographical signs, and buzzed about the picture like flies escaped from the casket. There was no way any order and meaning could be pinned down that turned me away from the attraction of that body; I could barely pay attention to the lines about her illness and the methods of taxidermy. But if cancer and its devastations had injections of formaldehyde as a response, if nitrate salts and distilled mercury tried to maintain her appearance of youth, then what was being revealed to me was in essence a secret I hadn't yet approached: adult love. Because Perón must have loved his wife a lot to keep her free of decay, even as a shell tugged at and abused by the avatars of politics, pushed and pulled every which way, with organs no doubt removed and stored for safe protection somewhere, prepared to be restored to the body when medical advances made her cancer reversible.

Evita was thus (she too) a parcel launched into the future, a dream of survival that hurtled through the space of myth and the possibilities of marriage (since Perón would die before his wife returned from the shadows) to locate her in the sphere of immortality.

Obviously, I wasn't interested at the time in any link to an archaic cult of resurrection, but the possibility opened by Perón's generous and visionary way of seeing—can a dictator also be a genius?—which considered the prospect of a long-term cure for his beloved wife to be viable, also pointed to the moment when science would discover the remedy for every illness, and therefore what encompassed each one of them: death itself.

In this respect, along with a multitude of scientists whose names were my true company, I too had to name that deposed president as my precursor. One with limits, because Perón left the solution to the problem in the hands of others and the ingenuity of times to come, while I was resolved to make all times come toward me—and if necessary go toward them. In spite of this, I couldn't help but consider the splendid way some elements of reality were presented. It was as if chance were putting things together in my favor so I achieved the desired results. No doubt I'd already learned a great deal, but I was still eager to go deeper into other revelations whose imminence made every second of my delay throb. I trembled with doubt, and still wasn't convinced I had to abandon Evita and move to the next page. Perhaps I was afraid that, searching for the new, involved in a "betrayal" at once sentimental, sexual and scientific, I'd lose everything good that I had gained. But at the same time, how could I discover anything without taking a risk? In any case, I told myself, if the next page didn't offer anything new, except for the illusion of oblivion, I could go back to the previous one, where the image of Evita's corpse called out to me. And anyway, flipping through the magazine would help me soothe the violence of the emotions that disturbed me so much when I looked at her . . .

I lick my finger; I turn the page. The next thing I come across is a regular section consisting mostly of agency cables, ones already published in all the country's newspapers and magazines, whose contents the editor has decided to refresh for the consumer of his product. But there are also fantasies that speak to an editor on deadline looking to fill the page: three-headed-calf births, pig hypnoses, extraterrestrial abductions, genophagic snake attacks, flea trainings, dwarf races, et cetera. The strange thing is that amid all this nonsense, the very information filters through (or materializes) that I need to move forward with the implementation of my design. A scientist in the United States has invented a time machine. And *How It Is* offers some clues about how to build it.

5

My first impulse was to rush to get hold of the scientific publications with the instructions I needed to put together the machine, then send myself to the time when the formula for immortality had been discovered.

Naturally, a second reading of that text box—titled *Believe It or Not*—helped me realize that before getting down to business, I'd need more information at every level: as regards the science, design, risks, et cetera, et cetera. Even if by miracle I were to obtain all these responses in some issue of another publication of the time, *Popular Mechanics*, those preliminary investigations would imply an effort and level of privacy that at the moment I didn't have. To set up a time machine in some corner of the house isn't the same as dedicating oneself to building model airplanes. But the difficulties didn't discourage me. I kept studying.

In 1917, Karl Schwarzschild discovered the stars collapse into points of an infinitesimal diameter, scattered throughout space of an infinite density. He didn't know what to call these points or how to describe the characteristics of this space, and he didn't know their specific arrangement. Today they're called black holes. In the mid-1950s Roy Kerr discovered that some stars don't totally close: they pass through a formative cycle that doesn't end, and collapse as they keep turning. During this rotation they generate rings (known as Kerr rings) which possess gravitational forces so intense they can distort space-time, allowing large objects to enter one side and leave another. According to Kerr, these black holes might work as portals to the past or future, and if one has a great desire to carry out the experiment, the only thing necessary is to find one and set off on your journey.

Now then, save for in the unlikely conditions of fantastic literature, in which proliferate magical objects able to condense the totality of the Universe into a small object, it isn't common for us to have the luck of stumbling across a black hole in the silence of our own room. Kerr offered an alternative: it was enough to create one's own ring, gathering up material equivalent to the mass of Jupiter, then compressing it to a mass of about five feet in diameter. The force necessary to squeeze such a mass would make the material start to spin, and once the speed of its rotation approached that of light, a black hole would form in the center, so the operator of this accomplishment could then enter the portal, pass through the black hole and be brought to another point in space and time. Unfortunately the domestic Kerr ring worked only in one direction, and it was a journey of no return.

For a brief period I grew enthusiastic about the warp bubble, which explored the possibilities of altered geometry, producing contractions in the space in front of and behind the spaceship, so it could travel faster than the speed of light. It was like rowing through the void, transformed into time. But after some calculations I understood that in order to form these contractions, I'd need more energy than was contained in our entire galaxy. In 1937, Willem Jacob van Stockum calculated that the only way of traveling to the past "would be inside an enormous high-density cylinder, which must turn at a speed near that of light." While rotating, the cylinder would drag space and time along with it, spinning onto itself and tracing out a "closed timelike curve." Obviously, for this to occur, the cylinder would have to be of an infinite length. But in 1949 Kurt Gödel discovered that if the entire Universe were in rotation, then there would be closed time-like curves everywhere: the Universe itself would be a great time machine. Since the Universe doesn't gyrate but rather expands, however, the idea of building a cylinder became, along with impracticable, unnecessary.

Directly picking up from the theories of Einstein, Kip Thorne claimed there were rips within space-time—so-called worm-holes—that served as direct access to other space-times, and it was only a matter of—precisely—time before we knew how to manage them so they'd perforate these dimensions according to our will, and could pass through those gates of the sky into both moments and spaces extremely far away, and distances just a few meters or minutes from our homes and places of departure. Thorne not only floated the idea of crafting a journey tailor-made to each user, but also proposed a way to make these trips happen. Four metallic plaques had to be set up, preferably rectangular and with a diameter no less than several kilometers long, arranged in parallel at an incredibly short distance from each other, so the force of attraction between the parallels generated quantum fluctuations in the void of the electromagnetic field. Once this environment had been built, the four metal plates were split into groups of two and connected through a wormhole.

But Thorne faced a practical problem: in order for the pro-cess to achieve the parameters of efficiency needed, the plaques could not be separated by a distance greater than the diameter of an atom, and the wormhole had to be of a proportional size in order to be completely included in this distance. Being so small, the result was that a human being would find it impossible to enter or leave its interior, even if the issues related to the radiation emitted, or the destructive effect of its gravity, were solved. With melancholy, Thorne concluded that the first trip through the walls would be undertaken by some nano-robot, equipped with various kinds of sensors able to register the details of its passage.

Although my euphoric starting point was precisely the limit where Thorne had grown discouraged, I wasn't unaware of the difficulties I faced: just getting hold of the kilometers of metal plaques I needed would be no picnic. It would require the support of the scientific community, of private foundations, of appropriate contacts at different levels of the State . . . all conditions out of my reach. That's why I decided to reverse the procedure based on the following conjecture: although the immensity of the plaques had forced Thorne to introduce elements at a micro scale, if I built a series of smaller plaques—which could be hidden in my room as if they were the Styrofoam panels of a school model—the worm-hole through which my machine and the objects inside it traveled would have a dimension larger than its entrance.

Given that a series of questions in theoretical physics had been resolved in advance by my precursor, even if they'd taken him down a dead end, all I needed was to apply the concept. The under-standing of the dimensions this involved made me delay carrying it out, however. Even though for me the machine of the future wasn't an aim in itself, but a simple means to obtain the formula of immortality—a formula I took for granted would be discov-ered in one of the futures I'd visit—the fact of knowing myself capable of building it, and therefore becoming the only human until now qualified to accomplish it . . . would form a milestone in the history of our evolution and thus turn me into . . . I didn't even want to think about it.

Let's be clear: it's not (just) about being a genius; there are geniuses galore, in every field. Geniuses trace out furrows in the terrain of the known and carve out passages for the fire of the new; these magmas rise to the surface and soon congeal. What was once lava turns to solid rock, a landscape that new geniuses must bore through in their turn so that then . . . and so forth. What I was going to do, in contrast, was gouge out a path for the new knowledge stolen from the future, in order to radically transform the possibilities for being in what existed in the present. I was on the verge of making the flame of the eternal cauterize the wound of death in our flesh. And here I imagined even further scenarios: lifting the torch of that conquered eternity, I'd go back in time to raise the dead from their tombs, guiding them toward life. Of course, I would start by bringing back my grandma . . .

6

Setting up the machine was easy. After carrying out my tests, I put it on a shelf of the library in my room. It had a "natural" presence, and its moving panels, connected by a tube, gave it a look between abstract and decorative, much in the style of the designer lamps made of aluminum or orange acrylic, shaped like squares or spheres, which in those years were the ornamental *summum* of the local petit bourgeoisie. And this is why, because it seemed to be one of those pieces of junk that crowded our house, which after being expanded had been arranged to harmonize with the criteria of interior design magazines, no one suspected its true character.

Now that I'm journeying to the center of my account, I want to say the following in a way that doesn't sound vain: art is a mental affair. Science, even more so. Science and art are the opposite of decoration, which takes pleasure in the random and offers as an ultimate justification of its existence the vacuous argument of freedom. In contrast, every serious activity reduces the margin for options and submits itself to a final objective. Nobody is free, not even me (especially not me), who chose to submit to what was necessary. This was so true that in the course of my work I had to leave behind everything and everyone, even someone who had begun to be important to me . . . my fourth-grade girlfriend, Alba.

Every Saturday that spring, at the hour of the nap, I stopped to pick her up at her house and we set out on an excursion, carrying big pieces of stiff poster board to a deserted suburban plaza, John Fitzgerald Kennedy, in whose center there began to rise up, before it was abruptly interrupted (just like the life of the honored president), a sort of elliptical monstrosity of iron and cement. There, in the shade of some eucalyptus trees, we cut up the poster boards and stuck them together with glue and Scotch tape. I'd convinced her we were designing the model of the mansion where we'd live when we grew up.

Clearly, those were my first attempts; I still hadn't distanced myself from Thorne's view, so I assumed a gigantic machine was a condition of the passage. At the same time, I was conscious that both the size and the materials within my reach differed from the standards required by the original project. Far from despairing, I considered this to be a stimulus and challenge; if Thorne's model was hypothetical, then my application could permit itself the luxuries of experimentation and extravagance.

As for Alba . . . as for Alba . . . she accepted my quirky decisions (the progress in my investigations) and enjoyed taking part in them. Maybe, when she was cutting the poster boards or sticking them together, she was dreaming of working as a fashion designer for María Fernanda, host of the program *Jean Cartier's Art of Elegance*.

One day I appeared with a few aprons that seemed to her "in poor taste." She laughed when she put hers on, and was astonished by their weight. I refrained from explaining to her that the cloth was lined inside with lead that would keep out radioactive elements, and instead told her that since "our house" still belonged to the realm of the imagination, whatever we did inside also had to fit the logic of dreams. Starting now, this was the path I was going to take. I encouraged her to follow me, but also said I wouldn't get angry if she preferred to call it quits. Alba looked at me with that luminous gaze of hers, and hugged me.

Owing to some disagreements with Thorne's conjectures, I'd begun to introduce a few modifications into the design of my machine. Sometimes the model seemed like a labyrinth, other times it took on the appearance of a boat, a California bungalow, a hydroelectric dam. It wasn't just about the form, but also the size. Sometimes I thought of putting down tracks to reach the speed of light, which according to calculations couldn't have a length of under a hundred kilometers, other times . . . I also had to locate, and with precision, the site where I'd put the wormhole. I was sure everything depended on it. In search of exactitude, I spent most of those afternoons shifting my girlfriend around all feasible points of condensation and transfer. Alba related this activity to the inscrutable representations of the women her mother called "mannequins," and at first she loved to imitate them. She thought she was performing a special version of the statue game, for which she had a great talent, since she could pass long periods standing still without moving, almost without breathing. Never did her beauty move me as much as it did then. Sometimes I'd interrupt my work to study her up close, the gleam of her pupils reflecting the sun, the wind fluttering her blond hair and making it ripple in swells, like the surf, which when observed with care revealed the tropism of the separate filaments. Statics and expansion, in different wavelengths. She herself, her body, filled me with new ideas . . . How right the physicists are when they claim that applied to their field, the conclusions of mathematicians are completely irrelevant! It wasn't from theory but from those capillary waves that I learned what I know about space-time. Those explosive instants let shards fly, glimmers of the immortality I sought, epiphanies of the real.

Was it because the poster boards collapsed, the glue stained her fingertips, the heat gave her a headache? Was it because our life as adults was too far away and I was too absorbed in my task to consider the details that make up the delight of first romances? One of those afternoons (it was summer now) I went to pick her up. I rang the bell and stood waiting at the door of her house. After a while her mother appeared and told me Alba couldn't go out, because she was studying. That attracted my attention, since my girlfriend was a good student who didn't need to make a special effort. But I didn't insist on seeing her or talking to her, because I knew her unexpected absence would make it easier to apply myself to certain experiments, with a greater intensity and openness. The egotistical part of my scientific passion chalked up that a repetition of these absences would be beneficial, letting me progress more quickly with my invention.

This certainty made me say goodbye to her mother and run quickly and happily toward Kennedy plaza. Yet even though what I did that afternoon was useful, my progress didn't achieve the dimensions I'd hoped. The part of my brain that had been occupied with evaluating strategies for misleading Alba was now taken up with confirming the effects of her absence. A gentle halo of melancholy surrounded me all day long, like an accretion disk, until in the evening I took down the poster-board encampment and went home.

The next morning, in the classroom, Alba walked over and told me she'd decided to break up with me.

I couldn't get in a word. Alba was leaving just when she'd started to become the love of my life. I walked backward as she went on berating me with a humiliating list of explanations, which came filtering through like an irritating high-pitched screech. I recited a litany of names, Vilenkin and Hartle and Hubble and Heraclitus and Bruno and Khoury and Ovrut and Turok and Ramanujan Aiyangar . . . but despite the protective aura of my invocation, I had to find out.

During breaks, while listening to him recount episodes of *The*

Man Who Came Back from Death, she'd fallen in love with Rodolfo Batista, a boy in the sixth grade.

I don't know—I didn't know then, I still don't know—what it was that captivated Alba, or pulled her away from my side. Whether it was Batista himself or whether he served as a vehicle to lead her toward the prior fascination some women experience for complicated plots, above all if they're ridiculous. So absurd and sordid was this series produced in our country, so grotesque and cheap was its conception and realization, so overacted and sinister did it seem in all its aspects, that a girl born and raised in the bosom of a family of precarious cultural development couldn't help but be mesmerized. Whereas, in my home . . . Exercising good judgment, my father had forbidden me from sitting in front of the television at the hour it was broadcast, so that I was the only boy in class who hadn't seen a single one of its episodes, even if through comments in the hallways I could at last get the thrust of its main plot: it was about the prolonged revenge over rivals by the protagonist, Elmer van Hess, a man who pretends to be dead and covers his face with a veil that shakes in the wind of his words.

7

I suffered. My entire life project and its tremendous implications now suddenly seemed alien to me. No longer did I want to be the first immortal, or the one to rescue the human species from the clutches of death; all I wanted was to get Alba back.

Due to my ignorance of the methods to seduce women, instead of tracing out a strategy, I proceeded by instinct. I prowled around her, and during breaks went after her by shielding myself behind the bodies of schoolgirls who jumped rope or played tag and soccer; I didn't want her to see me following the path of her movements that always ended up next to Batista, nor did I want her to notice my rictus of angst, the desperation that stretched the corners of my lips until it ripped them into a tragic grimace, while on her face the inverse expression of enthusiasm began to appear as she talked to her new boyfriend.

Sometimes, in order to gently prick myself on the thorns of my suffering, I took pleasure in the memory of her words, and renewed the torment by piercing myself with the gesture of joyful maliciousness that appeared on her face when she gave me the news that she was going to leave me. I was even able to recreate the click of her tongue against her palate, a display of satisfaction as if she'd just relished some tasty treat, and the dry smack of her lips that followed, like the one an owl makes when, after swallowing the entire body of a field mouse, it passes the last few centimeters of tail through its beak. Did I adore her because she made me suffer, or was it the pain of her leaving that made me realize how much I loved her? To make it all worse, her connection with Batista was going strong. They walked around the school patio holding hands; he always seemed to be introducing her to new visions of shared happiness, and she moved around with the air of a satisfied young wife.

Every attempt at recuperation involves a certain degree of firmness and personal equilibrium in the spirit of the one who carries it out. In the end, the approach is really a simple one, because you either triumph or go down swinging, and the consequences decide the matter: at least it's a result. In contrast I'd discovered a new vein whose riches I wanted to explore: the vein of heartache. In the classroom I spent hours looking at Alba, changing my desk to study her from various angles; I evaluated her perfections, yes, but above all I tried to detect whether in her heart there still existed any feeling of love (or even pity), and if this was lacking, whether I was capable of infusing it in her through the strength of my gaze and through telepathic transmission, helping her to come out of the delusion that linked her to Batista.

So I concentrated, and just as actors do to stimulate the crying mechanism, I pressed on my temples with my index fingers. Obviously, I didn't plan to turn on the waterworks without achieving victory. And against all odds, something did happen. Both to me—as everything started to grow blurred and my pupils were engulfed in a kind of vaporous fog through which luminous rectangles, colorful stars and quivering sparks immediately began to float, dashing across my retina like brief Roman candles before sinking in the east—as well as to Alba, who, although she concentrated on the dictation of the class, didn't remain unaware of the existence of a disturbing element whose cause was mysterious, and which imposed itself on her attention. Perhaps my intense mute prayer and its intended hypnotic character reached her in the form of a buzzing noise. In any case it distracted her, forcing her to drop her attitude of a good student and look for the source of her unease. Naturally if I'd continued to strictly follow the behavior she'd noticed in me, I should have taken advantage of the moments when Alba clearly wasn't herself to mercilessly launch the ray of my captivating gaze toward her (just like Elmer van Hess). If I'd done so, maybe she'd still be mine: destroyed as a person but in ecstasy, a zombie woman possessed by my love and forever in thrall to me. But as soon as I saw her turn her head, as soon as she looked one way and then the other, fear gripped my throat. I could predict her next movements in their every rotation and angle, the soft luster of her skin as it turned my way, but I wasn't sure about what the intention and meaning of her gaze would be at the moment it made contact with mine . . . and that devastated me. On the verge of capturing her, of exercising my absolute power over her soul, I suffered from an emotional jolt equivalent to an electric shock. And the fit left me defenseless. Terror overwhelmed me as I anticipated the crossing of our pupils. A microsecond before it happened, I lowered my eyes . . .

Finally, mad with love, I gave way to extremes of adoration. I rushed to take possession of the things she'd made some contact with: pages of crumpled paper, worn-out erasers, pens chewed at the tips. I kissed the surfaces she'd brushed against, even the floor, and tried to establish any sort of association with her friends, including the ones she'd cast away. After a few rejections, I went up to the girlfriends of girlfriends, the acquaintances, in a circuit that permitted me ever fainter gleams of the original radiance. One night, in my room, I understood this could go on forever, and the sustained exhibition of loss had made me a creature of contempt. I decided to end my life.

I got out of bed, grabbed some scissors and went outside. The act of death had to comply to the greatest extent possible with the dictates of an aesthetic act, since it had originated as an amorous tragedy. I decided to stealthily enter Alba's home, slip into her bedroom and, taking care not to disrupt her sleep, cut off the hair she wore down to her waist, braiding it to make the rope from which I would hang myself. Already I could see it: the deserted road, the jerk of the streetlight, my body dangling, the letter at my feet to explain it all.

Of course, beyond the lurid details provided by my imagination, taking into account my inexperience as a Romeo and ineptitude as a thief, the likeliest outcome was that the police would arrest me as soon as I tried to enter the house. The curious thing was that nothing like this happened. At the time, San Martín was a fairly safe neighborhood. People left their bikes on the street without chains, their cars with keys in them, and on hot nights like that summer's, their windows open.

I came in through the one in the front. As Alba's classmate, I'd been invited over several times for an afternoon snack, so I was familiar with the arrangement of that hideous living room. The chairs with the wide heavy legs that made noise when dragged, the table—the inheritance of a Spanish grandmother—voluptuously curved like a chandelier or gargoyle. The Alpine clock, with its cuckoo bird, above the cabinet full of little cups for vermouth. The photos of ancestors in sepia, huddled together in gold frames: dead people mute with horror, shining behind cheap glass. I went up the carpeted staircase. I also knew the drawing on the upper floor. Nothing made a sound, nothing crunched under my feet.

Alba was asleep on top of the covers, wearing only a white cotton nightie stamped with tiny yellow flowers. In her stillness, I discovered the forms always hidden from me under ridiculous school uniforms. Here was the body I'd never know as an adult. "Alba," I murmured. She was lost to her dream. She was a woman who while sleeping travels through time in a boat with white sails. Why, I asked myself, should I forgo possessing her? So far as I knew, there was no irreparable spell cast over her body. No one knew her better than I did; no one had seen her as I'd seen her. The stories parents tell their children to make them sleep were nothing as compared with the domination of my vigil . . . Alba opened her eyes, and for a moment the black pupils rolled up without awareness over the watery depth, then the eyelids dropped and she whispered something, a name or phrase that didn't include me, but didn't condemn me to eternal disappearance either. Afterward she turned over, with a smack of the lips. In this movement, her nightie rose halfway up her thigh. The part at hip level bunched so I was able to notice she wasn't wearing any panties underneath. At my age this discovery didn't suggest anything specific, but maybe I had my own ways of making her mine. I leaned over her lips until almost brushing them with mine; I felt the slightly acrid dampness of her breath. I breathed in those effluvia, where I could make out the substance of her diet and the fragrance of her acids, but also, to my dismay, the smell of someone else. The eerie thing about that perverse odor was that without sharing any feature with Alba's own scent, it still intended to mix itself with hers; in fact, I could perfectly sense the nature of its operation, like a dance of neutrons turning electrically around a nucleus, releasing their discharges, only in this case it wasn't to keep alive the functioning of an atom but to take possession of her soul. It was the smell of Rodolfo Batista dissolving into Alba's dream. He'd already entered in gusts, wafting inside on sultry currents, and was now perforating all of her resistance, submitting it to his harmful influence fatal to my desires. It was black magic, or perhaps the effect of a conjuration that Alba herself, in her innocence, had murmured.

With great gulps of rage, I started to breathe in that distinct condensation. I wanted to vacate my beloved of that presence.

Opening my jaws wide, I greedily inhaled the air. In the uncertainty of the combat, I felt I was purifying her, drawing her away from that pestilence, but all of a sudden the power of the other emptied me of all I'd won. I entered into her once more, and everything began again . . . At that moment, the moon, which had illuminated her body from an angle, fell directly on her face. The clarity of that light deformed her features, transforming them into a gruesome effigy of masculinity; then, for a few seconds, the distortion vanished and I could lay my eyes upon the beloved features, smooth and even. For a few seconds, it even seemed to me that without realizing it I'd achieved the hoped-for miracle, until suddenly—the disfiguring moon still pasted above—Alba's lips grew thinner and her nose elongated. Then I saw Batista's face imprint onto hers until fusing with it, and after doing so, as if he knew of my intentions and their uselessness, the resulting mask came away as if pulled by a magnet. Floating centimeters away from the original face, he opened his eyes and smiled at me.

I'm not saying this really happened, but I swear it's what I saw. And I understood it made no sense to travel back in time and arrive at the moment before the first meeting between Alba and Batista, getting there just in time to *prevent it from happening*. It was no longer about the possibility of twisting the past and modifying the path of the present, or about finding a way around the shock my present self would eventually give my self and the Alba of the immediate past—Alba wouldn't understand anything, and my past self would surely be astonished and happy to believe its dream had come true. But at this point in events, it was obvious that in all series of the Universe, and all lines of time, Alba was for Rodolfo Batista and would forever be, or to put it another way, and this sounds sadder now writing it down, she would never be mine again.

8

For a few days I kept a diary about losing Alba. I deluded myself into thinking I could record the totality of my pain in those instantaneous strokes, but the only thing I managed to do was draw asymptotic curves between lived experience and its narration, since I could barely account for a part of what had happened, and was always "behind" in capturing emotions or impressions. The very act of writing took place in time and created this deferral, but it didn't stop these emotions and impressions from continuing to accumulate, didn't even take the edge off them. So I gave up that activity, which in any case had already produced its real effect: obsessed with interpreting the meaning of events, I hadn't even realized that I had forgotten Alba.

The time machine . . . One day I went back to take a look at it . . . Now I notice that in the haste to recount my amorous misadventure I left out many details about its progress; how I passed from that prototype, a vast labyrinth of poster boards, to the mechanism of discreet size now waiting for me, glinting on the shelf. And perhaps it isn't worth dwelling on the topic. There it was, anyhow. All I needed was to try it . . .

As I've said, in the model developed by Kip Thorne, the time machine reaches a size bigger than several stadiums and can only transport small things, whereas I inverted the equation so that my machine was portable, and could move volumes bigger than it was. There's no reason to go into technical details about the way that without folding, destroying or changing anything, I was able to make the big fit in the small—or rather, the way that the machine shaped objects to its form. Each transportation could be quickly verified. With the machine located in my room, if I put an object inside it (a stapler, an iron, a stethoscope), this object would appear the next day in the living room. These modest proofs helped me to gain confidence. Then I moved to more complex matters, such as time within time. On the face of a wristwatch that traveled from the bedroom one Monday, and appeared in the dining room the Monday following, the needle of the second hand had barely advanced two positions. I made a calculation: if I were to slip inside the machine and show up at my home address again ten years later, my body would not have aged more than about thirteen and a half minutes. Therefore, traveling forward a century wouldn't take me more than two hours and a few minutes, and arriving at the next millennium would take twenty-four hours of my existence. Reaching the moment of history at which the formula for immortality had already been discovered, and which I calculated would occur within a period of at most five thousand years, would take me no more than a few days . . .

These hypothetical results turned out to be invalid in practice, however. Methodologically, I had to pass from experimentation with inert objects to a journey with living objects. My first attempt was with a spherical structure: a raw egg. Overcome by anxiety, I sent it into an immediate future: the next minute, just a meter away from the machine. To my unease, the egg appeared in the correct time and place, but fried. Was it possible that my machine could shift the positions of inanimate things without problems, but altered the coordinates of living matter, introducing a random dimension of the future into these organisms and aging them more quickly? If that were the case, I had to take care not to die of old age with my first attempt (if the forces of attraction in the wormhole hadn't already deformed or destroyed my anatomy in unthinkable ways). I sampled the fried egg, dipping a bit of bread into the yolk. It was exquisite: the trip hadn't modified its inner structure. Now all that was left was to evaluate its method of cooking. Why hadn't it turned into a hard-boiled egg, for instance? And also, did this mean that if I sent the egg on a trip to the past, its fate wouldn't be a temporal relapse into nothingness, but a passage into the original matrix, from egg to chicken, from chicken to dinosaur? Put this way, it sounds like a joke. But the consequences of such questions were dramatic. Instead of an immortal, a madman.

9

From the traveler's point of view, a time machine accelerates the physical evolution of the rest of the Universe; in contrast, from the point of view of an external observer who stays in place without moving, the machine works as an instrument of conservation, delaying all biological processes of the traveler so he can move forward or backward in time without aging. In some way I had altered this law, creating against all expectations a machine that could accelerate or modify the organic functions. I tried out ants, cockroaches and mice, and the results were always different: one critter grew, another split into fragments, a third developed a carcinogenic outer layer, a fourth was dispersed in the form of swollen and boiling ex-organs, a fifth . . . The machine didn't seem to answer to any norm whatsoever, which posed a danger to which I couldn't expose myself. And yet I had no choice but to investigate the matter.

When I got inside, the machine shook. Since I hadn't built it following the classic model from science fiction tales, its interior was a series of deserted corridors, a labyrinth within a ring-shaped Christmas cake that oscillated and trembled and veered from one side to another. The needles of my clock moved in opposite directions, coming and going, spinning and stopping. Everything was foggy and dark. Then there was a flash of lightning, and the shadow came toward me.

For a few seconds I took for granted that I was going into the future. But that was only until I noticed the movements of the machine seemed to have come to a standstill. I wasn't going into the future but *backward in time*, to the moment before the explosion of the Universe.

First I saw an oval shape, flattened, bisecting an enormous line of white gas, though it could well have been a cloud: it had the appearance of substance as well as the shine of colorful spun sugar, its exquisite texture produced as if from infinite crystallizations but at the same time admitting or incorporating reflections from elsewhere. In any case, it wasn't the line that mattered. The line was the accretion disk, committing the oval shape to existence. I didn't know what the shape was and, at the same time, I did: it was the Universe. I was the witness to how it unfolded at the same time as it twirled and melded, joining and sticking together its parts: a colored map I could see in its entirety even though I was inside it. The trip was extremely fast; there's no comparison to possible speeds, even extreme ones, like that of light. To see everything doesn't mean to perceive details, but to make out the first elements in the abyss. And there I was, seeing what no human eyes can see, the radiation in the depths, the light that emerged when the temperature cooled enough to let hydrogen atoms form. Their fluctuations expressed the different densities of the material, their moments of condensation. Obviously this was a prior moment, because my trip was hurtling me in time toward the origin . . . It was the demonstration of a magic trick, only in reverse: I watched the magician put his rabbits in the top hat, then the top hat and double-bottomed chest on which it rested vanish; then I saw the magician behind the chest walk in reverse, toward the moment before he rang the doorbell on my birthday, when the party still hadn't happened, my friends weren't there yet to celebrate and pounce on the crustless sandwiches my grandmother had specially ordered from the pastry shop, and no soda caps had flown through the air. Everything became the asphalt of time onto which they plummeted. But now San Martín and the school and my family had all disappeared.

And the origin began to arrive, or I started to go toward it.

I saw shining lumps that gave rise to thousands of stellar clusters boiled over from supergiant suns, massive stars that in my backward movement in time went from their final glimmer toward the ardor of their beginnings; I saw the hearts of these clusters vibrating, an echo of the clash of galaxies; I saw spiral galaxies lop off their elliptical movement to accelerate the formation of new clusters, their impacts unleashing torrents of radiation as their monstrous shapes bulged into mouths that fed off the leftover material of displaced planets; I saw gas escape these vortexes to be inhaled by vast black holes, creating waves that traveled hundreds of thousands of light-years and sounded in B-flat, fifty-seven octaves below C minor and a thousand billion times lower in pitch than the limit of our hearing; I saw buddings of hot blue stars surrounded by red hydrogen clouds that returned to them after having been expelled, hidden under dense masks of dust after they entered the mouths of these galactic cannibals, which engulfed them into their outer halo; I saw the struggle of these galaxies themselves to enter existence. Time came and went for me, but ultimately kept moving backward.

Before or after, the machine and I passed through a black zone with no light, no twinkling, no nuance of opacity. The blackness didn't gleam, or draw open like a theater curtain so over the course of the journey I could appreciate the oily silk of its ripples of sound. It was an absolute black, a uniform mass, and although I was crossing through it, the undifferentiated texture nullified time, or rather, time palpitated as it was cast against darkness. Then I understood I was heading nowhere but in the direction of my own death, as I plunged toward the center of a supermassive black hole. The machine was my coffin and my cat-afalque, and its limits and boundaries were also being consumed by that endless blackness. I couldn't help wonder who had sent me on this journey, and no longer knew what it had been meant to demonstrate. If in the beginning I'd harbored the desire to be immortal, now that I was on the way to annihilation, the path to the origin itself, I couldn't help but recognize the absurdity of my initial dream. If time has a beginning and there's something prior to it, then this something can't be touched or measured, as it's outside the existence of things, subsumed within the greater category of what doesn't yet have a form. It's impossible to get to this place, where what does not exist can be found, a place we cannot locate precisely, because we catch only a glimpse of its existence when it emerges from nothingness, showing us with its indiscreet throbbing what has been emerging for countless eons into being. And so, now that I was racing toward the direction of preexistence itself, I was being devoured by the cosmos, or rather the pre-cosmos. Perhaps, at some moment, the blackness would yield to the flame of this excessive, tremendous speed, and then everything would end for me. Whether these were seconds or millennia, I still didn't know, but I could settle accounts and laugh at myself. Why had I wanted to be immortal, I, who had lived almost no time at all, save for eight, nine years of a routine existence, submitted to the betrayal of my first girlfriend and the tedium of schooling? For what reason did I want to be eternal, I who had never known the features of adult love or the imper-atives of procreation or the experiences of lust and jealousy or the criminal impulse . . . ? And yet, in my inexperience, I'd tried everything. The only thing left for me to know—my end—was in some way contained inside what I'd already lived, and voided its necessity beforehand. Maybe the gratuitousness of my death would preserve me! Perhaps the very fact I wasn't needed for the continued working of the Universe, which has no plan anyway, would be my salvation . . .

I saw a flare. It came from a kind of spider of gas and dust—that is, a galaxy containing within it the radiance of a heavy burning mass, a thousand suns in one, or a cluster of stars that had burst, catapulting their light through space-time. That glow should have liquefied my body and every part of my machine in a millionth of a second, but although I could see it clearly, it appeared to me slightly faded by distance, which provided another explanation for the nature of my trip. I was going toward the origin of the Universe, yes, but on a parallel line, traveling along a string that transported me from here to there. That cluster had to be hundreds of thousands of light-years from where I was located. I regretted not having any measuring instruments to determine the exact temperature or predict the effects of the light absorption of interstellar dust, which assembled its material from such shimmering explosions of gold. After this, I could see a pulsing ochre, the systole and diastole of a heart of fire. The flickers gave me an idea of the mass of the star and its position in the cluster. Then I saw the youths that released their joyful blue near the gravity of an old red. Probably it was an enormous mass of gas (mainly hydrogen) and dust, some hundred light-years in diameter, an open cluster that served as a real factory for suns; ultraviolet radiation ionized the gas and made it shine at the same time as the pressure of the gas and gravity condensed the dust, turning it into burning stars that lit up the surroundings: a pink emission nebula furrowed by dark trails of stones, and beside it a blue reflection nebula. They spun in opposite directions, one clockwise and the other anticlockwise, and I noticed that my machine was going after them, as if it wanted to pass between them unscathed, or the opposite, as if it wanted to be shredded by the disintegrating effect of the vortexes. The gravitational pull shook my body. Since I hadn't thought to put in chairs or seat belts or any other way of holding myself down, I bounced against the corners and edges of my machine, tearing my skin and letting out jets of blood that separated into droplets that stayed suspended. I blinked to clear away a film that coated my eyes. It was a progression of scenes like curtains overlapping before the center, to hide the Event and its weight: the initial moment.

All of a sudden, what was missing was there. It was inconceivable and can be understood only through allusion, even if to do so presumes something preposterous, that a likeness can take on greater importance than a reality. What I saw, dark and brown, concentrating and condensing into the most solid mass possible, was the primary stone that existed before the bang, a stone so small it would fit within the tiniest casing and, damp and concave, might even dissolve, with all its smells and tastes, into that briefest instant of time: it was the Universe just prior to its unfolding, naked of any wrapping, like one of those hard bitter candies that taste of pitch and melt like a rock in your mouth. That's how it was, and it exploded.

10

Years before, in my bed at night, I'd wait for my mother's visit and kiss, which didn't come. I had to make do instead with the words of my grandma, her sentences half in Spanish, half in a foreign tongue, inviting me to dream . . . One day my grandma kissed the tip of her index finger and pressed it against my forehead. It was her goodbye. An impalpable dot, a mark of love, exact as an obsessive idea. Then she went away and I was left with this light pressure doing turns in the orbits of my mind. It was the start of my nocturnal parties. When the light of the room had been turned out, I began to dream the birth of the Universe. I imagined its explosion, following the shapes and pictures traced out when, in imitation of my grandma, I'd put my fingers over my eyelids and begin to press down on them, gently sinking the pupils until I saw sparks, electric rays, inklings of spheres and tubes and circumferences, squiggles of violet and yellow and green and black, comets overcome by the red backdrop, a pointillism of pressure. The memory of these childish spectacles, inspired by my grandma, had made me hope something similar would happen when I climbed into the machine. But what actually happened during my first and last trip, my only real journey, was something like the implosion of a star. The black mass expanded at an impossible speed, thousandths of microseconds that released eternity from the liberated material, but this substance was enclosed; the critical circumference of the ring kept it within bounds and obliterated its surroundings. The astonishing thing is that this tremendous, sudden obstruction activated the quasars and active nuclei of the galaxy, so at the very same instant what was compressed and liberated fused. And then I saw everything at once: the disappearance of the Universe into the black hole that absorbed it, and its multiplication into treelike networks that stretched out their radiant branches made of fiery stones and smoke and explosive gases, ramifications that unfurled their fronds toward every possible infinite to realize their own absolutes, as well as extended their branches backward, so far back they generated their own roots and recursive systems, and here I understood the Universe has no beginning but makes itself.

But before reaching this conclusion, within the simultaneity in which I was present, I verified something else, something I should have known from my own beginnings but revealed itself to me only at that moment: the map of my genealogy and the meaning of my existence.

The revelation came to me as if with a damper pedal, or as if the true meaning of events was reaching me from the depths. The time things took to happen and the space in which they moved were no longer important; now all that mattered was duration. Sounds and the way they combined were what was crucial, not music or something taken as such but indeterminate noises that linked together according to pitch and intensity. These sounds came from beyond the silence, not covering or substituting for it. On the contrary, they gave way to the silence and gave it texture. It was as if the essence of the void was its capacity to acoustically lodge in the center of one's hearing and make it vibrate. The song of the world, my teacher had said, speaking to us about that angelic music, that sound of the glasses illustrating the law of physics I've forgotten. I saw each planet sliding through space like a glass of water that rang out in accordance with the jolt given to it by an external stimulus. Obviously, this didn't come from something external to the Universe, but from something that had nothing to do with the trajectory of the planets, yet regulated them. I can say it only with words. It was the triumph of a systematic enigma, an arduous and perpetual mystery whose supreme harmony had managed to impose itself over the abyss: it had to do with beauty and truth. And this mystery opened up another, justifying what I'd never been able to explain in the slightest, what had tormented me until the moment I began my trip: the riddle of my mother's absence.

It isn't that she wasn't there when I needed her, but she'd kept what was most precious about her tucked away, in a kind of beyond where I couldn't glimpse even one detail. Those distant scenes, which had oppressed my soul throughout my entire childhood, found their explanation in the instant the Universe played its music. Because as the planets turned, and the music of the spheres made itself heard, I also discovered (in a moment both successive and simultaneous, as linear as it was infinitely ramified) the reason she'd been taken from me. I saw my mother writing the story of my family. I saw her moments of hopelessness, the descending spiral that consumed her when all at once, after believing for months and years she'd contributed to the glory and honor of our ancestors, she suspected that she'd been the victim of a tremendous initial mistake, a monstrous error of perspective. Maybe, she thought then, it would be convenient to burn every one of her pages, to accept they hadn't been the geniuses she imagined but poignantly wretched figures, bit players living out an illusion different from the truth she'd begun to open up through her way of writing their biographies. In reality, perhaps Frantisek Deliuskin was the original source of the confusion: a syphilitic libertine who in his arrogance had dreamed of being a groundbreaking artist, and died cuckolded and blind; and his plague-ridden blood had contaminated all his descendants: Andrei Deliuskin, a speck of dust who went astray in the hieroglyphs of Christian mysticism and the Eastern Napoleonic campaign; Esau Deliuskin, a yokel who anchored his life in the desert sands, trying to realize his father's utopian dreams; Alexander Scriabin, a feverish joker who hid behind clouds of cosmological aspirations and piles of spiritist trinkets, and whose *Mysterium*, which he intended to be an all-encompassing and cosmically transformative masterpiece, ended up a footnote in the history of composition, an extravagance that at best influenced psychedelic music and inspired the soundtracks of a few science fiction movies, in which Martians attacked and flying saucers landed; and after that painful trinity, my grandfather, her father, Sebastian Deliuskin, a virtuoso of the provinces, a failed pianist . . . She and her family chronicle, an outrageous absurdity, a pretentiousness without measure that would inspire laughter and pity in the few who read it. The surprise and compassion of friends, the contempt of strangers. She and her feeble, stuttering son. Mother, you never loved me, or you thought you saw in me the final, withered, sterile offshoot of that bloodline of dead vampires.

And so, in that moment that drew itself out, just as the pealing of a bell extends its tremor through the air and the purity of the skies, I pulsed against the secret of her melancholy, and could understand the sadness that would accompany her some nights, after hours of tracing her signs over the paper. In that moment, concentrated and precious, I could also read every one of the words she had written. And then I knew at some moment she'd risen above her tides of disquiet and finally seen with clarity the dimensions of the events of our family's geniuses, and understood that her task, under the mask of her abandonment, was to harshly instruct me in the school of our family tradition, now glowing and radiating its meaning. And it was then, at this moment of moments, that I saw how in another dimension of time (one of so many) I, too, was adding my writing to hers, extending her legacy. Your book, mother, wasn't finished. And so, in this endless return, I observed as past time the future moment when I'd lay the complete version on her worktable, the book we hadn't yet finished writing, the book nobody had read.

By the way, yes: the sound of those planets was the song of universal salvation, the *Mysterium* transfigured.

Translator's Note

Approaching the Absolute

Daniel Guebel's *The Absolute* is structured as six books that move from the eighteenth to the late twentieth century and recount a family's secret interventions in music, mysticism and revolutionary thought over the course of history. The reader meets with:

1: **Frantisek Deliuskin**, a libertine who experiments with the sensations of women to write a musical composition;

2: **Andrei Deliuskin**, a seeker disillusioned by love, who makes an annotated copy of the *Spiritual Exercises* of the Jesuit Ignatius of Loyola, later read by Vladimir Lenin and applied to politics, then joins Napoleon Bonaparte's Egypt campaign, where he seeks to decipher the Rosetta stone;

3: **Esau Deliuskin**, a political revolutionary who, after failing to assassinate the archduke Franz Ferdinand, is locked in a desert jail, where he engages in power games with his captor, breaks free and organizes a new society;

4: **Alexander Scriabin**, the famous Russian pianist, who works for Madame Helena Blavatsky (a Russian writer who cofounded the Theosophical Society of esoteric philosophy, which draws from Hinduism, Buddhism and Neoplatonism) and studies the teachings of Pythagoras, preceding his discovery of the mystic chord and his drafting of an unfinished symphonic masterpiece, the *Mysterium*;

5: **Sebastian Deliuskin**, the twin brother of Scriabin, separated from him in childhood, who reaches Argentina by ship and becomes a minor pianist in the provinces—as lovingly described by **Sebastian's daughter**, the narrator of the entire book, interested in probing her family's history;

6: **the daughter's ten-year-old son**, a kid who builds a time machine in search of immortality.

Each figure engages in obsessive, absurd acts that might be genius or madness, indistinguishable as they exist in a process in which one finds oneself and thus cannot objectively know; deemed one or the other by those who control a narrative, they remain somehow both and neither, wave-particle duality forever uncertain. In other words, free. Countless minor characters also appear, intersecting with these stories yet spinning out on their own trajectories that suggest infinite parallel narratives.

A book called *The Absolute* is destined for evocative incompleteness. What an attractive concept, but also—what an absurd attempt to take it on! To do so, one must be comfortable with the notion of a productive defeat. What is success? And in any case, can't the ill-fated striving to connect to an "absolute" nevertheless itself be art? Guebel's work draws attention to its status as a failed project, and is self-aware and humorous about this in a Jewish tradition. The capricious and suggestive cut may always fall short of a true Absolute, yet there need not be anything melancholy about failure. The very effort is a joyful throwing of oneself into the world, a taking up of everything at hand not just to capture life but to create it, within and through words.

Although the book contains an overwhelming amount of "stuff," it is never mere information. As the pages turn, there are both unfurlings and fallings short, moments of development and moments of rupture, mostly unanticipated. These change the course of self and society. Failure is as much a part of the personal and historical journey as success; Guebel is fascinated by the overly ambitious plans that end in unforeseen catastrophes and lead to new beginnings, leaving an object as testament.

Pluck the daisy petals: madman, genius, madman, genius. What seems to be bad, stupid, misguided, offensive or erroneous turns out, at a different historical moment, to be—instead or also—beautiful, intelligent, creative, visionary and avant-garde. How can one know which is which? Is there a greater reason or divine force behind our activity that keeps the wheel turning in revolutions? A vibration, perhaps? Here readers knock against a great, perhaps unknowable, philosophical question. In the meantime, Guebel narrates, and through his attention to detail and the stories of his individual characters, his work traces out a larger arc of events, both human and cosmic.

It's possible a reader will pick up a title like this one with some trepidation, as I did at first and perhaps still do, even after having spent a number of months with its pages. Yet what most astonishes me—and the book has much that astonishes—is its sensuous approach to the abstract. Every character or episode along the way seems insignificant when viewed up close, yet is a luminous and self-contained unit. And when viewed from a different temporal perspective, each of these units is shot through with the whole. Whatever its spiritual or cosmic forays, Guebel's book always continues to see, hear, smell, touch, taste. Forgive me if I put this in insufferable terms: *The Absolute* is an absolute of absolutes, but never forgets it has five (or more) senses.

History's scope is suggested here, but also boldly embodied in style and language, which unceasingly change. The sensual is rationalized and the abstract incarnated, while time seems to move in not progressive but spiral form, plunging forward yet forever turning toward an echo of the same. An eternal return—until cataclysm breaks the account, yet again, into further multiplicities. The single narrative of philosophical history is shattered into literature. What other work has done something like this? Here one can find views from the eighteenth, nineteenth and twentieth centuries, set out not by a historian with today's perspective but portrayed through the eyes of characters themselves in a stylistic free indirect discourse. The line between not only life and literature, but also history and literature, blurs and melts away.

As translator, it now feels strange to deliver up this absolute book—one that is philosophical, political, historical, literary, sentimental, erotic, religious, scientific and artistic—to the usual cycles of publication and criticism. It asks for so much more than that: a fuller interrogation, a deeper consideration. The salvation of the universe. Those who wish to go straight to "the thing in itself" are welcome, but if you've got a moment (or have already finished reading), I'd like to share a few thoughts—smaller infinities based on concrete objects, tangible ways I've found into this immensity, stylistic aspects that startled me into thinking.

Egg (Philosophy)

The egg on the cover is a symbol of the absolute, both contained whole and origin. (Which came first . . .) A single detail—for instance, an immigrant grandmother's pronunciation of "boiled egg" as "bodeg"—can contain infinite stories. The concept of the absolute is rooted in a paradoxical desire to encompass an abstract totality, yet simultaneously refer to each unique part. The German philosopher Georg Wilhelm Friedrich Hegel developed this in his version of idealism. Every possible being is fully itself yet dissolves into nothingness when contextualized in the greater whole of the Absolute Spirit. Through the use of reason, I, me, the ego, the subject, comes to know an object and acts. For Hegel, History was the unfolding of a universal Reason led by great men such as Napoleon. The Absolute Spirit is the perfection of this logic, the infinite self-conscious sum of being.

Or could one think of this another way, from different philosophical traditions? I and Other, Son and Father, Nature and Spirit, Atman and Brahman—each pair may be intimately related, as both recipient and wellspring; and ultimately the duality of these pairs or complements may prove to be illusory, a non-duality.

Guebel, as a novelist, avoids the hairsplitting, book-swallowing speculations of the halls of Jena or the rishi's ashram. But his characters and their actions give body to ideas and suggest new theories.

Magazine Page (Eroticism)

Guebel explores an array of erotic practices in intimate situations, from temporary infatuations to long-term partnerships, sadomasochist encounters to tender friendships, lesbian relationships to heterosexual marriages. Only a few pages in, the reader is treated to a description of how a libertine great-great-grandfather "composed" his musical masterpiece on the basis of the reactions of female bodies. Nowadays this might make for uncomfortable reading, but it would be a shame to stop there.

For this account—set in the eighteenth century—is very much in tune with the refined chronicles of scandal and treatises of eroticism by writers such as Pierre Choderlos de Laclos, Denis Diderot and Marquis de Sade, read all over Europe in their time. There is curiosity but no cruelty in Guebel's account, and the whole section is a tongue-in-cheek version of the Marquis de Sade's excess rationalism, in which the sexual act is obscured by a too logical attention given to poses and variations.

More importantly, Guebel's work, moving chronologically through history, adopts the tastes and styles of the people he describes, even if they're no longer "appropriate" from today's perspective. The reader may experience heady moments when coming across—in the very same set of pages—attitudes they consider barbaric, excessively rational, illuminated, disquieting or unfamiliar. Guebel's scandal is not conscious of itself in each scene, but is so within the context of the work. While a negative reaction to certain passages might be understandable, this disgust or repulsion, too, forms a part of the book's fascination. We are not in the realm of the safe and correct, and all seven of the traditional Catholic deadly sins are represented. If some parts are offensive to contemporary readers, that's because much of history is also offensive from today's perch. But to lose such "outdated" views, and the language that encrypts them, would also be to lose the history of ideas, the history of failures, the history of History.

Sex appears often in these pages—incarnated for a variety of tastes—but the real eroticism in Guebel's work is his tender description of sensual being in the world through *noticing*. The pleasure is in the anticipation, and all the characters of the

Deliuskin family hold dreams in their heads that make them savor what's around them, from a listing of edible delicacies at a country lunch spot, to ink leakages through the transparent pages of a magazine that inspire fantasies of Eva Perón. Often this attention is more satisfying than the final outcome, if it comes into existence at all. Imagination and the processes of creation are ultimately erotic, beyond the result—there's eroticism even in failure, if the ideas are caressed well enough along the way.

Talking Fish (Religion)

For Guebel, religion is based in the belief that all people and events are connected at the deepest level. The scenes slide from situation to situation, person to person, in absurd yet flowing transitions. Characters are sui generis personalities—again, thanks largely to the deft use of free indirect discourse—yet they form part of the same story, or *historia*. Shards from the same luminous whole.

The Kabbalah is important: Guebel's Jewishness is in the tradition of Kafka and Babel, and like his admired Borges, he always seeks the Aleph. A deep mysticism, the direct relationship between self and the absolute, is achieved by characters through an extraordinary variety of experiences, from the discovery of a talking fish by a shopkeeper in Finland, to the annotation of a Catholic manuscript, to the practical savvy of a Jesuit priest who advises Lenin, to the doubt-filled grappling of a mother unsure her story bears meaning, to the stubborn proofs of love by a young boy who builds a machine to launch into the absolute silence of the cosmos. And every fragmented part in this broken, impure world is a gleaming spark of a fractured totality.

The Jesuits play a key role too, for they are the enactors of abstract religious ideas and secret agents of history, an ideal combination of the spiritual and the practical. Ideally, the order is focused on helping others, and on seeking the divine where it is not obviously to be found. Yet its probabilistic sophistries are also able—flexibly, hilariously, dangerously—to justify about anything.

Japanese Battleship (History)

History is always a narrative, after all. This is a book about everything, but it focuses on the lived stories of a few beings. In Borges's anecdote "On Rigor in Science," a map is built of the same scale as a territory, but its obsessive level of detail is precisely what renders it useless. Mapping the world one-for-one as literature would be a similarly impossible project. One must select certain points that *represent* but also *contain* the absolute. Naturally, this requires techniques of exaggeration and caricature, selectiveness and a zoom lens, to condense and sharpen the narratives, which—like Borges's map—would otherwise suffer from an unwieldy excess of information. Or as Georges Canguilhem put it, "Often a caricature reveals the essence of a form better than a faithful copy."

Napoleon, Lenin, Eva Perón, Rasputin, Madame Blavatsky— Guebel shows us these great figures as obsessive megalomaniacs, eccentrics with foibles, well-situated actors on the "world stage." A writer can make us see someone we think we know with fresh eyes. Ricardo Piglia, through an essay, made Che Guevara famous as a reader as well as a guerrilla. Guebel, through his imaginary reconstructions, indelibly alters how we think of such "greats."

At the same time, he recounts a generational family history—a history of lesser-known figures with scattered ambitions, poorly placed or ignored, yet equally important to the story. And he recounts the story of the physical objects—books, bones, boxes, battleships—that shift the course of history as much as any human might.

Pyramid of Acrobats (Politics)

The absolute turns with ease into absolute power, the supreme God or dictator, the international trafficking of senselessness. Napoleon, on a whim, commands that a man be enclosed in a sarcophagus and sent as a spy to France, and that a pyramid of acrobats be ordered from this same France to stand still as long as possible. In parallel he conducts active maneuvers intended to prove his love for Joséphine and along the way conquer Egypt, with no better results; politics comes to seem a farce of personal passions and idealistic obsessions, with "action" the amoral conduit toward this or that fantasy.

Karl Marx famously criticized Hegel for his philosophy of absolute knowledge with a self-conscious, estranged mind that abstractly comprehends itself. For Marx, this was yet another form of alienation, given that "man is a corporeal, living, real, sensuous, objective being full of natural vigor" with "real, sensuous objects as the object of his being or life." Marx emphasized action upon the material things around us, and change undertaken not just by self-proclaimed great men but by entire oppressed social classes. Yet such ideas have resulted in their own complications and tragedies.

For his part, Guebel parodies grand gestures of both intentionality and action, which casting toward new visions of past or future, trample with oblivious violence through the present. *The Absolute* is an extended critique of the saying "You can't make an omelet without breaking a few eggs." But it also knows eggs will inevitably break, and there might be nothingness within: the ovule of would-be genesis, leaving behind its shattered, beautiful shell.

Micropolitics is macro: any character of his, with the smallest unintentional gesture, and without realizing it, can produce outcomes as grand as floods, wars, peace, the alteration of perception. Genius, an "absolute" idea from Romanticism, here could find a twenty-first-century twist. If genius is the single-minded pursuit of self-realization, then perhaps the concept remains a vital one— should "self" be capacious enough to contain alter egos and other people. Self-realization exists in infinite forms, and everything is bound to everything else. When the talking fish is cooked into a gefilte fish, sacredness is distributed throughout the community.

Note the supposed author of this book does not self-define as a genius, and although she suffers from doubts, she gets the work done. Individual geniuses burn fast and flame out, while perhaps those who create in a community are more like scribes, in the tradition of Kafka.

Ham-and-Tomato Sandwich (Sentimentality)

In an old notebook, I found scrawled a favorite line, by Rilke to his wife. It speaks of "we most changeable ones who walk about with the urge to comprehend everything, and (because we're unable to grasp it) reduce immensity to the action of our heart, for fear that it might destroy us." *The Absolute* is a great book because it is often a sentimental one, unafraid of emotions from love to jealousy to despair. The suffering of women and men, the close relationship of a boy with his grandmother (manifested through a loving description of the ham-and-tomato sandwiches she sat and ate with him), the heaviness of family expectations, the intensity of small affections, betrayals, sadnesses and loyalties, the impor- tance of tenderness, faith and nostalgia—if "the Russian novel," beyond its specific practitioners, has become shorthand for the expression of philosophy and human emotion in a big work of fiction, without fear of kitsch, then Guebel has written a Russian novel.

Rosetta Stone (Literature)

In *The Literary Absolute*, Philippe Lacoue-Labarthe and Jean-Luc Nancy describe literature as "the production of its own theory" and a "poetics in which the subject confounds itself with its own production." *The Absolute* is a novel that is fully aware of itself, and contains within it rewrites or parodies of almost every genre of novel, from the detective story to the adventure tale to the science fiction utopia. It abounds with aphorisms, the most condensed literary form, in which one line can allude to an entire unspoken tradition. Any "theory" in the book is embedded in its structure and infused in its stories, which are random yet coherent. Many mysterious signs are traced on the same stone for possible future decoding. Guebel himself has said in several interviews that the plots and preoccupations of all his previous novels are contained within this one.

The Absolute pays homage to specific writers, works and traditions, such as Thomas Mann's *Doctor Faustus* (Alexander Scriabin / Adrian Leverkühn), the Argentine movie *El Fausto criollo* (1979), Franz Kafka's *The Trial*, Fyodor Dostoevsky's *The Brothers Karamazov* (especially the Grand Inquisitor section), Jorge Luis Borges and Osvaldo Lamborghini's condensed writings, and Nabokov's various tongue-tapping works, from *Speak, Memory* to—perhaps especially—*Ada, or Ardor*. From the latter there are not only moments quoted (such as the line "to leave is to die a little, to die is to leave a little too much," in turn borrowed from Edmond Haraucourt), but also similar imaginaries like Anti-Earth, symbols and erotic episodes, as well as the broader theme of how a family might attempt to alter the Universe.

But, of course, this is a book chock-full of references, and looking for "influences," versions or thefts in Guebel's extended wink only gets you so far. What matters is how he transforms or transmogrifies them into his particular and moving style. Often lyrical, he is also fond of resources that poetically condense material, such as lists, anecdotes and jokes, as well as jack-in-the-box surprises and other forms of humor. Both the possible failures and the possible powers of literature are gloriously affirmed. As a writer, Guebel has been associated with the "Generación Babel," which published the '90s magazine *Babel*; while avoiding shock value for its own sake, the writers in this loose group did subscribe to the belief that no topic or style is off limits in writing if taken on with audacity, in the search for meaning.

Literature is ultimately a wager. *The Absolute* is composed by a mother writing a history of her family's geniuses. By imagining their various attempts at mastery and entering into details, she discovers the specific luminosity of each life; she *makes them geniuses*. Yet this activity eats away at her own life. Are these biographies worth her soul? What is the value of her productions within art and eternity? Literature is a time machine, but it is also the great consumer of time.

Keyboard with Lights (Music)

While translating I listened constantly to the piano music of Alexander Scriabin, a character but also the theoretical impetus behind Guebel's novel. Scriabin, a Russian composer and "tone poet," was linked to theosophical ideas and practiced an exhilarating synesthesia on the basis of mathematical chord progressions. In his works for pianoforte—from the études to the sonatas to the preludes to the symphonies—notes clatter, crash and thunder in dissonant sonorities, not a continuous flow but a discrete overlap of sounds. Yet somehow this remains satisfying to the ear.

A couple of years ago, Scriabin's notebooks were published by Oxford University Press, ecstatic declarations in Russian cursive that radiate freedom and bliss, torment and ecstasy. They do not touch earth, but remain high above in a mystic flight of the spirit, far from graspable material objects and tangible desires. There are no small moments of affection and humor; the senses are everything, but the body is missing. Only extremes reign, and a whole range of colors is absent from the palette. They are fascinating, yet I can live in his words for only a short time.

But his music—his music! His music is everything. It exalts, it melts ice blocks within you. What fatigues in literature intrigues in music. Scriabin aimed to play upon all the senses through his art, working with lights and sounds and colors to raise listeners to a higher plane of existence. To watch Glenn Gould play Scriabin's chords, raising a hand up and then letting it drift slowly down, is, indeed, ecstasy . . .

The special piano—the *tastiera per luce*—that Scriabin invented does truly exist, as does the mystic chord, even if he died before they were put into action. Scriabin's great project, to bring together humanity in a community through music and change the course of the planets and history, is perhaps the greatest failed project of the twentieth century, the awesome "what might have been." Or perhaps its failure is an acknowledgment that we cannot realize the absolute in mediated fashion, and will forever stop just short of knowing.

Music, as many have argued, is the purest art; it does not allow for representation, for concept, for the intervention of language or image. Scriabin's music does not seem abstract like this, however. It is more like literature, accessing fundamental ideas through superficial symbols, and through surfaces, colors, textures. Idea *and* substance. At its best, Guebel's writing extends the project of Scriabin's music, embodying a similar sensorial exaltation, lyrical yet avant-garde. It is art because of the intention and beauty of its process, but also as a created object—the work.

Time Machine (Science)

Guebel riffs on the "divine science" of theosophy, as well as on Pythagoreanism, doctors' jargon, popular science, alternative medicine and astronomy. These are treated as sources of wonder, even as they are affectionately mocked. Science comprises not just theories derived from experimental data, but also theories that cannot be confirmed—fictional constructions, hypotheses, alternative proposed versions that burst open and expand current visions of the known to form new Wissenschafts, anti-systems, other ways to understand or organize the world. Science includes its own paradigmatic critique, and need not be reduced to a system. It does not progress in an obvious way, but continues to discover the essential in kaleidoscopic forms—just as in the last scene, we zoom both toward and away from the Big Bang, as ending becomes origin and the labyrinths, tunnels and worm-holes that seemed so disparate connect via looping repetitions, constantly renewed.

Wormhole (Translation)

Is it possible to create a parallel work of art in another language, a wormhole from Spanish to English? The original novel is trying to act, do something, affect bodies and minds. Characters in the book dream of other lands, other forms of communication. *The Absolute* makes categories like the "national" or "global" novel seem miserly and all too human. Again, the reader comes back to the question of what literature can do. Often, while fiddling with this or that phrase, I thought of the entire translation as a mirror of Guebel's. A parallel system of relations. Not a ghostly double but solid and material, neither more nor less true. Mirrors hold both horror and fascination, as "fulfillers of an ancient pact / to multiply the world," as Borges put it. The *espejo fiel*, or faithful mirror, with its many significances of translation between worlds and texts, is at the heart of the Sephardic Jewish tradition. But faithfulness is an abstraction that can encompass nearly everything . . . Such were my thoughts as I engaged in the foolhardy task of "correcting the Absolute," at least this translation.

For this is the kind of mirror that doesn't just reflect and multiply, but lets one fall through to the other side. The word *transido* repeats throughout the book, and on one page we find the expression *transido de escritura*, racked by writing. Taking the meaning of rack as torture device, to be "racked" is to be "pierced through," in agony or ecstasy. The path from writer to page to reader is a wormhole, especially with a mystical and marvelous writing that forges systems of correspondences with a passion for detail. The writer is racked, the reader is racked. But what kind of a wormhole is translation? Is there an absolute of language? How can one set of symbols be racked by or pierce through to another? Is a translation a second wormhole that bifurcates from the first, the creation of a parallel universe?

Two or More Absolutes

Throughout his book, Guebel plays with ways of thinking about the self and the whole found in both nineteenth-century European Romanticism, and in Hindu and Buddhist philosophy. He also plays with Eastern settings in other novels; his latest is set in the world of Japanese samurai.

While differences between East and West are exaggerated and do not exist in any real sense anymore, if they ever did, perhaps the historically constructed dichotomies they represent still hold. This book flirts with two visions of the absolute, loosely mapping onto supposed Western and Eastern traditions. The Western

Absolute is time, events as unfolding process, with changes and developments in the material tending toward an end (possibly utopia); it favors scientists and revolutionaries, and is ultimately *self-creation*. The Eastern Absolute is the negation of time, events as illusory succession, with changes and developments in the material unveiling themselves as non-reality that reverts to impersonal silence; it favors mystics and contemplatives, and is ultimately *self-abnegation*. To reconcile these two visions of the absolute seems impossible. Perhaps any attempt at unity is destined to fail. Or perhaps, just as there are false divisions between geographies, there is also a false division between what is now and what could be.

The Absolute is about building things that are imperfect and transitory—whether these be sculptures, musical works, political structures, poems, relationships or families—but whose effects continue to resound in the universe. Both creation and abnegation form a part of what's made in practice, and theoretical contradictions cease to be so in the lived paradox of human experience.

Sometimes, when listening to a piece of extraordinary music— or reading an extraordinary novel—I feel myself poised on the brink of something between the physical and the mental, between reality and its negation. On the endlessly delicate, quivering line between This and That, an inviting abyss. Such a singularity, I tell myself, must be Art.

Jessica Sequeira